KNIGHTS OF THE SOLAR WINDS:

ABERRANT STAR

ABERRANT STAR

BENJAMIN BOEKWEG

Second Edition
Paperback ISBN-13: 9798986144245
E-Book ISBN-13: 9798986144214

Library of Congress Control Number: 2022921194

First paperback edition May 2022

Cover design by: MiblArt

Published by Heralds of Life in Provo, Utah

benjaminboekweg.com

A Note to the Reader

I do not use any profanity in any of my writing. Instead, I make up words that my characters use for "harsh language". When making up these words I did not simply change a swear word into a made-up word. Instead, I took a more linguistic approach. I created one word that is used as an exclamation or explicative. I made up a word that is used as an adjective and adverb. I also created a word that would be used interchangeably as either a noun or a verb. My goal was to simulate realistic dialogue without exposing you to anything offensive.

These made-up words do not have any word-for-word correlation with any real-world language. The only exception to this is the word Nova, which was used in place of references to God.

Contents

ACKNOWLEDGMENTS

First and foremost, I want to thank my dear wife, Ann. Thank you for believing in me, encouraging me, reading my early drafts, proof-reading my manuscript, and holding down the fort for me while our precious minions beat down the door demanding attention. I could not have done this without you, thank you.

I want to thank my brother-in-law Peter, for enabling me to find Writing in Community and encouraging me to publish this book. Thank you for your wonderful insights that helped me further develop the story plot.

Then to my brother Richard, thank you for helping me create this wonderous world of The Knights of The Solar Winds. Much of the strength of this story stems from the rich worldbuilding we did together.

And a big shout out to Isaac Elmer, the seventeen-year-old who utterly schooled me in Sanderson's Laws of Magic and helped me create a more interesting magic system. By the way, two of your grammar corrections I disagreed with, so I looked them up and then found myself bowing to your superior grammar. Thank you.

And to my older brother Buck, thank you for creating a writing group with me. It gave my stories wings to soar across the cosmos.

A huge thank you to Brandon Sanderson for posting your writing classes online. I devoured them. And I still re-watch them.

And finally, thank you Shad Brooks of Shadiversity, your YouTube channel inspired me to get my stories published, as well as inspire my love of heraldry. Notice that I included your chivalry explanation.

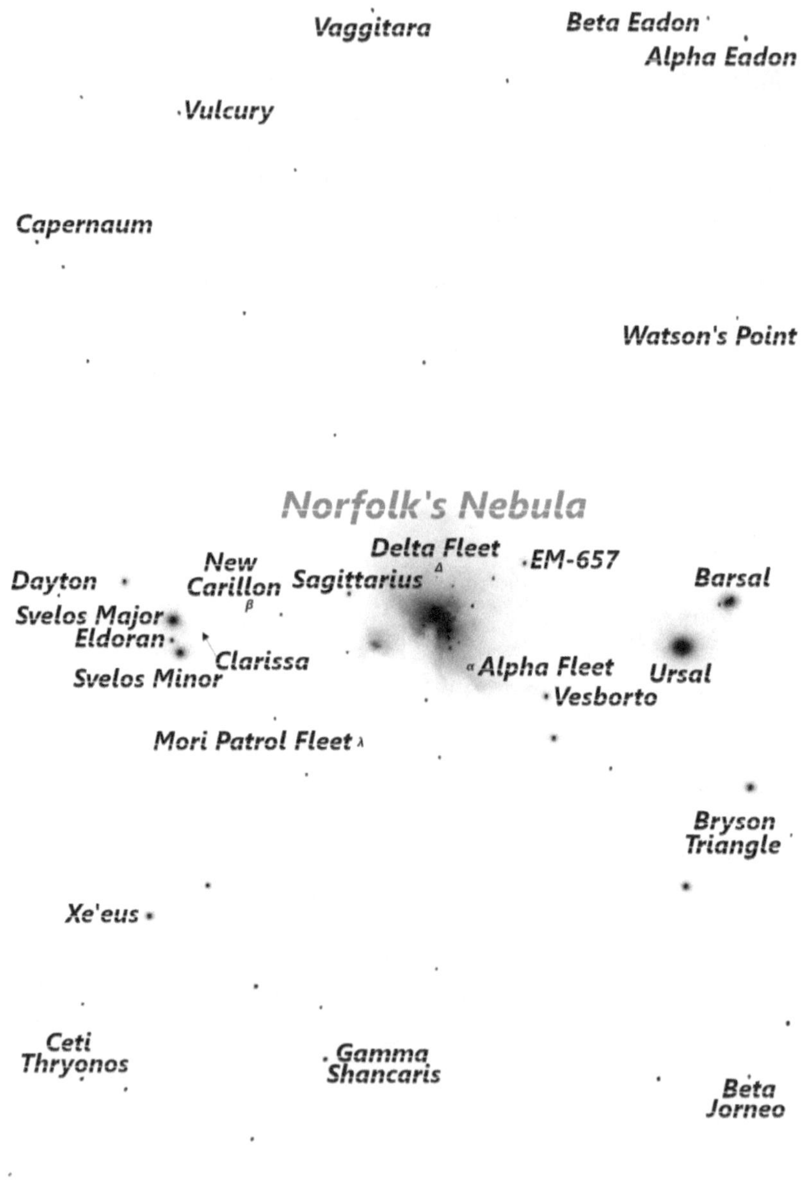

Vaggitara
Beta Eadon
Alpha Eadon
Vulcury
Capernaum
Watson's Point
Norfolk's Nebula
Delta Fleet
EM-657
New Carillon
Sagittarius
Barsal
Dayton
Svelos Major
Eldoran
Clarissa
Svelos Minor
Alpha Fleet
Ursal
Vesborto
Mori Patrol Fleet
Bryson Triangle
Xe'eus
Ceti Thryonos
Gamma Shancaris
Beta Jorneo

Chapter 1
THE JIBBER

*On the thirteenth day of the month of Ternary
in the four thousand seven hundred and seventieth
year of the Mori—known to us as Year Zero, the
Year of Infamy—the Mori destroyed our precious
planet Earth. They would afterward seek out every
human colony. Thus began the extermination of
mankind.*

—FROM "GALACTIC HISTORY VOL. IV" BY PROF. EZRA
DOUGHERTY

He knew twenty-hundred hours was far too late for any of the advanced scouts to return unless the mission had gone horribly wrong. Vance nervously tapped his hydraulic spanner against his leg. Sedston was flying in that patrol. Vance was only twenty-four years old and already Sedston was the last friend the war had not taken away. Hopefully, Sedston's luck would hold out. His patrol should have been back over three hours ago. A sick feeling sank into the pit of his stomach.

Only hours before, Vance had dreaded the overhead klaxon that would alert incoming danger. Now he wished for it; at least he would know *something*. Something was better than not knowing at all. He fingered the adjustment dial on his hydraulic spanner. Yep, still configured, still ready... but ready for what?

The dim lighting in the landing bay suddenly changed to a bright red. His entire spectrum of vision was now tainted with the red hue. The klaxon blared its monotone five note fanfare. Vance's heart rocketed up into his throat.

The loudspeaker blared, "General Quarters, General Quarters. All hands man your battle stations. Up forward on the starboard side, down aft on the port side. Inbound hostile starcraft."

Vance hopped off the railing and dashed across the bay. The klaxon repeated its alert. Anything non-essential for combat or medical needed to be stowed. For a mechanic like Vance, that was just about everything.

He reached the starfighter he was working on. He disconnected the diagnostic cables and hastily threw some tools back into their chest. Then he stopped cold. The unconscious nagging of a past first sergeant pulled him back over to the tool compartment. He retrieved the spanner from the lower shelf and instead placed it on the upper shelf. Another routine inspection was not going to make an example of him again. Not when two extra seconds could put it right, even though those seconds were always precious.

He slammed the lid shut on the chest and latched it securely. Other voices shouted in the bay as men and women hustled to their stations. Vance jogged the last few feet to the Comm Computer and pressed his hand to the screen. A laser scanned his handprint.

"AD3 Brewer reporting in!"

The screen flashed green. He stepped away as another three crewmen arrived to report in. Vance stood at his station. It was a station, at least, in name only. It was more or less a spot on the landing bay floor he was to stand ready at. His colleagues quickly joined him at their stations.

"AD2 Patterson reporting in!" A tall darker-faced woman shouted at the computer.

A skinny man with long limbs was right behind her. "ADSN Greensborough reporting in!"

A chubbier man—who somehow never failed a PT eval—followed behind him. It was like the man knew how to tap into all those stored calories when he needed them. "ADSN Stekler reporting in!"

More crewmen swarmed in. Stekler took his station a few feet away from Vance. Stekler wasn't only cool under pressure; he more or less thrived on it. Even as the man stood there panting, he looked almost like he was smiling. Vance wasn't sure if it was Stekler's adrenaline or his mentality that psyched him up so completely. Perhaps it was a combination of the two.

Vance didn't care much for the excitement. As an Aerospace Machinist's Mate, his first love was taking apart the aeon flow valve assembly and figuring out why the thrust ratio was off. He loved being the detective in his own little mystery world among valves, regulators, inlets, compressors, and turbines.

Close to two dozen of his Work Center mates arrived and reported in. The loudspeaker in the landing bay blared, "Starwrecker on final, pulling a jibber."

Even though it was a relief to hear Sedston's callsign, his entire work center began mumbling insults. And rightly so. Every pilot—every grease monkey for that matter—knew not to pull a jibber maneuver. If a pilot was having too much trouble getting his starcraft into the groove to land, he should ditch the craft. Damaging the runway with a risky landing was infinitely more expensive in material and manpower.

Vance's Chief deserved credit. He always had them running drills on a jibber landing even when they were never supposed to happen. If Sedston didn't have a really good reason for doing it, he was certain to get an earful from the landing signal officer and the Admiral.

Vance opened the large storage door behind him. It was full of tightly packed metal cylinders with shoulder straps. These were auxiliary fire suppression tanks. The Aerospace Boatswains mates usually handled fire suppression, but the Aerospace Machinists also suited up on a jibber. He started handing them out to his work center mates.

With the tank on his back and his goggles in place, Vance shifted his focus across the landing bay to the outer doors. Large yellow revolving lights spun. The light blue glow of the air pressure force field looked purple amidst the red lights. The space door moaned to life and clanked as it rolled open across the width of the runway. Large mechanical arms stretched a barricade net across the runway.

The muffled *pop pop pop* sound of the external gun turrets firing seeped into his awareness. His breathing momentarily stopped. Not only was Sedston's craft coming in at full speed, but there were incoming hostiles to deal with. Since no other pilots were scrambling, that meant there were only a few enemy craft. They must be chasing Sedston. The only reason starfighters would not be scrambled is when Long Range could verify only a few craft that the ZEUS system could easily knock out.

Moments later, a flash of steel and sparks flew into the landing bay. The second arresting wire extended under the pull from the tailhook of Sedston's craft. The barricade net caught the nose of the starcraft. The mighty engines of the captive craft powered down. The loud audible whine of the turbines faded away.

That was perhaps a picture-perfect jibber landing. He caught one of the arresting wires and didn't start a single fire. Perfect as it was, though, it still might not save him from getting an earful from the Admiral.

Overhead, the gun turrets had stopped firing. The engagement must be over. "Where's his wingman?" Vance blurted out.

Stekler shrugged and pointed to the massive space door closing. "Looks like his wingman must'a got vaped."

Sedston climbed out from the cockpit and down the skimpy pole-ladder, hopping the last few inches onto the cold metal deck. He took his helmet off as two crewmen approached with white coveralls. The first wrapped a blood pressure cuff around Sedston's arm while the other shined a small flashlight into each of his eyes.

They dismissed him and the clean-up crew swarmed the scene. After such a messy landing they needed to secure the craft and clean up the runway. The craft would soon be released to Vance's work center for inspection and repair.

The loudspeaker clicked on once more. "Secure from General Quarters, secure from General Quarters! All hands are to stand down from General Quarters, return to normal duties. The time on deck is twenty hundred thirteen. All Department Heads will muster with the Captain on the aft quarterdeck at twenty hundred forty-five."

Vance and his shipmates began the process of unencumbering themselves from the fire suppression gear and stowing it again, after cleaning it of course. A tight ship was a clean ship.

"ADSN Brewer!" An authoritative voice called out from a few yards away.

Vance shot a glance to his left. Sedston was standing a little way off with his helmet still under his arm. His blond hair stood in a crew cut with his green eyes hinting at the air of superiority about him. The patch on his green flight suit spelled out 'Zett Sedston, LT United Earth Navy'. Below the patch, 'Starwrecker' was embroidered.

When Sedston saw he had Vance's attention, he motioned with one finger. "A word with you."

"Aye sir." Vance hustled over to Sedston.

Sedston lowered his voice so that it would not carry. "Brewer, I wanted to—" Sedston eyed the new patch on Vance's coveralls. He looked back up into Vance's eyes with a smile on his face. "When did you make Petty Officer?"

Vance smiled back. "Passed the advancement exam last week, sir."

Sedston nodded. "Congratulations on becoming a Petty Officer 3rd Class. Now I'll have to start calling you AD3 Brewer. Keep it up, mister, and soon you'll be able to trade in those red stripes for gold ones."

He smiled again. "Thank you, sir." It felt good to be called AD3 now. He still had no idea what the letter 'D' was for; there was no letter 'D' in Aerospace Machinist Mate. Not everything about the Navy made sense.

Sedston straightened up his posture. "Well then, Aerospace Machinist's Mate 3rd Class Brewer, I wanted to personally thank you for the adjustment you made on my turbine compressor. I could really feel that extra power in the afterburner. And I can confidently say that may have been the single factor that got me home in one piece."

Sedston continued before Vance could reply. "Everything you touch seems to perform better. I even asked your Chief if I could have *only you* working on my engines."

Vance's eyes lit up, "You did, sir?"

Sedston nodded. "He told me that while it was a superb 'attaboy' to his division it would also be an inefficient use of manpower. Unfortunately, Ensign Nakito agreed. So I can only ask you unofficially, whenever my starcraft is in here, that you be the one to take the reins on my engines."

Vance nodded. "I'll do what I can, sir."

Sedston turned to leave. Curiosity still gnawed at Vance. "Can I ask you a question, sir?"

Sedston turned back and raised his eyebrows. "Okay, since you can't ask it, I'll ask it for you. 'LT Sedston, why in Nova's name did you bring your wildcat into the bay at full burn!'"

Vance failed to suppress a smile.

Sedston looked past Vance and off into space. "We found the Mori. At least their scout patrol. They shot down Cool Jerk's craft before we knew what hit us. He ejected, but those frazzin Mori..."

Sedston's jaw quivered a moment. "They broke off and circled around just so they could strike him in space. Those lousy canners were not content until they shot his helpless floating body."

Sedston paused before returning his gaze to Vance. "I was able to jam their comm so they couldn't report our position. That's when they went all sergeant on my six."

Vance stood stiff. "Do you think they will find us, sir?"

Sedston took a deep breath. "You know, I've never trusted Solwins. But if we're gonna have any hope of escaping the frazzin Mori, we're gonna need a few Solwins in here."

Chapter 2
ENTER THE SOLWIN

Just as these Solar Winds have stood and will continue to stand—timeless as to human standards—let us also organize ourselves into something just as timeless, just as majestic and eternal. And should we strive for this, we could even become as though an order of knights akin to those of our distant past, bonded together by life & limb and our profession too, swearing to one another—as did our forefathers of long past—this we pledge; our lives, our fortunes, and our sacred honor.

—SIR EDWIN NORFOLK, FROM "CONFERENCE OF ARTISANS: A SOLAR KNIGHT HISTORY" BY SIR ALEC TOLYUIN

Vance unlatched the tool compartment chest and opened it. Aside from being a little sloppily placed, it was perfectly in order. Not bad during a General Quarters call. He grabbed the hydraulic spanner and checked the setting dial. Good thing he checked; in its hasty return, the dial was off by a half-centimeter. His forefinger slid it back into place with a single practiced motion.

He reached up into the turbine cylinder of the mighty wildcat starfighter. The hydraulic spanner moaned as it loosened the bolts, one by one. He pulled off the cover panel and glanced inside the hollow tube.

"Let's see how you're doing, ol' boy."

He turned around and walked a few paces over to the Macron Scanner. He extended the diagnostic cables over to the craft. He ran his hand over the cover plate and the auxiliary port hatch slid open. He plugged the cables in. Turning to the Macron Scanner, he flicked the large green switch. The Macron Scanner hummed to life and the built-in monitor blinked on.

Vance typed a few keys on the keyboard. The Macron Scanner began communicating with the onboard flight computer of the starcraft. While the diagnostic was running, he went back over to the turbine and ran his fingers down the length of the shaft. Then he felt the interior of the tube, running his hand across the top of the cylinder.

"Hey Brewer," an annoying voice called out. "Making love to a wildcat again?" The voice belonged to Starman Greensborough. The skinny beanpole of a machinist never let a sarcastic opportunity pass him by.

Vance didn't even look back. "Go space it, canner!"

The turbine cylinder caught his attention as he passed his hand across it. There it was. Something was wrong with the thrust regulator.

Stekler poked his head around the aft of the turbine. "Hey Brewer, you gonna check the diag results? It's been sitting on that screen for a bit now."

Vance huffed. "Let me guess, the diag is givin' me the can by showing all systems are affirmative."

"It's a computer, Brewer. It doesn't give people the can. Now Greensborough on the other hand..."

Vance smiled.

Stekler straightened up. "So, if you knew the diag was gonna register everything affirmative, why all the disassembly?"

He pulled his hand back from the turbine and turned around. "'Cause I can tell there's somethin' wrong with the thrust regulator."

Stekler shook his head. "Negative. Patterson just reassembled the regulator personally. It's all on the up and up."

Vance's hands got more fidgety and animated. "That don't matter. I'm tellin' ya, something is wrong. You can feel it."

"Feel it?" Stekler inquired. "You mean like, woman's intuition?"

Vance grimaced. "Can it, Stekler! I'm being serious. When you have the diag running, you can feel the turbine vibrate. And when you feel the spot where it isn't vibrating, that's where the problem is, guaranteed."

"No way!" Stekler placed his hand up against the upper wall of the cylinder. "I don't feel anything," he admitted.

Vance placed his hand against the cylinder too. "You don't feel that at all?"

He shook his head. "I get nothin'."

"Hey Stekler," Greensborough called out. "Is Brewer teaching you how to make love to a wildcat?"

Vance and Stekler both shouted back in an unintended unison. "Can it!"

Stekler withdrew his hand from the cylinder. "Well, if you want to disassemble the regulator to have a look, don't let Patterson catch you. She'll think you're questioning her work."

"You're frazzin right I will!" a female voice sternly warned from behind.

"Ah kreket!" Vance cursed under his breath. Both men turned around to find Patterson standing tall with her hands on her hips. Her squinted eyes and pursed lips gave off the vibe that she was not in the mood to be questioned.

Stekler backed off, leaving Vance the sole target in the line of verbal fire. "AD2 Patterson, I, uh... think there's a problem in the TR-16 Thrust Regulator."

"Stekler is right, I just got the TR-16 back together and I didn't find anything wrong. Is it your opinion that I have missed something?" Her hands remained mounted to her hips.

Vance flinched. He desperately wanted to roll his eyes, but basic training had erased that habit with a lot of pushups. "My apologies AD2, just tryin' to follow up on a hunch."

Greensborough snickered. "A hunch huh?"

Patterson kept her stare piercing Vance. "No, Greensborough, Brewer here is right; we take safety very seriously in this work center. That's why Brewer is going to dismantle the TR-16. If he doesn't find anything wrong, he's going to polish and lube every piece before reassembling it."

Vance sharply exhaled. "Aye aye, AD2."

Vance spent all the rest of the morning polishing and lubing the thrust regulator assembly. He was so sure there was a problem with it. After all, he couldn't feel it vibrate. That always signaled where a problem was. That's how he found the microfractures in the fuel injector pod last time. When it was whole and perfectly sound, it seemed to vibrate. And until today, he thought everyone knew that.

Vance screwed on the cap to the TR-16 relay. It was finally back together. Maybe it would vibrate now? Perhaps a simple cleaning did the trick? He walked over to the Micron Scanner and pressed the big green switch to power it on. Then he walked back over to the turbine and placed his hand on the upper cylinder wall. He felt a little vibration. He moved his hand over to the TR-16 relay. No vibration.

"Somethin' hasta be wrong..." he mumbled.

He reached up and placed his finger over the connecting signal wire to the TR-16. No vibration there either. He pulled his arm out of the turbine. Walking halfway around the craft, he opened up the large maintenance panel under the wing. He ran his fingers across the circuit board wires. Convinced the problem was not there, he moved over to the secondary guidance board. He ran his fingers across the circuit connections. His finger stopped and backed up a couple of connections. There it was. He felt the vibration stop.

"Starman Brewer," a voice called out behind him.

Vance turned. The voice belonged to a familiar, short, dark-haired, speckle-faced man.

"AT3 Davies, I'm a Petty Officer 3rd class now," he said in triumph.

Davies stepped closer to admire the new patch on Vance's coveralls. "Ah man, get spaced! That's a total gabb! Congrats Brewer, welcome to the PO club."

"Thanks, Davies. It sure is gabb."

Davies looked behind Vance and at the open panel on the side of the starcraft. "What'ya doin' in the electronics? That's an AT's job."

"I know that's for the Electronics Technicians. But I've been tracking down a possible issue with the thrust regulator and now I'm thinking it might be electrical."

"Oh?" Davies stepped closer with a renewed interest. "Well for starters," he looked directly at Vance. "Let the pros handle the elec work." Then he turned his attention to the circuit board. "What did the diag say?"

Vance scratched the back of his head. "Well the diag just gives me the can; tells me nothin' is wrong. So either I'm chasing a ghost or there's a deeper problem the diag isn't picking up on."

Davies pulled a pen-shaped flashlight out of his breast pocket beneath his coveralls and shined it on the circuit board. "And you're sure it's this connection?"

"Pretty sure."

"Well, look at what we have here..." Davies maneuvered the flashlight to another angle, moving the shadow. "Looks like the soldering broke loose. It's still making contact with the leads, so that would explain why it still registers affirm on the diag."

"Does that mean it'll still work fine?"

Davies shook his head. "No, as soon as the pilot pulls a few G's it'll separate; either he'll get a flameout or a short. Neither one is good. I'll get my kit and fix it."

Davies switched off the flashlight and put it away. "How did you find such a canner of a problem anyway?"

"Long story short, I found out I'm weird," Vance concluded.

Davies chuckled. "Well it's gettin' late, you had chow yet?"

He shook his head. "Nah, I spent all morning on the starboard turbine. I'll head on over to the mess."

Davies caught Vance's arm as he was turning to leave. "Hey, did you hear the rumor? The Skipper has requested two Solars. They should be arriving sometime tonight."

Vance raised his eyebrows. "Real-life Solwins?"

Davies grunted. "Do yourself a favor, Brewer, don't call them Solwins to their face. They might rearrange *yours.*"

"Sure," he said, nodding. "Yeah, now that you mention it, I like my face the way it is."

Vance didn't eat much at the mess hall. His head spun with thoughts about the two new civilian Solwins that were being brought in. Well, at least most were civilians. The Fire Lance were military, but they had their own rank structure. He didn't know much about Solwins. He gleaned what he could pick up from rumors and jokes. The only certain thing was that he knew less about them than he thought he did. After all, he had just found out a Solwin was not to be called a Solwin publicly. If that didn't scream ignorance, what did?

After chow, the rest of the day went by rather quickly. His work center had completed the engine repairs and the Aerospace Electrical Technicians went to work on Sedston's craft. Davies even let Vance know when the electrical to the thrust regulator had been repaired. He wouldn't get a second attaboy in one day, but at least he saved Sedston a lot of potential grief. What satisfied his sense of pride most of all was that his suspicion was justified. He was right about the vibrating thing, even if he could not articulate it well or even if no one else could feel it.

Vance made his way back down to the landing bay. He walked back through the tight metal corridors of gray and white in deep thought. He passed by other shipmates, ever on the lookout for an officer so he didn't miss recognizing them. Descending the staircase, he entered through the hatch door into the wide-open landing bay. In the bay, an Aerospace Boatswains division looked to be in the middle of a drill. Off to the left, Sedston's starcraft was all buttoned up and ready to return to the hangar.

The loudspeaker clicked on. "X58 and X63 on approach. Scheduled time +3 minutes."

Vance spun halfway around toward the outer space door. The revolving yellow lights came alive. The space door moaned and clanked as it opened. The landing bay had two primary sections: the runway and the machinist stations. The runway took up most of the space. The machinist stations were where starcraft got repaired and inspected. Massive elevators lowered starcraft into the hangar below.

He leaned against the railing separating the runway from the machinist stations. The ground crew scurried about for the recovery of the inbound starcraft. Their movements looked very coordinated, like a well-timed ballet of men and equipment. Using radio calls and hand gestures, they communicated with efficiency.

The loudspeaker clicked on again. "Firefly on final. In the groove."

Vance wanted to walk down to the far side of the railing to get a better view of the approaching starcraft, but he also didn't want to miss watching the craft land. Supposedly the two Solwins were arriving tonight. While he was in mid-thought, a sleek red-winged starcraft glided into the bay at high speed and touched down exactly on the mark.

This craft did not have a tailhook to grab an arresting wire. Instead, it had magnetic plates that large electromagnet crane arms pushed against to slow it down. Electromagnetic arresting was not as troublesome as angling your craft to grab a wire, but you had to make sure your electrical was working.

A plane director in a yellow jacket gave the pilot hand signals. The engines revved up and the starcraft rolled forward, turning out of the recovery lane. It followed the directions of another plane director on deck. This part of the landing process was rather boring to Vance. The craft would taxi over to where it would be refueled and then stowed.

The loudspeaker clicked on again. "Gruesome on final. In the vibe."

Even though the rest of the landing process was boring, Vance still wanted to know more about the red-winged starcraft. It was an unfamiliar model. He looked around to see who else was on his side of the bay. Another shipmate also stood at the railing, watching.

She looked up at Vance. "First time seeing a starlancer?"

Vance looked back at the red-winged beauty, still taxiing into post-flight position. *"That's* a starlancer?"

She nodded. "State of the art assault craft. Build *by* Solar Knights *for* Solar Knights. We're also not allowed to touch them."

Vance snorted. "What, the Solwins are too high and mighty for the lowly grease monkeys to touch their crafts?"

She shook her head. "No, their crafts are not owned by the military. It's like a liability thing, I think."

She straightened up and headed back to her station. Vance kept staring at the starlancer. The cockpit canopy slid back to reveal a pilot dressed in a red flight suit with patches he had never seen before. The shoulder patch looked more like a crest than a squadron symbol. It had what looked like a red shield with a gold border and gold wing-looking shapes in the center.

The pilot descended the stairs that were wheeled up to the cockpit. When he stepped onto the deck, he took his helmet off and stared past the people in front of him. He looked directly at Vance. Vance quickly looked away and wandered back over to his station. He wasn't sure if he would be in trouble for staring at a Solwin. Getting caught staring was spooky enough so he wasn't waiting around to find out.

And what made matters worse, he desperately wanted to get close to that starlancer and check it out. What made it tick? What was the engine design? How did the turbines work? There were so many unanswerables swarming about his head. He wanted to risk it and see just how close he could get.

Chapter 3
THE STARLANCER

When joining the Fire Lance order, Solar Knight initiates must understand that to a Fire Lance knight their starlancer is not just a starfighter, it's an extension of who they are. We consider it a living thing. Flying with it is a symbiosis. You must learn to listen to it, learn its name, and master it.

—FROM "FIRE LANCE OPERATIONAL MANUAL" BY WIND COMMANDER ARIANA YATES

Vance glanced down at his wristband. The lousy thing never really did fit very well. He tapped it twice with his finger. The top glassy surface glowed to life, displaying the time. 2049 hours. That gave him 16 minutes before lights-out. He walked back down the hall passing several shipmates going in the opposite direction.

He descended the stairs and walked through the hatch doorway into the landing bay. The bay was now at low lights for the night. Just enough standing lights to see, and Vance knew exactly where he was going. Well, at least he had a good idea of where to start looking. Most of the crafts had been stowed in the hangar by now. Vance was betting that the high-

and-mighty Solwin would not want his starlancer stowed with the rest of the lowly starcraft.

He walked over to the ledge. It overlooked the starcraft pre-flight zone, where starcraft were relocated for pre-launch. He smiled as he gazed down on the magnificent red-winged starfighter. The wings were folded up into stowing position. Vance looked all around to see if anyone was watching. A few crewmen in yellow jackets exited the bay but not much more than that.

Vance quickly hustled his way down the stairwell to the flight deck. He paused a moment before emerging into the pre-flight zone. He waited for his pounding heartbeat and heavy breathing to slow down. It was ironic that he got a more rigid cardio workout doing something he wasn't supposed to rather than physical training. Somehow the nerves kicked the experience up by six more notches.

Overhead, the loudspeaker announced, "Tattoo! Tattoo! Lights out in 5 minutes. Stand by for the evening prayer. Silence about the decks..."

His heart rate began to speed up. Only five minutes to introduce himself to a sleek advanced beauty and then hustle his six back to his bunk. He'd done worse in trying to talk to a woman in a bar and that thought give him some measure of comfort.

He walked out of the stairwell and headed over to the starlancer. He walked casually because he wanted to look like he belonged. Sneaking about was a tell-tale sign that you weren't supposed to be there. He pretended he was going to assess a craft in his bay, hoping the extra mental exercise would help his stride look more normal.

He reached the smooth metal frame of the red-winged starlancer. He reached his hand out and touched the frame. Smooth and cold. Not a wintry cold but a relaxed cold. He slid his hand across the body of the craft over and under the folded wing.

Then he heard it. It sounded like a faint voice. It was soft and subtle. The complete opposite of the military. Vance crouched down to look below the craft. He didn't see anyone's legs on the other side, nor did he see anyone beyond. It sounded like a female voice. He shuddered to think if it was Patterson because she'd eat him for breakfast. But this voice wasn't her harsh tone, this was almost melodic.

His hand was right next to the maintenance hatch. Did he dare open it up and see what was inside? He pulled his hand back. Nope. He only had a few minutes left to get back to his bunk before lights-out, but that wasn't the real reason. It just felt wrong. Like he would be invading somebody's personal space. He hadn't felt that way about any starcraft he worked on. But then again, he was always ordered to work on them, not the other way around.

Vance stood up and backed off a few steps, admiring the majesty of the craft. He glanced back down to his wristband and tapped the screen. Two minutes left. It was time to hustle.

"See something you like, Starman?" A stern male voice spoke just a few feet behind him.

Vance's heart leaped into his throat. He closed his eyes. "Kreket..." he mumbled. He was sure he could talk his way out of a confrontation with an Aerospace Boatswain's mate. But it would be a little harder if it was a chief, or, worse yet, an officer.

He opened his eyes and turned around. A few feet before him stood a tall man with brown hair and piercing blue eyes. He wore a red flight suit with a patch that read, 'Royce Williams, S-CPT Fire Lance'. Below that, he had the embroidered word, 'Firefly'. On his shoulder was the mysterious shield-shaped patch that he saw from a distance earlier that evening. Now that he was up closer, it looked more like a medieval coat of arms.

Vance stood at attention. "I'm sorry sir... I am realizing I am out of line, sir."

Royce casually walked up to him. "Kreket is right. You sailors know not to monkey around a starlancer."

Vance resisted the urge to look down. Basic training had taught him that no matter how bad he felt, he must always look at a superior who was addressing him. "Aye sir."

"Then what in Nova's name are you doing around my starlancer?"

Vance hesitated a split second. "I thought I heard a voice, sir." It wasn't exactly a lie; there was a voice, but that wasn't why he wanted to snoop around the starlancer. It was, however, the safer of the two options to admit.

Oddly enough, Royce's eyes twitched slightly and he stared at him with a renewed interest. His facial expression betrayed nothing but professional annoyance.

Overhead, the loudspeaker announced, "Taps! Taps! Lights out! All hands turn into your bunks. Maintain silence about the decks."

Vance's shoulders dropped a half-inch and he exhaled. Now he was going to be late to his bunk also. Royce took two steps closer, his face inches away. His stern expression and piercing eyes could have drilled holes into Vance. He stood a long second before speaking. "What did she say?"

Vance's mind caught hold of the word, 'she'. How did this pilot know it was a woman's voice? He swallowed. "You know it's a woman's voice, sir. Does that mean you've heard it too?"

Royce's eyes narrowed and irritation oozed from his calm voice. "I'm going to ask you one more time, sailor: what did she say?"

Vance stammered a moment. "L, Lleona, I think..."

Royce's eyes eased up and his face softened. He pulled back his intimidating posture, staring into Vance's eyes. It was as if he was searching for something. Vance remained at attention, not daring to move or breathe.

Royce backed up a step. "Goodnight, sailor."

Had this pilot found what he was looking for in his eyes or had he simply given up? Vance hastily nodded and scooted past Royce over toward the stairwell. Then he stopped in his tracks. One question burned inside his head. Did he dare ask now? Now that he was dismissed from his 'talking to' did he dare risk getting into the bad graces of a mysterious officer? His curiosity got the better of him.

He turned around. "Captain Williams, sir,"

"*Sky* Captain Williams," Royce snapped.

Vance's jaw instantly shut. He exerted extra effort to open his mouth again. "Sky Captain Williams, sir, what does 'Lleona' mean?"

The corner of Royce's mouth crept up ever so slightly. "It's her name, sailor. Now get to your bunk."

Vance obeyed.

Chapter 4
EVALUATION

When seeking those destined for The Crusade, you will know them because they listen to The Winds. They will seem, as it were, to tap into the knowledge that the galaxy keeps hidden away.

—FROM "LECTURES ON THE CHOSEN" BY SAGE DOROTHY VLAVSKISK

Vance was still a little wary in the morning. Though he hadn't received any adverse consequences last night from the Solwin, that didn't mean it would not be reported in the morning. So, he was pretty much a bundle of nerves heading out from morning's chow down to the landing bay.

He descended the stairs and crossed the threshold into the bay. He glanced over to his right to see the Aerospace Boatswains mates getting the flight deck prepped for the day. It was easy to tell what jobs everybody had on a starcraft carrier by the color of their jacket.

Yellow was worn by starcraft handing officers and plane directors. Green was usually worn by the catapult and arresting gear crew as well as cargo and maintenance. All the really dangerous jobs required a red jacket, such as ordnance handlers and firefighters. Fuel handlers—or grapes, as they were affectionately called—wore purple. Plane captains, who were responsible for ensuring a starcraft was ready to fly, wore brown. White jackets were worn by inspection, safety, and medical personnel.

Vance returned his gaze forward and narrowly missed bumping into a senior chief petty officer. It was quite relieving to have missed that encounter—that would have been bad. He was already uptight about the possible consequences of last night's escapade and didn't need any new drama. He silently promised himself to pay attention to where he was going. Then he looked up and his heart sank into the pit of his stomach.

Ensign Nakito stood at the machinist station talking with Patterson who was nodding her head. Ensign Nakito was the head of the Aerospace Machinist Starfighter division. Vance's legs turned to lead and his pace slowed to a halt. The thought of turning around and leaving the bay popped into his head. And for a fraction of a second, he entertained the idea. But experience had taught him it was better to get disciplinary actions over with as quickly as possible. He forged on, forcing his legs to continue walking to his station.

Patterson glanced in his direction and pointed at him. His legs utterly refused to move. The uncooperative limbs pinned him in place. His heart raced. Ensign Nakito was a short man with darker skin and narrow eyes dressed in a white button-down uniform shirt and slacks.

Patterson and Ensign Nakito were wearing their covers. The rest of his work center wore their covers too. On board a ship, wearing a cap was usually reserved for official business. Hopefully, it was a uniform inspection and not anything to do with his late-night escapade. He pulled out his cover from a pocket, unrolled it, and placed it on his head.

Ensign Nakito turned and looked at Vance, beckoning him to approach with two fingers. Vance's legs were instantly released from their captivity. Behind Ensign Nakito, stood Chief Petty Officer Caldwin. It looked like the entire brass of his division was assembled. He saluted and stood at attention, bracing for shock.

Nakito returned the salute and gave a satisfied half-smile. "Aerospace Machinist's Mate 3rd Class Brewer, your Work Center Supervisor has recommended you for an assignment."

Vance glanced over to Patterson. She had a scowl on her face. This was not a good sign. If Patterson was still sore that he had questioned her work, this 'assignment' might end up being more of a punishment. He glanced back to Nakito. "Aye sir."

In the distance, the *beep beep beep* sounds announced the arrival of the flight deck tractor maneuvering a starcraft into their machinist station. Vance waited until Nakito turned to look before he did. That was the unspoken signal it was okay to break eye contact for a moment. The flight deck tractor pushed the red-winged starlancer into his work center's service station.

Vance blinked to be sure it wasn't a mirage or a trick of his eyes. He blinked a second time. Still there. Was his dream coming true? Was he being asked to inspect a starlancer? His head started buzzing with questions. What kind of compressor did the turbines use? How had they solved the aeon overflow conversion?

Patterson walked up to Vance and whispered in his ear. "Don't goose this one up!"

If Vance hadn't been so enamored with the aerospace masterpiece, he would have been in the right state of mind to be insulted by that remark. As far as he could recollect, he hadn't ever goosed up a repair in his entire career—if you didn't count that old Crusader; which he didn't.

The tractor finished backing the craft into place and detached. The operator of the tractor spun his chair around and the tractor moved out and back down the way it had come. Vance walked up to the starlancer. Before he touched the fuselage, Royce walked around the other side of the craft. He was not wearing his red flight suit this time; he wore a red button-down shirt and slacks with a navy-blue trim. Pinned to his breast pocket were his gold-colored metal pilot's wings.

"AD3 Brewer," Royce addressed.

Vance quickly stood at attention, bumping his head on the folded-up wings of the starlancer. He saluted. "Sky Captain Williams, sir."

"At ease," Royce directed, returning the salute.

Vance widened his stance and put his hands behind his back.

Royce walked up close. "I'm told you are the most knowledgeable in your division for starfighter engines."

Vance's heart rate accelerated. This also wasn't a good sign. Rarely did a compliment come down from a stern-looking superior that wasn't immediately followed by something harsh.

Royce motioned to his starlancer. "There's a problem in the afterburner. I want you to find it."

Vance couldn't believe his ears. He was being asked to inspect the most advanced starfighter in existence. But before he was able to respond, Royce amended, "And Petty Officer, you are being evaluated."

Nope. His dream was not coming true, in fact, it was looking more like a nightmare. He should have trusted his instincts about Patterson. She most likely recommended him because if he succeeded, she could take credit for her work center. But if he failed, then he would look like a fool in front of the Chief, the Division Officer, *and* a Solwin.

"Aye, aye sir," he responded. Although it was not specifically mentioned, he would be timed. The military spelled efficiency T-I-M-E. "Sir, may I ask that you open the diag ports on your starlancer?"

Royce waved his hand over a small panel near the engine thrusters and the panel slid open, revealing three connector ports. Vance waited for Royce to take a few steps back. Once he did so, Vance dashed over to the Macron Scanner. He extended the diagnostic cables and connected them to the starlancer's ports. He turned back to the computer and punched a few keys on the keyboard to start the diagnostic sequence.

He'd need every edge he could get, so he wasn't about to rely wholly upon the diagnostic report. That meant he was going to have to use every trick he had picked up to solve this issue pronto. He unlatched the tool compartment and lifted the lid. His hydraulic spanner was right where it should be—another reason a few extra seconds to put things in the right place was desirable. Not having his primary wrench at a time like this would spell disaster early on.

He quickly moved to the thruster housing and eyed the bolts. They looked a bit larger than the standard wildcat assembly bolts. Without looking, he fingered the adjustment dial on his spanner and rotated it slightly to the left. Then he placed his spanner to the bolts—perfect fit, he had correctly eyed the bolt size. The spanner moaned as it removed all the bolts. He dropped his spanner—which was a bad idea, but his nerves seemed to have given a very persuasive argument to his muscles. So, the spanner clanked to the ground as he removed the external housing of the thruster assembly.

He *gently* set down the housing case—no need to insult the Sky Captain by mishandling the parts to his craft. Then he reached up into the turbine and began feeling around the cylinder wall. He swiftly completed feeling down the entire cylinder. There must be some mistake, everything was vibrating as it should. If something was wrong, it would not vibrate. At least that was his experience with military starfighters. He hadn't tried this on a starlancer before, but the principle should be the same.

Just to be thorough, he felt around the inside of the turbine once more. He felt all around the edges and on over the valve regulators and the electrical connections. This time he was sure he did not feel anything wrong. Everything was all vibrating as a healthy system should.

Vance stood and faced Royce. "Sky Captain Williams, sir, there must be some mistake. There isn't anything wrong with the thruster assembly."

"You mean, nothing that you can find?" Royce offered.

Something in the back of Vance's brain was screaming that he was walking into a verbal trap. He was sure nothing was wrong, but the clarification he was being offered was, 'nothing that he could find'. And that was not the truth. Vance's breathing accelerated. If he insisted nothing was wrong, he might end up polishing and lubing again. But he also didn't want to publicly accept that he could not find the problem. That would be an insult to his professional pride.

It took a few eternal seconds for Vance to hastily make up his mind. "Negative, sir. Everything is working correctly."

Royce took another step closer. "That's a bold statement when the diag hasn't even come back yet."

Vance took a breath and heard the faint beep of the Macron Scanner. That was the signal the diagnostic cycle just completed. If he was wrong there was not going to be a way out of it. So, he simply stood back at attention. "Aye sir."

Royce stared him down a few moments. It was not an uncomfortable 'you are in trouble' kind of stare. It was more like the previous night when Royce was searching his eyes.

Royce finally spoke. "You're right. There is nothing wrong with it." He turned to Nakito. "Your division is the fastest and most thorough I've ever seen. I hope you're proud."

A large smile of pride crossed Nakito's lips. He turned to Chief Caldwin. "Good job. Have everyone return to normal duties."

Royce looked back at Vance, motioning toward the thruster housing lying on the ground. "If you'd kindly button her back up."

"Aye sir." Vance knelt and retrieved his hydraulic spanner. He unconsciously felt the adjustment dial with his forefinger. The setting was off by quite a bit. He adjusted the dial with a fluid motion of his finger, then he began reassembling the thruster casing.

Royce leaned in close and whispered to him, "Why do you even bother with the diag?"

Vance paused with the reassembly for a moment. "If it isn't running, I can't feel the vibration in the cylinder." He wasn't sure why he decided to be entirely honest. It might have been the intimidating officer that provoked his complete confession.

Vance reassembled the housing and disconnected the diagnostic cables. Royce had left. He knew he had aced the inspection, but he still had a sinking feeling in his stomach that had he somehow failed an unspoken evaluation. It was best that he worry about it later, much later.

After the flight deck tractor had moved the starlancer back to where it was being stowed, Vance went to the mess hall. Once again, he simply sat there, poking at his mashed potatoes. Even though he loved mashed potatoes, the current course of events seemed to have banished his desire for food. What was the purpose for the evaluation? His brain also kept coming back to the question of who this 'Lleona' woman was and where she had been when he heard her speak.

As he walked back down the hallway to the landing bay, he stopped short. Patterson stood at the doorway at the bottom of the stairs. She shot a glance up to him. "Brewer," she addressed, holding out a folded piece of paper toward him.

Vance descended the stairs and took the paper. He unfolded it and quickly perused its contents. His eyes shot back up in alarm. "I'm bein' transferred?"

She pursed her lips. "Ensign Nakito wants you to report to him first thing after reveille tomorrow morning. I warned you not to goose this one up."

Chapter 5
THE TRANSFER

I always wondered why we don't ever see any heroes born with talent and fame. Perhaps Nova has already rewarded the talented and famous, leaving the real heroism to the mundane among us. He was no exception. He didn't have the most exciting of beginnings; quite the opposite, in fact. His early career was like a dull pencil, rather pointless.

—FROM "MEMOIRS OF THE EXODUS" BY HANS THE BRONZE

Vance lay in his bunk, staring at the paper. He questioned his sanity in entertaining his curiosity with the red-winged beauty. He reviewed the destination on the transfer order again and again. He was not able to make heads or tails of where he was going. There was no ship name. Usually, there would be the name of the ship he was being transferred to but the order just had the department acronym: KSW.

If no ship was mentioned that usually meant he was being transferred within the same ship. But he had never heard of a department starting with the letter 'K'. His thoughts turned to Sedston and how proud he had been when he saw Vance had earned the rank of Petty Officer 3rd

Class. Would his last friend now be taken from him? His vision began to blur as his eyes began collecting moisture.

Thoughts of his shipmates that he worked with in his work center coalesced in his head. There were Stekler and Davies. Though they were not friends, they were certainly better than starting over. That meant not knowing anyone and having to prove himself to everyone all over again. Next was Patterson. Even though she was a hard leader, she was still familiar and predictable. That was something else he would lose by starting over again.

The loudspeaker called out, "Taps! Taps! Lights out! All hands turn into your bunks. Maintain silence about the decks."

Vance reached over to the light controls on the wall near his bunk. He pressed his thumb to the plate and the lights slowly dimmed into blackness.

If Vance could have dreamed that night he would have, but he tossed and turned until he heard the loudspeaker call out, "Reveille! Reveille! Reveille! All hands heave out and trice up. Reveille!"

His body responded automatically. He rolled off his bunk and his feet hit the floor, and then he tilted his bunk up against the bulkhead. Last, he opened his eyes. His bunkmates had heaved out already and were getting prepared for the day.

Vance still had the transfer order paper in his hand. He would have to go to physical training a little later today. He was expected to report to Ensign Nakito first thing after Reveille. He grabbed his towel and headed for the showers.

After dressing in his coveralls, he climbed up the steps to the topside deck and put on his cover. The topside deck and the Bridge were the only places on the ship where sailors always needed to be covered. It was one large open floor with compartments around the outer edge. Above was the ceiling with transparent sections to give a view of the surrounding space. Seeing the naked stars was a humbling reminder of just how far away they were. Away from the nurturing soil and natural gravity of a planet.

He walked down the long stretch of compartments, looking for the cabin with Ensign Nakito's name. When he found it, the door was already open and Nakito looked up. "AD3 Brewer," he called, motioning with two fingers for him to enter.

Vance stepped over the threshold, stood at attention, and saluted. "Sir, AD3 Brewer reporting as ordered."

Nakito returned the salute. "At ease, Petty Officer."

Vance widened his stance and put his hands behind his back. Nakito picked up a file folder that was lying on his desk and opened it. "So, have you given it any thought?"

"Just confusion, sir," Vance admitted. "Did I do something wrong?"

Nakito looked up from the folder and into Vance's eyes a moment. After an expressionless eternal second, Nakito chuckled. "Oh, I guess you didn't read it very thoroughly. It's not a transfer order, it's a transfer *request* order."

The puzzled expression on Vance's face gave Nakito the cue to continue explaining. "We don't see these very often. It's where one department requests a specific individual be transferred into their department. It needs clearance from both department officers, and it is optional. That means if you want to stay where you are, you can decline the offer."

"What department is KSW?" Vance asked.

"Well, it's treated as a department for clerical purposes," Ensign Nakito explained. "But it's actually an exclusive organization outside of the military, that supports us."

"Then, if I may ask sir, who are they?"

"The Knights of the Solar Winds. How much do you know about them?" Nakito inquired.

Vance shrugged. "Only that they fly gorgeous starfighters and that I should not call them Solwins to their face."

Nakito smiled and nodded. "That about sums up the majority of the crew's understanding. Think of them kind of like an elite unit of engineers, doctors, pilots, and Nova knows what else."

Nakito plopped the folder back onto the desk. "I'm going to put it to you straight. If you were to live ten lifetimes, you'd only see this opportunity once. You're a gabb fine machinist and I hate to lose you, but this would be a great opportunity for you."

Nakito pulled out another copy of the request form and slid it into a clipboard. He handed the clipboard to Vance. "If you want to accept this transfer, sign on the line. If you'd like to decline and stay where you are, just initial on the right side."

Vance's heart lifted when he thought of staying with his shipmates and being Sedston's favorite machinist. He eyed the small line on the right for his initials. He then patted his coveralls looking for a pen. He normally kept one just under his coveralls but had neglected to replace it this morning.

Nakito took a fancy pen from his desk and handed it to Vance. He took it and placed it on the initial line and hesitated. His eyes caught sight of something that stole his attention. Just above the signature line were the following words; Requested by: S-Cpt. Royce Williams.

His eyes widened. He looked up at Nakito. "This was requested by Sky Captain Williams?"

Nakito nodded. "That is affirmative. It would seem you impressed him with that evaluation yesterday."

Vance took the pen tip off the initial line and hovered over the signature line. "Sir, would I be accurate in assuming I'd be a real canner not to accept this opportunity?"

"Officially," Nakito explained, "I can only say that it is a great opportunity. But if you'd like my personal opinion, you'd have to be one blasted canner not to accept."

That settled the matter. A Solar Knight wanted him and was willing to give him some kind of great opportunity. It had to be better than polishing and lubing regulator assemblies. And although he didn't know exactly what this great opportunity was, Vance signed his name on the long line.

Vance handed the clipboard back to Nakito. He glanced at the form. "Accepted," he confirmed to himself. He detached the paper from the clipboard and put it back into the file folder. Picking up a small circular stamp from the desk, he stamped the paper. Then he detached the lower half and handed it back to Vance.

"This is your official transfer order. Please take it to the Aerospace Department Officer, Lt. Commander Dawson."

Vance took the paper and studied it for a few seconds before looking back at Nakito. "Thank you, sir."

"May Nova speed you on your journey, son. Dismissed."

Vance saluted. Nakito returned the salute. Vance turned on his heel and exited. His head was now spinning. Was this for real? Was he going to be able to work on a starlancer now? Would he be able to get answers to his questions about how the starlancer worked? Then his smile drooped. Or would he be subject to rigorous evaluations and endless scrutiny? The truth was that he didn't have any idea what he was getting himself into.

His mind buzzed with notions of returning to Ensign Nakito and asking to change his mind. After all, he did say he was a gabb fine machinist and hated to lose him; maybe he would gladly take him back. Then Nakito's other words surfaced in the soup of thoughts under his skull: you'd have to be one blasted canner not to accept.

Now he had embarrassment adding to the fuel to keep his legs moving along the row of compartments toward Lt. Commander Dawson's cabin. Somehow, he had hoped it would have taken him a lot longer to reach it. Unfortunately, basic training had bred military efficiency into him from day one. Even the way a sailor walked was trained.

Dawson's cabin door was closed. He knocked and waited. Then a woman's voice called out, "Enter."

He opened the door and looked in. A woman in a white button-down uniform shirt and slacks sat in a chair across from Royce. Royce wore his red with navy-blue service uniform.

"Come in," Dawson beckoned.

Vance stiffly walked over, stood at attention, and saluted. "Ma'am, AD3 Brewer reporting as ordered from Ensign Nakito."

Dawson returned his salute. "Have a seat."

Vance stepped closer and handed her his paper before removing his cover and taking his seat. She looked it over with a quick trained eye. She nodded and looked back over to Vance.

"AD3 Brewer," she motioned to Royce, "this is Sky Captain Williams. You will be reporting to him from now on. He is stationed at this starcraft carrier currently so you will remain on board until further ordered."

Vance nodded. "Aye ma'am."

Royce pulled something out of his pocket and tossed it to Vance. He caught it with both hands. It was a gold-colored metal pin in the shape of a hollow shield.

Royce answered his unspoken question, "It's to be worn on your uniform. You're a squire now."

Vance looked up, not able to speak. Question after question filled his mind. He could not decide which question to ask first.

Royce stood and walked up to Vance. "Squire Brewer, let's take a walk topside and give you some answers."

Chapter 6
CORRECT QUESTIONS

Date: 27 Ternary
Subject: Discovery
Notes: This one was easy to find; not due to his
clumsiness but rather to the strange aptitude he
has toward The Winds. Abilities that take years to
learn across multiple Orders seem to flow to him
as naturally as his crude accent. Such a rare
aptitude is not only worthy of additional study but
warrants it.

—FROM "DOSSIER #13" CLASSIFIED

Vance exited Dawson's cabin with Royce. Royce unfolded his cover and put it on. Vance did the same. As they strolled the topside deck, Vance sorted out questions in his head. There were a few he really wanted to be answered. Some would be nice to have answered, and others that wouldn't hurt to get an answer. They walked for a few moments in silence, passing by other shipmates. Finally, Vance ventured to try opening up the conversation.

"Permission to ask a question, sir?"

Royce kept looking forward as they walked. "Fire away."

Without thinking, he began listing off question after question. "So what are the Solar Knights? Are they a civilian unit? Ensign Nakito said

I could kinda think of 'em like special units. Alls I know is that you fly a really gabb starfighter. Will I get a chance to look at your starlancer's aeon overflow assembly? I've wondered how that problem was tackled in the newer designs. Have they really been built just for Solar Knights?"

Royce calmly replied. "That's a lot of questions, but you haven't yet asked the correct question."

Royce turned and looked at Vance. "Why don't we start with the correct question?"

Vance was taken aback for a few long seconds. Royce was right. The first and biggest question was not related to the impressive starfighter. Nor was it related to the back story of the organization. Vance swallowed and asked the big question. "Why me, sir?"

Royce returned his gaze forward during their walk. "*That* is the correct question."

Royce stopped walking and Vance stopped short of bumping into him. He glanced at Vance and looked him over, sizing him up. Then he turned to the crewman standing at the commissary. "Medium."

After being handed a folded-up uniform, Royce turned back to Vance. "What first caught my attention was that you could hear Lleona's name."

"Sir, may I ask who Lleona is?"

Royce walked up close and spoke in a low voice. "You've met her twice; the night you were out of your bunk, and then again during your evaluation."

Vance raised his eyebrows. "You named your craft Lleona?

"No," Royce corrected, still speaking very quietly. "My starlancer was not named by me. One day when I was cleaning out her aeon overflow valve, she whispered to me that her name was Lleona and that she prefers a cleaner coolant to fuel ratio than what I was giving her."

Vance looked around to make sure no one was listening in. "Beggin' your pardon, sir, but you're asking me to believe a craft speaks to you?"

Royce shook his head. "That's not the correct question, Squire. The question you should be asking is: why were you able to hear it also?"

Vance's eyes widened. Royce was right again. He couldn't deny that he had heard a voice say Lleona—or could he? It was late at night and he was doing something he wasn't supposed to. Perhaps it was more likely that he imagined it.

Royce read Vance's expression. "If it was just your imagination, then how did you know her name?"

Vance was at the point of exasperation. He shrugged, unable to find words. His mind had stopped thinking of questions about the starlancer's engines. Instead, he began questioning the reality he knew. Was there something mystical in this reality? Something beyond his understanding?

"Now let me help you with your next question," Royce offered. "How is it that you can *feel* where a craft is damaged?"

"The vibrating?" Vance asked.

Royce nodded.

Vance briefly cocked his head to one side before straightening it. "Well, up until two days ago, I thought everyone could feel it. But when I tried to show Stekler, he couldn't feel nothin'." He shrugged again. "Suppose I'm weird."

Royce's next words were quiet and stern. "I can feel it too."

Vance's power of speech completely failed him. He wanted to ask more questions but his brain seemed to idle on only one thought; what did this all mean? "Sir, are you sayin' that you can do the same thing I can do?"

Royce pursed his lips and turned his head slightly to one side. "That's not the correct question."

Vance closed his eyes briefly and exhaled. He was getting tired of not asking the correct questions. He looked back at Royce. He was still standing there, still waiting for the 'correct question'. Vance sifted through his thoughts, looking for any other question that might be better to ask. But his brain kept coming back to the evaluation, back to feeling the starcraft vibrating. Then his eyes widened. Royce was right yet again. He asked the right question, but he had it backward.

Vance took a slow breath. "What you're sayin' is, I can do somethin' the Solar Knights can do?"

Royce nodded. "Affirmative."

Vance stood expressionless for a few moments. Then his face contorted into a confused expression. "But, if Solars can already do what I do, why do you need me?"

Royce looked away and exhaled sharply. He stared off into the distance for a brief moment before returning his gaze to Vance. "Squire, you have about as much idea of the world you just stepped into, as an infant in its mother's arms. You are not here to be my personal grease monkey."

He paused to allow Vance time to reflect on that statement. Vance took a breath in preparation to ask a follow-up question, but the words did not come out of his mouth.

Royce concluded. "You are to become a Solar Knight."

Vance's breathing stopped. His heart pounded. Just what had he got himself into? He was an aerospace machinist, nothing more and nothing less. What would be expected of him now—and could could deliver?

Royce started walking down the hall again but stopped short. He noticed Vance was still motionless, staring with blank eyes. Royce tossed the uniform bundle to Vance, who caught it like a football, snapping him out of his trance.

"More answers to come, Squire Brewer," Royce declared. "Get suited up and meet me on the flight deck in twenty—and until you get a proper patch, wear your pin."

Vance held the top of the uniform bundle and allowed it to unroll. He was holding a green flight suit.

Chapter 7
FIRST FLIGHT

*When the starcraft is ready to launch, it is the
responsibility of The Shooter, a specially
designated flight deck operator wearing a yellow
jacket, to check that all stations are reporting 'go'
by signaling with a thumbs up. This check is made
once the pilot has saluted with his stick hand.
Once the flight deck operator at each station has
signaled The Shooter with a thumbs up, The
Shooter will signal the catapult operator by
dropping to one knee with one arm extending
outward down the flight path. The catapult
operator will then lower his hands and engage the
electromagnetic catapult system.*

—FROM "STARCRAFT CARRIER OPERATIONS MANUAL" BY THOMAS
J. SUTTON, UNITED EARTH NAVAL COMMAND

Vance stood on the flight deck of the landing bay, nervously
tapping the helmet he now held in his hands. He wore his green
flight suit with his gold hollow shield pin. The Aerospace
Boatswains mates with their colorful jackets were all treating Vance as
another pilot. There was still the feeling of being a fraud.

Piloting starcraft was the domain of officers, not junior enlisted. He tried not to make eye contact with anyone. He hoped not to be recognized and called out for being somewhere he felt he should not be.

"Squire Brewer," Royce called out.

Royce walked up to him, dressed in his red flight suit. "You don't look very confident," Royce observed.

Vance looked down before his military training corrected the issue. It alerted his reflexes to look into the eyes of the officer addressing him. "I feel like I don't belong among the officers, sir," he admitted.

"That's a tough spot to be in, Squire. Would it help if I clarified that the rank of squire is equivalent to a navy ensign?"

Vance's jaw dropped.

Royce smiled. "That's another question you failed to ask."

As soon as Vance regained control of his voice, he stammered a moment before responding. "Why are you making me an officer? I haven't earned that."

Royce stood up close to Vance. "Would you like the long answer or the short answer?"

"May I start with the short answer, sir?"

Royce nodded. "That's the lowest rank we have."

Vance's face twisted in confusion.

Royce gave a half-smile. "Looks like you're going to need the long answer. As knights, we practice chivalry. But before you let your mind wander, the truth of the word is far less romantic," he explained. "Chivalry is simply the anglicized version of the French word 'chevalerie', meaning 'horse soldiery'. We just use starfighters instead of horses."

Vance took a breath and exhaled calmly. "So every knight is a pilot?"

Royce nodded. "And pilots are all officers. Hence, that is the lowest rank we have."

Sedston walked up to Royce. "Sky Captain Williams, I was ordered to report—" He stopped short when he saw Vance. "Brewer?"

Vance stood at attention, not knowing what to say. Either the expression on Sedston's face was confusion, disapproval, or both.

Royce glanced at Vance and then looked back at Sedston. "I see you are already acquainted with Squire Brewer."

Sedston's eyes widened. "Squire?"

Royce nodded once. "He will be flying with me today. You will be taking me to where you last encountered the Mori. My orders are to assess their strength and position."

Sedston glared at Vance for a long second before turning back to Royce. "Let's get underway."

Sedston walked away. Royce motioned for Vance to approach the starlancer to their left. A man in a yellow jacket rolled a staircase up to the starlancer. Royce climbed the steps and then waved his hand across a plate near the cockpit canopy. The canopy hummed as it slid back, revealing an opening to climb into the cockpit. Royce climbed into the front seat and motioned for Vance to get in the back.

Vance put his hands on the railings and placed one foot on the bottom step. His brain was screaming at him, inquiring what he thought he was doing. He was climbing into a starfighter that he could only have dreamed of. The weight of his thoughts pressed his foot down firmly on the flight deck. Yet the swelling of his heart urged him onward into the starlancer.

He lifted himself onto the first step, then hesitated a moment. His heart and head were at war giving him conflicting orders.

The starcraft handling officer, who held onto the rolling staircase to steady it, looked at Vance. "Sir, we have a schedule."

That was the secret ingredient that broke the stalemate in his mind. The military's efficiency with time was baked into Vance's subconscious. A product of basic training. Without waiting, Vance ascended the stairs and climbed into the seat behind Royce.

The canopy closed over their heads and sealed shut. Royce began running through the pre-flight checks.

Realizing he hadn't yet done so, Vance put on his helmet. "Sky Captain Williams, sir. I thought the pre-flight was normally run before the pilot got into his craft?"

Royce continued pressing buttons and checking gauges. "Normally yes, but sailors aren't supposed to monkey with starlancers, remember?"

Vance jerked his head back. "Right."

The plane captain on the ground gave a hand signal to Royce, who then turned on the starlancer's engines. The gentle whine of the turbines wound up faster and faster and the low growl of the thrusters begged to be let loose.

Royce glanced at his instrumentation one final time. Then he gave the plane captain a thumbs up. A crewman in a blue jacket removed the wheel blocks and wing fold locks. A plane director signaled with both arms for Royce to taxi out of the pre-flight stall.

Royce pushed the throttle up ever so slightly and the groan of the thrusters roared to life. The starlancer crept forward. A second plane director waved both hands in the air, again signaling Royce to taxi forward. Royce gingerly pushed the throttle. The starcraft rolled out of its position and along the pre-launch corridor, toward the runway.

Vance looked to his left and saw Sedston in his wildcat zooming down the runway and out the large open space door. He had seen starcraft launch before, but somehow being this close made it seem much more real. Royce continued following the directions of the plane directors on the flight deck. Within moments, his starlancer stopped in position at the head of the runway.

Vance heard the radio chatter in his ear from his helmet. "Firefly, you are Golden O-two to Mother."

"Roger Allstar," Royce replied.

"Sky Captain Williams, sir. What does Mother mean?" Vance asked.

"Mother is our home carrier. We've been assigned the squadron callsign of Golden Two."

"Golden two, cleared for launch," the voice said. "Clear stars today, sir."

"Golden, roger and thank you." A catapult crewman on the runway with a green jacket ran up to the nose gear of the starlancer. His job was to connect the front wheel to the launch track. Two gigantic electromagnets on crane arms swiveled around behind the craft. The catapult crewman rushed out from under the starlancer, holding one arm in the air. That was the signal that the starcraft was connected to the launch track.

Royce gave a salute to The Shooter, who was dressed in a yellow jacket. The Shooter crouched down, signaling to the catapult operator with one arm extended forward. A few seconds later, Vance was thrown into the back of his seat. The catapult propelled the starlancer to launch speed in a matter of seconds. Vance pulled his head forward again and looked around through the transparent canopy. He saw the black emptiness of space. The glittering of distant stars beckoned to him and his imagination.

"Doing okay back there, Squire?" Royce inquired.

"Aye sir," he replied, still in awe of the scenery.

"It's a little different than staring through a window, isn't it?" Royce asked.

Vance nodded, not realizing Royce couldn't see his head nod. "It certainly is, sir."

Royce clicked on his transmitter. "Starwrecker, I'll form up on your wing. Take us to the zone."

The slightly garbled transmission responded, "Roger Firefly."

Royce turned off the transmitter. "You know, this is where it all began. Nakkaron particles expelled from exploding supernovae, permeating space... we call it The Winds."

"Is that the 'Solar Winds' the org is named afta'?"

"More or less," Royce replied. "Eddison Frank can give you a more scientific answer."

"Who's Eddison Frank?"

"He's the other Solar Knight that came in when I did. He's a Blue Planet engineer."

"Blue Planet, sir?"

Royce chuckled. "By Nova, you certainly are starting at ground zero. The Knights of the Solar Winds are divided into eight Knightly Orders. I am a Solar Knight after the Order of the Fire Lance." He tapped his shield-shaped shoulder patch. "And this patch is my Order's arms."

"As for you," Royce continued. "The pin you wear is a hollow shield, signifying that you have not yet been accepted into an order. Which," he amended, "will come later."

"Firefly, Starwrecker. On approach," Sedston's voice announced over the transmission.

Royce switched on the transmission. "Roger. Let's—Starwrecker break right!" Royce also rolled his starcraft into a high turn. The canopy illuminated as bright red beams of light streaked past.

Vance's breathing accelerated. "We bein' attacked?"

"Affirmative," Royce said. "We've encountered the Mori."

Chapter 8
THE MORI

The L.A.N.C.E. is the starlancer's signature weapon. Every Fire Lance knight must learn the skill of harnessing the energy of that weapon, but instead of discharging it, enveloping the entire craft in the destructive field. Failure to learn the LANCE Ram technique will disqualify them for rank advancement.

—FROM "FIRE LANCE OPERATIONAL MANUAL" BY WIND COMMANDER ARIANA YATES

"Starwrecker, jam those bandits," Royce directed.

Sedston's voice came back through the transmission, "Roger Firefly."

Royce glanced down at one of his gauges and then flipped a switch. "Brewer, how many bandits do we have?"

Vance looked around at his instrumentation. He saw a large array of screens, gauges, keypads, and switches. "Uh..."

"On your right-hand screen," Royce coached. "You will see a circle with crosshairs. That's your Sensor Detection and Ranging, or SEDAR. On the SEDAR you will see several colored dots."

Vance looked. "Oh... four bandits."

"Negative," Royce corrected. "The yellow dot close to the center of the circle is our wingman."

"Sorry," he said. "Three bandits."

"Starwrecker has jammed their transmissions. They cannot report back to their carrier unless they bug out or destroy us."

Vance swallowed hard.

"We are going to do a little fancy maneuvering to splash them first. I will need to ask you to remain silent so I can concentrate," Royce instructed.

"Aye sir," he replied.

Royce switched on the transmission. "Starwrecker, bandits are the cats. My sign is mouse. Swing wide until they are all on my six, then roll in behind. Splash bandit two. I say again, splash bandit two."

"Roger that Firefly," Sedston's slightly distorted voice replied.

Royce pulled the throttle back slightly and the starlancer started losing speed. Vance watched the orange dots get closer and closer to the center of the SEDAR screen. A bead of perspiration ran into his eyebrows. He reached up to wipe it away but instead, the whole starlancer rolled to the right. Bright red beams of light bolted past the canopy, illuminating it.

Royce danced the starlancer around in small tight maneuvers. The more he did so, the closer the three orange dots clumped together. Royce must be making himself appear a tantalizing target. Either that or he was annoying them to no end.

The yellow dot pulled away and circled around the outer edge of the SEDAR screen. Soon it was behind the orange dots. He smiled. Royce made the Mori starfighters forget all about Sedston. This must be what Royce was talking about when he mentioned cat and mouse.

Sedston's voice called out over the transmission, "Tally bandit 2."

"Get into the saddle and let him have it," Royce directed.

Royce then switched off the transmission. "Brewer, in a moment the Mori are going to figure out our little game and the roles will switch. Hang tight for a very sharp break."

Vance wasn't sure if he should say 'aye sir' or remain silent as he was instructed. He remained quiet, figuring it was safer to be obedient rather than to be understood.

Sedston's voice called out, "Splash bandit 2. Starwrecker sign is mouse."

Suddenly, all Vance's insides lunge to the left, along with this head. After a second of being pinned to the side of the cockpit, he felt everything normalize. He glanced down at the SEDAR screen. The two remaining orange dots had peeled off in opposing arcs, circling around toward Sedston.

Vance looked out the front of the canopy. The small glowing yellow thrusters of two starcraft appeared in the distance.

Royce switched on the transmission. "Tally on bandits 1 and 3."

Royce pushed the throttle to maximum and hit the afterburner. The engines groaned louder and Vance was again thrown against his seat-back. The two enemy fighters got closer. Small details of their starcraft became large enough to see. They did not look like any kind of winged craft he was used to. They were more or less a cylindrical fuselage with four wings on the aft. They looked a lot like throwing darts.

Royce angled the starlancer toward the craft on the right. Royce snapped his trigger and a bright yellow glow flashed from the right side of the canopy. A missile sped toward the Mori starfighter, its yellow glow steadily closing the distance.

The Mori craft fired red bolts of light at Sedston just moments before the missile struck. The Mori craft exploded in a neon green flash of light and spinning debris. The last Mori starcraft peeled off to their left.

Royce hit the braking thrusters, attempting to stay behind the last craft. "Splash bandit 3."

"Bandit 1 is bugging out!" Sedston's voice hollered.

"Starwrecker," Royce ordered, "keep jamming his transmission. We're going to follow him home and see what their strength is."

Vance eased up his strangling grip on the instrumentation panel. He wasn't sure if he was terrified beyond belief or utterly thrilled. Royce kept his distance behind the last Mori craft. That would keep the pressure on the Mori without accidentally overtaking him.

Vance was rather surprised that the technologically advanced Mori starfighter was slower. Or maybe it was just that the starlancer was faster. He hadn't thought about that. This impressive craft was starting to intrigue him more and more by the minute.

"Bogey at twelve o'clock low," Sedston's voice alerted.

Royce pressed a few buttons on his instrumentation panel. "I'm betting that is bandit 1's boat." Then he exhaled. "Not good."

Vance glanced down at his SEDAR screen. Multiple orange dots popped up at the top of the screen. First one, then three, then seven, then he stopped counting them. His breathing became erratic.

Royce turned his head as far as he could to give a token glance at Vance. "Breathe easy Brewer. I know this is a lot heavier than what I intended for your first flight but stay with me. Control your breathing."

Vance forgot all about his earlier decision to remain silent. "Aye sir," he said.

Royce switched back to the transmission. "Starwrecker, return to base immediately and submit your sensor logs. I will be on your six as soon as I foul the enemy carrier's runway. It should prevent them from chasing us with any starfighters."

"Negative," Sedston's voice returned. "I do not leave my wingman."

Royce huffed. "Roger Starwrecker. Hold a delta then, I'll be back in under five."

Royce then pushed the throttle back up to maximum. The starlancer zoomed toward the metallic speck in space that the Mori craft was heading for. In a few moments, the speck grew larger; large enough to see details on the large ship. It was gold in color with blue lights strewn about the hull.

Royce switched off the transmission. "Brewer, I know you've been through quite a lot today. Nova only knows how you must be feeling right now."

Vance wasn't quite sure how he was doing; his hands were a little shaky and he felt a little numb emotionally.

Royce continued. "But I'm going to need you to trust me and hang in there. What you're about to see is probably going to freak you out a little. Close your eyes if you have to and control your breathing."

Vance was able to mutter a weak "Aye sir".

"We're going to spoil their runway, so they can't scramble more starcraft. We can't have them following us back to Mother," He explained.

Vance watched as the golden enemy carrier got closer and closer. Royce flipped a switch and a low hum grew louder and louder. The hum became loud enough that it bothered Vance. A blue light started flashing on Royce's instrumentation panel.

To distract himself from the noise, Vance focused on the SEDAR screen. A very large orange circle was extraordinarily close to the center of the screen. His heart rate accelerated and the hair on the back of his neck stood out. He glanced forward out the canopy. They were flying at full burn straight at the enemy carrier.

Hundreds of large red bolts of light came streaming toward them. Royce jinked the starlancer around to evade the enemy carrier's turret fire. Then he placed both hands on either side of the canopy. The loud humming noise died down. Neon red flames enveloped the starlancer.

When Vance looked forward again, his heart launched into his throat at high velocity. They were on a collision course with the enemy carrier.

Time seemed to slow down. The enemy carrier's hull had a strange golden hue to the metal. Lights pulsed around the perimeter of a large rectangular opening; the enemy runway space door. They entered through the space door at full speed. The strange faces of the people inside were not human. Their elongated bluish heads held large dark eyes far apart. Pointed teeth outlined their facial expressions of utter confusion. His judgment of the colors was probably off, seeing through the neon red flames all around the starlancer.

Walls and machinery flew around them. They moved deeper and deeper into the interior of the carrier. Explosions moved in slow motion. Several more walls and odd-looking machinery passed around them. Then there was the familiar black of space. It took him quite a while before his brain registered what just happened. They had just passed through the enemy carrier.

The neon red flames around the starlancer faded out and Vance could again see in true colors. Royce rolled and turned around to head home. When the sight of the enemy carrier came back into view, Vance spotted a hole straight through the vessel. Green fires raged in defiance of the cold vacuum of space. Vance coughed a few times.

"Brewer, you still with me?" Royce called out.

Vance's nerves screamed at him, and his vision blurred. He knew something was wrong and it frightened him. Blackness eroded his vision as he slipped into unconsciousness.

Chapter 9
PAYING THE PRICE

*The Fire Lance have one of the most intriguing
heraldic arms among the eight orders. The red
field signifies the order's namesake, fire. The
offset twin chevronels along with the disjointed
chevron form a unique symbol that resembles
wings—a very appropriate image for the masters of
the starlancer.*

—FROM "GALACTIC HERALDRY" BY JEAN-CLAUDE ARMAND
DuBois

Vance was not sure how long he had been unconscious, but he heard a voice through his helmet. "Golden two, Allstar marshal."

Royce's voice replied, "Golden two, go."

"Golden two, you are cleared to land. Call the ball."

Royce responded, "Paddles, Golden two, starlancer, 'Firefly', ball, fuel state 3.1, manual."

Vance slowly opened his eyes. He was still in the back seat of the starlancer. He lifted his head and looked forward. His home carrier was ahead, growing larger as they got closer.

The voice in his helmet replied, "Roger, ball. You're fast."

Royce gently eased up the throttle and made a few more adjustments. The carrier ahead steadily got closer. The open space door they were heading for got closer. Instantly, images flashed back through his mind of the enemy carrier. His heart started beating faster and his breathing accelerated.

They flew through the space door and touched down on the runway. Two seconds later, Vance's harness straps dug into his shoulders. They held him back as the starcraft was brought to a complete stop. His insides wanted to continue forward through the canopy. His equilibrium took a few seconds to normalize.

The starlancer soon taxied along the recovery lane as Vance struggled to remain conscious. What was wrong with him? His strongest desire was to get out of the starcraft and breathe while standing on solid ground. Moments later a plane director on the ground gave a hand signal to Royce, who then shut down the engines.

A starcraft handler wheeled the rolling staircase up to the canopy. The canopy slid back and Vance felt the gentle breeze from the flight deck.

Royce stood up and turned all the way around. "Brewer, glad you're back with me. How are you feeling?"

Vance coughed once more and gave Royce a thumbs up.

Royce leaned a little closer. "I want you to report straight to medical. I'll see you when I can; I have a debriefing to attend."

He nodded. "Aye sir."

Royce descended the stairs. Vance slowly stood with shaky legs. He leaned over and grabbed the railings. Slowly, step over step, he climbed down. When he touched the floor of the flight deck, the warmth of familiarity spread all over. A renewed feeling of well-being surged into him. He was home.

He took off his helmet and let it hang from his left hand. The starcraft handler motioned toward the stairwell. "To the stairs, sir."

Vance nodded and walked over to the stairwell. It served as a reminder of the night he came down similar stairs to get a closer look at the starlancer. Now he was climbing up with a small sense of belonging.

Vance made his way over to the infirmary and checked in with the corpsman. It didn't take very long before they had him sitting on a bed. They attached devices to his arm for monitoring and testing. He appreciated the cushiony bed to sit on and the nice white lights.

After a few moments, a man walked over to Vance with a clipboard in his hand. He wore a white button-down uniform shirt and slacks. He carried a stethoscope draped around his neck.

"Squire Brewer, I am Lieutenant McMasters, the ship's flight surgeon. How are you feeling?"

Vance raised his shoulders a little. "Feeling a little lightheaded and a bit weak, sir. But I'm feeling loads better than an hour ago."

McMasters lifted the top paper on the clipboard and wrote down a note. "Well, your vitals are all good." He set the top paper back into place and looked at Vance. "It would seem you experienced a panic attack."

Vance widened his eyes. "Am I gonna be okay?"

McMasters nodded. "Yes. Your record shows you've had no history of panic attacks or psychological disorders. My guess is that this was brought on by combat stress."

Vance took a deep breath; relieved he didn't have a serious medical condition. "Thanks, doc—I mean, sir," he corrected himself.

McMasters chuckled to himself. "I'm ordering a day of rest before your next flight. Let me know if you experience this again. I can prescribe a few therapy sessions to train you how to work through intense emotions."

Vance nodded. "Sounds like a plan, sir."

"I'll have the corpsman give you some paperwork to give to your C.O." McMasters clicked his pen and put it away before exiting.

Vance slumped a little and glanced upward. His mind replayed the images of passing through the enemy carrier again. Then the obvious question finally rose to the surface of his thoughts. Just how did they pass through an enemy ship?

Before he was able to ponder more on that revelatory question, a familiar voice called out, "Brewer."

Vance turned his head toward the sound. Sedston stood a few paces off. Vance's face brightened up at seeing him. "Lt. Sedston!"

Sedston walked up to Vance. Somewhere in the back of Vance's brain, he thought something was off. He knew he was happy to see Sedston, but Sedston didn't seem happy to see him.

"So," Sedston continued, "a squire now?"

Vance was afraid his cheeks might show the embarrassment he felt, so he lowered his head. "Yeah, it all kinda happened, rather sudden like." He returned his gaze to Sedston. "I kinda feel like I'm in over my head."

"That's because you are," Sedston stated flatly.

Vance took one short, startled breath. What had he just heard?

"Look at where you are, Brewer," Sedston pointed out. "You're in the infirmary after one flight."

Vance's heart sank.

Sedston continued. "Pilots are trained officers that have put in the hours and the years to become so." Sedston stared at Vance a few moments before going on. "I don't know what that Solwin is trying to pull. You're not pilot material until you've earned the right to sit in the cockpit and take the stick. Jumping you up from junior enlisted—skipping eleven ranks—up to an officer is gonna do you a lot more harm than good. I just hope it doesn't ruin your career."

Vance's eyes drifted downward as his heart was pulled down under the weight of Sedston's words. Tears formed in his eyes. He blinked quickly to eradicate any evidence of his emotions.

"I never did trust those Solwin canners," Sedston amended. "It's because of them that Earth was destroyed." With that, Sedston left the infirmary. The corpsman entered just as Sedston was leaving and handed a paper to Vance.

Vance took the paper with a weak hand. His hand muscles were a little jittery. The corpsman was giving him some final instructions, but Vance could no longer hear anything. He felt cold all over. A strange absence of sorrow, anger, or happiness. Numb.

Vance slid off the bed and onto his feet. His feet still worked correctly, which he was thankful for. He looked at the squire pin on his flight suit; the golden hollow shield. He stared at it a moment, tensed up his hand, and then yanked it off.

He looked at the pin. It somehow lost its luster, its mysterious appeal. Now it was just a small gold pin in the palm of his hand. Why was he still holding onto it?

He heard a faint noise that grew louder. "Squire Brewer!" Royce called out, just feet in front of him.

Vance snapped out of his stupor and gazed into Royce's face with a perplexed expression.

Royce looked down at the slightly bent pin in Vance's hand. His face softened. "Your rough day still hasn't ended yet, has it?"

Vance tried to speak but only managed to weakly shake his head.

Royce put one hand lightly on his shoulder. "You've discovered in one day just how high a price you're required to pay to become a Knight of the Solar Winds."

Vance was no longer able to keep his tears back; they began sliding down his face.

"After all the danger on the outside—that we have all sworn to defend against," Royce explained. "We find avarice and contempt toward us among our own shipmates. It eats away at the soul—I know; I've been there many times."

Vance looked up into Royce's eyes.

They were soft, yet intense. "Shakespeare once said, 'Be not afraid of greatness: some are born great, some achieve greatness," Royce smiled. "And some have greatness thrust upon them'."

Vance's eyes relaxed as tears continued to stream down his smiling face. He breathed normally again. "Thank you, sir."

Royce's smile intensified into a satisfied smirk. "Come, I want to introduce you to Eddison Frank, the other Solar Knight."

Chapter 10
THE MYSTERY OF THE WINDS

*The Knights of the Solar Winds are organized
into eight orders, each specializing in a particular
profession. Fire Lance are the starfighter combat
specialists. Wind Dancers make even the most
skeptical of scientists believe in magic. Lily of the
Valley are medical professionals and biological
researchers. Orbiting Star are force field
manipulation experts. Blue Planet are super-
engineers and scientists. Gun Stars are
sharpshooters, trick shooters, gunslingers, and
artillerymen. Virtus Occulatum are the masters of
espionage and intel. Rising Sun are hackers and
saboteurs.*

—FROM "HISTORY OF THE SOLAR KNIGHTS" BY SIR ALEC TOLYUIN

Vance followed Royce down below to the engineering section of
the ship. Vance hadn't spent much time at this end of the
carrier. Most of his days had been spent in the landing bay, so
his eyes wandered about. Red deck plates on the floor highlighted the
large rows of gigantic machinery. They had computer screens, gauges,
monitoring lights, and high gantry walkways.

"Sky Captain Williams, sir. Permission to ask a question?"

"What's on your mind, Squire Brewer?"

"When we spoiled the enemy carrier's runway..." Vance wasn't sure how to ask his question. Was he even allowed to ask?

Royce sensed the tension and stopped, turning around. "You want to know what I did?"

Vance nodded. "How did we pass through a carrier?"

Royce stood silent a moment as if deciding how to respond. "Squire, you have just stepped into a whole new world of wonder. One that you could only have dreamed of. A complete explanation won't mean much to you until you've learned some basics first. For now, just know that you have stumbled into the gray area between what's possible and impossible."

Royce continued walking. Vance followed him around a corner and into the large engine room. Vance's eyes lit up. The room was two decks tall and as wide as a soccer field. Enormous house-sized machines were humming and grumbling along. Dozens of crewmen in gray or blue coveralls worked all around. They made repairs, adjustments, and who knows what else.

Vance's eyes followed a young engineman. He was reassembling what looked like a massive aeon regulator. As a result, Vance failed to notice when Royce stopped walking and bumped into him.

Royce turned around and looked right at Vance. "Problems applying the brakes?"

He sheepishly grinned. "Sorry, sir, I'll pay better attention."

A voice called out from behind Royce. "With Royce, you always need to pay extra special attention."

Royce smiled and turned around to meet an older man in fancy coveralls with a toolbelt. The man had thinning white hair, a white beard that entirely hid his neck, and a contagious smile.

Royce shook hands with him. "Juleay vis epron coneay."

The man nodded. "Meh koos gusay, vinioh lef es voley."

Royce turned halfway back to Vance. "This is the new squire: Vance Brewer. And Squire Brewer, this is Chief Engineer Eddison Frank of the Blue Planet Aerospace Chapter."

Eddison reached out his work-roughened hand toward Vance. Vance took his hand to shake it but was surprised by the firm muscular grip of the older gentleman. Eddison then smirked, "Has Royce taught you the old tongue yet?"

Vance shook his head. "Negative, sir. He has not."

"So, whenever I need to make a snide remark about you I should use that language, right?"

Vance stammered a moment not knowing what to say. Both Royce and Eddison chuckled, bringing a warm smile to Vance.

"Eddison, I brought Squire Brewer here hoping you had some free cycles. He has a lot of questions about The Winds."

Eddison nodded, "Well sure! I have the Enginemen reassembling the tertiary reaction cylinder as we speak. We have time right now."

He turned to Vance, "So Vance, how much do you know about The Solar Winds?"

Vance felt a little awkward hearing his first name used. That was always inappropriate in the military. "Well, Chief Frank, sir, I kinda–"

Eddison held up his hand, "Whoa, back off the thruster just a moment, son. I am a civilian and you are soon to become a Solar Knight; so I insist you call me 'Eddison'."

Vance looked toward Royce, "Is that allowed?"

Eddison burst out laughing and turned to Royce. "You have a cautious one here."

Royce smiled. "Cautious and teachable." He turned to Vance. "Chief Engineer Frank will be your instructor on The Solar Winds. You will obey his instructions as if they were orders."

Vance exhaled with a satisfied smile. "Aye sir." He then turned to Eddison, "Aye sir—I mean Eddison, sir."

Eddison chuckled again. "Well, first I'm going to warn you, young Knight-in-training. The eight Orders of the Solar Knights do not view The Solar Winds in the same way. The Fire Lance and the Wind

Dancers have an almost spiritual connection with The Winds. The Orbiting Star generally see all this as some kind of funny adventure. The Gun Stars see The Winds as a spiritual manifestation of their destiny on a 'holy crusade'. As for the Virtus Occulatum, well, Nova only knows what they believe. Lily of the Valley and Rising Sun see the Winds as an extension of human evolution. But for those of us Blue Planet knights, The Solar Winds is purely a principle of the natural world; nothing spiritual or supernatural about it."

"You guys seem a lot more diversified than I would have thought," Vance said, venturing his opinion.

Royce smiled. "Yes, but you should ask Eddison's opinion on scientific advancement and warfare."

Eddison laughed.

Vance raised his brow. There was something deliciously mysterious in the topic. "May I ask what your opinion is, sir?"

"Royce sure knows how to start up a massive conversation," Eddison began. "You see, it is still a matter of discussion whether science and war go hand in hand. But as for engineering and battle, the question has already been decided. Everything from slight modifications on contemporary systems, on down to the birth of the starlancer class starfighter has resulted from this."

Eddison turned around and pointed to a large machine up against the far wall. Vance peered at it. It looked like a giant motorized suit of armor, painted blue with gold trims.

"That," Eddison proudly announced, "is the current culmination of engineering and battle. We still don't have a gabb name for the powered armor suits. You see, we aren't as creative with nicknames as the navy."

Vance snickered.

"Now on to that first lesson," Eddison decided. He took out a small device from his tool belt and handed it to Vance. "This is an Aeonometer. It measures aeon drift, but that's not part of the lesson. I want you to hold it and tell me what you feel."

Vance took the long rod-shaped device into both hands. He looked it over and hefted it to approximate its weight. "I don't feel nothin', sir."

"Correct," Eddison appraised. He then reached over and flipped the power switch on. "Now what do you feel?"

The device vibrated. It was just like he would feel when checking starcraft engines. He looked up at Eddison, "I can feel it vibrating. Like when I'm inspecting aerospace thrusters."

"Good," Eddison concluded. "Now tell me why you didn't feel the vibration until I turned it on?"

Vance shrugged. "'Cus there's no power runnin' I guess."

He nodded. "And why was it, that when you inspected Royce's starlancer, you first started a computer diagnostic?"

"'Cus, I can't feel the vibrating if it ain't runnin'," Vance replied.

Eddison smirked, "Now tell me why you think that is?"

Vance thought a moment.

Eddison added, "And if you need a hint: there's a reason I first handed you the Aeonometer."

Vance's eyes widened. "'Cus it needed to be turned on!"

"Yes. Now let's go a step deeper." Eddison took back the Aeonometer. He unscrewed the bottom cap and emptied two large batteries into his other hand. "These are simple, everyday items you see all the time. What can you tell me about them?"

Vance shrugged. "They're batteries. They store power."

"Very good, very good. But do you know how we get that power out of there?"

"Well yeah," Vance said. "When you have a wire touching both ends you have a closed circuit and the electricity starts flowin'."

"Very good, Vance. We could go a whole lot deeper into the principles that make that possible. But, if I've correctly gauged your level of understanding, we'll stay right here for now. That circuit creates an electrical field—well it also creates a magnetic field too. But special relativity reveals that to be just another electrical field anyway."

Eddison stopped when he noticed the confused look on Vance's face. "Sorry, sometimes simplifying the complex is more of an art than a formula. But this is at the heart of what Solar Knights can do."

"They can feel electrical fields?"

Eddison shook his head. "No, but an electric field must be present. Without it, you can't interact with the Nakkaron particles that make up The Solar Winds. You weren't feeling the vibration of electrons moving in concert. You were feeling the Nakkaron particle effect *by way of* the electrical field."

Vance looked warily at Eddison. "...okay..."

Eddison smiled. "Here's your homework." Eddison screwed the cap back on the end of the Aeonometer and switched it on. Then he held it out to Vance. "Touch this."

Vance obeyed.

"Your homework is to tell me why you are feeling the vibration."

Vance wrinkled his nose and squinted one eye. "Is that a trick question? It's because it's turned on."

Eddison opened his other hand to reveal the two batteries he had not put back into the device. Vance froze at the sight. He quickly glanced back at the Aeonometer. It was running and he felt the vibration. "Get spaced!" he said in amazement.

Eddison let go of the Aeonometer and it lost all power. Vance no longer felt any vibrating. He looked at Eddison's hand. Eddison politely opened his hand and showed it to Vance for inspection.

Vance looked at Eddison's bare hand, then back to the Aeonometer, then back to Eddison's hand.

Royce laughed. "You are pure evil sometimes, Eddison."

Eddison smiled as he looked at Royce. "A magician is nothing more than a physicist having fun."

He looked back at Vance. "This homework assignment is open-book. I expect you to spend some time on the library network and read what you can on electrical fields and circuits. I expect a well-thought-out answer tomorrow."

Bewilderment still decorated Vance's face. "Aye sir."

Chapter 11
THE DISCOVERY

In the two-thousand two-hundred and twentieth year of the Mori, the Mori's scientific aspirations had waned to such a degree that no new experiments or exploration were attempted. The very concepts and fundamental knowledge that still drives their colossal machines had become an afterthought. As a result, the entire Mori society forgot how to run the technological wonders that had been built by their ancestors. To this day, they rely on the automation these magnificent machines afford but have forever lost the ability to even repair them.

—FROM "GALACTIC HISTORY VOL. III" BY PROF. EZRA DOUGHERTY

Vance spent the rest of the evening sitting in his bunk with a large flat tablet computer from the ship's library. He perused the library network. He read and watched everything he could find on electric fields.

He then spent two hours with a little flashlight; turning it on and off, on and off, over and over again. Then he unscrewed the bottom cap and removed the batteries. He stared intently at every inch of the flashlight's interior and exterior.

He put the batteries back in, screwed the cap back on, and turned the flashlight back on. Then he unscrewed the cap once more and let the batteries fall back into his hand. Then, one by one he placed the batteries back into the flashlight but had trouble screwing the cap back on. The cap slipped out of his hands and the batteries dropped out and onto his bunk.

"Kreket!" he cursed.

He picked up the batteries and then began looking for the flashlight cap. He slid off his bunk and onto his feet, then shined the flashlight under the bunk and saw the missing cap. He grabbed the cap and froze.

He examined the cap and the two batteries in his right hand. Then he looked over to the flashlight that was shining light in his left hand. He turned his wrist to look at the back end of the flashlight; he saw the empty flashlight cylinder.

"Get spaced!" he blurted out. "What is goin' on?"

He dropped the batteries on the floor, and the flashlight stopped working. Vance stared at the flashlight with a dumbfounded expression. Then he picked up the batteries, and instantly the flashlight turned back on. He dropped one battery, and the flashlight faded and went out.

Vance smiled. "I get it. It still needs power, but somehow I'm completin' the circuit."

Vance then heard the loudspeaker announce, "Taps! Taps! Lights out! All hands turn in to your bunks. Maintain silence about the decks."

Vance turned out the lights and fell softly into a deep sleep with a wide grin on his face. The next morning, he showered, ate morning's chow, and headed on over to the flight deck to meet Royce. Vance took his flashlight with him.

Vance stood there with his mind running circles. He was so pleased with the flashlight and the batteries. Then a familiar voice called out to him. "Squire Brewer."

Vance smiled at Royce, holding up his flashlight. Royce walked up and glanced at the flashlight. "Well, you look happy," he observed. "Does this mean you have found an answer for Eddison?"

Vance eagerly nodded. "Sure have sir. Look." Vance turned on the flashlight and waved it around. Then he opened his other hand displaying the batteries.

Royce grinned wide. "Attaboy Brewer! You've probably set a new record."

"I still don't know exactly how I'm doin' it," he admitted, "but it's gabb strange, sir.

"Good," Royce observed. "Eddison will have fun answering your questions." He motioned over to the starlancer. "Ready for round two?"

Vance eagerly nodded, then his eyes widened. He sullenly shook his head. "Negative sir, the flight surgeon prescribed me a day of rest before going back out."

Royce gave a nonchalant grin and tilted his head to the side for a moment. "Well, do you feel rested?"

Vance nodded. "Affirmative sir."

"Then hop in."

Vance put his helmet on and quickly climbed the stairs and got into his seat. Royce followed and climbed into the front seat. As Royce started through the pre-flight sequence, Vance allowed his mind to wander. He thought about the flashlight. What mystery had he stumbled onto? How did he make it work? What changed about him that allowed it to work?

Before he knew it, Vance was once again thrown back into his seat. The starlancer launched out through the space door at the end of the runway. He was once again reacquainted with the wondrous starry blackness of space.

"We're on a routine patrol with Ponzer as our wingman," Royce notified. "So we shouldn't see any Mori this flight."

"Permission to ask a question, sir?"

Royce nodded. "Fire away, Squire."

"Does anyone know why the Mori are still chasin' us? I mean, they already destroyed Earth. Why do they hate us so much they have to make sure we're all dead?"

Royce took a long breath. "You don't go for the easy questions, do you, Brewer?"

"'Course not, sir," Vance said, smiling. "I was instructed to go for the correct questions."

Royce smiled. "Tell me what you know already about the Mori, and I will fill in the gaps."

Vance shrugged, "Well I know the Mori are the big kids on the block, so to speak. We must've given them the can somehow because they want us all dead."

"The Mori are a part of current events," Royce explained. "And they are also a part of old history—there's also an ancient history before that, but we won't go there yet. In old history, the Mori forgot how to repair or even run the technological wonders their ancestors built."

"Firefly. Ponzer," a voice reported through the transmission. "I have just formed up on your wing."

"Roger Ponzer. Let's lay out a large scanning grid and see what's out here."

"Roger that Firefly."

Royce turned off the transmission. "Anyway," he continued. "The Mori didn't care enough about humans to even acknowledge our presence. That is, until they learned about the Solar Knights."

Vance tilted his head off to the side, "What do ya' mean, sir?"

Royce exhaled hard. "If it were not for the Solar Knights, the Mori would not be hunting us down to extinction."

Vance blinked a few times, not trusting his ears. "Are you saying it's our fault?"

Royce waited a moment before answering. "Affirmative." He pulled the starlancer into a gentle turn. The wildcat gracefully followed in formation.

Vance swallowed hard. "I don't suppose it's somethin' we can fix?"

"The real problem is this," Royce explained. "The Mori no longer know *how* to interact with the technological wonders of the ancients. They lost that ability more than twenty-five hundred years ago."

Royce leveled out from the turn. He glanced back through the canopy and took visual note of Ponzer's position. "And then along comes the little not-worth-recognizing humans with a home-grown secret." Royce paused.

Royce waited as if he wanted him to guess. Vance replied, "The ability to move The Winds?"

"How eloquently put," he appraised. "As fate would have it, The Winds is precisely how the ancient wonders are controlled."

Vance's eyes widened. "You mean, they can no longer control the ancient machines, but we could?"

"Affirmative, Squire."

Vance cast his eyes downward in thought. "Talk about a security risk... that's like not bein' able to fly your own starfighter but a potential enemy could."

"...which is why," Royce amended. "On the 13th day of Ternary, in year zero, the Mori began the systematic extermination of all human life..."

"The Year of Infamy." Vance identified. He lowered his head. "No sir, I don't think it's anything we can fix."

"Brewer, are you watching your scope?" Royce alerted.

Vance's eye focused on the SEDAR screen. "Three bogeys, sir. And I'm not counting our wingman this time."

Royce smiled. "Good. Now can you tell me their position?"

Vance shrugged. "Uh, well... if it was a clock, they'd be halfway between noon and one o'clock, sir."

Royce shook his head. "Reserve clock notation for a visual sighting. For a SEDAR contact, just use the bearing notation you see around the outer circle."

Vance reassessed the screen a moment. "Oh, got it. Three bogeys bearing 035, sir."

Ponzer's voice sounded through the transmission. "Firefly. Ponzer. Three bogeys inbound bearing zero-three-five. Heading three-one-seven. No tally yet."

"Nicely done, Squire Brewer," Royce praised. "Ponzer even confirmed it."

"Thank you, sir."

Royce switched on the transmission. "Roger, Ponzer. Let's go in for a closer look." He switched it back off.

Royce pushed the throttle to maximum. Vance felt himself be pushed against the back of his chair. Royce then rolled the starlancer into a wide turn. Vance watched the SEDAR screen. The three orange dots slowly moved to the top of the SEDAR screen.

"Okay Brewer," Royce directed. "Now on the left of your instrument panel, there will be an IFF readout on those SEDAR contacts."

Vance looked over to a square screen that read, INVALID IFF RESPONSE. SCP-003. He looked back up to Royce. "Uh, it says it's an invalid response, sir."

"That means there's an 80% chance they are Mori scouts," Royce explained. "So much for not encountering them today."

"They're movin' sir!" Vance panicked. He watched the orange dots start moving erratically. Then he looked up and saw the distant yellow engine glow of the three fighters.

He saw one of them swing out wide to the right. Another one swung out wide to the left, while the third started into a wide climbing loop.

Ponzer's voice rang out over the transmission. "Confirmed three bandits, rolling into attack vectors."

Royce switched the transmission back on. "Roger Ponzer. Take Bandit three, I'll take Bandit two."

Royce briefly hit his afterburners. The sudden extra jolt of acceleration helped Royce stay behind the Mori starfighter. Moments later, Vance heard the growling sound of the targeting computer in his helmet. Royce snapped the trigger and a missile rocketed away from under their wing. It sped off toward the starfighter in their sights.

Royce did not wait to confirm the impact. He broke hard to starboard, again hitting his afterburner. He quickly circled about and was heading toward the first of the three starfighters.

"Splash Bandit three," Ponzer called out.

Royce grunted. "Ponzer. Tally bandit one. Forming up on your six. Scissor him to port."

Ponzer's wildcat rolled to the left side. The trailing Mori starfighter fought to keep him within his firing arc. Royce again hit his afterburner and closed in. Soon Vance and Royce heard the growling of the targeting computer. Royce fired another missile.

The missile rocketed toward the Mori starfighter. It tracked each course adjustment the starfighter made. The Mori starfighter exploded in a neon green flash of light and debris.

"Splash bandit one," Royce called out. He then switched off the transmission. "Brewer, do you see that other bandit on SEDAR or did we get him?"

"Negative, sir."

Royce switched on the transmission. "Ponzer, negative confirmation on bandit two. Let's finish our sweep of the area and RTB."

"Roger, Firefly.

Chapter 12
THE BIGGER PICTURE

Eddison's first law of The Winds states: in order to manipulate The Winds on a given system, a person must first have at least a rudimentary understanding of how that system works.

—FROM "THE SCIENCE OF THE WINDS" BY PROFESSOR-EMERITUS PING CHENG

Vance stood tall, shining the flashlight around in front of Eddison. Then he opened his other hand to reveal the batteries. Royce and Eddison applauded.

"Truly you are one of the fastest learners I've encountered," Eddison appraised. "Now, are you ready for your quiz?"

Vance's smile faded. "A quiz?"

Royce tilted his head straight up and closed his eyes. "I think I know where you're going with this, Eddison, and you are truly evil."

Eddison chuckled. "Okay Vance, but be careful; it doesn't work all the time. Sometimes it can fail you at the very moment you need it."

Vance's eyebrows furrowed and his mouth silently parted. "You mean, it can break?"

Eddison nodded. "Yes. Now for your quiz. Let's see you do it one more time, and hope it doesn't fail."

Vance fingered the batteries in one hand and turned on the switch to the flashlight in the other hand. Nothing happened. Vance flicked the switch a few more times. Still nothing. "Ah, nah, nah, nah, not now. It was workin' so perfectly!"

Eddison laughed out loud. "You believed me, and you doubted."

"I don't understand," Vance admitted.

Eddison leaned closer. "The first law is, you must have at least a basic understanding of how a system works. That is why you needed to do some homework before you could command The Winds. The second law is, it cannot work unless you expect it to."

Vance glanced back down at the flashlight. He caressed the flashlight switch with his thumb for a brief moment and then turned it on. The flashlight shined brightly.

Vance exhaled sharply with a wide grin on his face. "That's just gabb weird!"

Royce nodded. "That's why a lot of the Orders emphasize faith and belief so much. If you can't believe it, you can't do it."

Vance widened his eyes and narrowed his brow. "Eddison, sir. Does this whole belief thing mean that I can intentionally break it?"

Eddison and Royce were both silent a moment and exchanged glances. Eddison broke the silence. "You say he's a first-year student?"

Royce nodded. "Nova as my witness."

Eddison turned back to Vance. "Well, Vance. Tell me, can you intentionally break it?"

Vance glanced at Royce. His expression did not divulge any information. He turned back to Eddison. He placed both batteries back into the flashlight and screwed on the end cap. He turned the flashlight on and off a few times to verify it was assembled correctly. Then he glanced back up to Eddison.

Eddison held his beard with one hand, while his other hand supported his elbow. His eyes were glued to Vance's flashlight. Vance turned the flashlight on again. Nothing happened this time.

"Get spaced!" Vance said in excitement. "No way!"

"Vance," Eddison said. "No first-year student has ever thought to ask that question, let alone actually do it."

Vance looked up in shock. "What?"

Royce smiled. "Seems you're a fast learner, Brewer."

Eddison turned to face Royce. "I guess he is ready to begin his rounds."

Royce shook his head. "He has to complete flight school first."

Vance looked at Eddison, then Royce, then back to Eddison. "Rounds?"

Eddison smiled. "When you become a Solar Knight, you must petition to join one of the eight knightly Orders. So it is customary for young knights to make their rounds spending time with members of each order. It's also called going on tour with the orders."

"I thought I was going to be in Fire Lance, with Sky Captain Williams?" Vance looked over to Royce.

Royce shook his head. "You still have to qualify. Fire Lance is not a walk in the park. We are the masters of the starfighter—and not just the starlancer. We can quickly adapt and get the feel of any fighter craft. To become a Fire Lance is to be able to threaten any fleet with any craft." He swallowed a moment. "Brewer, I would love for you to become a Fire Lance Knight. It would mean sending you away to flight training school, though. Upon graduation, you could begin your rounds."

"Do I gotta do the rounds before I decide to be a Fire Lance?" Vance inquired.

Eddison snorted. "Yes, of course. You have no idea just where your talents lie. It's best to explore each of the Orders and in what ways they specialize in using The Winds."

"Okay," Vance decided. "When do I get started with flight training?"

Royce smiled. "I'll get it scheduled. A member of the Orbiting Star order will accompany you to the flight school—but be careful around those clowns. They wouldn't know dignity if it were embroidered on their uniform."

Eddison laughed. "That's a bit harsh, Royce."

"They're not much more than a joke; their blatant levity is a disgrace to the Orders," he stated flatly.

"Perhaps so," Eddison offered. "But everyone has their place in the tapestry of this existence—yes even the Orbiting Star. It is worth noting, that the Lily of the Valley order routinely prescribes spending time with the Orbiting Star. It helps Solar Knights suffering from stress and anxiety." He turned to Vance. "Lily of the Valley is the Solar Knight order consisting of medical professionals."

Royce huffed and turned back to Vance. "Just remember to keep the conduct of an officer."

Vance nodded. "Aye sir."

"In the meantime," Royce continued. "Get some chow; I want you with me for the next flight briefing at fourteen-hundred hours."

The mid-day meal hadn't seemed so menial to Vance until that day. He spun the spaghetti around his fork and lifted his utensil to watch the noodles unwind off his fork. He spun the spaghetti up on his fork again, and in like manner watched it unwind. He watched gravity pull apart his creation several more times. What laws governed the system he was observing?

In the end, the demands of his stomach won out over his curiosity, and he reluctantly ate his food. After lunch, he made his way to the stairwell leading to the topside deck.

As soon as he found the Ready Room, he entered without any invitation. Inside he found several people seated around a large table. Many more stood in the back with mugs of coffee in their hands.

He saw Royce sitting down talking to Eddison and another uniformed officer. On the other side of Royce, was Sedston. Sedston glared at Vance for a few seconds before turning his eyes away. All the muscles in his stomach tightened and his heart felt heavier.

He took the first available seat and tried not to look anyone in the eye until he had to. Somehow it felt safer to be invisible for as long as possible.

"Attention on deck!" a voice called out from the back of the room.

Everyone who was seated, including Vance, jumped to their feet and faced the door. The admiral, a short muscular man in his mid-fifties, had just entered the room.

"Carry on," he said as he strolled inside.

Everyone took a seat around the table, including the crewmen who were sauntering in the back. Why was the admiral attending this briefing? He forgot all about Sedston and was now self-conscious for a new reason.

"Sky Captain Williams, and Eddison Frank," the admiral addressed. "Thank you for your continued support."

"Our pleasure, Admiral," Royce smiled.

Eddison nodded. "No thanks necessary, Rear Admiral Hauls, we're all in this together."

Rear Admiral Hauls turned to the officer that Royce and Eddison were talking to. "Captain Thompson, let's hear your report."

Captain Thompson stood up and walked around to the front of the table, carrying a tablet computer. He pressed a button on the tablet and a wall-mounted screen turned on and displayed a grid map of outer space.

He produced a laser pointer from his uniform jacket pocket and shined a red dot on a spot on the star map. "The first sightings of Mori scouts were reported in sector 7439 by 4312 by 173. Since then, Mori have been sighted in these surrounding sectors." Captain Thompson traced a large area with the laser pointer.

"And with the intel brought back by Sky Captain Williams and Lieutenant Sedston," he continued, "we've identified a patrol fleet in this sector, heading right for our position. They're traveling at a slow pace. That suggests they are in a search pattern and have no idea they're going to run right into us."

The room erupted into muffled whispers. Captain Thompson pressed another button on his tablet. The wall-mounted screen changed to show still shot photos from Royce's starlancer. Vance looked at the images; they were from his first flight with Royce.

"From these images," Captain Thompson continued. "We can estimate this trailing fleet has a starcraft carrier, eight destroyers, two battleships, and about twenty to thirty smaller support craft."

Royce raised his hand. "What does the tactical simulator predict?"

Captain Thompson exhaled. "Tactical simulations theorize we could win a head-on encounter. But, we'd lose so many ships it would be just as if we lost."

Rear Admiral Hauls turned to Royce. "Can the Solar Knights improve those odds?"

"With the right strategy," Royce explained, "any odds can be improved. But in an all-out confrontation, you're playing a numbers game any way you look at it."

Sedston raised his hand, "Does this mean we need to move the fleet?"

Captain Thompson lowered his head a brief moment. "That is the advice of the A.I.O."

"I'm hesitant to pull back," Rear Admiral Hauls stated. "We've not yet rendezvoused with Delta Fleet, and if we relocate, we may never meet up."

Captain Thompson looked at Eddison. "Chief Engineer Frank, how much time can you buy us?"

Eddison took a long, deep, thoughtful breath. "We can improve your sensor jamming. And depending on how Sky Captain Williams can manage the Mori scouts, we can give you as much as three weeks at best."

"And at the end of three weeks?" Captain Thompson inquired.

"At the end of three weeks," Eddison clarified. "This fleet will be unavoidably discovered by the Mori."

Rear Admiral Hauls exhaled slowly. "Rendezvousing with Delta Fleet is our standing order. So if you can buy us three weeks, we stay here for three more weeks. Then we pull out at flank speed."

Vance's thoughts wandered off. Their fleet was waiting to join up with another fleet, and the other fleet had been delayed. If he went off to flight training now, would this fleet be here when he got back?

He allowed his worry to get the better of him and his attention faded out until he could only hear his doubts and fears. It wasn't until he heard the Captain say 'Dismissed', that he snapped out of his internal haze.

Vance stood up and filed out of the ready room but lingered near the door until Royce joined him. "Hey Squire Brewer, what's on your mind?"

"Sir, is flight training more than three weeks?" he asked.

"Twenty-two weeks," Royce replied.

"Kreket," He mumbled. "The fleet won't be here in twenty-two weeks," he complained.

Royce placed one hand on Vance's shoulder. "Nova only knows what is in store for you. If it is the will of The Winds that we meet again, we will meet again."

Vance felt a sudden sense of loneliness. He was no longer an Aerospace Machinist's Mate. He no longer had a work center with people to talk to. And his last friend, Sedston... well, he figured that was gone as well. He probably shouldn't feel any hesitation to leave the carrier. All he had left was the familiarity of the corridors, the mess hall, and his bunk. His last anchor was Royce, the man who believed in him. That was, perhaps, the one thing he could not let go of.

"Can I do it in three weeks instead?" he asked. "Like if I cram and study like Nova himself, could it be done?"

Royce tilted his head slightly off to one side. "It's not a good idea to rush flight training. Especially if you're wanting to qualify for Fire Lance."

Vance's hand began to tremble, and his breathing became shallow. "Sir, I don't want to go if I can't ever come back to you."

Royce's eyes softened. "Brewer, becoming a Solar Knight is what you were born to do. Life will always test you to see if you're serious about it. It will throw friends, relationships, money, prestige, and anything it can find at you. All to see if you are serious about becoming something greater than the sum of your experiences."

Vance diverted his eyes.

"Our paths will cross again," Royce promised, "you can be sure of it. For Nova put us together in the same place at the same time for a reason. Trust in The Winds, and not even the Mori will be able to keep us from reuniting."

Vance sniffled as a lone tear traced its path down his face. He was once again losing his only friend.

Royce looked into Vance's eyes. "I have sent word to Hans Christian. He is an Orbiting Star knight—one that I trust. I still think he's a joke, but he's as loyal as a moon in orbit. He'll fly out here tomorrow morning. He will accompany you to flight school."

"I'm scared sir," he finally admitted.

Royce exhaled with a half-smile. "Be not afraid of greatness, Brewer, just be believing."

Chapter 13

THE ORBITING STAR

*Eddison's second law of The Winds states:
successful manipulation of The Winds is directly
proportional to a person's belief that their
manipulation will be successful.*

—FROM "THE SCIENCE OF THE WINDS" BY PROFESSOR-EMERITUS
PING CHENG

Vance sat in the back seat of a starlancer looking through the canopy at the landing bay he had come to know as home. Royce was not in the front seat of the starlancer; it was another Solar Knight he just met. He had introduced himself as Hans Christian only an hour before.

The starlancer taxied over to the runway. It followed the guiding hand signals of the plane directors on the flight deck. Vance observed the Solar Knight in the front seat. He wore a green helmet decorated with cartoon characters. Vance wondered if the decorated helmet was what made Royce consider them a joke.

Hans seemed to be just as detailed in his pre-flight operation as Royce had been. But then again, if all Solar Knights were pilots, it would make sense that they would all be professionals behind the stick. Hans flipped a few switches. The groan of the engines died down as he straightened out his alignment on the runway.

Vance heard the radio chatter in his ear from his helmet. "LazyDuck, you are Outgoing O-six to Mother."

"Roger Allstar," Hans replied.

"Outgoing six, you are cleared to launch. Watch the magnetic wind from Sagittarius bearing zero-nine-three."

"Outgoing, Roger. Thank you boys for your hospitality, and have a fabulous day," Hans replied.

Vance's heart sank. He was leaving his home and might never again return. His thoughts were interrupted when he was thrown back into his seat. The starlancer bolted forward along the runway and sped out the open space door.

"Yeee-hah!" Hans shouted. "I *never* get tired of that!"

He turned his head toward Vance, as much as possible. "So what's your story, Mr. Brewer?"

Vance cleared his throat. "I, uh... I guess I'm to become a Solar Knight."

Hans laughed. "I know *that*, what I don't know is who you are and where you come from?"

"Well," he recollected. "I was born on Driscal on the 28th of Novenary.

"Hey, I have a Novenary birthday too!" Hans cheered. "Mine is on the 12th."

"Get spaced, that's gabb." Vance smiled.

"So, Driscal," Hans further inquired. "That's a volcanic world. So were you a water farmer or an ore miner?"

"Hydroponics technician, actually."

"Ah, the one choice I didn't think of," Hans admitted. "And how was it working under the iron fist of Queen Marsha Va'Laross?"

Vance snorted. "It was the biggest incentive to join the military."

Hans chuckled. "Yeah, I hear that."

Vance frowned. "Wait, you tellin' me you know about Queen Va'Laross?"

"I wasn't born on Driscal," Hans began, "but I lived there for about 12 years. I was a rad ore miner. Pretty successful one too, until her royal hiney decided we were making too much money and raised the costs of living."

"Never in a million years would I have thought I'd meet another Driscan way out here."

Hans laughed. "You'll find that the galaxy really is a small—hello?" He readjusted his helmet visor. "We've just been scanned."

Vance darted his eyes down to the SEDAR screen. No dots. "I don't get anything on SEDAR, you sure?"

Hans nodded. "Yep, I felt it."

"Felt it, as in the Solar Winds, kinda 'felt it'?"

"Affirmative, Mr. Vance. Hans the Bronze has a suspicion we are being followed." He flipped another switch and gently rolled the starlancer to the right. "Let's go see who is so curious about us."

Vance kept his eyes on the SEDAR but then looked out the front of the canopy, hoping to see something.

"Whoa, did you feel that, Vance?"

Vance shook his head and then realized Hans could not see his head shake. "No sir, I got nothin'."

"Give it time," Hans directed. "It takes a little practice to hear The Winds."

A blaring alarm stole Vance's attention back to the SEDAR. A fast-moving red dot streaked toward the center of the screen. "Fast incoming, bearing one-seven-two!"

Hans rolled the starlancer hard to the left and hit his afterburner as a missile streaked past the canopy.

Hans shook his head a moment. "Mori don't use missiles. This is getting more interesting by the minute."

"But why would any *human* want to fire on us?" Vance inquired.

Hans shrugged. "Probably a lazy pilot who didn't bother to get a confirmation before firing. That alone could get a pilot in big trouble." Hans looked back toward Vance. "Hey, do me a favor, do you know how to trace the trajectory?"

Vance looked at his instrumentation panel in confusion. "Uh…"

Hans smiled. "Not to worry, the small square screen on the far left. Hit the triangle button." He snickered. "Get it, the 'triangle' button to 'triangulate'?"

"I'm afraid I don't get it," he admitted.

Hans laughed. "Not to worry, my friend, we will have you unwound and loose as a goose in no time flat. It's not healthy to be all strict and serious for too long, in my opinion."

Vance hit the button and graphing lines started flashing on his screen. "Okay, I'm seein' red, blue, and green lines."

"Don't worry about the green and blue, for now, just find out the bearing on the red line."

Vance checked the gauge again. "Oh, got it. Bearing one-seven-nine."

Hans rolled the starlancer in a tight turn to his left and then leveled out. "Okay, will the mystery guest please sign in?"

Vance watched his SEDAR screen. Two yellow dots popped up at the very top of the screen. "I have two bandits at zero-nine-zero."

Hans shook his head. "No, no. Even though they shot at us, we're still going to count them friendlies—misguided and in need of an earful from their squadron leader—but friendlies nonetheless."

"Aye sir." Vance said. "Two friendlies at zero-nine-zero."

Hans switched on the transmission. "You know you fellas can put an eye out if you're not careful."

Vance heard the reply through his helmet. "Stalker to unidentified starcraft. You are ordered to identify yourself immediately."

Hans giggled. "Stalker, this is LazyDuck. Starlancer class starfighter. Please be so kind as to stop shooting at an unidentified friendly while you still have the privilege of holding onto your wings, pilot."

The transmission was silent for a few minutes. Vance was about to give up waiting for the reply and ask Hans a question of his own. The voice on the other end finally replied. "There may have been an instrumentation failure causing a misidentification."

Hans switched off the transmission. "Yeah, right. They all say that when they don't want to own up to their own mistakes." He switched it back on. "Roger, Stalker. Proceed back to Mother and we'll follow you in. We'll gladly assist in the debrief so this 'malfunction' doesn't happen again."

Hans switched it back off and then laughed.

Vance failed to hold back some snickering of his own. "He probably suspects he's in trouble."

"Oh, he *knows* he's in trouble," Hans corrected. "Had he owned up to it, I'd have let it pass. But anyone who will not admit their mistakes is not worthy to wear their wings."

"So you gonna' submit a formal complaint?" Vance inquired.

"I don't know the whole story yet. Until I know what the conditions were for those pilots, I won't make up my mind. Sorry for the detour, Vance."

Soon, multiple specks appeared in the distance. When they got close enough, they resembled large capital ships. The largest one in the center was a starcraft carrier. It had the number CV-319 painted on the outside near the large space door.

"Oh, the Tiger," Hans recollected.

"Tiger?" Vance asked.

"The Ticonderoga, Mr. Brewer. We affectionately call her the Tiger," Hans explained.

Vance looked at the hull around the space door. Black marks, holes, and bent metal plating decorated the outer hull with hastily welded patches. These were the signs of battle damage—extensive battle damage. "Hans, this fleet has seen some major action."

"Now that you mention it," Hans agreed. "A lot of these ships are showing signs of damage. If these guys are in strung-out condition, that would explain a few things. But what I don't understand, is why this fleet is still here? They could easily meet up with Alpha Fleet, and get some proper repairs."

"I guess it's a good thing that pilot didn't apologize; we never would have found them."

Vance heard a voice in his helmet. "Incoming six, Tiger marshal."

Hans switched on the transmission. "Incoming six, go."

Vance heard the reply in his helmet. "Incoming six, you are cleared to land. Call the ball."

Hans replied, "Paddles, Incoming six, starlancer, 'LazyDuck', ball, fuel state 30.8, manual."

"Hans, what does 'call the ball' mean?" Vance asked.

"Oh, that?" he replied. "That's just the LSO checking in. I need to verify I can see the lineup lights as well as some other information. You see, they angle the lineup lights based on what type of craft is landing."

"LSO?" Vance asked.

"Landing signal officer. Whom we affectionately call Paddles."

"Roger, ball. Left for lineup," the voice said.

Hans adjusted his trajectory ever so slightly. Moments later, they flew through the large space door. The straps dug into Vance's shoulders. His insides wanted to keep flying forward. Vance wasn't sure he'd ever get used to coming to a complete stop in two seconds.

Chapter 14
DELTA FLEET

Following the nine months of the Mori's merciless purge of human life, nearly all human colonies and outposts were wiped out. Fortunately for humanity, their purge was sloppy. There were survivors scattered abroad. Acting-President Susan Bower issued an evacuation and a call to rendezvous at Norfolk's Nebula. The remains of the Earth Naval ships gathered up all the survivors they could find in whatever spaceworthy ships could be used—forming several fleets—and then proceeded to the rendezvous.

— FROM "GALACTIC HISTORY VOL. IV" BY PROF. EZRA DOUGHERTY

Hans taxied the starlancer, following the directions of the plane directors on the flight deck. Vance watched out the canopy seeing the flight deck crew staring back at him. A chill went up his spine as every set of eyes was directed at him and Hans.

At a hand signal from a plane director, Hans cut power to the engines and opened the canopy. Hans unbuckled and stood, facing Vance. "By Nova's name, stick close to me."

Vance stared back with wide eyes. He finally blinked. "Aye sir."

Vance took off his helmet and followed Hans down the stairs. Hans struck up a conversation with the starcraft handler and Vance surveyed the scene. The landing bay looked very similar to his home carrier. There was a lot of structural damage that was either poorly patched up or forgotten. The walls and deck were not perfectly painted, but instead charred and disfigured.

The hair on Vance's neck stood up on end. He slowly looked around. Everyone who was not actively recovering the starcraft was staring at him and Hans. It was better to not show his discomfort, so he shifted his weight to one leg hoping to look casual. He wasn't sure how well he did.

Hans nodded to the starcraft handler. "Thank you, Starman." He turned to Vance. "Follow me to the ready room."

Vance warily followed Hans who looked like he was perfectly at home without a care in the world. Hans had a sort of bounce in his step as though he were oblivious to the creepiness all around. Was Hans simply unaware? But then what of his stern warning, 'By Nova's name, stick close to me'? No, Hans had to know what was going on, at least enough to caution him.

Hans was, after all, a Solar Knight, and he had seen marvelous things from two Solar Knights so far. Part of him hoped to see more incredible things. The other part of him just wanted a simple stay and to quickly leave. He did still have flight school he needed to attend and graduate so he could apply for the Fire Lance order.

Hans and Vance rounded a corner and stopped just inside the ready room. Several officers were already seated, one of whom looked up at Hans and Vance and motioned for them to come in. "Please come in, Solars."

"Thank you, Captain Hawthorn," Hans addressed, taking his seat. Vance took a seat next to Hans.

"We didn't expect to see any Solars way out here."

Hans smiled. "It would seem Nova has smiled upon you. We were heading through this sector."

Several other officers huffed before Captain Hawthorn spoke what they all were murmuring. "I doubt very highly Nova has smiled on *this* fleet. We're two weeks behind rendezvousing with Alpha Fleet. And the attacks on our carrier have crippled us—we're dead in space until we can effect repairs."

Hans raised his eyebrows. "You need some expertise and two Solar Knights just happen to cross your path; I'd still say Nova *has* smiled upon you." He turned to Vance. "This is Squire Brewer, he specializes in repair. Just introduce us to your damage control team, and we'll help them get you underway."

Vance's eyes lit up. He had been volunteered to fix something a whole lot bigger than a starfighter engine. Hans had better know what he was talking about and not just blindly assuming he knew how to repair capital ship systems.

Captain Hawthorn looked around at the other officers at the table. One of them shrugged. Captain Hawthorn turned back to Hans. "We'll take all the help we can get. But we've had such a canner of a time getting the engines online. It seems one system after another keeps burning out."

"Solving mysteries," Hans identified, "is *my* specialty." He then stood up to take his leave. "Will you give my best to the admiral?"

Captain Hawthorn stared down at the table in front of him. "Admiral Betts died during the first encounter..."

Hans pursed his lips. "I'm very sorry to hear that, skipper."

Captain Hawthorn glanced up and nodded once, then spoke with a sullen voice, "dismissed."

Vance rose to his feet and followed Hans out the door. "Hans, I have a bad feeling about this whole place."

Hans nodded and kept staring forward as they walked. "Well, I'm no Lily, but I can tell this entire crew has been running on adrenaline for quite some time now."

"Hans, sir."

Hans exhaled. "Let me guess, you don't know much about fixing boats."

"Aye sir," he admitted.

He looked over to Vance as they descended a long staircase. "No problem. Royce said you know how to feel where something is wrong."

Vance widened his eyes and half nodded. "Starfighter engines, yes; anything bigger, no."

Hans stopped on the last few steps and pointed his finger at Vance. "Tell me this, Brewer, what's the difference between the electrical field in a starfighter, and the electrical field around a star?"

Vance stopped cold and studied Hans's finger and his question for a few moments. "I suppose the star is bigger and so the field must be stronger."

"It's a trick question," Hans admitted. "For a Solar Knight, the only difference is here." He pointed to Vance's head. "The only limitation is the mind. What is possible and impossible is not determined by scale, quantity, or distance. It's all determined in the mind. What you believe to be impossible, will become so for you."

Hans retracted his finger. "To a Solar Knight, stubborn faith *always* trumps what is realistic."

Vance weakly grinned. "I guess what I meant to say is, let me at those engines."

Hans smiled and winked. "*Now* you're talking like a Knight."

They finished descending the last few steps and entered the engine section. They had not gone far before the hallway in front of them was barred by five crewmen with cross expressions. Hans and Vance stopped. Another five or six crewmen blocked their retreat.

Hans forced a wide grin. "So good of you to meet us. Please lead the way to the main engines."

The man in the center of the front five men took a step forward. He had a thick mustache. His beard stubble hinted at sleepless nights and constant turmoil. "You Solwin canners caused this. We don't want you around to cause more."

"You can't be serious," Hans retorted. "You're sitting ducks out here in space and you want to run off the first helping hands that come your way?"

The man reached under his shirt and pulled out a pistol. He effortlessly pulled the slide back. The first round clicked into place in the chamber. He pointed it at Hans.

Hans exhaled. "I'm only going to tell you this once. So you'd better listen good. First, we're going to forget all about brandishing your sidearm and talk about attempted murder. Not only will you get to spend the rest of your tour in the brig, but you will be facing a general court-martial."

Hans pointed his finger back at the man. "And second," Hans grinned, "you have no idea what kind of combat training a Solar Knight goes through. It's not advisable to pick a fight you cannot win."

"Nothin' personal, Solwin, but protecting my shipmates is worth the risk." The man pulled the trigger. Vance stopped breathing, watching the small flash from the barrel of the pistol. A split second later the air between them and the shooter shimmered like water. The bullet hung suspended in the shimmering air for a brief moment. Then it dropped to the ground.

Vance blinked and shook his head. What had he just witnessed? Was it for real? He had seen the flash of the barrel and then the bullet stopping in mid-air. His brain replayed the event twice over.

After the bullet clinked to the floor, Hans cocked his head to one side. "I stopped the first round. If you choose to shoot again, I guarantee the next one will ricochet."

A second man turned to the man with the pistol. "Jay, let's forget this."

Jay shook his head. "I'm already in too deep. I'm gonna have to see this one through to the end..."

"My friend, you're not going to win this one," Hans cautioned. "Cut your losses now."

Jay shook his head. "Can't." He fired another round.

Hans balled his hand into a fist and threw a punch into the empty air toward Jay. Again, the air between them and Jay shimmered like a stone hitting water. This time, however, Jay cried out in pain and dropped to his knees. His pistol clattered to the ground.

Hans slowly walked toward Jay. The crowd of sailors rapidly dispersed like dew before the approaching sun. Hans reached Jay and lifted his head and looked into his eyes a moment. Then he turned around to the crewmen who stood behind them. "Get a corpsman down here, this man has been hit."

Chapter 15

INTRUDER

Those with the strongest affinity for The Crusade often demonstrate an accelerated learning curve. These individuals seem, as it were, to stumble upon the mysteries of The Winds almost as if they were falling into the gravitational pull of their ultimate destiny. Lineage and birth do not seem to be an indicator of who will hold such a strong affinity. Whether they are selected by Nova or chosen by fate, it can only be guessed.

—FROM "LECTURES ON THE CHOSEN" BY SAGE DOROTHY VLAVSKISK

Vance sighed in relief as two corpsmen lifted Jay onto a stretcher. A third was finishing up a field dressing around his wound. Vance turned his head at the sound of quick steps pounding against the stairwell steps. Four armed men exited the stairwell and advanced over to the scene.

One of the men approached Hans, who was standing prominently in the center of the corridor. "Sir, I am Chief Caldwell, Master-at-Arms. I'm going to need a statement."

Hans scowled at Caldwell. "Your small arms training is severely lacking, Chief Caldwell! If your junior enlisted cannot handle a sidearm without injuring themselves, it tells me your training has been insufficient."

Caldwell was taken aback for a moment.

Hans cocked his head slightly to the side. "Do you prefer this statement be made in writing?"

Caldwell shook his head. "No sir, that will not be necessary. You informed me you witnessed a weapon handling error in which a sailor was injured."

Hans waited for Caldwell to finish jotting down the details in a little notebook. "Can I be assured, Chief Caldwell, that another sidearm training will be coming soon?"

"That is affirmative sir. You may carry on with your duties."

Hans nodded before walking up to the stretcher. Jay was being hastily prepped for transport to another part of the ship. Hans placed one hand on Jay's arm. Jay, who was breathing with the aid of a breath mask, looked at him with regretful eyes.

"Got it," one corpsman announced to the others after securing Jay to the stretcher.

"Clear!" The second corpsman commanded. He pushed the stretcher down the hallway with the others in tow.

Vance walked up to Hans and whispered, to ensure his voice would not carry to the Masters-at-Arms. "Why didn't you tell them what really happened? That man belongs in the brig; he tried to kill us."

Hans leaned in toward Vance. "Right now, we need allies. If we're ever going to patch this place back together, we need people working *with* us instead of *against* us. We just lucked out that a foolish man's actions have given us the leverage we need."

Vance looked around him once more to verify their conversation was private. "What happens when they ask the other sailors what happened?"

Hans raised his eyebrows and tilted his head. "Admittedly, I am gambling on the hope that everyone else will corroborate my story. Call it a hunch, that I figured they would. They know they were in the wrong, and I provided a way out for them."

Vance lowered his eyes, studying Hans's words. He disagreed on many levels. His military training taught him to never break the rules and to never tolerate anyone else breaking the rules. And this was pretty close to a violation of both. Then his mind caught hold of the eerie feeling he had when they first came on board. The feeling when everyone was watching them. Hans was right; they needed allies.

"Sir," Vance whispered. "I hope this doesn't become a regular practice."

Hans smiled. "I love your integrity, Vance." He then motioned with his head toward the end of the hallway. "Now, let's get to the engine room."

Hans and Vance strolled down the dingy fire-bathed halls. Vance cleared his throat. "Hans, sir, how did you do that thing with the bullet?"

Hans stopped walking and turned to Vance. "Simple physics."

Vance twisted his face into a confused look. "Nothin' simple about stopping a bullet in mid-flight."

Hans smiled. "You've seen the hangar space door. You know how it allows starcraft to fly in and out without letting all the air in the ship get sucked out into space, right?"

Vance nodded. "Yeah, the pressure seal around the space door keeps air pressure in while larger, faster-moving objects can pass through it."

"In other words," Hans clarified, "the air is held in by a force field."

Vance nodded slowly, trying to find where this line of questioning was leading. "And somehow, knowing this makes it possible to stop bullets with The Solar Winds?"

Hans laughed. "You make me feel like such a magician when you over-think something so simple." He tapped a small box fixed to his belt. "Here's the magic."

Vance leaned in and inspected it. It had a small indicator light and a blue half-moon logo on it. "What's the logo mean?"

"Oh, that?" Hans asked. "That's just a warning label. Every force field generator is required to have that label. It basically lets you know it generates a force field. You know, in case you're worried about getting cancer or something from long-term exposure. You'll see that logo on anything that generates a force field."

Vance's eyes lit up. "It's a portable force field generator?"

Hans nodded. "And it doesn't need to be very strong, because—"

"Because it's an electric field and The Winds allows you to enhance it," Vance said.

Hans nodded in approval. "Welcome to the expertise of the Orbiting Star Solar Knights. We are the masters of force field manipulation." He smiled, "That, and one other thing."

"What's the other thing?"

"I'll give you a hint," Hans offered. "What happens when you cross-breed a cow and a shark?"

Vance's eyes darted around, searching for whatever tidbits of genetics he could remember. After a moment of stammering, he gave up. "I got nothin'. What happens?"

Hans leaned in closer with a stern glare. "I have no idea," he admitted. Then he burst into a smile, "But I wouldn't try milking it!"

Vance practically choked on his laugh. His brain still took a few extra seconds to realize Hans had told a joke. The silly mannerism in which he told it tickled Vance's funny bone long before his brain caught up.

Hans swatted Vance on the shoulder. "Vance the Lance needs to lighten up some more."

Both men continued walking to the Engine room. Once they entered the massive room, Vance observed men and women all over the place in a sea of human traffic. They were spot welding machinery, running cables, and programming computers. It resembled a construction site more than a room under repairs.

An officer dressed in a white button-down uniform shirt and slacks approached. "I am Lieutenant Ross Kimball. You are the two Solar Knights I was informed about?"

Hans nodded. "Yes, Lieutenant. I understand you've had a real canner of a time repairing this place."

Ross ran one hand through his hair. "It's been a perpetual nightmare. Every time we get close to fixing the engines, another system burns out, shorts out, or catches fire."

Hans looked deep into Ross's eyes. It wasn't clear if Hans was looking into him or past him. The corner of Hans's mouth crept up into a half-smile. "I encountered a problem that sounded very much like this one."

Ross's eyes perked up with hope glimmering. "What did you find?"

"Well," Hans began, "the ship I saw this on had a direct encounter with the Mori."

Ross nodded. "Well, we've had several."

"And they were once boarded by Mori soldiers."

Ross nodded again. "When we were first hit, a Mori assault shuttle raided our landing bay."

Vance gasped. "What happened?"

Ross turned to Vance. "There was a long firefight on the flight deck. We eliminated the intruders and cut down their shuttle for scrap."

Ross returned his look to Hans. "So what did you find out on the other ship?"

"They had a zandor'an," he replied.

Ross closed one eye in a confused expression. "A what?"

"An invisible Mori saboteur."

Ross's eyes widened. "Blast you Solwin! I hope you're frazzin kidding me."

Hans smiled. "Believe me, Lieutenant Kimball, I would have a whole lot more fun if I were."

"You're on a Typhoon class carrier," Vance blurted out. "The most advanced starcraft carrier built. And yet you report encountering system after system blowing out. Either your ship is a lemon and your whole dam-con team are all canners, or you have a saboteur."

Ross was silent for a few moments. He eyed Vance up and down. Either he was wondering how to reply or how to condescend.

Ross exhaled. "We have some of the best Damage Controlmen in the fleet," he admitted. "And this carrier would never have passed inspection if the primary systems kept going down at the drop of a hat. I guess the only logical answer would be a saboteur." He looked back at Hans. "I can get the Masters-at-Arms down here. But how do we flush out a saboteur that has remained undetected with so many crewmen around?"

Hans smirked. "That's where things get fun. We only need to threaten to repair the ship, and he will try to strike again. And all we have to do is introduce a nice juicy target."

Ross's mouth curled up into a weak smile. "I can get on board with that."

Hans turned to Vance. "Okay Vance the Lance, help these gentlemen find what is broken and they will fix it. The faster we find and fix, the more active the saboteur will have to be."

Vance nodded with a smile and walked over to the main reaction chamber. He began by feeling the chamber walls. He didn't feel anything. He wanted to curse but figured that might not send the best message of confidence. When working on the starcraft engines, he had to turn on the diagnostic software. He didn't know why at the time, but Royce had alluded to the electric field the diagnostic provided.

Vance had no idea how to run a diagnostic on a capital ship engine, let alone if one even existed. He closed his eyes a moment, waiting, wondering. Then he had a thought; this thing has power running. It should already have an electric field.

He thought about it a moment. What could the problem be from among so many possibilities? He mentally ran through the rules Eddison had told him. Was he believing too little? Was he wrong about the electric field? Was he missing a basic understanding of how the system worked?

Vance opened his eyes and turned to the closest engineman. "Tell me where the last system blow happened?"

The young woman in dark blue coveralls pointed to the gigantic turbine pre-compressor behind him. "Blasted pre-comp blew yesterday. We're about ready to space it all."

"Please give me a brief rundown of how the pre-comp works."

She nodded. "The pre-comp charges the particle fuel. Then accelerates it up to speed before the hand-off to the compressor." She scratched behind her ear and continued to elaborate on the complex function of the massive machine.

Vance's eyes glazed over. It was like drinking from an informational firehose. "Okay, okay, thank you Petty Officer 3rd class, uh," he glanced at her name embroidered on her coveralls. "Thurston."

He walked over to the pre-compressor, mumbling to himself. "I understand in a small way how you work. So you better frazzin speak to me..." He touched his hands to the cylinder wall and smiled. Bingo! It vibrated.

He slowly slid his hands around the cylinder wall. Then he ran his hands up inside the pre-compressor chamber. "You have a break in the electrical between this doohickey here and the outer chamber wall."

Upon hearing Vance's words, two enginemen immediately sprang into action. They dismantled the circuit housing in preparation for probing the electrical circuits.

Vance continued to slide his hands around the rest of the pre-compressor. "Hold it!" he shouted. "Somethin' is very wrong over here, and if I'm not mistaken, this is electrical too."

One of the enginemen pulled out his multimeter and placed the probes onto the spot Vance was feeling. "Kreket!" the engineman cursed. "We have a circuit overload just waiting to happen. If we try to repair the circuitry first, we could end up canning the entire pre-comp."

The second engineman abandoned his repairs. He joined the first in diagnosing the new problem. Vance stood back to give them room.

Ross walked up to Vance. "I hope you're not making this up..."

Vance instinctively lowered his head. But then a glint of indignation flashed in his eyes and he looked directly at Ross. "I believe your men can vouch for what is and is not real about the condition of your engines, sir."

Vance was not sure he could keep his confident composure for very long. So, he broke eye contact and moved on over to the main reaction chamber. "Okay, who can tell me how this one works?"

One by one, Vance went around to every single massive machine in the large open engine room. Hour after hour, he ran his hands over every square inch of the machines. His hands felt raw. System by system and part by part, the entire damage control crew was patching together the broken parts and damaged pieces.

Hans watched in amazement as Vance went around from place to place calling out the problems and the potential problems. He occasionally laughed when Vance had a hard time explaining how doohickey A and doohickey B were not 'jiving' together.

Vance now sat on a hand railing beside Hans. "How much longer ya think it'll take 'em before they get it all up and operational again?"

Hans shrugged. "Fixing things wasn't exactly my strong suit either. But solving mysteries is my passion. I was the canner kid who would rather read a book and figure out who done it, than go play with the other kids."

Hans snapped his fingers. "Which reminds me." He hopped off the railing. "I need to give you some basic combat training."

Vance wrinkled his nose. "What do ya mean? I had plenty of that in basic."

Hans snickered. "No, I mean *Solar Knight* combat training."

Vance's eyes widened. "You have special combat training?"

Hans's eyes narrowed and he tilted his head forward. "You know, we're called *knights* for a reason. Aside from all our specialties, we are first and foremost, combatants."

Vance hopped off the railing. "That's gabb! Yeah, let's train."

Hans looked around. He spotted a relatively secluded corner of the engine room. It was almost miraculous to find considering all the manpower that was currently employed in repairing the ship.

Vance followed and stopped behind Hans. He smiled, "Okay, first let's start with a few punches." He held up his hands for Vance to hit. Vance punched at Hans's left hand. Instead of feeling the soft pink skin, his fist felt like it collided with the metal bulkhead of the ship. A stinging pain raced through his hand and the air between them shimmer like water.

"Ahhh! Kreket! Kreket! Kreket!" Vance clutched his aching hand.

Hans chuckled. "Boy, judging by your reaction, you hit harder than I would have guessed."

"You said you were gonna *teach* me, not gloat over me! That was hardly fair..."

Hans narrowed his eyes and tilted his head off to one side. "In what way was it unfair?"

Vance pointed at Hans. "'Cus you got a force field generator!"

Hans smirked. "You're a gabb fast learner, Vance. So I'm going to ask you: *is it* unfair?"

Vance opened his mouth to shout out that it was, but then he caught himself and said nothing instead. There was something in the way Hans asked that question. Could this be another trick question?

He opened his mouth a second time to answer but hesitated. If this was a trick question, what was the trick? Where in this scenario was there a false assumption? One side with a force field and the other side without was definitely not a fair match. But if that was the trick question, then something in it was an assumption.

Is one side having an advantage the assumption? If it was going to be a fair fight, both sides would need to have force fields. And in that one thought, his mind caught hold of a question. Perhaps the very question that Vance needed to ask.

"Hans, sir," he sheepishly asked. "Does it matter who owns the force field generator?"

Hans's grin bloomed into a massive smile. "I'm willing to bet you probably already know the answer to that."

Vance held up both of his hands in the air, pretending to touch an invisible wall, like a pantomime. Then he suddenly pushed both hands forward. The air between them shimmered and Hans fell backward.

Vance stood there, stunned, and wide-eyed. His jaw hung open. "Did you see that?"

Hans rubbed his nose and chin. "Yup, Vance the Lance. And I felt it too."

"Did you see that?" Vance repeated, oblivious to Hans's words. "Did, you, see, that?"

Hans chuckled. "A gabb fast learner but a kid at heart. By Nova, I'm really starting to like you, Vance."

"I put my hands up and I pretended I knew what I was doing," he explained all in one breath. "And it happened like I was picturin' it in my head!"

Hans stood and placed both hands on Vance's shoulders. "Okay, cool the jets and kill the turbine. You have every reason to be excited. Quite frankly, you're acting exactly the way I did on my first successful attempt."

"Hans, this means I don't got just my equipment to work with, but I got everyone else's also." Vance's eyes lit up, "This probably means I can use an enemy's weapon against him, right?"

Hans nodded. "Yes, the possibilities are endless. But your practicality rests with how much practice you put in." He backed up a few paces and pulled out a coin from his pocket. "I'll toss the coin at you, and I want you to block it with a force field."

Vance nodded.

Hans threw the coin and it struck Vance on the forehead. He silently cursed. Hans picked up the coin. "Not to worry, Vance the Lance. We probably have a few hours. We're going to practice it until you can pull it off like a reflex."

Chapter 16
ZANDOR'AN

The Orbiting Star order has developed a rather surprising variation on the simple force field. By varying the harmonics of the field resonance, they angle the field into a dome-shaped curve that crackles with electrical discharges. I had the misfortune of touching one of these electrical discharges and my left arm was numb for two hours. When asked how they manipulate the field with such precision, their official response was, "very carefully".

—FROM "THE SCIENCE OF THE WINDS" BY PROFESSOR-EMERITUS PING CHENG

Vance stood with perspiration running down the side of his face. He stared intensely at Hans, waiting for the slightest motion. Hans smirked. "Why do I feel like I'm in a wild west showdown?"

Vance snickered.

Hans flung the coin as Vance threw his hands forward. The coin bounced off the force field and clattered to the ground. Hans cheered. "Woohoo! That's nineteen in a row!"

Vance smiled.

Hans looked around. "Ah darn, that was the last of my small change."

Vance felt his hands shake. He looked at them, quivering. "Hans?"

Hans looked. "Oh dear, you got the shakes," he said as he pulled out a small tablet from a pouch on his belt.

"The shakes?" Vance asked.

"Here, chew this." Hans gave him the tablet. "You're low on electrolytes."

Vance chewed the tablet and cringed at the taste. "Aw, that's awful."

Hans chuckled. "Yeah, it's an acquired taste. But at least you don't need water like with the gel caps."

"What's in it?" he asked.

"Magnesium, potassium, sodium, calcium, phosphorus, and a few others I don't remember," Hand replied. "They're called electrolytes. They're the stuff your body uses to regulate its electrical system. And using The Winds burns through your body's electrolytes fast."

"How fast?" Vance asked.

Hans shrugged. "Depends on how extensively you use The Winds. The more grandiose, the more you burn through."

"What happens if you run out?"

"Out of electrolytes?" Hans asked.

Vance nodded.

"First your hands start to shake," Hans explained. "After that, you'll experience mental fatigue—like a strong fog in your mind. Following that, your muscles will start to cramp. And by that time you should stop using The Winds until you take some electrolytes. If you keep using The Winds, you'll start to have breathing trouble. And then finally, fatal irregular heartbeat."

Vance's eyes widened. "You can die from using The Winds?"

"If you don't keep up your electrolytes when extensively using The Winds, yes, you can. Oh, and only take the recommended amount of supplements. You can also have health issues with too many electrolytes."

Vance nodded. "That's good ta know."

"How are you feeling now?" Hans asked.

Vance smiled and showed his hands. "Loose as a goose and ready to rock."

Hans laughed.

Vance's smile faded as a new question surfaced. "Hans, sir. How does a Mori become invisible? Do they use The Winds or somethin'?"

Hans shook his head. "No, the one we found used some kind of energy field. It negatively charged light photons and then deflected them. The technology is still light-years beyond our ability to duplicate though."

To Vance, it didn't seem feasible that anyone could go about trying to fight something they couldn't see. It seemed like an unfair advantage. But then again, he had thought Hans's portable force field generator was an unfair advantage. The memory of the flashlight demonstration with Eddison Frank flooded into his mind. He remembered stopping it from working, preventing the electricity from flowing. What if the Mori's technology wasn't the unfair advantage? What if *he* had the unfair advantage?

Vance stood up straight. "Sir, can I try somethin'?"

Hans cocked his head in curiosity. "Sure, what?"

"Put up your force field again."

Hans took a few steps back and held up his hand. The air between them shimmered. Vance held his hand out toward the force field for a few moments.

"Okay," Vance said.

Hans lowered his hand and the force field disappeared.

"Again," Vance said.

Hans eyed him curiously but threw his hand forward. The air between them again shimmered as a force field appeared. Vance held out his hand and closed his eyes. He concentrated on the electricity flowing through the force field generator. He imagined the electrons stopping their motion. Then he opened his eyes. The force field was still there, almost as if mocking his attempt.

Hans smiled. "If you're trying to sabotage it, good luck. That's a tough skill to learn. When I was doing my rounds with the Rising Sun order, the best I could do was turn off a reading pad."

Vance lowered his hand and shrugged. "Well, I was curious."

A young man in dark blue coveralls rushed over to Hans and Vance. "Excuse me, sir. Lieutenant Kimball has ordered a final briefing now that repairs are almost complete."

Hans smiled. "Ah, Ross the Boss is ready to set our trap. Please tell him we'll be right there."

He nodded and left. Vance looked over to Hans. "I hope I've had enough practice."

Hans walked up close to Vance. "Now don't forget Eddison's third law of The Winds: It'll only work if you expect it to."

Vance tilted his head off to one side. "I was told that was the second law."

Hans squinted and looked up. "Well then, which one is the third law?" He abruptly looked back at Vance. "Oh, it's the one about the size of the electric field not being as important as the flow of the Nakkarons."

"Wait, what?"

Hans simply smiled. "The first two are the ones I remember, the other two are a little sciencey for my taste." He put one hand on Vance's shoulder. "Come, let's not keep Ross the Boss waiting."

It took them a few minutes to find Ross, sifting through the sea of manpower. Everyone was moving all about performing diagnostics and last-minute inspections. Ross stood on a low gantry overlooking the final repairs. He hollered to a man below. "Double check the gravity field generator. The last thing I need is for the skipper to ask me why his coffee is floating away."

Ross turned around when he heard boots clanking on the metal gantry. "Where did you two disappear to for the last couple of hours?"

Hans smirked. "Top secret Solar Knight stuff; if I told you, I'd have to space you."

Ross snickered. "You know, I'm real pleased to find a Solar with a sense of humor. It sure has eased the tension."

Hans smiled and nodded. "That is the backbone of the Orbiting Star's philosophy. There's enough tight-canned seriousness in the galaxy to last ten lifetimes and we only live once."

"Well said," Ross appraised. "Now how about setting our trap? I've got the mains to the primary turbines unguarded. All the other systems have Masters-at-Arms stationed."

"That's a start," Hans appraised. "But I want to plan on our uninvited guest being more clever than that."

Ross's smile smeared off. "What's wrong with my setup?"

"I said it was a good start. Now I want you to pick one of the places you have Masters-at-Arms stationed and triple the number of men."

Ross narrowed one eye and tilted his head to one side. "What in Nova's name is that going to accomplish?"

Vance failed to suppress a chuckle. Ross's eyes were on him in an instant. He stood silent, hoping Hans would bail him out of the embarrassment. No such luck. Hans was quiet.

It was time to explain. "Begging your pardon, sir. But since you have guards posted, a smart saboteur might expect a trap and will avoid the obvious target. The enemy will probably judge one system is more important than another based on how well guarded it is."

Hans nodded. "And just in case he *does* choose the unguarded system, we'll need to be ready to pounce on both.

Ross huffed. "What's to stop him from picking a system at random?"

Vance felt his irritation rise. He was sure Ross had his reasons but was probably overthinking things. However, Vance's mouth acted before he fully thought things out. "Oh come on, with that line of thinkin', what's ta stop the canner from listening in on what we're planning right now?"

The men fell silent. The only sounds they heard were from the crew moving around and working. Ross glanced around suspiciously. Vance felt the blood rush to his cheeks. "Yeah, that kinda got awkward fast."

Hans smiled and looked at Ross. "We might be overthinking this. How about you just trust me?"

"All right," Ross conceded. "I'll get a few more Masters-at-Arms down here. When do you think he will strike?"

"Well," Hans explained, "as of right now, he could hit anytime between now and Thursday. But if you fire up the main engines, he's guaranteed to strike tonight."

Ross gave a half-smirk. "I'll see to that."

Ross retreated from the gantry and climbed down the short ladder. He walked over to the enginemen. Hans turned to Vance. "So, either we split up and each watch one of the potential targets, or we both pick the one target we will watch together."

Vance's heart rate climbed. His fingers twitched at his side. "I... uh..."

Hans smiled and his eyes softened. "Never fear, Vance the Lance. I would rather not leave a Squire to fend for himself. Let's fight together and hope we pick the correct target."

"Which one should we pick?"

Hans shrugged and searched his pockets. He eventually pulled out a coin. "Heads or tails? Call it in the air."

Vance's eyes gaped wide at the incredulity of what he was hearing. "You're not seriously gonna flip a coin to decide?"

Hans smirked and tilted his head to the side. "Well, I'm not a Virt-O, so I kinda have to resort to the old-fashioned ways."

"Virt-O?" Vance asked.

"Virtus Occulatum. They're the seventh order of the Knights of the Solar Winds. They are the daggers of the mind, the finders of secrets, the learners of all things. They specialize in reading thoughts and seeing the possible future. If one of them were here, they'd predict with high accuracy which target would be hit."

Hans snapped his fingers again. "Vance the Lance, when you do your rounds with the Virtus Occulatum, be sure to ask them about it."

Vance nodded. "Aye sir, I will."

A deep mechanical groan filled the engine room as multiple massive machines came to life. The whole room shuddered for a few moments as each turbine revved up. The reaction chambers began processing fuel and reactant. In moments, the reverberation of the walls and floor subsided. A gentle hum from the main engine thrusters sounded in the room.

Vance heard the familiar hum. It reminded him how much he missed that sound from being on his home carrier. "Ah, that's a beautiful sound."

"Woohoo!" Hans cheered with one fist in the air. "Ross the Boss has had his first victory in a long time."

Vance and Hans clapped from the gantry and soon other enginemen joined in the applause. Then Hans flipped the coin, caught it, and smoothly slapped the coin on top of his wrist. "Heads, the unguarded target. Tails, the super-guarded target. Agreed?"

Vance exhaled slowly. "I can't seriously be flipping a coin in place of a strategic decision..."

Hans revealed the coin. Vance looked at it a moment, then hung his head. "Kreket!"

The rest of the evening flew by. They caught the evening chow from the mess hall but didn't spend much time eating. Vance just poked at his spaghetti. His appetite was in hiding while his nerves were pacing back and forth in his head and his stomach. Hans, on the other hand, wolfed down his meal as if he were late to an inspection.

After the mess hall, Vance and Hans returned to the engine room. They staked out a position on top of one of the large machines. It overlooked several drive fuel reaction chambers. They sat down as low as they could.

Hans leaned over to Vance. "I'll take the first watch. I'll wake you up when it's your turn."

Vance nodded and closed his eyes. Getting some sleep high off the ground, lying on a warm metal machine with Nova-knows-what going on inside, wasn't going to be easy. Let alone while waiting for a lethal encounter.

Vance wasn't sure how long he slept when a hand was placed over his mouth. Vance's eyes shot open to see Hans with one finger in front of his mouth, motioning him to keep quiet. Vance awkwardly nodded and Hans withdrew his hand. He pointed down toward the target area.

Vance quietly turned over onto his stomach and peered down. Small sparks popped quietly out from a reaction chamber. He looked closer. The air around that circuit panel quivered the way hot desert air distorts images.

Vance looked over to Hans and mouthed the word 'Invisible?'

Hans smirked, nodded, and whispered. "Game time."

Hans reached around to his force field generator on his belt and pressed a button. A tiny red light turned on. Then he reached his hand out toward the invisible saboteur. Large blue and white electricity snaked all around the invisible enemy like a domed cage.

Vance heard a shriek that made the hair on his neck stand on end. It was not a sound he had ever imagined a human could make. It was high-pitched yet with a deep growl.

"Gotcha!" Hans shouted with glee.

A red bolt of light shot out from the electrical cage and flew up at Hans, striking the metal casing just in front of him. Hans hastily shifted his position and lost his balance. He slid over the side of the large machine. Vance reached out and snatched Hans's shirt. It tore, and Hans fell to the ground below.

"Hans!" Vance hollered clambering to make his way down from the top of the machine. He found the ladder and quickly climbed down. He hopped off the ladder when he was close to the ground. His feet landed with a loud *thud* next to Hans. He quickly looked ahead to make sure he could see the electricity cage. To his horror, he no longer saw it. When Hans fell, it must have deactivated the cage.

His heart rate soared as his brain screamed at him that he was not safe where he stood. He quickly looked down at Hans. Then his attention was stolen away when he heard a faint growling sound in front of him.

In a panic, Vance threw his hands forward. A flash of red light streaked down the walkway right at him. The red bolt of light struck the shimmering air of the force field Vance hastily threw up. The beam slowed down a little but still cut through the force field and struck Vance's upper leg.

He cried out in pain and dropped to one knee. His force field dissipated. He looked back up toward the invisible enemy. A second shot would be coming any second now. And if he was not able to deflect the first shot, he didn't have a prayer of stopping the next one. If only he had practiced how to strengthen the force field instead of just raising it quickly.

The pit of his stomach sank deep. Was this the end then? His brain flashed images of his life in front of his eyes. One image that lingered was the memory of Eddison Frank, the Blue Planet Solar Knight. Then he remembered the flashlight and the last question he asked Eddison.

Vance saw the slight shimmer of the invisible saboteur. It moved closer to Vance. The closer distance might afford the saboteur a better shot. Vance reached his hand out toward the approaching enemy. He imagined seeing little yellow dots of electrons flowing in a circle around the Mori. He imagined the little dots suddenly stopping.

Still, the invisible enemy drew near. *Maybe I don't believe it will happen,* Vance wondered. He began chanting in his mind. *You're all out of power. I can see you plain as day. You're all out of power, I can see you plain as day...*

The slow-moving shimmer stepped closer. The footsteps sounded very near. He continued his mental chant with renewed vigor. The shape of the enemy walked a few steps closer and the tall alien faded into view. The large head with off-set eyes, the jagged teeth in the mouth. He had seen a Mori once before when Royce rammed into their carrier.

They looked strange then. But now, seeing a Mori soldier with vile anger in his expression—only feet away from him—was terrifying. The Mori pointed a sleek orange-tinted metal pistol at Vance.

Vance's hands shook and he felt tired. He closed his eyes and braced himself for the next shot, the one that would end his life.

The Mori pull the trigger. *Click.*

Vance stopped breathing and flinched. Something wasn't as he expected it. There wasn't any new pain. He opened his eyes. The Mori looked at his pistol in confusion.

"Freeze!" A voice called out from across the room.

The Mori spun around and pointed his pistol toward the voice.

BANG BANG BANG BANG BANG! The Mori flinched multiple times as bullets ripped into his flesh. He staggered under the repeated punches of the bullets and then he fell to the ground never to move again.

Chapter 17
FLIGHT SCHOOL?

*A knight-initiate must complete flight school
training and obtain a passing grade in order to
qualify for consideration into the Fire Lance order.
Failure to obtain a passing grade will disqualify the
initiate from further consideration.*

—FROM "FIRE LANCE OPERATIONAL MANUAL" BY WIND
COMMANDER ARIANA YATES

Vance once again found himself sitting in the back seat of the starlancer. Hans taxied over to the runway. It wasn't until now that Vance realized there were so many bumps along the way. His bandaged leg complained at every little thump. Vance had decided to postpone taking his pain medication until they arrived at their destination. It was a decision he was now regretting.

The starlancer turned and straightened out its position on the end of the runway. The large crane arms swiveled around behind the craft. The massive electromagnets waited for the launch sequence.

"You know, Vance," Hans thought out loud. "I'm starting to second guess my decision to leave so soon."

Vance rolled his eyes. "You and me both didn't want ta spend any more days in the infirmary."

Hans smiled. "Yeah, it wasn't the most exciting 72 hours I've ever spent. But you and I both got banged up real good."

Vance heard the familiar radio chatter in his helmet. "LazyDuck, you are Outgoing O-six to Mother."

"Roger Tiger," Hans replied.

Vance lowered his eyes. "Yeah... my first combat and I take a hit to the leg—and almost bit the big one."

Hans frowned. "Don't tell me you think you goosed that up?"

Vance hung his head. "Affirmative sir. I didn't exactly demonstrate Knight material back there."

"Blast you, Vance. Those negative thoughts will pull you down faster than a nosedive on afterburner! Tell me this," Hans challenged. "How did the Mori die?"

Vance shrugged. "One of the Masters-at-Arms shot him."

"And why wasn't he shot weeks ago?"

"Well, he was invisible with a light-bending doohickey."

"And why wasn't he invisible this time?"

Vance swallowed. He saw where this line of questioning was headed, and there wasn't any way out of listening to Hans's point. "'Cus I turned it off, sorta."

"Exactly! You sabotaged the enemy's electrical systems. That's something *I can't* teach you! You figured out how to do something the Rising Sun Solar Knights specialize in. Now I don't want to hear you berate yourself for not playing the part of the immortal soldier. Rather, I should be hearing you jumping for joy that you are something of a savant."

The radio chatter sounded in Vance's ear. "Outgoing six, cleared for launch. Clear stars today, sir."

Hans clicked on the transmission. "Outgoing, roger. Thank you boys; it's been a real pleasure serving with you."

"With all due respect, sir. We should be the ones thanking you. We owe you one. May Nova speed you on your journey."

Hans smiled wide. "Acknowledged Tiger."

Hans switched the transmission back off. "Vance?"

"Sir?"

"For what it's worth," Hans said, his voice quieting down. "Thanks for fixing my goose-up. Who has ever heard of a Solar Knight falling and knocking himself out at the start of a fight?"

Vance huffed a partial laugh. "I guess we both kinda goosed it in our own ways."

"With one difference," Hans clarified as he saluted The Shooter. "Your goose killed the snake. And you know what we call any goose that can kill a snake right?"

Vance cocked his head off to one side. "Nah, I don't know what that's called."

"A mon-goose." Hans laughed as he and Vance were suddenly thrown back into their seats. The starlancer bolted down the runway and flew out the space door.

"Waahoo!" Hans hollered. "I *love* that feeling!"

Vance opened his eyes and slowly started relaxing his stomach muscles. The launch was a cruel reminder about his sore leg. It felt like all those little bumps on the runway, magnified a few hundred times. After a little concentration and patience, he was able to relax all his muscles again.

"Vance the Lance, you'll probably want to get some sleep, we have a nine-hour trip ahead of us."

"*Nine* hours! Where in the galaxy are we going?"

"Vaggitara VII," Hans replied. "It's one of our last outposts, and the best flight school this side of Wayson's Nebula."

"Forgive me, sir." Vance rubbed his sore leg. "I thought the Mori canned all our planets and outposts."

Hans shook his head. "We still have three they haven't found yet. Vaggitara is one of them. The big-wigs in charge are trying to retrofit a destroyer into a floating flight school. That way we can take it with us to the Frontier."

"Have you ever seen the Frontier?"

Hans again shook his head. "Negative. I've only ever heard stories. The Great Frontier of the Ancients is how it is known in old galactic history. Or maybe that's in *ancient* galactic history."

"What have you heard?" Vance inquired.

"Not much more than the usual. I've heard that it was built by the Ancients more than four thousand years ago. And that it is some kind of impenetrable barrier of gravimetric force."

"Wait, it can't be impenetrable if that's where everyone will be going."

Hans pulled the starlancer into a gentle turn. "Vance the Lance, you are once again at the top of your game. Yes. The Rising Sun Solar Knights think they have some ideas on how to break through the Frontier and forever leave behind the lousy Mori."

"How long ya' suppose it will take us to get there?"

Hans leveled out the starlancer from the turn. "That's probably a better question for a Blue Planet knight. If memory serves, it would take several years traveling faster than light. But for us, it would seem more like several months. Which somehow translates into even more crazy relativity mumbo-jumbo."

Vance laughed. "How long until we've gathered everyone and can start heading that way?"

Hans flipped a few switches and pressed some buttons on his instrumentation panel. "I heard we finished evacuating Driscal. That means we just have two colonies left. Once we have them spaceborne, and we have enough food and fuel for the trip, the exodus will begin."

Vance nodded, again forgetting Hans could not see his head movements. He was silent a few moments before he smiled. "Hey Hans."

"Mr. Vance?"

"You know, I got attacked by a goose once."

Hans turned his head toward Vance. "Really?"

"Needless to say, I used some 'fowl' language."

Hans chuckled a deep belly laugh. "Vance the Lance, you are on a roll!"

Vance felt proud of his joke's reception. He finally felt at home since leaving his carrier several days ago. But even though he felt at home, it still took him a long time to fall asleep. His thoughts about the exodus and flight school and becoming a Solar Knight were all swarming his mind. When he finally did doze off, his brain replayed the night he fought the zandor'an.

The fear of danger crept over him once more. If only he could have erected a stronger force field. One strong enough to repel the enemy's weapon shot. What he would have given to have taken down the Mori single-handedly. He imagined receiving a hero's reception like a champion boxer winning the title.

Hans's words crept into his thoughts from his recent memory. 'You sabotaged the enemy's electrical systems. That's something *I can't* teach you!'

Vance drifted back into consciousness. He heard the sounds of the starlancer around him. What sort of power had he stumbled onto? Was it as mundane and useless as he thought? Royce could ram a starfighter through an enemy carrier. Hans could reflect bullets at an attacker. Whereas he could turn off electricity and feel where something was broken. These did not sound like the wondrous powers of the Solar Knights. Rather, they seemed more like consolation prizes.

He fully awoke to his name being called. "Vance. *Vance.*"

Vance opened his eyes and yawned. "Aye sir."

"Sounds like you got a good sleep. I thought you might want to know; we're coming up on Vaggitara now. Home to the flight program and some of the best deep-sea diving since Earth."

Vance looked out the canopy. The fast-approaching planet had a brownish-blue hue with one small moon orbiting it.

Hans switched on the transmission. "Vag-Com this is LazyDuck on approach. Request clearance to land."

Vance's stomach tingled with emotional butterflies as they approached the planet. Vance saw cloud formations in the atmosphere. He had finally arrived. What exactly was he in for? If it was as simple as studying for his advancement exam, he'd be fine.

"I say again, Vag-Com this is LazyDuck. We're coming up on final approach. How about some clearance and directions?"

"They always this quiet?"

"Not really," Hans admitted. "Usually they're all over my six about which approach lane to take and which port I'll be docking, yadda yadda yadda."

The starlancer flew down into the atmosphere. Vance clutched his leg during the bumpy jostling of turbulence as they descended through the clouds. Once they broke through the clouds the lighting in the canopy turned orange. Down below, hundreds of volcanoes dotted the landscape. Lava poured out, collecting into rivers of magma which wound their way across landmasses and into molten oceans.

"By Nova..." Hans said, a little stunned.

Vance dropped his mouth open. "This would *not* be my first choice for an outpost..."

Hans stared out the canopy for a few eternal seconds. "That's because Vaggitara is not volcanically active. It resembles Earth in many ways."

"That," Vance pointed out the canopy. "Looks nothing like the Earth I remember."

"Nope. It looks exactly like the Earth *after* you remember. After the Mori obliterated all human life and left it uninhabitable."

Vance stopped breathing and tensed up the muscles around his lungs. "You're sayin' the Mori were here?"

"Affirmative Vance. The Mori found Vaggitara and destroyed her."

"How?" Vance asked in disbelief.

"One of the many technological terrors the Mori have. I've never seen it, but I'm told it looks like an enormous satellite in space. It shoots a powerful beam of energy into the planet's core, superheating the crust all around. I guess you could say it boils the core and causes massive volcanic activity. On an apocalyptical scale, that it."

"But... the flight school?" Vance's heart rate elevated and his breathing increased. "How can I become a Solar Knight? Sky Captain

Williams said I had to complete flight training or I can't become a Fire Lance knight."

Hans pulled the starlancer up and began ascending through the clouds. "It's a tough break, Vance. I don't have the answers either, but I will take you to New Carillon. It's the starship acting as headquarters for the Grand Council of the Solar Knights. Maybe you'll have to do things a little out of order and begin your tour before flight school."

Vance's eyes began to blur amidst the moisture forming in his eyes. His chest ached like a major piece had just been ripped out and cast aside. He tried to say 'aye sir' but only managed to get out a slight moan. The starlancer rumbled through the clouds and finally punched through the atmosphere. It streaked back across the star-laden landscape.

Chapter 18
THE GRAND COUNCIL

The eight orders of The Knights of the Solar Winds are self-organized and self-governed for the most part. The orders are unified in one ruling body: the Grand Council of the Orders. It was first organized when the Knights of the Solar Winds was founded, 172 years before the Year of Infamy. Lady Merilla Crandall was the first Supreme Grandmaster of the Orders, and Lexa Novinensky was her Seneschal of the Orders. Sir Edwin Norfolk, the one who discovered The Solar Winds, was nominated as the first Marshall of the Orders.

—FROM "HISTORY OF THE SOLAR KNIGHTS" BY SIR ALEC TOLYUIN

Vance didn't sleep anymore. He couldn't sleep anymore. The weight in his chest kept aggravating the pain of the loss. His mind kept one question spinning in his head: why? It didn't seem fair to him that he had lost the chance to attend flight school. He had done everything right; why was fate actively working against him?

He didn't want to cry, so he faithfully wiped away every tear that broke free. What then would become of him? In the end, it wouldn't be so bad to return to the Aerospace Starfighter division on his home carrier. After all, he still could find and repair starfighter engines like no other. Then his thoughts returned to Sedston. How Sedston had told him he didn't belong amongst the pilots and officers.

Perhaps Sedston was right after all and destiny was catching up with him to confirm the truth of Sedston's words. Maybe he didn't belong, to begin with. He looked down at the Squire pin on his flight suit. Even after straightening it, it still looked slightly bent in one place. He remembered how he bent it, tearing it off of his flight suit after wallowing in Sedston's words. Then he thought of Royce and the comforting words he had spoken to him.

Royce had quoted Shakespeare and that brought a warm light to his chest. It felt like the exact opposite of Sedston's words. Royce's piercing blue eyes had peered deep into his own. He had said: Be not afraid of greatness, Brewer, just be believing.

Vance involuntarily took in a sudden deep breath. The breath filled his lungs to capacity. And as he exhaled, two fresh tears coursed down his cheeks. But these two tears were not the heavy dark tears of despair. These were the bright and welcoming tears of hope. The hope that Royce had given him.

Vance snapped out of his daydream state by the whining of a small console alarm. Hans silenced the alarm with a press of a button.

Hans shook his head. "That's not surprising..."

"What's the matter, sir?" Vance inquired.

"Well," Hans began with a bit of hesitation in his voice. "I was expecting to refuel at Vaggitara. So naturally, we are now officially running on our fuel reserve."

Vance's eyes widened. "You're sayin' we're out of fuel?"

"No, I am *not* saying we're out of fuel." Hans paused a moment. "I'm saying we're *almost* out of fuel."

"That's just as bad!"

"Watch your tone, Brewer," Hans warned.

Vance felt disarmed. "Sorry, sir."

There was silence for a few minutes. Vance could only hear the small digital sounds from his instrumentation panel. "Hans, sir. Are we gonna make it?"

Hans's voice was quiet and solemn. "Well, I can cut the fuel usage and coast for a while. We'll keep moving but we'll slowly drift off course, so I'll have to engage the engines now and again to compensate."

"What's the catch?"

"The catch is... with an undetermined time frame to get to New Carillon, I don't know if we'll have enough oxygen."

Vance's SEDAR screen beeped. Two yellow dots appeared at the top of the screen. "Two bogies inbound bearing zero-nine-zero!"

Hans let his head fall back onto his headrest. "Yeah that's exactly what we need right now; a good old skirmish to exhaust the last of our fuel."

Vance then heard a voice in his helmet. "CodeBreaker to unidentified starlancer, please report your fuel state."

Hans jerked his head off the headrest. "CodeBreaker, this is LazyDuck. Almost out of fuel."

"Roger LazyDuck. Open your tow port and receive my cable."

Hans breathed a deep sigh and relaxed. "Roger CodeBreaker. And if I may say so, I'd like to petition to change your callsign to Deus Ex Machina."

"Too many syllables," came his reply.

Hans smiled and flipped a small switch. Vance heard a motor moaning as the exterior hatch opened.

"Sir, can I ask what's going on?" Vance inquired.

Hans switched off the transmission. "Vance the Lance, Nova has smiled upon us! My good friend CodeBreaker is one of those Virtus Occulatum knights I told you about."

"You mean the ones that can read thoughts?"

Hans nodded. "Yep, and they can glance into the future, something they call precognition. So apparently CodeBreaker was watching out for me and 'saw' I would run out of fuel."

116

Hans and Vance heard a clanking noise as the tow cable connected. CodeBreaker's voice came through over the transmission. "LazyDuck, cut your engines and save your fuel for landing."

Hans pressed a button and flipped two switches. "Roger CodeBreaker."

The next two hours seemed like an eternity. They watched the two starlancers, towing them onward like a crippled vehicle. Vance felt excitement tingle in his stomach when he noticed small dots in the distance. As they grew larger, they looked like a fleet of ships, but somewhat different than the fleet he was used to seeing.

He did see destroyers and cruisers, but he didn't see the battleships. Nor did he see starcraft carriers or escort ships. Instead, it contained a mismatched fleet of various ships of all shapes and sizes. The vast bulk of them did not look military. This was not a military fleet, it was a refugee fleet of evacuees. In the center of the fleet was a long slender ship with an ornate crest and shield painted on the hull. It reminded him of the shield patches worn by Royce and Hans only it was much more detailed and ornate.

"Home sweet home-away-from-home," Hans gleefully addressed.

"This is New Carillon?" Vance asked.

"Affirmative. This is the temporary HQ of the Knights of the Solar Winds. It's probably the only non-military ship equipped with military weapons."

As they neared the open space door, Hans reignited the engines and disconnected the tow cable.

Vance heard a voice in his helmet. "Incoming six, Carillon marshal."

Hans switched on the transmission. "Incoming six, go.

Vance heard the reply in his helmet. "Incoming six, you are cleared to land. Call the ball."

Hans replied, "Paddles, Incoming six, starlancer, 'LazyDuck', ball, fuel state 0.01, manual."

"Roger, ball. Power."

Hans gently increased the throttle.

"Watch your lineup!" The voice cautioned.

Hans cautiously adjusted his angle. Moments later they flew through the open space door. The safety straps dug into Vance's shoulders. He cried out in pain as his wounded leg insisted on following inertia out through the canopy. The large electromagnets that brought the craft to a two-second stop started pushing the craft backward.

Hans powered down to idle. In response, the arresting electromagnets turned off. The crane arms swiveled out of the way. A plane director on the flight deck waved Hans to pull forward.

Hans revved the engines and slowly began taxiing around the runway. He was passed off to another plane director who guided him over to the recovery lane. Then a final plane director guided him to where he was to secure the craft. With a hand signal from the plane director, Hans cut power to the engines and it whined as it revved down.

A rolling staircase was wheeled up to the starlancer and the canopy slid back. Hans unbuckled and stood to stretch. Vance still clutched his aching leg but wanted dearly to stand and stretch after such a long flight. He placed his hands on either side of the open canopy wall and hoisted himself into a standing position. Keeping all his weight on his good leg, he stretched as much as he dared.

Their visit to the infirmary was brief. Vance got an earful from the physician about taking his pain medication. Vance and Hans found their way to a small waiting lounge outside a large set of double doors. Vance slowly sat and kept his hand on his throbbing leg, wishing the pain meds would kick in sooner.

"I thought we was goin' to get some chow?" Vance inquired.

Hans lowered his eyes. "Sorry Vance the Lance, I wanted to get some answers for you about the next step in your training. I was instructed to bring you here as soon as the infirmary released you."

"Where is here?"

Hans motioned toward the doors with his head. "Through there is where the Grand Council of the Orders meets. I get the feeling this is going to get a little hairy."

"Hairy? Like how?"

Hans bobbed his head from side to side a few times. "Well, nobody is giving me a straight answer. And now we're going to address the Grand Council of the Orders in person—something just smells of goose."

Vance hung his head in exasperation. "Just space me now..."

"Hey hey hey, Vance the Lance, don't worry. I'll guide you through the whole thing. Just don't mention toilet seats and we'll be fine."

Vance lifted his head and gave a confused look. "Toilet seats?"

Hans nodded, "Yeah, some blazar stole all the toilet seats from the bathrooms. The worst part is, security says they have nothing to go on."

Vance silently chuckled. "Okay Hans the Bronze, even when I'm not in the mood to be cheered up, you still make me laugh."

Hans folded his arms and smiled. "It's a gift."

Two men opened the great twin doors. They wore fancy dress uniforms with knee-high boots and long capes. One of them motioned to Hans and Vance with one white-gloved hand. "The time has arrived."

Hans stood. "Come, Vance the Lance, we'll either make history or history will make us."

Vance slowly stood. He smiled as he noticed the pain medication was kicking in and he only felt stiffness in his leg now. He followed Hans into the large room.

The large oval room was ornately decorated with flags, tapestries, and heraldic arms. It had raised benches and tables around the perimeter. Immediately opposite the entry door, along the far wall, were two prominent seats. They were made of fine wood and colorful fabric. They looked more like thrones than chairs. A lady and a man sat in them.

Vance whispered to Hans, "Is that the king and queen of the Solar Knights?"

Hans cupped his head in his palm, desperately trying to muffle his hysterical laughing. He was only able to answer Vance's question by vaguely shaking his head.

"When you're quite through with whatever ails you to persist in carrying on in this manner, the Council would greatly like to disseminate your stewardship's plight."

Once Hans was able to get a hold of himself, he turned to the woman who had addressed him. "Forgive me, your ladyship. The young squire, by no fault of his own, had mistaken the Supreme Grandmaster and your Seneschal for a sort of monarchy."

Several men and women around the outer benches muffled their laughter. The woman half-smiled. "By what name is this squire addressed?"

"Squire Vance Brewer, your ladyship."

"Squire Brewer," she addressed. "I am Anna-Lexa Novinensky, Supreme Grandmaster of the Orders." She motioned to the man sitting in the chair at her side. "And this is Scott Frederick Crandall the third, Seneschal of the Orders."

Vance stood at attention. "My apologies, ma'am."

"You are the squire Sky Captain Royce Williams initiated, are you not?"

Vance nodded, "Affirmative, ma'am."

Hans motioned to Vance, "My instructions were such that the young squire was to be escorted to Vaggitara for flight instruction training. And upon arrival at the said destination, our discovery of the footprint of the vile Mori was as horrifying as it was disheartening. And to this end have we sought the wisdom of the Council as to the proper course of action in regards to the knightly training of the squire, seeing as Vaggitara is no more."

Anna-Lexa turned to a red uniformed man at her right. "Twin-Star Commander DeCampbell, perhaps the Fire Lance may prove a superior schoolmaster for the young squire in regard to flight training, and also seeing as the youth was initiated by the same Order."

DeCampbell stood up and descended the few steps until he was on the floor. "Your ladyship, members of the Council. Indeed, every knight is afforded the right to seek out the gifted children of Nova, but hindsight has illuminated that no such provision nor precedent has been established to encumber an order simply upon the membership of the initiator." He turned and pointed at Vance. "The fact that the Mori have made a vagabond of the youth does not invalidate the mandate of flight training completion. Until such time, the squire cannot be considered for acceptance. The lad is therefore not Fire Lance and should be under the tutelage of his own order."

Scott, who sat beside Anna-Lexa, raised one hand to gain DeCampbell's attention. "Surely, it sounds like circular logic being presented. To deny assistance to the youth until he shall become a member of your order—when the means of acceptance into that order requires the very assistance being denied—is not this the absence of civility?"

"I contend that upon written contract, it is not so. Are not all knights without order, in fact, members of Orbiting Star de facto? And upon what rite, duty, or expectation is one order answerable to the obligations of another in respects to its membership?"

A lady stood up from the opposite side of the tall benches. "Forgive the impertinence of the forthcoming remarks, but upon what sound judgment does a Knight of the Solar Winds look into the face of Nova's judgment, seeing the next pupil of destiny, and commit him to uncertainty. If it was not the will of The Winds that the lad become a knight, then he would not have been discovered, or he would have sooner arrived at Vaggitara only to perish under the hand of the Mori. Nova brought him to us for a reason."

DeCampbell gave an annoyed look in her direction. "If Sage Vlavskisk wishes to evoke the endowment of Nova, then I suggest we let Nova decide the lad's fate by observing happenstance yet to come, and not wasting the Council's time any further."

Anna-Lexa turned to Scott, at her side. "Rhetoric aside, what duties are in writ?"

Scott turned a page in a packet of papers he held. "From the Charter of the Orders, the sovereignty of each order is as Twin-Star Commander DeCampbell depicts. Accordingly, in light of the absence of the flight training grounds, the responsibility for the squire would fall to Orbiting Star respectfully."

Anna-Lexa turned to a man in a green uniform. "Reginald Owens, the squire's fate will be at your hands. May Nova guide you."

Reginald stood up. "May I express my gratitude for your confidence. May this Council always know that the Orbiting Star are ready and willing to bolster up the moral failings of any member of the Orders."

DeCampbell spun around with intense eyes. "Blast you blazar of a joke!"

"Out of order!" Anna-Lexa commanded. She then looked directly at Hans. "You and the squire are dismissed."

Hans and Vance exited the room and the doors closed behind them. "Well, that could have gone better."

Vance impatiently waved his hands around. "What does this mean? The Fire Lance won't train me?"

Hans shook his head. "They say you're our problem to solve."

Vance stood there, staring off into space, not sure if he should be feeling sorrow or indignation.

"But I will say something for Dorothy Vlavskisk. She is a typical Gun Star; you'll never find a more fiercely loyal friend than in a Gun Star. They will fight for any knight as if they were their own blood."

Vance placed one hand on his forehead. "What do I do now?"

Hans's eyes suddenly widened. "Vance the Lance, never fear, for Hans the Bronze has just thought of an outrageous idea."

Chapter 19
THE BANQUET TABLE

*The Orbiting Star have one of the most
beautiful examples of elegance in simplicity. The
gold and green field features a simple ring
counterchanged with the opposing colors of the
field. The effect gives almost a yin-yang feel to the
design. A simple star is added next to the ring—
giving the appearance of the star orbiting the ring.
The entire magnificent design thus spells out the
name of the knightly order that bears it.*

—FROM "GALACTIC HERALDRY" BY JEAN-CLAUDE ARMAND
DuBois

Hans grabbed Vance by the wrist and swiftly pulled him down the hallway. Vance shouted in pain. "The leg, the leg! Remember, the leg!"

"Sorry, Vance the Lance. But we have to get you a dress uniform, pronto."

"Why pronto?"

"I just remembered the Banquet Table is today," Hans answered. "Now let's haul some jets while we still have some time."

Vance hobbled along after Hans. Vance did his best to not outwork the pain medication; if he worked his leg too much, his leg would shout at him in throbs. They stopped by the cafeteria to quell Vance's stomach. Almost immediately, they headed for the second deck.

Vance was still eating his sandwich when Hans pulled him into a small clothing shop. The overhead sign read, Wardrobe of the Order. It hung with a heraldic arms shield beside it. The green and gold shield had a hollow ring in the center and a small gold star in the upper right corner. It was the same shield that Hans wore on his flight suit.

A man walked up to Vance with a long measuring tape in his hands. He wore a sleeveless green leather button-down shirt, baggy black trousers, and knee-high boots. Hans saw him approach. "We need a dress uniform for this squire."

"Formal wear?" the man raised his eyebrows. He turned to Vance, "Are you a lawyer?"

Vance shook his head, "Negative, sir."

"Good," the man concluded. "I won't have to fit you for a lawsuit."

Vance snickered. "Get spaced, even the tailor tells jokes? That's real gabb."

The tailor smiled.

Hans chuckled. "Vance the Lance, I told you we'd have you loose as a goose in short order. That's part of being an Orbiting Star."

The tailor spread out the measuring tape across Vance's arms, taking measurements. He turned to Hans. "Will this be standard or rushed?"

Hans frowned. "Very much rushed. I need to get him to the Banquet Table."

The tailor stopped suddenly as if frozen in time. He widened his eyes and stared at Hans. Hans put up his hands in surrender. "I know, I know, I'm asking for a miracle because I need one right about now. This squire here is almost at bingo on his chances to get into his preferred Order."

The tailor straightened up and crossed his arms. "I'll do it on one condition."

Vance craned his neck to look at the tailor. "What's that?"

"You have to know the difference between a well-dressed man and a tired dog," he announced.

Vance thought a moment. "Oh, wait a minute, wait a minute. One wears a suit and the other just pants."

Hans laughed out loud. "Vance the Lance, you are on target!"

The tailor smiled. "Okay, Cinderella, let's see about getting you to the ball on time."

The next two hours passed like a speeding comet. Before he knew it, Vance was standing alongside Hans in a large ballroom. Elaborate tables were set out in rows. He flexed his fingers a few times. He was not used to wearing gloves, and it was still nagging at his senses. He wore a sleeveless green jacket that was so long it draped across his ankles. This too was an adjustment for Vance. The clothes were not only fancy; they were a strange fancy.

He was used to wearing his coveralls and on occasion, his dress white uniform. But the silky gold shirt with a string-tie in place of buttons, and the baggy black trousers were about as far removed from his naval uniform as he could imagine. He wasn't sure if he was dressed like a pirate or a nobleman—or some strange joke in between.

Vance looked around the open room and saw large banners draped down the walls. They bore embroidered heraldic arms. He identified Fire Lance and Orbiting Star, the two he knew, but there were others that he hadn't been introduced to yet. One was pure black with what resembled four claw marks rending downward. Another was a silver flower on a purple background. As he was looking at yet another heraldic arms, he noticed a man in ornate black robes. The man walked down the tables flicking his fingers at candles. One by one, as he flicked his fingers at a candle, it lit. It was almost mesmerizing to watch. Was this some use of The Solar Winds?

Hans noticed Vance's gaze and leaned over to whisper. "That is Sir Gaius. He is a Wind Dancer Apprentice of the 1st tier."

"Is he lighting the candles with his fingers?"

"The Wind Dancers are the Solar Knights that do not carry weapons; they are weapons. They specialize in harnessing every electrical field in reach. Whether as great as a thermal reactor core or as small as the electrical field in the human body. They can hurl flaming balls, absorb laser fire with their hands, and yes even light candles with their fingers. Nothing says 'wizard' like a Wind Dancer."

Vance's jaw fell open. "That must be so gabb to be one of them."

Hans tilted his head to one side and shrugged. "Well, that level of precision costs them a lot of time and energy spent in ritual and meditation. They spend years learning to control their emotions, idle thoughts, and dark desires. The slightest loss of control could be disastrous for a Wind Dancer."

"Ahhh, that's a steep cost," Vance admitted.

"Some like it hot, and some like it not," Hans concluded.

A swarm of blue and white colors moved through Vance's peripheral vision. He turned to see a young woman in a blue and white dress with long curly black hair and two pistols strapped to her waist.

Vance whispered to Hans, "Who is that? In the blue and white dress."

Hans looked and then sighed. "Let's... not go there."

"Hey, you dragged me here. So, tell me who that is."

Hans rolled his eyes. "*That* is not why we're here."

"Oh come on," Vance goaded, "you afraid I'm gonna goose this up and embarrass you?"

"No, no, it's—okay, yes I am *confident* you are going to goose this up," Hans admitted.

Vance tried to think of a rebuttal but his mind was blank. He stammered a moment. "Maybe... it'll be some good comedy?"

Hans sighed and glanced heavenward a moment. "The blue and white signifies her Order's ceremonial colors. She is a Gun Star. And judging by the twin pistols at her hips, I'd say she is a member of the Quick Draw clan."

Vance broke his gaze from the woman and looked at Hans. "Can I go introduce myself?"

Hans hesitated. "Ah... well, it's customary when at these ceremonial proceedings to speak in High Novan."

"Everybody speaks Novan."

Hans shook his head, "I said, *High* Novan. That means you start pronouncing the 'g' on words ending in 'i-n-g' and use twice as many words to say what you mean. Do you remember the Grand Council? They were speaking High Novan."

Vance squirmed where he stood. "Ah c'mon Hans the Bronze, could you teach me to at least say hi?"

Hans exhaled sharply. "You'll first need to resist the urge to stand at attention. Second, you'll need to bow. Then you say something to the effect of, 'If it please you, miss, may I introduce myself as Squire Vance Brewer, Solar Knight initiate and admirer of your Order."

"I have ta say all that?" he complained.

Hans chuckled. "Vance the Lance, you got to talk the talk if you want to walk the walk. Just remember that this is *your* idea."

Vance shrugged, fidgeting with his hands a moment before making up his mind to go for it. He walked over to where the young woman was standing. She was nodding, listening to another gentleman converse. He would first need to get her attention.

He panicked. Should he try clearing his throat or would that be too lowly of speech? He was relieved, however, that once he walked up to her, she turned and looked at him. Her eyes were a lovely brown and she had delicate curls in her hair. He could have gone on staring at her but his sense of danger alerted him that it was time to speak.

"It is pleasing, ma'am, I am AD3 Brewer—I mean, Squire Vance Brewer. I'm... I'm, uh, initiating and an admirer of you."

She widened her eyes and stared. Vance's heart rate climbed. He was sure he had accurately stated everything Hans had told him. Yet she was not reacting in the way he anticipated.

He closed his eyes. "I just said somethin' wrong, didn't I?" He felt the blood rushing to his cheeks and forehead. While keeping his eyes closed, he quickly bowed, about-faced, and walked away. He bumped into a chair and remembered he still had his eyes closed. Upon remedying that small oversight, he marched as casually as possible back to Hans's side.

Once he was safely at Hans's side, he felt a familiar feeling of awkwardness—like the annoying friend you can't seem to get rid of. He looked into Hans's eyes, dreading what he might find. "You must be real disappointed in me."

Hans had his arms crossed with one hand casually covering his mouth. There was not anything harsh in Hans's eyes. The corners of his eyes were pulled up slightly as if an undisclosed smile was speaking through them.

Hans recomposed himself before removing his hand from his mouth. "Vance the Lance, it has been some years since I have been so thoroughly entertained."

Vance looked down and closed his eyes tight. "Did I embarrass you, sir?"

Hans put one hand on Vance's shoulder. "No Vance, you have a certain goofy charm about you that I can't help but admire."

Vance looked back up into Hans's eyes.

Hans smiled. "The primary mission of the Orbiting Star order is to help alleviate stress and anxiety for the Knights of the Solar Winds. So, if your Fire Lance petition doesn't pan out, you could do so much good with *us* as an Orbiting Star."

"I wish I had your confidence, sir. I sorta goosed up my first impression with that, uh... that—sir, what's the High Novan word for a gal?"

"That's probably a more complicated subject than you're ready for. Age, grooming, station, and other factors all play a part," Hans explained. "So for you, just stick with 'young lady' for now."

"I sorta goosed up my first impression with that young lady."

"Yes, and in a very memorable way, I might add."

In the distance, music started playing. It was a pair of violins, identifiable only because of the iconic sound. As soon as the music began, everyone began claiming seats at the various tables.

"Okay Vance, the only rule on seating is that you cannot sit directly next to another member of your order. And once you choose a seat, wait until all the ladies are seated before you take yours. Oh, and it is polite to assist any lady with her chair."

Vance eyed Hans curiously. "What part of sitting could they possibly need help with?"

Hans stroked both hands slowly down his face as he took a deep breath. "Nova grant me patience please—Vance, imagine that you are being evaluated. Pretend your performance on this exam will be judged by how well you do all these quirky little details."

"Got it, sir."

Hans motioned for Vance to move forward. "Now go ahead and find yourself a seat."

Vance nodded and walked up to the closest table and took hold of the back of a chair. He looked across the table. Several men stood behind their chairs.

Vance quickly removed his hand from the chair back and stood at attention. He enjoyed feeling proper and was glad his leg was not complaining. Several men around him were standing next to women. They pulled out the lady's chair and gently pushed it in as the lady sat down. Vance took note of the curious custom and nervously looked to either side. Maybe happenstance would free him from the obligation.

He glanced to his left. He looked straight into the mahogany eyes of the young lady he had tried to introduce himself to. She stared right back at him. Vance stopped breathing with only a half-breath that made its way into his lungs. Her eyes were not intense nor glaring. On her lips, she betrayed no smile, but her eyes seemed to hint at one.

Vance's eyes were a welcome captive. But his unfettered ears alerted him that people were sitting down now. He blinked and reached for the back of her chair. She took a step aside and allowed him to pull it out for her. She crossed in front of her chair and stood there. Vance hesitated a moment. Was he supposed to start pushing in her chair now or should he wait until she started sitting?

She glanced back at him. He took that as a sign that she was waiting on him. He gently pushed her chair in as she gracefully sat down. She was quite practiced at this since she looked to be at the perfect distance from the table.

Vance felt the silky dark curls of her long hair brush his hands when she sat down. He wasn't sure why, but he wanted to feel that again. His brain conjured up a few possible excuses before his better judgment locked them away. He pulled out his chair and sat down, then scooted several times to get his chair close enough to the table. The chair gave an audible squeak as the legs rubbed across the solid surface of the floor. He completed his journey toward the table while avoiding eye contact.

Several men and women in fancy white clothes and gloves brought out large trays. They had several plates of food on them. They placed the plates in front of each of the women seated at the tables before serving the men. He was noticing a pattern.

Other white-dressed servers came around. They poured a clear bubbly drink into the tall glass cups. Vance reached for his glass but then quickly retracted his hand. Better observe what other men were doing before taking any chances. They all waited. He smiled that his decision had rewarded him with avoiding another blunder.

"Miss Valerie," a man addressed, sitting directly across from Vance in a purple dress coat. "It is truly a pleasure to see you diverted from your previously intended seat. Surely I cannot be a more interesting conversationalist than Sage Jor'del Smith."

The young lady beside Vance brushed aside a stray lock of curly hair. "Certainly you have unmasked my pretensions, Dr. Rychen. May the truth then be known that my boundless curiosity demanded that I learn about," she turned and looked at Vance, "my admirer."

Vance instinctively looked back at Valerie. Then quickly diverted his gaze to the table as he felt the blood rushing to his cheeks. "Yeah...somehow, that sounded different in my head than it did comin' outta my mouth."

"'Tis a common ailment in youth—more so when they are close to graduating from the reference," Dr. Rychen mused. "I need only imply that the majority seated here this evening have not passed through unscathed."

"Perhaps then, Dr. Rychen, you can prescribe something for his condition."

"Oh no doubt, my dear Valerie, it would probably read along these lines: Take thrice daily, good judgment, sound advice, and world experience. The peril, however, is when the patient neglects to take the medication."

Vance looked at Dr. Rychen. "No problem here, just remind me of this evening, an' I'll be back for a refill."

Dr. Rychen smiled. Then Vance heard an angelic giggle to his left. He dared a glance at Valerie. She was smiling as she recomposed herself from her giggle.

"Oh, wow, I made you laugh," Vance observed. "That's, that's a good thing... I think. Better than my first impression, I suppose."

"No," she admitted. "It rather complements the first."

"Wait... you sayin' I didn't end up makin' a goose of myself back there?"

"Oh on the contrary," Dr. Rychen clarified, "on that score, let there be no doubt that you proved to be quite accomplished."

"...then how was that a good thing?"

Valerie smiled again. "Then allow me the pleasure of expounding what I saw amidst your actions. After your unfortunate introduction, your bumpy retreat told me just how much courage you must have garnered for the attempt."

"It would appear the diagnosis would of necessity change," Dr. Rychen observed. "Now that it is apparent the admired is now taking part in the admiring."

Valerie turned to Dr. Rychen. "I contend then, that it is contagious."

A server placed a plate of food in front of Valerie and moved on.

"Well then, by what name is this contagious young admirer called?"

"Oh, I'm Squire Vance Brewer, sir." He nervously held out his hand to shake and, in the process, bumped his glass which tipped.

Vance instinctively stood and grabbed his napkin. "I'm so sorry, I—"

A blue gloved hand had caught his glass. Only a single drop was spilled onto the white tablecloth.

He looked into her mahogany eyes once more. "You have very fast reflexes."

Vance slowly sat back in his chair while keeping his eyes on her.

"Valerie here is a Gun Star of the Quick Draw clan. It stands to reason then, that the single most coveted trait among her clansmen would be quick reflexes."

"Sir, may I ask what Order and clan you belong to?"

Dr. Rychen huffed a chuckle. "I am a Knight after the order of the Lily of the Valley."

"Oh, that's the purple flag with the flower, right?" Vance pointed to the banner on the wall.

Dr. Rychen nodded. "Yes, but we do not have a clan social structure like the Gun Stars. We are organized into committees. I am the Grandmaster Surgeon in the Delegation of Medicine."

A server walked up behind Dr. Rychen and placed a plate of food in front of him. A plate of food was also placed in front of Vance and he diverted his eyes to this new distraction. It looked like fish with a white sauce lightly drizzled over it. Ornate sprigs of green leaves along with steamed vegetables and a few other items he wasn't sure about decorated the plate. The smell trickled up his nose like a snake charmer's cobra.

"Oh, just the smell alone, sure beats the mess any day o' the week!"

Valerie gave off the slightest hint of a smile. "Tell me, admirer, from where do you come?"

Vance's cheeks burn red again. He smiled sheepishly and looked down at his plate. "I, uh... I'm... I'm from the starcraft carrier Saratoga. She's stationed with Alpha fleet near some nebula I can never remember the name of."

Dr. Rychen picked up his fork and knife. "On such a large vessel, I would imagine a multitude of occupational opportunities would abound. To which particular duties did you attend?"

Vance raised his eyebrows. "I'm sorry sir?"

Valerie clarified, "What job did you have?"

"Oh, if'n you don't mind me braggin', I'm the fastest Aerospace Machinist's Mate on that whole ship. I can find and fix any problem with a starfighter's engines. I think that's how Sky Captain Williams found me; he evaluated me diag'n his starlancer."

"Forgive me for overhearing your conversation, young Squire, but my understanding was that the evaluation was only to *confirm* his suspicions."

Vance turned around in his seat. A tall man dressed in a red dress uniform with navy-blue trims stood staring at him. "The way he *found* you happened the night you stole out of bed."

"Aye sir, thank you for the correction."

"Enlighten us then, young Squire, what happened that night," the man urged.

Vance lowered his eyes. "Well, I hadn't ever seen a starlancer before. To me, it was a mysterious red-winged beauty that came into the landing bay one night. And I really wanted to get a closer look at her engines—I still haven't seen those engines. I'm curious how they managed to correct the aeon flow regulation issue. And I figured if I went down just before lights-out, I could get a closer look."

Vance looked back up to see all the surrounding people at the man's table and his table were listening to him. "Then Sky-Captain Williams caught me trying to get a closer look."

"No," the man challenged. "Expound upon what happened just prior to that; what name did you hear."

Vance hesitated a long moment. "Lleona."

Valerie abruptly stood and walked away. Vance watched her graceful upset stride to the end of the large room and out the door. Vance looked back at the man in red, who had just taken his seat. He wore a satisfied expression on his face.

Vance turned to Dr. Rychen, "Did she leave because of what I said?"

"Without being acquainted with her past, I could only conjecture that something about that story has indeed upset Miss Vlavskisk."

"Wait, *Vlavskisk*?" Vance inquired. He remembered the name from the Grand Council. He didn't wait for further explanation as a more pressing question surfaced. "And who is that guy askin' me ta tell that story?"

"That is Wind Captain Marlon Dawes of the Fire Lance."

"Does he have it out for me or what?"

Dr. Rychen shrugged. "I am afraid I do not have the advantage of being within his confidence. But just between you and me, I would venture to assume he knew what he was doing."

"What a real *canner*. I don't even know him, and he's like, already willing to goose me over. Have I done something to offend the Fire Lance?"

"Yes," came a response from an aging gentleman with gray hair on his right. He wore a black velvet hooded robe with ornate white patterns dancing about. He swallowed and took a sip of his glass. "The Fire Lance are a tight-knit military organization who hold pilots and fellow Fire Lance knights in higher regard."

"And how does that make me his target?"

"You're not a pilot. They feel a certain sense of indignity that Royce Williams chose to initiate a mechanic instead of a pilot."

"In smaller words, I'm not worthy to sit in the same room as 'em."

"For what it's worth, Squire Brewer, not all orders of the Knights of the Solar Winds view initiates in the same way. I, for example, am a Wind Dancer; we value self-control and ambition in our initiates."

He motioned to Dr. Rychen. "Lily of the Valley along with Blue Planet is very excited with scholastic progress." He took another bite of his food.

Vance motioned to Valerie's empty chair. "And I guess the Gun Stars value fast reflexes."

He shook his head and swallowed. "No, the Gun Stars are rather unique in their selection. The clan sages and the clan master will interview the initiate. The decision of whether they will be accepted into their order is based entirely on that interview. No other qualifications are considered." He turned around and looked behind at a tall woman in a blue and white gown who was walking in his direction. "Is that not so, Dorothy?"

Dorothy walked up to him. "Lord Baltris, I must beg your pardon and ask that you repeat your question."

Baltris motioned to Vance. "I was just educating young Vance Brewer here on the criterion the order of the Gun Stars employs when selecting an initiate for acceptance into their order. I related that no qualifications aside from an interview with the clan sages and clan master are considered."

Dorothy shook her head "Upon technicality, one does not join the Gun Stars order as a whole; one must petition a specific clan within the order. Then the initiate will be interviewed by the clan sages and the clan master. But you are correct that no other criteria beyond that exist. Who am I to protest anyone from wishing to join the Gun Stars Order? If it is the will of The Winds, then they have been destined and will be endowed with the gifts for The Crusade. And should that be the case, then they were my brother before I even met them."

"Mr. Brewer," Dr. Rychen addressed. "May I introduce you to Lord Baltris, Wind Dancer Master of the 3rd tier; and Sage Dorothy Vlavskisk, Sniper Clan of the Gun Stars."

"Vlavskisk?" He snapped his finger. "That's right, you was the one who stood up to the Fire Lance guy for me in your council meeting. I want you ta know I appreciate that, ma'am."

She smiled gingerly. "You're becoming quite the folk hero around here."

"I am?"

"Certainly." She turned around and motioned to three tables away. "Hans Christian has been relating to us your stories; fixing the primary engines of a starcraft carrier and your battle with a Mori soldier."

Vance glanced across the room. Hans stood in place at a table and moved his arms around, telling a story to a captive audience.

"Which is primarily the reason I came to see you," She admitted. "A number of us have discussed advancing your studies and beginning your tour right away."

"...ah...I'm sorry, ma'am, is the 'tour' where I spend time with each order gettin' ta know them?"

She nodded. "Correct, Squire Brewer. You will have quite the advantage here on New Carillon; representatives of every order can be found here. If it is agreeable, I will schedule some time for you with Number 1, of the Virtus Occulatum."

Vance swallowed, wide-eyed. "Ma'am, that would be so gabb; I have heard so much about them—er, I uh... I mean, yes it is agreeable. Very much so. Really agreeable. Truly."

She warmly smiled and nodded once. "Until tomorrow then. I will send word by way of Hans Christian."

Chapter 20
NUMBER 1

Eddison's third law of The Winds states: the strength of the electrical field used to manipulate The Winds is not as important as the relative distance between a person and the flow of Nakkaron particles.

—FROM "THE SCIENCE OF THE WINDS" BY PROFESSOR-EMERITUS PING CHENG

"**A**n' I can't believe that frazzin canner put me on the spot just to upset Valerie! Or maybe it was to get me away from her... either way, what right does he have to make a goose out of me?"

Vance followed Hans around the small apartment. It consisted of two bedrooms each joining a central sitting room with a couch. Two small appliances stood on a small, tiled floor section.

Hans glanced heavenward momentarily and then spun around. He placed his hands on Vance's shoulders. "Okay, I realize you're very upset about that blazar giving you the can but you're probably low on potassium. Also, it is late and we have an early morning tomorrow."

Hans pointed to a wall-mounted clock made of silver wire and gears with a frosted-glass face. The big hand of the clock was pointing to the number 22. Vance looked at the clock and then back to Hans.

Hans picked up a pillow and shoved it into Vance's arms. "I'll see you in the morning—showered and ready—at 0600."

"Yeah but—"

"Taps! Taps! Lights out, Vance. If you need something to get your mind off that blazar, think of Valerie; her subtle smile, her emerald eyes—whatever it takes!"

Vance closed his mouth tight, turned around, and meandered the few feet over to his room. "She has brown eyes."

"And silence about the decks," Hans amended.

Vance quickly found that thinking about Valerie only led him back to Wind Captain Dawes and how he used him in some way to offend Valerie. And that only brought up more questions to keep his brain awake and spinning endlessly. It was only when he turned his thoughts to meeting with a Solar Knight from Virtus Occulatum that his mind started winding down. He dreamed of what they might be like.

The morning came quickly. Vance found himself wide awake for the first time without hearing Reveille from the overhead speakers. He followed his first instinct to heave out of bed, hit the shower, and then dress in his flight suit and his squire pin.

He exited out the slender double doors that divided his room from the sitting area. He found Hans placing some fruit on the coffee table.

Vance bounced in his steps over to Hans. "Reveille. Reveille, Hans. All hands heave out and trice up."

Hans grinned. "Here, put something in your mouth." He tossed a small red fruit to Vance.

Vance examined it. It was as red as fire with yellow and orange highlights, along with a leathery shell. "Get spaced! I haven't had a sunspot since leaving Driscal!"

"Thought you might like it."

Vance peeled back the tough shell and took a bite of the soft orange center. "Hmmm... oh yeah, that's a piece of home right there."

"Be sure to eat all of it, there won't be time for a proper breakfast. You're expected at 0630 hours, which for the Virtus Occulatum, means 0629."

"Aye, aye, sir."

Vance finished it as they left the apartment and descended an elevator. The elevator stopped and the doors parted. They both exited into a busy hallway with people walking every which way.

Vance turned sideways to avoid colliding with a mildly distracted pedestrian. When his eyes returned forward, he noticed several children laughing in the distance. They were gathered around a young woman in a skirt with two pistols at her hips. She quickly drew them, then spun them around her trigger fingers and re-holstered them. The children jumped up and down cheering.

"Vance the Lance! We've got to get moving."

"Hey, I think I see Valerie. I gotta talk ta her."

Hans caught hold of Vance's arm. "On your own time, Brewer. Now let's haul some jets."

"Blast it!" he mumbled under his breath. Hans was right. "Lead on, Hans the Bronze."

Hans led him down several hallways until they reached a cargo room. "I'll meet you here at 1700 hours."

"1700! Ah, this is gonna take all day."

"Vance the Lance, you can play the part of the schoolboy with a crush *after* you're off duty."

Vance closed his eyes and pursed his lips, allowing Hans's sanity to soak in. "Sorry sir, must be the hormones. Won't happen again. See you back here at 1700."

Vance then pressed a small button beside the extra-wide door and it slid open. Vance walked inside and the door closed behind him. The wide room was empty except for a table in the center with four chairs. A deck of cards was left on the table outside the tuck case.

Vance approached the table with cautious interest.

Pick any card, Vance.

Vance looked around the room. "Is someone there?" Finding himself alone, he picked up the top card and turned it over. *It's the three of clubs*, he thought.

The challenge will then be, 'Three of clubs'.

Vance dropped the card and once again looked all about the room. "Either I'm hearin' things or that sunspot was overripe."

Now pick another card.

"Hello?" He looked around a third time before spreading the cards out into a fan. He pulled a card from the middle and turned it over. He glanced at it and placed it back face down.

Good. The answer will then be, 'But the Jack is wild'.

Vance jumped back. "Okay, who's messin' with me?"

"Over here." A low and controlled rough voice announced.

Vance shot a glance to his left and jumped back another two feet. "Whoa! Where'd you come from?"

The man, dressed in black military fatigues with dark sunglasses stood up against the left wall. "What are you doing here?"

Vance stood at attention. "Squire Vance Brewer, reporting as ordered, sir."

"How do I know you are who you say you are?"

"Wha...? I wasn't briefed than I needed some kind a' identification or nothin'."

The dark man took three steps closer. "I'm gonna give you to the count of 'three' to answer my 'challenge' before I beat you with 'clubs'."

Vance froze. His lips slowly parted as he stared at the man in all black. Was this for real? Was he going to be bodily harmed or was this just some kind of evaluation? A smirk slowly crept up Vance's left cheek. "But the Jack is wild?"

"Very good," he replied.

"You was the one messin' with me?"

"You may call me 'Number 1'. And I will call you 'Number 13'."

Vance squinted one eye in confusion. "Thirteen? Isn't that a bad luck number?"

Number 1 took a few steps closer. "Thirteen is the misunderstood number. It is the odd one out, the number that breaks a few of the rules. It is the aberrant prime number."

"Wow, I didn't know that, sir."

Number 1 held up his hand. "Do not address me as 'sir'. Sir conveys rank and seniority. The way you move and the way you talk must never reveal anything to the enemy."

"Sorry, sir—er, I mean..." It was time to stop talking.

Number 1 walked over to the door and pressed the button to open it. "Time for duty, Number 13."

Vance looked around the rest of the room. "You mean, we're not stayin' here?"

"We're not Blue Planet; we don't hold a classroom. All knowledge is O.J.T."

"On-the-Job-Training?"

Number 1 nodded, then motioned toward the open door with his head. Vance scurried up to Number 1's side and followed him out the door. They walked over to an elevator and Number 1 pulled out a small rectangular thin metal card. He inserted it into a small slot that Vance hadn't even realized was there.

The elevator doors opened and chimed three times. Number 1 retrieved his card and stepped into the elevator with Vance right behind him. The doors closed and it began its descent.

Vance tried to retain his excitement but the questions started flooding his mind. "So you can read my thoughts, right?"

Affirmative, Number 13.

"Aw man, that's gabb—wait, your mouth didn't move when you talked..."

Number 1 just stared at him through his dark sunglasses. Vance's eyes darted around as his brain was stitching pieces together. "Ah, you can send thoughts as well as read them, am I right?"

What do you think?

"Oh, man! That's so gabb! So, how far back in my head can you see?"

It doesn't work that way; only what you're actively thinking in the moment.

"Hey, can you teach me to do the whole mind-talking thingy?"

I can show you the motions to go through, and the actions to take, but only one-third of the students are ever able to learn it. And if they cannot learn it, they cannot be a Virtus Occulatum.

"Oh wow. Okay, what do I need to learn?"

You don't need to learn it right now. For now, you can simply think about what you want to say. Any Virtus Occulatum will be able to read your thoughts and respond.

The elevator slowed to a gentle stop but the elevator doors remained closed. Instead, the back wall of the elevator slid open. Number 1 turned and walked out. Vance followed.

They entered a large open hangar. Starfighters, shuttles, and cargo transports were all lined up. Small tractors pulled and pushed them into and out of lanes. Number 1 descended the brief flight of stairs, with Vance on his heels, and walked up to a starlancer. A rolling staircase had already been wheeled up to it. Vance and Number 1 climbed up the steps and into the cockpit. Vance picked up a helmet that was resting on the back seat and put it on. He clicked his safety harness straps into place as the canopy closed.

Number 1 began his pre-flight checks. *Your dossier mentions that you were not able to attend flight school.*

"Sir, what's—ah kreket! Sorry sir—I mean, sorry Number 1. Blast, that 'sir' has been drilled into my head."

You want to know what a dossier is.

"Aye si—" Vance quickly shut his mouth. "Aye, Number 1."

Your dossier is the collection of documents we have about you. You could call it your file.

At a hand signal from the plane captain on the flight deck, Number 1 started his engine. He taxied the starlancer toward the runway. *Your dossier doesn't have much in it yet. Just your military records and your personal history at the Driscal colony. And recently added, the reports from Royce Williams, Eddison Frank, and Hans Christian.*

"Wow, that's a little spooky that you got all that. But you're right, the Mori canned it before I could get there."

"Wormwood, you are Phantom O-four to Mother," the radio chatter began.

Number 1 replied, "Roger Carillon."

"Phantom four, you are cleared for launch. Be advised there is an ion storm bearing two-seven-three, please steer clear."

"Phantom, roger and thank you."

"You're callsign is Wormwood?"

Number 1 rolled his eyes. "Don't ask." He saluted The Shooter. Moments later, Vance was thrown against the back of his seat. The starlancer thundered down the runway and out through the open space door.

Vance winced in pain from his leg injury. "Ah kreket, I forgot to take my pain meds this morning."

I want you to report to Dr. John Rychen, of the Lily of the Valley, as soon as we return.

"Oh, I already have some meds, I just forgot to take them."

That's an order, Number 13.

"Aye sir—I mean, Number 1."

Vance sat as patiently as he could before his questions got the better of him. "So, uh, beggin' your pardon, Number 1. Where we goin'?"

Number 1 pulled the starlancer into a sharp turn and then leveled out. *I will show you in a few minutes.*

Vance waited while Number 1 flew for a while in one direction. He occasionally checked his instrumentation to verify coordinates.

There it is.

Vance looked all around out the canopy on all sides. "Sir, I don't see nothin'."

Do not address me as 'sir'.

"Sorry Number 1."

Number 1 pressed a few buttons and flipped a switch. The transparent surface of the canopy faded into a red hue, then cooled into a blue hue. Then Vance saw a white light flashing in the distance. He strained to see where it was coming from.

"Hey, I see that star flashing!"

Say hello to Clarissa. She's a class 7B pulsar. She pulses every second more accurately than an atomic counter.

"Hello Clarissa." Vance snickered.

There was a moment of uncomfortable silence. The blood rushed to his cheeks.

Save the clowning around for when you are with the Orbiting Stars.

"Very sorry, sir—ah, I mean very sorry Number 1."

Number 1 flipped another switch and the canopy changed to a magenta hue. Vance now saw what looked like funnels of colorful vapor shooting out the top and bottom of the pulsar.

"Whoa, what is that?"

Those are the jets of the pulsar; streams of new particles of various elements being flung out into the galaxy. Pulsars like this one are where Nakkaron particles come from.

"You mean, the stuff that makes the whole Solar Winds stuff work comes from pulsars?"

This is where Eddison's third law comes into play: The strength of the electrical field is not as important as the distance to the Nakkaron flow.

"I have no idea what you just said."

It doesn't matter how strong the electrical field is, what matters is how close you are to the flow of Nakkaron particles. Out here, close to a pulsar, we are nearer to a flow of Nakkarons, hence your abilities will be stronger. This is where we come to catch glimpses into the possible future.

"Wow. How close can we get?"

Not very close since it has enough gravity to pull you apart, atom by atom. But I can safely get us a little closer to the jets.

Number 1 pulled into a gentle turn. Vance stared at the pulsar, nearly mesmerized by its rhythmic flashing. As the pulses flashed into his eyes, he felt a wetness on his hands. He looked down at his hands and saw blood. He looked up in alarm, wanting to inform Number 1. But he did not see the cockpit of the starlancer anymore. He was kneeling on a planet with brown sandy rocks and a green sky.

He felt a warm sandy breeze at his neck. Then he heard coughing. He looked around and saw a woman collapsed on the ground, facedown and struggling for breath. Vance dashed over and turned her onto her back. He looked into her mahogany eyes and saw blood running down the corner of her mouth.

"Valerie!"

She coughed again and reached her hand up and touched his cheek. "I was right about you." Her breathing grew shallow and slow. Then her body completely relaxed, her hand fell from his cheek, and she became limp.

"Valerie!"

"Squire Brewer." A familiar voice called out.

Vance turned around and saw Royce in his red flight suit standing a few yards away. "Sir?"

"Goodbye," he said as his image faded from view.

"Sir! Wait!"

"Number 13." A very nearby voice called out.

Vance shot his eyes open and flailed his arms around. He inadvertently jabbed his elbow into the side of the starlancer canopy wall. His breathing accelerated. He struggled against the safety straps holding him into his seat.

"Number 13! Calm down! Relax!"

Vance felt a plastic breath mask placed over his nose and mouth. He struggled against it but found he wasn't as strong as the hands that held the mask in place.

"Breathe deep, and calm down."

Vance heard the words but the meaning didn't register in his brain. All he knew was that he was scared. He continued to pant and struggle against his restraints. After a few minutes, the fog in his head started to clear, and rational thoughts started to surface.

Vance struggled against his instincts and forced a long deep breath. His heart rate began to slow, and his mind became a little clearer. He inhaled another deep breath and then relaxed his arm, leg, and back muscles. His breathing normalized, and Number 1 removed the breath mask.

Number 1 handed him a gel capsule and a little plastic pouch of water. "Here. Swallow this."

Vance put the capsule in his mouth. He tore off the top of the water pouch and drank. He noticed a cool breeze on his face. He looked to his right and saw Number 1 standing up in the cockpit, hunched over him. The canopy was open and an orange sunset painted the distant sky.

"Where are we?" Vance asked. "I didn't think there were any planets close to the pulsar."

Number 1 shook his head. "There aren't any nearby. I had to go hunting to find something with an atmosphere. You scared me Brewer— I mean, Number 13." He knelt on his seat. "What happened out there? One minute we're observing the pulsar and the next you're having some kind of panic attack."

"I don't know, I guess I musta' blacked out or somethin' 'cus I had a weird dream that someone was dying. It freaked me out."

Number 1 exhaled slowly. "I'm sorry, Number 13, I should have anticipated this. I usually don't tour with initiates that are so new. Usually, they've had a good hundred hours behind the stick and visited a few pulsars already. You weren't ready to get that close to the flow."

"So ya think I blacked out because I'm not used to it yet?"

Number 1 nodded. "Either that or you're very low on electrolytes. I'm very sorry."

"Nah, that's okay. I'm sorry you had to land on this rock just to check on me."

Number 1 held up one finger. Vance recognized it as the non-verbal cue to remain silent. Number 1 turned around and looked into the distance.

Number 13, I can hear another one of our operatives on this moon. Come quietly.

Number 1 hopped down from the cockpit and helped Vance down. Vance was careful not to put any strain on his leg. Once they were both down, Vance followed Number 1 as they walked down a lonely trail of rocks and debris.

Vance looked up at the grayish-blue sky with few clouds. How close was the air to Earth norms? Maybe he should have taken the breath mask with him.

Vance looked forward just in time to see Number 1 stop, and Vance was able to avoid bumping into him. Ahead, sitting on the ground, a man rested up against a large rock. He was dressed in all-black military fatigues. He held one hand against his stomach while the rest of him lay sprawled out up against the boulder.

Number 1 ran up to him. "Number 22, what are you doing here? We're supposed to rendezvous on Capernaum VI."

Number 22 removed his hand to reveal it was bloodied. "They won't kill him, because he can tell them where we are."

"Who?"

"I saw in vision the crimson shield of the Fire Lance and three silver bars. When the vision closed, I knew this was the place. And it looks like I was right, the Mori shot me to bury their secret."

Number 1 shook his head. "The Mori don't take prisoners, they exterminate all human life they find."

"They know we have a fleet on the run. They're desperately searching for it. I can only guess they intend to extract its location from their prisoner."

"They're looking for New Carillon." Number 1 turned to Vance. "The medkit is under the front seat in the starlancer."

"I appreciate the gesture," Number 22 sighed. "But it won't make a difference at this point. I've lost too much blood."

"Don't be a neutron-head!" He turned back to Vance. "Help get him up. We'll take him in our starlancer. It'll have to get real cozy back there since the two of you will be sharing a seat."

"Aye, Number 1."

Chapter 21

DENIED

I never thought about regrets or even repercussions. I did what was right and that was all there was to it. It never ceases to amaze me how prickly some of these bureaucrats can be. They're worse than porcupines; at least with a porcupine you can crossbreed it with a sheep and produce an animal that can knit its own sweaters.

—FROM "MEMOIRS OF THE EXODUS" BY HANS THE BRONZE

Vance hobbled down the rolling staircase that was wheeled up to the starlancer. Each step he took painfully reminded him it was a good idea to take the prescribed pain medication. When he got to the bottom of the staircase, he looked forward. Number 22 was lying on a rolling stretcher, being whisked away by four men in hospital scrubs.

Number 1 stood beside the starlancer talking to a man in a long white medical lab coat. The man took notes on a tablet device. If only his leg wasn't still injured, he could keep up with the men and the gurney. Hopefully Number 22 would live.

He started his slow pain-ridden walk over to the closest elevator, one slow stinging step at a time. After several steps, he stopped to rest a bit.

After panting a few times, he again wished he had taken his pain meds. The starlancer's launch and recovery both had been hard on his leg and it felt almost as sore as the day he was shot.

He felt someone grab his right arm and put it around their neck. A soft voice spoke, "You'll never get to the infirmary at that rate."

Vance looked into her mahogany eyes and could smell the sweet scent of Valerie's dark curls. She put her other arm around his waist and helped him hobble quickly to the elevator. Once they arrived, she pressed the button to call the elevator down.

Vance shyly smiled. "I appreciate this, ma'am."

"Ma'am is my mother," she flatly stated.

"Sorry miss–I've been strugglin' with how ta talk straight here–I am very grateful for your assist."

Her eyes hinted at the smile she held in reserve. "At least we're not at the Banquet Table, so you don't have to worry about speaking too properly."

"Yeah, there's a plus."

The elevator chimed once and the doors parted. Valerie helped Vance inside and pressed the button for the 2nd deck. "I finally got to hear your stories today."

He eyed her in a little surprise. "You mean they're still talkin' about me?"

She nodded. "Hans Christian has been telling everyone. I didn't know you were shot; you didn't look injured last night."

"Yeah, last night I remembered the cardinal rule to take my pain meds."

The corners of her mouth curved upwards ever so slightly but did not produce a smile. Her eyes, however, betrayed her. "We should get you to see Dr. Rychen. He'll get you fixed up."

"Yeah, Number 1 ordered me to report to him when we got back. I'm glad you know the way, that saves me from havin' ta ask around."

"Dr. Rychen is the Lily *I* toured with. He's very smart and exceptionally skilled."

The elevator slowed to a stop and the doors opened. Valerie put Vance's arm back around her neck and helped him hobble the long distance to the infirmary.

Once they walked in, an orderly in light blue scrubs walked over to Vance with a tablet computer. "Please fill this out while you wait."

Valerie took the tablet. "We request Dr. Rychen when he is available."

"Why does everyone keep requesting Dr. Rychen? It might be a long wait."

Valerie kept her composure. "We'll occupy ourselves by filling out this form."

The orderly shrugged and walked back to the front counter. Valerie assisted Vance in taking a seat. She took the seat beside him. "What did the Mori look like?"

Vance's brain swiftly replayed his last encounter in front of his eyes. "He was pretty freaky. He had a large bald head with two big eyes that were kinda farther apart than yours or mine. His teeth were all jagged and sharp-lookin'. But that wasn't what scared me; it was the horrible sounds he made that truly got my heart pumpin'. I felt like I was bein' stalked by a wild animal."

A wisp of air fluttered across Vance's face. He looked up to see Dr. Rychen in a long purple lab coat and a stethoscope draped around his neck. "Mr. Brewer, I have just received a personal request from Number 1 to have a look at you."

"Hey, you can talk normal?"

Dr. Rychen smiled. "You'll find most people do. It's only at formal gatherings that High Novan is spoken. It would get rather tiring otherwise."

Vance huffed a chuckle. "Yeah, I s'pose."

Valerie assisted Vance in following Dr. Rychen into an examination room and helped him ease onto the cushioned exam table. Dr. Rychen walked up and placed a hand on Vance's shoulder and closed his eyes. He simply stood there with his eyes closed for a few uncomfortable minutes.

Vance slowly turned his head toward Valerie and cast a confused look in her direction. She lost her composure and looked away as she broke into a smile.

Dr. Rychen opened his eyes. "Thermal penetration wound to the thigh, narrowly missing the femoral artery." He looked Vance in the eyes. "You're lucky to be alive."

"Story o' my life, sir. The flight surgeon on the Ticonderoga said I'd need to keep off it for a few days, but that hasn't happened." He sighed. "I guess what can't be done just can't be done."

Dr. Rychen walked over to a counter, pulled out a drawer, and produced a small metallic band. He brought it over to Vance. "Here, lift your leg a bit, I need to wrap this around it."

Vance obeyed.

"Tell me, Vance, why do you think there isn't anything that can be done about it?"

He shrugged. "I just know there's some things you just can't do nothin' about. I'm guessin' this leg is one of them."

Dr. Rychen cocked his head off to one side. "No, I don't believe you quite understand yet. You see, there are no problems, only procedures. There are no complications, only new directions. There is no disparage, for everything interconnects in one. And no limitations, for everything is modifiable. You see, there is no death when we have sufficient time."

Vance was silent for a few moments while Dr. Rychen placed his hand on the metal band around Vance's leg. Then, Vance took a breath and asked, "Are you sayin' you can fix anything?"

Dr. Rychen looked up from what he was doing and into Vance's eyes. "You mean, like fixing up an aggravated leg wound?"

Vance shrugged.

Dr. Rychen took off the metal band from around his thigh. "I'll leave that up to your judgment." With that, he swatted Vance's leg twice.

Vance instinctively winced, then his eyes widened. "What!" He rubbed his leg a moment. Then began systematically feeling around his leg, searching for the wound. "You gotta be frazzin kidding me!" He stood up and hopped from one leg to the other several times. "This is, this is like, a miracle!"

Dr. Rychen put one hand on Vance's shoulder. "Vance, when it comes time for you to tour with me, I will show you the many different miracles *you* could do as a Lily of the Valley."

Vance's breathing grew heavy as the air in the room thickened. Vance's heart felt bright and hopeful. His lungs forced in an overdue breath of air. "It would be an honor, sir."

"Before you leave, Vance, let me give you a list of exercises for your leg to prevent your muscles from getting stiff." Dr. Rychen walked out of the room.

Vance looked over at Valerie. She wore an emotional smile with misty eyes. "Valerie, did you hear that?"

She nodded, but before she could speak, Dorothy walked into the room. "Well well, Valerie, it looks like you've run into the famous squire after all. I hope you didn't have to scour all of New Carillon."

"It was by chance; his starfighter only just arrived."

"It's sweet that you're willing to assist Squire Brewer, just be careful not to taunt gravity, if you know what I mean."

"Mother please, not here."

Vance shifted his glance between both of them. "Mother?"

Dorothy smirked and looked over to Vance. "Squire Brewer, would you mind excusing Valerie for a few moments?"

"Uh... yeah, certainly ma'am."

Dorothy beckoned to Valerie and they both left the room. Vance exhaled and looked up at the ceiling.

I heard the best place to dance is at one of the three clubs on New Carillon.

Vance quickly looked around. He sighed and dropped his shoulders. "But the jack is wild."

"Very good," Number 1 replied.

Vance shot a glance over to his left and was startled. "Man, how do you do that comin'-outta-nowhere thing?"

Number 1 took a few steps over to Vance. "The human mind takes in a lot of information yet only allows the consciousness to be aware of a small amount. The subconscious filters what we notice. It is a simple task then, to tell someone's mind that seeing me is of no more consequence than the last step they took or the last light fixture they passed."

"Get spaced! That's totally gabb."

"Number 13, the reason I'm here is to inform you of the debrief you were not able to attend due to your injury."

Vance sat back down on the table.

"Number 22 glimpsed a possible future and saw a Fire Lance pilot abducted by the Mori. I've informed our cell leader and he is organizing a meeting with the other cells to discuss our next move."

"It's Sky Captain Williams, sir."

"I told you *not* to call me 'sir'," Number 1 corrected. "And no, we have not had enough intel to establish *who* has been captured."

"Sorry Number 1, but you gotta trust me, it's Sky Captain Williams."

"So you think the three silver bars Number 22 mentioned are rank stripes, do you? Well, let me clue you in, squire. Silver bars are also a measurement of deployment time as well as the pecking order in Fire Lance. You think you have this whole mystery figured out? You, who can count your field experience on one hand, think you have enough training and experience to solve any mystery greater than where a thruster is broken? You have no right to ask for my belief in your intuition... and I have no reason to give it."

Vance sat there, slowly collapsing under the weight of Number 1's words. His head succumbed to the emotional weight and hung. "Forgive me sir, I, I... thought I could help."

Number 1 exhaled loudly. "Look, don't take it personally. I have nothing against you, Number 13. In fact, I kinda like you. But the truth is that noble intentions and pulsaric ideals cannot replace experience. We've both had a traumatic day. Your order is to go home and relax. I'll call for you tomorrow evening and we can have another go at the pulsar."

Vance slowly looked up and nodded. "Aye sir—I mean Number 1."

Number 1 walked out the door just as Dr. Rychen walked back in, and handed a small packet of papers to Vance. "I found the ones with picture diagrams. Take it easy, and make sure to stretch."

Vance weakly took the papers.

"Vance, is something wrong?"

Vance took in a slow, deep breath and then let it all out. "Thank you, sir, I just need a little air."

Vance walked out of the infirmary and strolled down the hallway. The image of Royce bidding farewell and fading away kept circling in his head over and over. He clenched his hands into fists as he walked, trying to keep back his tears by sheer will. Then he stopped cold in his tracks. He took in a half-breath with wide eyes and stood there. After an eternal second, a determined smirk crossed his lips. He bolted down the hallway, dodging other pedestrians until he came to the apartment he shared with Hans.

He walked in and headed straight for a little cooler box on the tiled section of the floor. He took out two clear bottles of water. Then he turned around and grabbed a piece of fruit from the counter. Next, he looked around for something he could pack them into.

The door opened and Hans stepped in. "Hey! Vance the Lance, I heard you had a big day!"

Vance stared at him, expressionless, motionless.

Hans looked at the water and fruit he had in his arms. His smile slid off his face. "Where are you going?"

Vance swallowed. "I have to help a friend."

"Who?"

"Sky Captain Williams, sir."

Hans scowled at Vance for a long, uncomfortable minute. "You're going to disobey orders, aren't you?"

"Hans the Bronze, I just have this terrible feeling that somethin' bad is gonna happen ta him if I don't try ta help."

Hans was silent another moment before speaking softly. "Vance, I can't allow that."

Vance's chest felt heavy and his shoulders sagged.

Hans turned and walked over to the front door. "You are to remain here until I get back with food for dinner."

Vance looked at the floor. "Aye sir."

"Vance. Vance."

Vance looked up.

Hans unclipped a small device from his belt and placed it on the nearby counter. He held his hand on the device and stared straight at Vance. Vance looked back at him curiously. Then he eyed the device under Hans's hand, and then returned his gaze to Hans. Hans intensely stared back and patted the device on the counter twice before leaving.

Vance stood there in silent solitude a few moments before approaching the counter. His slow sullen breaths enlivened into deep energized panting. A smile crossed his lips and a tear ran down his face as he picked up from the counter Hans's force field generator. His finger caressed the blue half-moon logo.

"Thank you, Hans." He picked up his helmet and headed out the door.

Chapter 22

ON THE TRAIL

Date: 01 Tetrad
Subject: Initial exposure
*Notes: Since the subject's initial exposure he has
proven to exceed even my expectations. The
unfortunate side-effect is that his talents are
becoming a nuisance to my work. A shorter leash
and a tighter grip will need to be maintained to
ensure control.*

—FROM "DOSSIER #13" CLASSIFIED

Vance rushed down the hallway, walking in long strides. He wanted to look casual and yet get as much distance covered as possible. He decidedly slowed down after noticing a few odd looks from people he passed.

He reached the elevator and entered. He quickly scanned the control panel and pressed the button marked 'H', hoping it meant 'hangar'. The elevator began its descent and hummed as it went. Vance nervously tapped the force field generator against his leg. His mind once again replayed the picture of Royce saying goodbye and then fading away.

Not this time, he thought to himself. *I'm not gonna lose another friend.*

The elevator slowed to a stop and the door opened. Vance stepped out and stopped suddenly. He looked around the brightly lit hallway in confusion. This wasn't the hangar. He quickly backed up into the elevator and looked at the control panel. The light had ended on #1 instead of H.

"Ah don't tell me I need a keycard to go down there."

He looked around the elevator, hunting for ideas. Then his eyes locked onto the red emergency button. He hadn't ever seen much of elevators but figured there had to be an emergency escape if the elevator got stuck between decks. He waited for the elevator doors to close and then started looking. He searched the carpeted floor for any sign of a hatch, panel, or anything that might denote a way into the elevator shaft.

"Blast it! There's gotta be a way out." He sighed and looked heavenward as if to ask 'why me?' And that's when he noticed a trap door on the ceiling. He smiled wide. "I gotta learn to look at things from different angles."

He stepped onto the handrail and hoisted himself up to the hatch and pushed it up. It clanked open and Vance put his arms through the small opening and hoisted himself up. He closed the hatch door behind him and crawled over to the edge of the elevator. He saw a small indentation in the wall with a metal ladder leading down.

He reached over to the ladder and noticed he was trembling. He retracted his hand and took three deep breaths with his eyes closed. Then he reached over again and grabbed hold of the ladder and climbed onto it. "It's okay, I can do this."

He reached back to the elevator roof and retrieved his helmet and the force field generator. Then he started his slow descent, one rung at a time. When he reached the bottom, he saw the door marked: Hangar Deck.

Smiling, he opened the door and walked through. On the other side of the door was a long stairwell. He paused and looked at it for a few moments. "You're tellin' me, I could have taken the stairs!" His voice echoed up the stairwell.

Vance looked over to the exit door, the one that would lead him to the hangar. He reached for the handle but the door swung open and crashed into him. It knocked him back up against the railing that overlooked the flight of stairs going down.

"Oh, I'm terribly sorry!" Came a voice from the other side of the door.

Vance was distracted by the sight of the force field generator, that had slipped from his hands. It tapped against the railing, and then tumbled over the edge.

He watched in slow-motion horror as the device fell from view, down the long shaft. He instantly felt pressure on his chest. He smelled the sweet scent of curly locks of hair tickling his face. The arm that had reached across his face extended over the railing. He looked up at the owner and was delighted to stare into those mahogany eyes.

Valerie pulled her arm back up over the railing with the force field generator she had caught. Then she looked into his eyes. Their faces were uncomfortably close. His heart started to beat faster. Valerie eased herself off Vance. She had practically climbed over him to reach for the falling device. She recomposed herself, dusted off her dark leggings, brushed off her blue and white skirt, and readjusted her twin pistol holsters.

"...you have fast reflexes..." was all he could say.

"What are you doing here?"

"Please, don't stop me," he begged. "I gotta help Sky Captain Williams before it's too late."

"What's wrong with Royce?"

"I seen him in a dream, he said goodbye to me, and then he disappeared." The image flashed again before his eyes. He felt a tear escape his eye and race down his cheek.

"A dream?"

He nodded. "When I was up in the starlancer with Number 1, we were watching a pulsar and—"

"Pulsar? Vance, did you see into the future?"

Vance took a few silent breaths. "I think so, and it scares me."

"Did you tell Number 1?"

"Yeah, but it didn't go so well."

She exhaled slowly and a saddened expression befell her face. "Let me guess; you were promptly dressed down for arrogance and inexperience?"

He nodded. "Apparently my 'noble intentions and pulsaric ideals' are no match for experience."

"Some of these knights wouldn't know a pulsaric virtue if one fell on them and began to wiggle."

Vance snorted. "Beggin' your pardon miss, but you sound like you been there."

She nodded. "I was told I could have been the greatest Fire Lance Knight. But when I saw arrogance parading around as sophistication, I decided I did not want to be one of them."

"I take it Wind Captain Dawes feels like you gave him the can when you decided to become a Gun Star?"

"Oh, that's only half the story with Dawes." She held out the force field generator to Vance, but before he could take it, she retracted the offer. "You don't know how to fly. How are you planning to leave?"

Vance sat motionless for a moment. "I hadn't thought that far ahead..."

She thought for a moment. "I can take you in my mother's starlancer."

Vance hesitated. "That's... not such a good idea."

"Please don't be a neutron-head; you can't fly, you need me. Why wouldn't it be a good idea?"

Vance opened his mouth to reply, but nothing came out. The memory of seeing her dying came tumbling back into his memory. His hands started to tremble.

She looked deeper into his eyes. "You saw something else, didn't you?"

Vance's mouth tried to make words to reply but no sound wanted to come.

Her voice softened to a whisper. "Did you see me?"

Vance nodded. "You were injured somehow, and I saw you slip away."

She looked down. Her eyes seemed to shift all about as if in thought. "Even just knowing about this possible future has already introduced some changes. Now that we know, we can be careful to avoid that fate."

"I would rather not risk it."

She looked at him with commanding eyes. "It is my choice whether or not I accept the risk."

Vance lowered his head. "Yeah, but if I have ta be the one to break the news to your mother..."

Vance felt her blue gloved hand pulling his chin up, causing his eyes to meet with hers. "Your concern for others, your courage to do what you feel is right, and your loyalty to your friends are what truly make you pulsaric."

"That's pretty high praise, miss, I hope I can live up to it."

"You will." She straightened up and held out her gloved hand to Vance. He took it, and she helped him to his feet. Then she handed him the force field generator.

"How do ya know?"

She leaned in closer to him. Her mahogany eyes peered deep into his. "Because your heart only masquerades as a squire, when in reality it bleeds blue and white."

Vance smiled. "Are there any openings in the Gun Stars?"

She blushed and exited the stairwell. Vance took a deep breath. "I can certainly feel *her* gravity," he said under his breath, exiting after her.

They descended a few steps onto the flight deck. Vance kept up with Valerie who paraded around as though she were the commanding officer. She pointed to a rolling staircase off to the side. "Bring that."

Vance jogged over to it and rolled it after Valerie. She helped him position it up to the canopy. They climbed up the steps and she waved her hand across a panel near the canopy, and it slid open. She stepped into the front seat, picked up the helmet that was lying on the seat, and sat down. He settled into the back seat.

She closed the canopy and switched on the rudimentary power. She clicked on the transmission. "Carillon tower, this is Bullseye, requesting launch schedule."

"Bullseye, Carillon tower. Ma'am, you are not scheduled today."

"Yeah, it was a last-minute change in the duty roster, I get to pick up the slack."

"Yeah, I hear ya. That will place you sixth in line for launch; we'll have the flight crew tag you for position in under ten."

"Roger, and thanks."

"Bullseye?" Vance asked.

She switched off the transmission. "My mother's callsign; she's the sage of the Sniper Clan."

"You got a callsign yet?"

"No, I'm not officially in the squadron yet. Not for another few months."

"What would you like it ta be?"

She shook her head. "It's bad form to try to make your own callsign. Your squadron gives it to you. So depending on my rapport with the squadron, I could end up with 'HotHead' or—"

"Or Ace?"

She smiled. "I like your positive thinking, Vance."

"Hans has been helpin' me cut out the negative thinkin' in my head."

A plane captain, wearing a brown jacket, walked up beside the starlancer and gave Valerie a hand gesture to start her engines. She ignited them and the turbines whined to life. Valerie started systematically going through the pre-flight checks.

Before long Valerie was following the directions of a plane director, taxiing the starlancer to the head of the runway. Vance watched her hands over the instrumentation panel and on the flight controls. Her hands seemed to fly from one control to another with the smooth rhythm of a practiced pilot.

"Bullseye, you are Caliber O-one to Mother," the voice said.

"Roger Carillon," she replied.

"Caliber one, you are cleared for launch. Clear stars today, ma'am."

"Caliber, roger and thank you," she said.

Moments later, the starlancer bolted forward. It rocketed out the open space door and into the starry sky. "I'm starting to get the hang of launching," Vance admitted.

"Where to?" she asked.

"There's a moon with an atmosphere near the Clarissa pulsar. That's where Number 22 was shot."

"Probably Eldoran IV-b," she surmised. "It'll take a while to get there."

"Not a problem, miss; I'll be watching the SEDAR—It'll give me some more practice."

The time seemed to pass by swiftly and before Vance knew it, they were in orbit of Eldoran. Valerie pressed a few buttons. "Vance, are you getting anything on SEDAR?"

"Sorry miss, I got nothin'."

She flipped some switches and pressed more buttons. "I learned a little trick from Blue Planet," she offered. "If the aeon trail is less than 72 hours old, we can sometimes pick up a trace."

"I'm not sure what all you said, but it sounds very brainy and gabb."

She giggled. "If it works, you'll be saying that; otherwise you'll probably be saying, 'Who's neutron-brained idea was this?'"

They laughed together until her console started beeping along with a small flashing light. "Gotcha!" she declared.

"You found somethin'?"

"There are three aeon trails. Two look to be made by starlancers—they don't emit as much as other starcraft. So the last trail is the one to follow."

"You can follow their exhaust trail?"

She bobbed her head from one side to the other. "Not exactly, the cosmic weather always pushes things around. Nothing is ever truly stationary in space. But it will give us something to follow, with about 60-80% accuracy."

"The planet I saw had brown sandy ground and a green sky. And we were breathing without masks."

"That... cuts down the possibilities considerably." She pressed a few more buttons on her console. "Vance, on this trajectory, there is only one class M9 planet in range; Dayton II."

Vance looked out of the canopy. "Hang on sir, we're comin'."

Chapter 23
INTO THE DEN

If it is the will of The Winds that a knight-initiate become a Gun Star, they will be endowed with the gifts of The Crusade. The foremost of these gifts being the ability to feel the angle of the shot, reducing the need to take aim. The Quick Draw clan utilizes this skill more prominently than any other clan within the Gun Stars.

—FROM "LECTURES ON THE CHOSEN" BY SAGE DOROTHY VLAVSKISK

The alarm on Valerie's instrumentation panel screeched its two-note distress. A red light flashed on her console. A fog of thick clouds plastered the canopy. "I can't see anything Vance!"

"What do I do?" he asked frantically.

"To the right of the altimeter, are we in the red or the green?"

"Red!" he replied.

"Too fast," she muttered to herself. She slowly pulled back on the stick. "Now one gauge down, watch my glideslope. Keep me inside the blue lines!"

Vance kept his eyes glued to his control screen. "I got it! Uh, we're lookin' too shallow!"

Valerie readjusted.

"That's it, miss, now level out a little more and we're still comin' in too fast!"

She flipped a switch to deploy the atmospheric flaps and then steadied her gaze on her gyroscope. She struggled to keep the craft level. "Vance, I'm engaging the vertical thrusters, keep watching my glideslope!"

"Aye miss!"

Valerie snapped a button on her stick and Vance felt twice as heavy. The starlancer's descent slowed. Suddenly, the visual fog vanished and Valerie was able to see the rocky ground rushing up to meet them. She flipped another switch and pulled the nose of the craft up a little more. The landing gear scraped the rocky surface and stopped with a solid *thud.*

Valerie cut power to the engines and then slumped down in her seat, panting. Vance took deep breaths to slow his erratic breathing. "Well now," he took another breath. "That was an adventure."

"Yeah, let's have that be the adventure we only go on once." She opened the canopy, rested in her seat a moment longer, and then stood up. She turned around and looked at Vance. "Thanks for guiding me in."

"Thanks for helpin' me help you." Vance stood and realized he was too close to Valerie. In response, he turned to get down off the starlancer. The landing gear shifted under the sandy ground and they caught hold of each other for balance.

Holding onto her felt really exciting. His heart rate accelerated. The wide-eyed momentary panic in Valerie's eyes vanish away in favor of hinting at a smile she kept locked away. Vance took a deep breath and let go of her.

"Sorry miss, I uh..." Vance hopped down from the canopy to the ground. Then he turned back and offered her his hand. She eyed his offer a moment and then looked at him.

His hand was too low to be of any use. "Ah, yeah—well maybe the thought counts for somethin'."

She opened a little compartment in the cockpit and pulled out a bandolier with pistol magazines. She hopped down as the canopy closed.

She slung the bandolier over her head and one shoulder. Then she reached down to a small zipper pocket on one of her boots and pulled out two shiny metal hair clips. She pulled back the left side of her long black curls and clipped them back. Then she did the same for the right side of her hair.

She reached into another zipper pocket and pulled out a handful of tablets. She opened her hand to show Vance six tablets. She handed him half. "That's all we have."

"Electrolyte tablets?" Vance asked.

She nodded and then drew her pistols. She inspected them a moment before replacing them in her holsters. "Ready?"

Vance unzipped a pocket on his flight suit and put the force field generator inside and zipped it back up. Then he pocketed the three tablets. "Ready as I'll ever be, miss."

She nodded and turned around to face the surrounding scenery. "Where to?"

"Well, assumin' we're still pointin' the same direction when we started the descent, it should be just over that rise."

She started after the large hill in the distance and Vance followed. As they started the uncomfortable climb, Vance stumbled. Valerie caught his hand, preventing him from sliding back down. "That's three times now, you've saved me with your fast reflexes."

She continued climbing up the hill. "What about you," she inquired, "how good are you with that force field generator?"

"Well, I sure can throw it up real fast... everything else could use some practice."

She momentarily stopped to look at him. "You didn't think that far ahead either, did you."

Vance shyly smiled. "I guess I walk a fine line between pulsaric virtue and neutron-brained impulsiveness."

She rolled her eyes and continued walking up the steep rise. Vance continued after her. "That goes without sayin', miss, that I appreciate your help; without you—"

"Shhhh!" She held one finger to her lips.

Vance obeyed and listened. A faint humming sounded in the distance. "Vertical ascent thruster," he identified. "Too high-pitched to be one of ours."

"You can tell that just by listening?"

"I'm a starcraft grease monkey, don't forget."

When they reached the top of the rise, they got down on their hands and knees. They peeked over the ledge and into the valley beyond.

Valerie's eyes lit up and Vance's jaw dropped. "There must be a million of 'em..."

Valerie reached down to her other boot and pulled out a small finger-sized telescope. She peered through the glass and surveyed the scene. Multiple metal buildings and long paved runways filled the valley. Countless starcraft lined the runways and filled up several holding zones.

"Vance, do you know what kind of starcraft those are?"

"Yup. They're Mori starfighters. I got to see some up close when I was flyin' with Sky Captain Williams."

Valerie turned to face him. "Vance, this is not a fringe location, this is a staging post for a starborne assault. And they're in range to strike New Carillon and the fleet."

Vance scratched his forehead. "I was afraid that was the case."

"We don't even know which building he is in?"

Vance shrugged, "Well I was figurin' the big one on the left looks like it has a space door for letting craft in and out."

"Why does that matter?"

"Why would a building need a space door?"

She returned a puzzled look.

"Space doors are only for lettin' starcraft leave the landing bay while keepin' the air inside the ship—which they have no need of on a planet. The runway is outside on the ground. So that means outta all these buildings, that one is not a building at all, but a landed ship."

She blinked. "You have a feeling Royce is on that ship?"

"Well unless I'm wrong, those Mori starfighters only have one seat. They would need a bigger ship to bring the Sky Captain back in."

Valerie looked through the telescope once more at the landed starfighters. "Looks like we make a good team, you and I." She put her telescope away and started climbing down the other side of the rise.

Vance smiled wide. "Why thank you miss." He started after her. They kept low. It helped reduce their chances of being seen by a sentry or patrol. Once they reached the valley floor, Valerie drew her twin pistols. She slowly advanced toward what seemed to be the rear of the landed ship. Vance followed behind and felt for the force field generator in his pocket. Just touching it gave him a boost of confidence. It was as if some part of Hans's competence could be gained by the simple contact.

When they came up behind the large ship, Valerie looked back over at Vance. "How can we get inside?"

"Well," he assessed, "Their space door looks closed, so we can't get in that way. I do know from deployments that whenever you put to shore, so to speak, you always take the opportunity to recirculate your air. Maybe they do the same thing."

Valerie looked up and made a visor with her arm to block the intense sunlight. "There," she pointed with one of her pistols.

Very high up, an open hatch protruded from the top of the sidewall. "I'll bet you anything that's it."

"How do we get up there?"

Vance smiled. "That, miss, is where I come in." He reached out toward the ground in front of the ship. The air shimmered in front of them. Valerie walked up the force field like an invisible ramp to the open hatch.

Vance cautiously stepped onto the force field. He noticed when he put some weight on it, the force field shimmered like running water splattering over rocks. He breathed in a faint smell of ozone and walked up the ramp to Valerie.

Vance motioned for Valerie to enter the hatch. "Ladies with weapons first?"

She smirked and climbed into the hatch. Vance followed. Once he was inside, he relaxed his hand and arm muscles. He flexed his fingers and extended his arm a few times, shaking out the stiffening muscles. "I hope we don't get into a prolonged fight."

"Shhh."

"Sorry miss," he whispered.

They were inside the ductwork that carried air from outside into the various parts of the ship. Vance pointed to an air return duct. "Miss, we can use these ducts to wander all about the ship. That means we should be able to find Sky Captain Williams without bein' seen."

She nodded.

Vance walked over to the other end of the duct and heard a loud *pop.* The air duct floor gave way under Vance and he fell through the ceiling down into the room below.

Vance shook his head and looked around. His heart rate accelerated at the sight of three Mori in the room, staring at the new surprise that crashed down. Their wide bald heads and spaced apart dark eyes highlighted the eeriness of their sharp, jagged teeth. One of the Mori growled and bared his teeth like a wild animal and pointed to Vance. The other two each pulled out a small shiny orange-tinted metal pistol and pointed it at Vance.

BANG BANG BANG! Each of the three Mori jerked in pain and fell to the ground. Vance looked up and saw Valerie partially hanging out from the air duct with her smoking pistol poised.

"Come on, Vance, take my hand."

Vance quickly got up and took her hand. Then the rest of the duct floor gave way and Valerie fell on top of Vance. "Okay," she conceded, "time for plan B."

She got up off Vance and he slowly climbed up onto his feet. "I'm thankful you don't weigh much."

"This is so *backward!*" she complained. "We're supposed to be shooting our way *out* not *in!*"

"I guess plan B is to bust our way in ta every room lookin' for Sky Captain Williams?"

Valerie picked up one of the Mori pistols and tossed it to Vance. "Here, I hope you can shoot."

"Hey hey hey, I did graduate basic training."

Valerie pressed a button near the door. It slid open and she peeked out the door and looked both ways. She motioned for him to follow.

"Don't you want one of these fancy weapons?"

She shook her head. "I can do a lot more with a projectile than I can with a beam of light."

Vance hustled to keep up. Valerie swiftly crept along the hallway. She kept one pistol facing forward and the other one facing up. They rounded a corner and saw a long hallway ahead of them. It had several passageways branching off.

Valerie sighed. "We're going to be caught long before we find where Royce is."

Vance looked up at the ceiling and followed its path with his eyes. "We're already caught."

Valerie shot a glance back at him. "What are you talking about?"

He pointed up to a black glass orb attached to the ceiling. "I'll bet that's a security camera."

"Blast!"

"Nah nah nah, miss, all cameras link back to a central control—well, assumin' the Mori think similar to us." He placed his hand on the wall nearest he could to the black orb. He felt small vibrations in the metal wall. Some vibrated slower and others faster. He closed his eyes and pictured in his mind the different speeds of vibrations.

There's always a pattern, he thought. *Where is the pattern?*

He opened his eyes and huffed a half-chuckle. "I'll bet you money the control room is one floor up and a few doors down."

Valerie took one step forward before she ducked. A red bolt of light streaked past her. A few strands of her hair billowed in the slight breeze as the bolt passed. She fired back several shots and then pushed Vance into the wall. "Don't stand in the middle of the hall when someone is shooting!"

"Sorry miss. I can't see where the shots are coming from."

Another red bolt struck the wall behind Vance's head. The bolt sparked and left a smoking black mark. Valerie fired off another round. A distant grunt echoed down the hall followed by a heavy *thud.*

"Nice shootin'"

She glared at him, "You have a gun too, use it!"

Her glare reminded him of one of his drill sergeants in basic training. "Ma'am, yes ma'am."

Valerie and Vance rushed to the hallway intersection and peered down both directions. Vance pointed down one of the hallways. "Stairwell." Just then a klaxon started belting out a whiny alarm.

Vance and Valerie bolted down the hallway toward the stairwell. A door opened in front of Vance and a Mori soldier stepped out. Vance tried to stop, but his forward momentum pushed him onward. He fell back and slid into the feet of the Mori, toppling him right over the top of Vance.

Valerie fired off one round and the Mori stopped moving. She released the magazine in one of her pistols. It clattered to the ground. With pistols in hand, she pulled a new magazine from her bandolier. She inserted it into her pistol and slapped it in place with her palm.

She holstered one pistol as she ran up to Vance, helping him up with her free hand. "Unorthodox, but effective."

He smiled. "Yeah, I guess you could say it went down well."

Valerie smirked. "Very funny. Now let's get—" A terrible roar echoed down the hallway behind them. They looked back and saw Mori soldiers running down the hallway. Multiple red, hot bolts of light came raining down the hallway. Vance held out his hands desperately. The air between them and the Mori shimmered like water. Bolt after bolt harmlessly smacked up against the force field.

Vance's eyes lit up. "I'm doin' it!"

"Doing what?" she asked.

"I finally got the force field strong enough to stop enemy fire!" he said with excitement.

Valerie aimed and fired one round. It hit the force field from their side and bounced off. "I can't shoot through it!"

"Up the stairwell then?"

She nodded and started charging up the stairs. Vance backed up until he was on the stairs and then ran up after her. He abruptly bumped into her. "Why'd you stop?"

Another red bolt flew past his ear and hit the wall. Valerie grabbed his shirt and pulled him down into a crouch. "That's why!"

"Good reason."

Valerie swiftly leaned her head around the corner of the stairwell. She took a quick peek and returned to safety. Two more red bolts flew past her head and burned into the wall behind. She aimed at the sidewall for a few moments, then fired three shots. The bullets ricocheted off the opposite wall and struck flesh. The Mori pistols clattered to the ground.

Valerie jumped up and rounded the corner. Vance followed after her to find three dead Mori. "Oh," he said excitedly, "you can do trick shots too?"

"That's like me asking if you can lube an engine as well."

"That's really gabb, miss."

"Left or right?"

Vance closed his eyes to recall the memory. Valerie grabbed him by the shirt and yanked him toward her as two more red bolts of light whizzed past from the stairwell. Vance tumbled to the floor around the corner. Valerie crouched around the corner and started returning fire.

Vance sat up only to see additional Mori soldiers coming from the opposing side hallway. Vance threw up a force field, blocking them. "Miss, we need to go through the Mori I'm blocking. So on the count of three, we'll switch targets. I'll switch the force field toward the stairwell and you shoot the guys in front of us."

"Just a second." She released both pistol magazines, letting them clatter to the floor, and reloaded. "Okay, now you can count."

"On three; one, two, three!" Vance dropped his arm from in front and raised his other arm toward the stairwell. Valerie fired off five rounds, dropping each of the Mori.

"Let's move!" she commanded.

Vance followed Valerie across the hall intersection to the other side. He pulled on one of the doors. It didn't budge. Vance raised his Mori pistol and shot the door. He stared at the door, puzzled. His gun had only produced a black burn mark on the metal.

Valerie snickered. "Let me try." She fired both pistols a few times each, pounding holes into the door's lock. She smirked.

Vance shrugged. "Bullets: two, lasers: zero." He pulled the door open and was met with multiple hot red bolts of light streaming out from the room. Vance dropped his pistol and threw his hand out in front of him. One bolt grazed his shoulder just as he raised the force field.

Vance instinctively grabbed his shoulder, dropping the force field. A bolt flew straight for him as if in slow motion. It raced toward his chest as a bullet from Valerie intercepted the bolt. Vance dropped to his knees as Valerie shot the three Mori inside the room.

Valerie holstered her pistols. Then she pulled Vance into the room, closing the door behind her. She knelt by Vance. "Are you hit bad?"

Vance's breathing was erratic. "I almost bought it." He gasped for another breath. "Such a *canner* of me to drop my arms." He gasped for a few more breaths.

Valerie searched him until she verified he wasn't shot anywhere else. She tore off a thin piece of her skirt's hem and tied it around Vance's shoulder. "You'll be just fine..." she muttered as she worked.

Vance turned and looked deep into her mahogany eyes. "I don't know how I would have managed without ya."

She faintly panted as she stared back into his eyes for a few silent moments. "As I said, we make a great team."

She stood and walked over to the front of the room. Vance stood and walked over to Valerie's side. She stared at a whole wall full of camera feeds, each playing on a small square section of a wall-mounted screen. Some displayed the interior of rooms, others showed hallways.

Vance pointed to one monitor. "They're bringing in armored troops."

Valerie sighed. "Well, at least they're learning. However, that is going to make our departure a lot more difficult."

"There he is!" Vance pointed to a monitor showing Royce strapped down to a table and three Mori standing over him.

"Can you tell where he is?"

Vance looked at the scene. "I got nothin', miss. That room could be anywhere."

"Then what was the point of coming here? We're still going to have to search *every single room* on this blazing ship!"

"Wait wait wait... I have an idea." Vance closed his eyes and put his hand on the screen.

After a few moments, Valerie heard noises close to the door. She drew her pistols and crouched behind the edge of the desk. The screen Vance was touching shut off and he opened his eyes.

She glanced over to the screen. "What did you do?"

"I killed its electrical. Now whichever room does not vibrate is the room where the camera is not working."

"Can you find it from here?"

He shook his head. "Negative miss, I need ta feel the walls."

"Well in a moment, the Mori are going to burst through that door shooting. Can you push them back with your force field?"

He aimed his confused look in her direction. "You can move it?"

"I've seen spectacular creativity with Orbiting Star knights and their force fields. I guess you haven't learned that yet."

Vance extended his arms out toward the door. "When I was on the Ticonderoga with Hans, I saw him do this punching thing and it reflected a bullet. I guess now's as good a time as any." The door flung open and grunts and growls filled the air as a hailstorm of red bolts of light flooded into the room. They pelted the force field Vance still held up. He punched the empty air in front of him. Nothing happened. "Yeah, that's what I figured. Prob'ly more to it than that."

Valerie stood up, grabbed him by the collar, and yanked his head inched from her own. She stared at him with narrowed eyebrows and intense eyes. "Vance! If Nova blessed you with the gifts for The Crusade, then you *are* a Solar Knight! Where's your faith, Vance?"

He swallowed. "I—I'm...I'm just—"

"Your ability to harness The Solar Winds is the very manifestation of your destiny! Where's your faith?" She let go of his collar.

He turned around to the screen behind them, remembering the image of Royce. He heard Royce's words echoing in his mind: Be not afraid of greatness, Brewer, just be believing.

He turned to face the Mori, and with his free hand, balled up his fist. He began rehearsing over and over in his mind, *My very punch sends things flying. My very punch sends things flying...*

He stood stationary for a few more nervous moments. He purposely increased his breathing rate trying to override his doubts and hesitation. He threw the hardest punch he could at the emptiness between them and the Mori. The shimmering air of the force field sprang outward. It plowed into the Mori and smashed them up against the far wall of the hallway. Helmets cracked and bones snapped. Vance dropped his arm and the force field dissipated.

Valerie's wide eyes looked at him. "I thought you said you were just going to reflect their weapons fire back at them."

He stared at the scene with a dropped jaw. "Yeah... I was tryin' to bounce their shots back..." He pointed at the doorway, "I wasn't intendin' that."

She swiftly kissed him on the cheek and ran to the open door. "Great work, Vance. Let's find Royce."

He brought his hand to his cheek and smiled. Then he noticed his hand was shaking. He quickly popped the first of his three tablets into his mouth before rushing after her. Valerie led the way down the hall as Vance followed, running his hand across the walls on his way. He searched for where that particular vibration stopped.

They rounded another corner and skidded to a halt. They saw a dozen armor-clad Mori soldiers running down the hall. Vance put up a force field and then threw a punch in their direction. A few of the red bolts of light reflected off the force field.

"Oh come on! That's not what I was tryin' ta do and you know it!"

"Vance, let's go the other way!"

She pulled his other arm, towing him back and down the opposite hallway. She fired a few shots with one pistol, hoping to slow the enemy's advance. Vance held out his hand and resumed feeling the wall as they hustled down the hall.

"We're gettin' close," he reported.

She slowed down and peeked around the next corner. Six Mori soldiers with armor were coming up the hallway on the right. Another eight were coming down the hallway on the left. She crouched down by the corner of the wall and drew her second pistol. She reloaded both pistols and then started shooting down both hallways. Vance erected a force field behind them.

Her bullets glinted off the Mori's armor. "This is bad," Vance said.

Valerie stopped firing and pulled her head back around the corner to safety. Red bolts of light, fired from both hallways, zipped past them. "What? Are they not afraid of cross-fire?"

"Valerie! We need to go down the left hall!"

She looked at him strangely for a moment, "Can you stop the Mori from the right hallway too?"

Vance nodded and held out his other hand toward the right hallway. "Can you punch through their armor?"

She shook her head. "Not with standard rounds. But I can probably do the next best thing."

She peeked back around the corner and aimed both pistols for a few seconds. She fired them both in rapid succession. Most of the bullets bounced and ricocheted off the charging troops' armor. A few of them sliced into the Mori rifles.

Valerie pulled herself back around and holstered one pistol. She pulled out a tablet from her boot pouch. It slipped from her fingers and fell to the floor. She briefly looked for it before giving up and pulling out her second tablet and swallowing it. Then she reloaded her pistols.

"Vance, they may not be able to shoot back, but I don't want to fight hand-to-hand. Is there anything you can do with your force field?"

"Yup," Vance said, dropping one arm. He charged down the left hallway toward the Mori soldiers with broken rifles. Valerie charged after him.

The Mori soldiers counter-charged, barreling down the hall at Vance and Valerie. Vance dropped to the ground and threw up both hands in front of him. Valerie slid to a stop behind Vance. The charging Mori collided with the force field, knocking them out cold as if they had hit a solid metal wall.

Vance stood back up and surveyed the unconscious troops. "Yeah, it hurts, don't it? I found out the hard way too."

Valerie shoved Vance to the wall as hot red bolts of light streaked past where he was just standing. She returned fire behind them while backing off down the hallway. Vance put up another force field behind them to block the assault.

"Where to?" Valerie inquired.

Vance dashed over to the wall and felt it with his free hand. "Very close," he announced. He hurried down the hallway running his hand along the wall. Then he stopped and backed up one door. "Got it!"

Valerie reloaded her pistols. Vance looked at Valerie's bandolier. "Looks like you've gone through more than half your ammunition."

She crouched down and pointed her pistols at the door. "On my mark, open the door. We saw three Mori on the camera, right?"

"Careful, we could hit Sky Captain Williams by mistake, and that would ruin this whole day."

Valerie lowered her aim to the bottom third of the door. "Noted," she replied.

Vance kept his arm up, holding the force field behind them in the hallway. He reached over and held his free hand over the button to open the door.

"Mark!"

Vance pressed the button and the door slid open. Valerie fired off several shots and the Mori dropped to the floor, never to move again.

She holstered both pistols and hopped inside the room. She dashed up to the table Royce was strapped to.

Royce looked at her. "Miss Vlavskisk?"

"Long story," she replied. "How are these straps fastened?"

Royce motioned with his head toward the nearby wall. "It's automated. They push a button on the wall."

She reached over and pressed several buttons. On one button press, the straps released, and Royce untangled himself from them and got off the bed.

He looked out the open door with wide eyes. "Brewer?"

"Aye sir. You ready to leave?"

Royce and Valerie exited the room and started down the hallway. Vance dropped his hands and followed after them. "Sky Captain Williams, sir, I don't suppose you know the way to the flight deck from here?"

"The blazars wheeled me down this corridor and took only two lefts. So I'd say hang two right turns and we should be there."

Valerie ran down the hallway and slowed down only to peek around the right corner. Then she motioned for them to follow and she dashed down the next. Vance and Royce followed quickly. When she stopped at the next right turn, she again peeked around the corner.

She motioned for them to stop. "We've reached the hangar, but there are a lot of armored troops around your starlancer."

Royce peeked around the corner, "We need some kind of diversion to get them away from the starlancer. I'd rather not risk a stray bullet igniting a missile or rupturing the fuel tank."

"Miss, can you shoot far enough to hit that yellow tank at the far end of the bay?"

She studied the distance a moment. "It's not impossible, but quite a challenge with a pistol."

Royce looked around the rest of the bay. "That's not our only problem." He pointed. "The space door is closed."

Valerie hung her head. "There's always something else."

"You two get those Mori away from my starlancer," Royce directed, "and I'll take care of the space door."

"Man," Vance complained. "What I wouldn't give to have learned that Virt-O invisibility trick right about now."

Royce put his hand on Vance's shoulder. "You cannot learn everything, Brewer; the jack of all trades is the master of none."

Valerie looked at Vance. "The purpose in picking an order is to find a specialty that you are good at, and then master it."

Royce turned to Valerie. "Don't do anything until the space door opens. Then give them the biggest reason to forget about my starlancer. Once I'm in the air, I'll give these blazars something a lot more pressing to worry about than you two." He patted down the breast pockets of his flight suit. "Either of you have a tablet?"

"Here," Vance said, handing him his second tablet.

Valerie gave Royce a half-smile. "If we're not in the air in 15 minutes after you, please call the cavalry."

Royce looked at her with his piercing blue eyes and smiled. "You have my word as a Fire Lance." He broke eye contact and quietly crept around the corner and into the hangar.

Valerie holstered one pistol and pulled out the magazine on the other. After checking her remaining bullet count, she put it back and slapped it into place with her palm.

"Vance, I need you to watch for anyone coming in the halls; I have to give this shot all my attention."

"You got it, miss."

Valerie sat down with one knee pointing up. She briefly repositioned her skirt and then took her pistol in both hands. She rested her arm on her upright knee, using it to steady her aim.

Vance flexed his hands a few times in anticipation. He glanced down both ends of the hallway watching for any trouble that might come. For the first time, he felt powerful standing there like a sentinel, ready to defend his companion.

Large revolving lights on the ceiling of the hangar started flashing. Loud cranking sounds echoed in the bay as the large space door slid open. The open air revealed the fading sunset in the distance.

Valerie held her breath and steadied her aim for a few seconds, then she fired. The bullet bounced off the far wall, inches from the metal tank. She fired again; the tank exploded in a ball of fire. A ringing bell erupted in the still air. Mori flight deck crew ran to the sidewall of the bay, snatching up fire suppression equipment.

Valerie rolled back onto her feet and drew her second pistol. "Okay, let's haul some jets!"

Valerie charged into the bay, heading away from the starlancer and Vance followed. She fired off multiple rounds into a landed Mori starfighter and it began leaking fuel. Roars and growls filled the air, drowning out the screech of the bell. Valerie fired a few more shots and the Mori starfighter caught fire. Valerie ducked below several hot red bolts of light flying across the bay from the troops that were guarding the starlancer.

Vance put up a force field between them and the Mori troops. "Keep goin'! I'll watch our six-o-clock!"

Valerie reloaded her pistols. Vance saw the advancing armored Mori troops through the force field. Behind them, Royce climbed into his starlancer. "Just a little longer, miss!"

Valerie continued pelting equipment and starfighters in the bay with numerous bullets. She took one more step forward and the Mori starfighter that had caught fire exploded. The force of the explosion threw her to the side, impacting up against a pillar. The blast pushed Vance into his force field and he fell to the ground.

Vance opened his eyes and looked around. He could only hear a ringing in his ears. He lifted his head and saw the Mori troops lying on the ground several feet farther away. They were stirring and slowly recovering from the blast. Behind them, the starlancer taxied down the runway toward the open space door.

The ringing in his ear slowly subsided and he could hear his name being called. He looked back at Valerie. She had a large piece of the starfighter wreckage laying on top of her.

"Vance!" she called after him.

Vance scrambled to his feet, realizing just how sore his muscles were. He dashed over to Valerie and started pulling up on the large piece of metal. He tugged and pulled for a few seconds. Then he panted a moment and then reasserted his will against the heavy wreckage.

"There's no time; Vance, the space door!"

Vance spun around. The large space door was closing while the starlancer still rolled along toward it. "He's not gonna make it before the door closes!"

"Get me my pistols!"

Vance looked around and saw one of her pistols lying on the ground. He snatched it up and handed it to Valerie. She fired off several rounds at the large metal space door gears. The bullets bounced and sparked off the heavy metal gears.

"No no no!" Vance sprinted over to the nearby wall of the bay and grabbed a hold of a large conduit running up the height of the wall. He closed his eyes and began mumbling a repetitious chant to himself.

Valerie released the spent magazine and fumbled around on her bandolier for a new one. When she found one, she loaded it into her pistol and slapped it into place. She aimed at the large turning gears of the space door but before she squeezed off another round the large gears ground to a halt. Valerie looked up from her gunsight. The ringing bell suddenly fell silent and all the lights in the room shut off. Now the only light was coming from the burning fires and the expiring sunset through the half-open space door.

The starlancer roared its engines and picked up speed. It crossed over the threshold of the space door and continued taxiing outside. Vance stumbled back to Valerie's side. He dropped to his knees beside her, panting.

She looked at him. "Did you do that?"

"Affirmative, miss. Now let's get this off you…" He leaned on his hands and knees with his head drooping.

"Vance, you need a tablet," she urged.

He panted a few more times, then pulled out his last tablet and put it in his mouth. He rested a few moments more before looking at her. "Forgive me, miss, but I need to get my arm under this metal; I swear, I'm not tryin' ta get cozy or nothin'."

She let an exasperated giggle escape.

Vance reached between Valerie and the wreckage as far down as he could squeeze his arm. "Okay, here we go." Vance erected a force field and lifted his arm. The force field expanded, pushing the fallen debris upward.

Valerie crawled out from her prone position. She snatched up her second pistol as she got up onto her hands and knees. Vance let the debris fall back down and then helped Valerie to her feet. When she put pressure on her left foot, she gasped in pain and fell to one knee. She instinctively covered the left side of her abdomen with her arm.

She tried to stand again, and then cried out in pain and dropped her pistols in favor of clutching her side. Vance picked up her pistols and put them in her holsters. He took her arm and draped it around his neck and pulled her up to her feet.

She turned to him, "This looks familiar."

He smiled. "Happy to return the favor, miss."

She looked past him. "Vance!"

He turned and saw the armored troops, who had recovered, rushing over to them. One of them fired their rifle at Vance. He desperately threw up a hand and a shimmering wall of air appeared between him and the armored troops. But his timing was off. The red bolt had already flown past where he erected the force field. The force field flew across the bay. It plowed into workbenches, tables, stray equipment, exploded wreckage, and everything else in its path and dragged them to the far wall of the bay. The bay echoed in a loud crash when the troops and debris were smashed against the wall.

The red bold struck Vance on the left side of his chest. He let go of Valerie and she collapsed to the floor with a sharp inhale. Vance fell to his knees. He felt a burning heat against his chest. He gasped for a breath. Then a growl came from his right. He didn't have enough time to look before a strong large hand grabbed him by the throat and lifted him into the air. Vance tried to free his neck and managed only to take a deep breath.

The Mori soldier pulled Vance's face close to his. Vance's image was reflected in the two cold black eyes of the strong soldier. The Mori bared his teeth and bellowed a hideous roar. The Mori's breath reeked like a dead rodent.

Valerie held her breath and moved one arm toward her holstered pistol. A stinging pain forbade her and she returned her hand to clutching her side.

Vance stole another breath through his now-aching neck. He struggled against the strong hand that held him in the air. Fear permeated his thoughts. His brain shouted at him that he needed to act quickly. Scenes of his life flickered in front of his eyes. Then he heard Hans's voice in his head, explaining that electrolytes regulated the body's electrical system. *If there's an electrical system in the body,* Vance thought. *Then maybe that system can be turned off?* He didn't have time to practice his theory. He would get only one attempt. And if he failed it wouldn't matter soon, the Mori would see to that.

Vance let go and grabbed either side of the Mori's head, closing his eyes. The heat of stray fires in the room grew warmer and closer. That feeling soon gave way to his lungs screaming out for air. Vance started feeling light-headed but held his concentration. Then he suddenly collapsed to the floor. His neck was released and he gasped for air. After a moment of breathing and coughing. He opened his eyes and saw the unconscious Mori beside him.

He coughed. "Lights out, canner!"

He rubbed his sore neck and looked over at Valerie. She was back hunched down and leaning against the remains of a workbench. Vance slowly rose to his feet and looked around. The bay fires were raging out of control. Mori flight deck crew were futilely combating the raging inferno. The heat intensified on his left. He glanced and saw the flames slithering toward him. They crept toward the oxygen from the open-air coming in through the space door.

Vance swallowed and winced in pain. Then he took Valerie's arm and draped it over his neck. She gasped in pain. He helped her to her feet and then assisted her in hobbling toward the half-open space door.

"What did you do?" she inquired in between short painful gasping breaths.

"I figured if I could turn off a space door," he explained, hoarsely. "I might as well try ta see if I could turn *him* off. After all, if there's an electrical field, there's somethin' to sabotage."

"Vance, you haven't trained with the Rising Sun yet, how are you able to sabotage like that?"

He swallowed and again winced in pain. "I don't know, miss. But I'm hopin' they'll be able ta tell me."

They crossed the threshold of the space door and into the rose-colored dimming sky. The heat of the sun had passed and the cool night air was rushing in. Step by step, they hobbled toward the mountain rise. Behind them, explosions thundered in the night air as Royce's starlancer strafed buildings and landed starfighters. It seemed that Royce shot at everything that looked interesting.

Scores of Mori starfighters exploded while others zoomed down the runway, taking off into the air to retaliate.

"I hope Sky Captain Williams will be okay with all them starfighters on his six."

"Royce," she said, "is the best," she groaned, "starfighter pilot..."

They came to the rising hill. Vance held his hand out. "Let's see if I can make this easier." Nothing happened. He tried to erect a force field again. Still, nothing happened.

Valerie looked over him and noticed the burn mark on the chest of his flight suit. "Vance, have you been hit?"

"Yeah, but it doesn't feel that bad."

"You're not bleeding," she noticed.

Vance looked down at his flight suit and put a finger through the charred hole. "Ah no, not now." He unzipped the pocket the hole went through. He reached in and pulled out the lifeless force field generator.

He paused a moment, plastering a mournful expression across his face. Valerie looked into his eyes. "I'm sorry about the force field generator."

He caressed the charred blue half-moon logo.

Valerie shivered in the chilly air. Vance snapped out of his stupor. He gingerly helped her back over the hill and down to the awaiting starlancer. He set her down next to it.

She groaned in pain. "Vance..."

He looked into her mahogany eyes. Then he noticed blood running down the corner of her mouth. "Oh no, Valerie, I've got to get you home quick."

She reached up and touched his cheek. "I was right about you; you have the heart of a Gun Star."

Vance closed his eyes tight and tilted his head heavenward. "Why is it happening the same way? Why hasn't it changed?"

Valerie coughed. Vance opened his eyes and looked into hers. She took a deep breath. "I think you should know," she ran her blue gloved finger down to his lips. "I think my heart is being pulled into your orbit."

Vance sighed. "Beggin' your pardon, miss, but that's prob'ly the adrenaline talkin'." He reached over to the zipper pouch on her boot and pulled out her last tablet. "You should prob'ly take this—"

She reached her hand around to the back of his head and pulled her lips into his and gifted him a sweet, tender moment. Vance carefully laid her down on her back. Then he noticed the tablet was not in his fingers anymore. He sighed in frustration. It was already too dark to search the ground.

"I gotta get you outta here." Vance looked up at the starlancer. "How am I gonna get you up into the cockpit?"

Valerie softly moaned, "The gear."

Vance spun back toward her. "What was that?"

She coughed. "The landing gear."

Vance's eyes widened. He hastily climbed up the small handhold near the wing joint and pulled himself up onto the wing. He scooted as close to the canopy as he dared and reached his hand over and waved it across the plate. The canopy slid open and Vance climbed into the front seat.

He looked at all the dials, gauges, buttons, and switches all across the instrumentation panel. He closed his eyes and focused on his memory of Valerie starting up her pre-flight check. He opened his eyes and flipped a switch and the initial electrical system turned on. He reached over and flipped another switch and then felt the nose of the craft lowering to the ground. *Oh,* he thought to himself. *I guess only the nose gear can retract while I'm on the ground.*

He stood up and stepped out onto the ground. He hoisted Valerie up into the back seat amidst her painful groans. He latched her safety straps and put her helmet on her. Then he sat back down in the front seat, buckling up. He pressed a button and the canopy closed. He flipped the switch for the landing gear again. He heard a metallic whine but the starlancer didn't move.

Valerie shook her head. "The nose gear is not strong enough to lift the nose of the craft. Angle the ascent thrusters to compensate for the decline."

"How do I do that?"

"Left side, fourth-row green switch. Flip it and then adjust the dial beneath it."

Vance obeyed. "Listen, miss—"

"I liked it when you called me Valerie."

"Listen, Valerie, please stay awake, I'm gonna need all the help I can get ta fly this thing."

"Welcome to flight training, à la Vlavskisk." She smiled and then abruptly winced in pain. "Vance, I have a feeling we need to hurry..."

Chapter 24

SACRIFICE

Due to the extreme complications involved in studying the Nakkaron particles directly, we still only have a basic understanding of how the particle operates. It carries either a positive or negative charge and switches that charge periodically. We don't know how this is possible. One theory is that Nakkarons flow opposite the linear flow of time, in which case, the charge would be relative to the observer and all our previous assumptions would be null and void.

—FROM "THE SCIENCE OF THE WINDS" BY PROFESSOR-EMERITUS PING CHENG

"**E**ase up on the throttle," Valerie directed. "We have to conserve enough fuel to make it back to New Carillon."

Vance pulled the throttle back slightly.

"A little more please."

Vance pulled it back more. "Like that?"

"That's good... hey Vance," she winced a moment in pain. "I'm showing seven SEDAR contacts bearing two-six-eight."

"We won't be able to outrun them *and* make it back to New Carillon, will we?"

She breathed out with audible discomfort. "They're not chasing us—it's Royce; the other six are chasing *him*."

Vance's breathing and heart rate climbed. "He's gonna make it though, right? You said he's the best pilot."

She exhaled with audible shivers in her breath. "I'm now showing eleven bandits in pursuit."

Vance pursed his lips.

"Vance, we have to help him."

"Negative! If I don't get you to infirmary quick, you're not gonna make it."

"Vance," she clenched her muscles and halted her breathing while a stinging pain passed. Then she took in a deep breath. "Vance, if Royce dies this whole trip was for nothing."

A tear broke free from his eye. It flew on down his cheek before he could wipe it away. "You're askin' me to choose between him and you."

"Vance. I'm asking you to help your friend—our friend. He needs you."

Two more tears paraded down his face. He took in a deep breath that fought against his chest muscles. "What about you, Valerie?"

She groaned a moment and then recomposed her face. "Vance, look out the canopy. Every star you see will eventually die—that much is certain. The only question that remains is when you and I die, will we simply burn out and fade away? Or will we offer up everything we have and explode in a supernova—being reborn into a life-giving neutron star?" She took a short shallow breath and winced. "Vance, a pulsar is a neutron star giving elements back into the galaxy—including Nakkarons."

Vance heard Number 1's words circling in his head: Noble intentions and pulsaric ideals cannot replace experience. Then Valerie's words intruded upon his thoughts: Your concern for others, your courage to do what you feel is right, and your loyalty to your friends are what truly makes you pulsaric.

He wiped away two newly formed tears and sniffled. "Valerie."

She took in a slow painful breath. "Yes, Vance?"

"It was an honor servin' with you."

She sniffled. "Let's show these blazars what Solar Knights can do."

Vance pressed his lips together tightly and nodded once. He rolled the starlancer into a turn and hit the afterburner. Valerie moaned in pain.

"Sorry about that, miss," Vance said.

"Don't pay any attention to me right now, Vance, you need to close in on those starfighters."

Vance saw the small glittering dots in the distance. "Okay, when can I shoot?"

She coughed. "The switch on the stick, make sure it's set to missiles."

Vance clicked a switch. "Okay, then what?"

"Pick a bandit and close in on his six o'clock. That's called 'getting into the saddle'."

"He's movin' all around! He won't stay still."

"That's bec—" she moaned, enduring a long throb of pain. "That's because Royce is jinking all around, trying to stay out of their sights."

"Once I'm in the saddle, then what?"

"The targeting computer will growl in your ear when the missile has locked on target. Then you pull the trigger to fire the missile."

"Blast it! Why does this have ta be harder than it looks?"

She took in another shallow breath. "Don't fight the stick, let them drift into your sight."

Vance took a deep breath and exhaled much of his anxiety. He eased up his grip on the control stick and watched the enemy starfighter drift in and out of this line of fire. Then a growling noise sounded in his helmet.

"Vance, that's it. Fire!

Vance pulled the trigger. A missile detached from under the wing of the starlancer and rocketed forward. The missile slammed into the Mori starfighter and it exploded. Vance watched as the other enemy starfighters broke formation and started to scatter.

"I did it! I did it!"

"Good... good job. Need to... tell Royce..."

Vance looked down at his instrumentation panel and found the transmission switch. He switched it on. "Sky Capt—I mean Firefly, sir. I got 'em off your six. Hopefully, that will give you some breathin' room."

He heard Royce's slightly distorted voice over the transmission, "Roger. Brewer, what are you doing on the comm?"

"The miss has been hit; she's been walking me through this."

A small light flashed on Vance's instrumentation panel accompanied by a beeping sound. "Valerie, what's that sound mean?"

"...scanned... check your six..."

"Miss, you stick with me! I need you." He turned the starlancer hard to the left. He caught sight of a Mori starfighter from the corner of his eye. He pulled the starlancer around to intercept.

"Brewer, there are two bandits on your six! I want you to jink; move around erratically and don't give them a clean shot."

"Aye sir." He pulled the starlancer into a small climb. Then rolled to the right, then he pushed into a dive while pulling out to the left. Red bolts of light flew past the canopy.

"Valerie," Vance called to her, "hang on, we're in a little trouble but Sky Captain Williams is takin' care of it."

Vance continued to roll and pitch all about until he saw a starfighter moving across his line of fire. He settled the starlancer into a turn and lined up with the starfighter. He heard the growl in his ear and he pulled the trigger. A missile flew out from under his wing.

He fought the urge to watch the missile and instead continued jinking the starlancer. He wanted to see if the missile hit, but he also didn't want to be a combat statistic. He rolled to the left and narrowly evaded several bright red bolts of light flashing past the canopy. He nearly jumped in his seat and his heart rate accelerated.

Vance tried to steer the starlancer in more unpredictable ways and each time, narrowly missed being shot. A light on his panel started flashing along with a whining alarm. Vance glanced at it. "Oh, no no no; Valerie, this looks like the light I saw when flyin' with Hans." He leaned back toward Valerie. "Is that the fuel reserve alarm?"

Vance waited for a reply but there was only silence.

"Valerie, please stay with me. Is that the fuel reserve alarm?"

Again, silence.

"Valerie!"

He heard Royce's voice through the transmission. "Brewer, you have the leader on your six and he looks bound and determined to shoot you down."

Vance's chest tightened and his eyes watered over. He clutched the stick with a renewed vigor. His jaw tightened as his tears fled from their captivity. He rolled the starlancer in time to avoid several more shots from the Mori starfighter.

"Fine!" he grumbled. "You want me, you're gonna have ta *earn* me!" He looked over to a side screen on his panel and pressed a few buttons. Coordinate numbers displayed on the screen along with the caption: Clarissa.

Vance hit his afterburner and rocketed into a tight turn and broke away, heading in a new direction. He continued to jink around seeing stray red shots fly past him. His heart rate kept building momentum. His breathing became shallow and faster. *I gotta get my breathing under control,* he thought.

With every turn and jolt he made, the furious Mori kept sending red tokens of his intentions flying past. Vance suddenly felt a wave of an odd sensation pass through him. He took another short quick breath, and then pressed a button on his console and flipped a switch. The transparent surface of the canopy changed to a red hue that cooled into a blue hue.

Vance saw the pulsing flashes of light from the pulsar. "Hello Clarissa. If you pardon my intrusion, ma'am, I'm hopin' you can help me take care of this blazar on my six."

Vance felt a sudden jerk in his seat, causing his helmet to smack against the canopy. A red indicator light flashed. A small screen showed a diagram of the starlancer and a rear portion flashing in red. His starlancer had been hit. He wasn't able to tell how badly and quite frankly, there wasn't time.

He rolled to the right and hit his afterburner. The starlancer turned but the afterburner did not engage. "Kreket!"

He steered directly toward the pulsar, still jinking around the best he could. "I'm as close to the Nakkaron flow as I can, please let this work."

Vance closed his eyes and focused his thoughts on the Mori starfighter. He pictured in his mind the long fuselage, the four triangle wings, the canopy with the Mori pilot inside. He pictured the engine—what he imagined it might look like. He followed with his imaginary eyes up the exhaust port, into the turbine, and through the compressor. He imagined himself reaching out with his hands and ripping out the electrical cable. He imaged what it would look like for the Mori starfighter to lose thrust and glide into Clarissa's pull.

An alarm sounded on his console and he opened his eyes. The bright flashes of the pulsar were large; he was too close. He broke right and hit his afterburner—which was still inoperative. He kept the stick tightly clenched in his fists as if the extra exertion could somehow push the starlancer further away from the pulsar's covetous grasp.

He saw movement out of the corner of his eye and he looked. The Mori starfighter lifelessly drifted straight toward the pulsar. The enormous gravity pulled the craft in ever faster. Tiny glittering pieces of the starfighter were stripped off in a long line toward the center of the pulsar. In a matter of seconds, the long glittering line was all that remained of the Mori craft.

Vance saw another flash from the pulsar and he blinked. He turned back toward the pulsar but he didn't see the pulsar, he didn't even see the inside of the starlancer. He was kneeling on a carpeted floor. In one arm he was holding a little dark-haired girl who seemed to be hugging him for want of comfort. In his other hand, he was holding a pistol. A faint trickle of smoke rose from the barrel.

He looked past the end of the pistol and saw Number 1 standing at the other end of the room. He clutched his stomach and dropped to one knee. "Do you have any idea what you've done?" He gasped for another couple of breaths and then collapsed to the floor.

"Brewer!"

Vance shuddered and opened his eyes. He heard Royce's voice in his helmet. "Brewer!"

Vance took in a deep breath. His heart was thumping and his hands were shaking. "Firefly, sir. I'm here." He gasped for another breath.

"I thought I lost you. What were you doing so dangerously close to the pulsar?" Royce asked.

"Can't...breathe..." Vance said, struggling.

"Sounds like you're very low on electrolytes. Take another tablet," Royce directed.

Vance leaned his head back and placed his hand on his aching neck. He strained for another breath. "All gone, sir."

"Cut your engines and open your tow-port. I'm going to extend a tow-line."

Vance looked at his instrumentation panel, but his mind was muddled and foggy. A strong sense of fatigue bore down on him, urging him to simply close his eyes. Something in the back of his mind was shouting at him to stay awake, but his body was so weary. His hand slid from his neck down his chest to the hole in his flight suit. Then he felt the rough texture of an electrolyte tablet pressed against the front zipper.

What was a tablet doing there? The memory of Valerie's kiss flashed in his mind. He plucked the tablet loose and put it in his mouth. He chewed it, the taste hardly registering to his brain.

"Brewer! Brewer!" Royce's panicked voice sounded in his helmet.

"I read you, sir," he finally said, his mind starting to clear. He felt his lungs pulling in the air more freely. He shut down his engines.

"Good, now open your tow-port."

Vance surveyed the instrumentation panel again. "Um... I seen this once before, where did I see the switch for the port?"

"Left-hand side, third row down."

"I see it." Vance flipped the switch and heard the moan of the motor as the port opened.

Royce flew in front of Vance and settled into formation. A long line was extended. Royce gently maneuvered his starlancer until the cable connected.

"Cable connected, sir."

"Roger Brewer. How are you feeling?"

"I found a tablet I thought I had dropped," he replied.

"I will tow you in, but you're going to have to land," Royce explained.

"Aye sir."

"When you're in a starfighter, say 'roger' instead of 'aye'."

"Roger, sir."

"By the way, Brewer, thank you for coming after me."

"You're welcome, sir. I may not know much, but I knew I needed ta help you."

"I owe you one."

"Not anymore, sir. As I see it, you're saving me now."

Royce chuckled over the transmission. "Anyway, we're soon going to be on approach. When you get clearance to land, they're going to ask you to 'call the ball'. You're going to address the LSO as 'Paddles'. State your flight callsign, your starcraft type, followed by your own callsign. Indicate your fuel state, and then say 'Ball' if you can see the landing indicator lights. Do you remember seeing them?"

"Aye sir, the line of lights for if'n you're too high or too low."

"That's correct. Keep that lined up, and you'll need to turn on your ACLS."

"What's the ACLS?"

"Think of it as auto-pilot for carrier landing. Fire Lance try never to use it so we can keep our skills sharp. But in the unforeseen situations—this one included—it is a nice feature."

"Oh," Vance remembered a question, "what's my callsign sir?"

"For now, your callsign is Aberrant Star. Because so far your training has been all backward."

Vance chuckled. "That's an affirmative with a capital 'A'."

The trip back didn't seem nearly as long. Before he knew it, the large fleet of ships was in sight.

"Okay, Brewer, now is the time where you disconnect from the tow cable and re-engage your engines."

Vance flipped a switch and heard the *clank* of the tow cable detaching. Then, he ignited the engines. They sputtered and then roared to life. Off in the distance, the large capital ship of New Carillon steadily grew larger. A sense of relief that he was coming home washed over him, but it was tarnished when he thought of Valerie. His heart sank and his breathing required more effort.

A voice in his helmet spoke, "Caliber One, Carillon marshal."

"Uh... Caliber, go ahead."

"Caliber One, you are cleared to land. Call the ball."

Vance looked at a small square glass screen attached to the window of the canopy. He looked through the glass and noticed the light was filtered through it. The natural colors looked dim. He looked at New Carillon—which was fast approaching—and it looked pale and gray through the glass. And then he saw a bright array of lights near the space door. The glass filtered the light so he could clearly see the alignment lights. The lineup lights showed he was pretty close to the center.

"Paddles, Caliber one, starlancer, 'AberrantStar', ball... and uh, my fuel state is critical."

"Roger, ball. You're low."

Vance flipped the switch labeled ACLS. The nose of the starlancer raised slightly. The gyroscope tilted a little as the starlancer auto-corrected the trajectory. Then the engines sputtered one final time before completely going silent. Vance glanced at his fuel gauge. The needle was resting on the very bottom of the dial.

He looked back through the glass. His alignment was still good but it was starting to veer off to the right. He flipped the engine switch off and then back on again. Nothing happened. He looked up at the fast-approaching space door and clenched his eyes closed. A moment later, he felt thrown forward, his safety straps digging into his shoulders.

He might never get used to the feeling of stopping in under two seconds. But a feeling of gratitude for being safely on board climbed up to his eyes and spilled over. He panted for a few moments trying to slow his heart rate. A plane director signaled for him to taxi forward.

Vance shook his head and waved his arms. The plane director turned to someone out of Vance's sight and gave them a few hand gestures. A few seconds later a small runway tractor pulled up in front of the starlancer. A tractor driver in a blue jacket hopped out and attached a hook to the starlancer's nose gear.

The tractor driver hopped back inside the little tractor and pulled the starlancer down off the runway and down the recovery lane. Vance's angle didn't afford him a good look but he saw Royce's starlancer come through the space door. Tired of craning his neck, he turned back around. A rolling staircase wheeled up to him. He flipped a switch and the canopy slid open.

Vance quickly unbuckled his safety straps and turned around to see Valerie slumped in the seat, motionless. Vance released several more tears as he stood there. His eyes became too blurry to see anything, and he didn't care to see anything anyway.

Voices were trying to talk to him, but he didn't care. Soon his arm was pulled in one direction and he was assisted down the staircase. He still couldn't see through his storm of tears. He didn't care what sounds were all around him. But he could feel the railing, the tugging on his arm, the solid floor beneath his feet.

For a while, Vance lost all concept of time and only found some little measure of comfort in sleep. He was still able to sleep. He didn't have any dreams, or if he did, he didn't remember them.

"Vance the Lance, can you hear me?"

Vance slowly opened his eyes. His stomach felt empty yet he had no appetite. The air smelled sterile. He focused his eyes and saw Hans sitting on a chair beside him. Hans intensely looked into Vance's eyes. "Hey Vance, you've had us all worried."

Vance took in a deep breath and lifted himself into a sitting position, realizing he was on a gurney in the waiting room of the infirmary. He looked around the room. Dorothy Vlavskisk stood at the other end of the room. She nodded her head as Dr. Rychen spoke to her. She brought up a small white cloth to her eyes and dabbed away tears.

"What happened up there?" Hans asked.

Vance turned back to Hans and let another tear betray his emotions. "I had ta make the worst decision of my life, Hans; Sky Captain Williams or Valerie."

Hans stared into Vance's eyes for a few silent moments. "That's a blazar of a spot to be put into. I'm sorry you had to go through it."

Footsteps approached behind him and Hans looked up. Vance looked back around and saw Dr. Rychen take the final steps up to him.

Dr. Rychen put his hand on Vance's forehead and closed his eyes. "Mr. Brewer, how are you feeling?"

"Responsible, doc. Very much responsible."

"Well, that would account for your acute bereavement attack." Dr. Rychen was silent for a few moments before he continued. "Marginal hypokalemia, acute hypocalcemia, severe hypophosphatemia, moderate hyponatremia, and severe hypomagnesemia." He opened his eyes.

"What does all that mean, doc?" Vance asked.

Dr. Rychen smiled. "It means you're critically low on your electrolytes. It would seem you haven't been taking your tablets following extended use of The Winds."

Vance shook his head. "Negative, sir. I took one prob'ly 15 minutes ago, and another one not too long before that."

Dr. Rychen stared at him. "The only way you could be burning through your body's electrolytes that fast is if you're performing very extensive manipulation of The Winds. Something way beyond what a trainee would have been taught."

"It's been a busy day," Vance replied. "But what's really rough on me is when I get close to those pulsars. Those visions really take everything out of me."

"I'll have to talk with the Virtus Occulatum. They should not be having trainees perform precognition. That's too much of a drain for an untrained knight."

"Doc, I wasn't tryin'," Vance explained. "It just happens. Is there anything you can give me to make 'em stop?"

"There isn't a treatment for that, Vance, because what you're describing shouldn't even be possible."

Vance stared at Dr. Rychen for a few silent moments. "I guess I just need ta steer clear of pulsars for now."

Dr. Rychen nodded. "I think that would be wise. I'm also going to prescribe ten electrolyte gel capsules. They're prescription strength. Keep them on you in case you end up near a pulsar again."

"Thank you, doc."

"You also took a huge hit of magnetic radiation. Technically, I'm supposed to temporarily ground pilots in this condition. But since you're not technically a pilot, I'm just going to recommend that you get plenty of rest in the next 72 hours."

Out of the corner of his eye, he saw Dorothy walk up to them. Amidst her tear-reddened face, she smiled. "I want to thank you for everything you have done for Valerie."

Vance's chest muscles tightened. "I'm so sorry ma'am." He wanted to explain, but his powers of speech were weighed down by his heavy heart, and his sentence ended there.

She placed one hand on Vance's shoulder. "I am forever in your debt."

Vance was at a loss for words while Dorothy walk away. Then he turned back toward Hans and Dr. Rychen. "Why does she feel she owes me one?"

"Because you saved her daughter's life, Mr. Brewer."

"Valerie's alive?" he said, half stunned.

Dr. Rychen nodded. "Yes, her body was saturated with Nakkarons; it slowed her body's degeneration and gave us time to operate."

"Time," Vance said, wiping away two fresh tears. His breathing accelerated, and he smiled. "The one thing I thought I was all out of."

"It was a very clever idea to get her into the path of the pulsar's jet stream. What made you think of it?"

Vance glanced heavenward momentarily, "If I tell you the truth, doc, you're gonna know I'm not that smart. I thought she was already gone."

"Well then, Mr. Brewer, it would seem Nova has smiled upon you." Dr. Rychen put his hand on Vance's shoulder and squeezed it a moment before leaving.

Hans sat back in his chair. "Vance the Lance has come out on top. How was your first combat?"

Vance smiled. "Well, I had 1, 3, 5, 7, and 9 all piled up on top of each other—the odds were stacked against me."

Hans burst out in laughter. "Vance the Lance, if you ever decide to stay on as an Orbiting Star, you are a perfect fit."

Vance's smile faded slightly. He reached into his chest pocket and pulled out the laser-blackened force field generator. The sad-looking half-moon logo showed only a little blue color left. "So sorry, Hans the Bronze. It gave its life to save mine."

Hans curiously eyed the blackened device. "I'd say the two of you now have some history together. Why don't you keep it as a souvenir?"

Vance smiled appreciatively and placed it back into his pocket and zipped it back up. "Oh," he remembered, "where's the doc? I wanna know if'n I can see Valerie."

"I already asked; it's family only at this point. For now, let's get you something to eat. With all the growling your stomach has been making, I'd swear you've got a missile lock on me."

Vance smirked. "Yeah, I think I could eat a whole cow."

He stood up and walked alongside Hans toward the doors. A man in a military uniform stopped in front of them and handed Vance a folded paper.

"Squire Brewer, you are officially ordered to appear at a debriefing of the latest incident. Debrief will be held in 48 hours."

Vance took the paper while displaying a confused expression. The man left and Hans peered at the paper in Vance's hands. Vance swallowed. He was at least glad his neck felt better. "I guess my impulsiveness is catchin' up ta me."

Hans shrugged, "Well... maybe they want to pin a medal on you?"

Vance frowned. "I disobeyed a direct order, Hans. This may become my court-martial."

Chapter 25
RECOVERY

Naval aerospace aviator callsigns serve two primary purposes: to facilitate communication transmission brevity, and more easily distinguish one aviator from another. The unofficial cultural significance of callsigns facilitates comradery and unit cohesion. Callsigns are assigned by the squadron and are subject to approval by the flight commander. UEN brevity requires callsigns to be no longer than three syllables (increased from the previous limit of two) or no longer than four syllables if the callsign can be reasonably spoken as three.

—FROM "STARCRAFT CARRIER OPERATIONS MANUAL" BY THOMAS J. SUTTON, UNITED EARTH NAVAL COMMAND

Vance walked through the white hallways inside the infirmary and stopped just outside an open door. He peeked inside and saw Dorothy standing over Valerie, talking to her. Vance tapped on the open door to get their attention.

Valerie lit up. "Vance! Come in!"

He sauntered in carrying a small bundle of flowers neatly wrapped with foil paper and ribbon. He felt the blood rushing to his cheeks as Valerie and Dorothy spotted the gift.

"Vance, you brought me flowers!"

"Sorry I couldn't come yesterday; I'm told it was family only."

He handed Valerie the flowers. She promptly brought them to her nose and breathed in the pleasant scent and let it linger in her lungs for a moment.

Valerie turned to Dorothy. "See mother, my admirer has brought the appropriate gift."

Vance's alarmed eyes complimented his cheeks. "Ah yeah, my introduction at the Banquet Table..."

Dorothy looked at Vance and then returned her gaze to her daughter. "Perhaps, to be suitable, there won't need to be as much training as I initially thought."

Valerie nodded. "Agreed."

Vance looked at Valerie, then her mother, then back to Valerie. They were obviously continuing a previous conversation that he was not privy to. Valerie held out her hand to Vance. He eyed it suspiciously but sauntered over and took her hand. Her soft warm hand was a pleasure to hold.

"What?" she asked.

"I get to touch your hand without a glove, and I kinda like it."

She blushed. "Thank you for saving me, Vance."

"I gotta be honest with ya miss, I didn't have any brilliant idea or nothin' about helpin' you out. I keep hearin' people compliment me on my quick thinking and great idea, but the truth is, miss, that I didn't know."

Valerie's expression slowly fell. "You weren't trying to save me?"

Vance's jaw quivered. His eyes threatened to spill out and stream embarrassment down his face. "I don't mean to disappoint ya miss, but you asked me to choose Sky Captain Williams, so I did. An' when you stopped responding, I thought you were gone. I only went near the pulsar because I needed a way to fight off that canner on my six."

Vance looked up to Dorothy. "I know you might be thinkin' I'm some pulsaric hero or somethin', ma'am—and I'm sorry if I disappoint you too. But the truth is, I'm not that clever, and the doc says Nova must've been smilin' on me or somethin'."

"Thank you for setting the record straight, Squire Brewer. But I think I'll keep my own counsel on what is and is not pulsaric," Dorothy said with a hint of a smile.

Vance nodded and then looked into Valerie's mahogany eyes and was surprised at what he saw. She was beaming with a glossy sparkle in her eyes. The air thickened. It was time to retreat. He squeezed her hand before letting go.

He backed up a step and gave a short bow. "Valerie." He then gave another short bow to Dorothy. "Ma'am." He then turned to leave.

"Vance," Valerie called.

He turned to her.

"Will you come and see me again tomorrow?"

He shook his head. "Negative, miss. I'm afraid I'll be at the formal debriefing most of the day tomorrow."

She blinked. "Wait, they're holding a *formal* debriefing?"

"Hey, I knew I was gonna get myself in trouble for disobeyin' orders. So I can't complain too much."

She balled her hands into fists. "After saving Royce, they're going to *punish* you? Ahhh! This is so backward!"

Vance huffed a half-chuckle. "Speakin' of backward, I got my callsign yesterday."

"Get spaced! Are you serious?"

Dorothy interjected, "Valerie, your language."

She glanced at Dorothy, "Sorry mother." Looking back to Vance, she cleared her throat. "That is thrilling, please, do tell?"

He nodded with a smirk. "AbberantStar".

She glanced at her mother. "What does Aberrant mean?"

Dorothy replied, "It means to depart from the ordinary or accepted standard. I suppose you could say it means: backward."

She turned back to Vance. "Oh, that is just so fitting!"

They laughed together for a few moments until the excitement had run its course. An awkward sense of foreboding slowly crept back into the air.

Valerie looked deep into his eyes. "May Nova be with you tomorrow."

"Thank you, miss." He walked to the doorway and stopped. "Just so you know, miss, even though I prob'ly need Nova with me tomorrow, I kinda would rather have you." He smiled and then left the infirmary.

Vance casually walked down the halls of New Carillon. He reveled in every inch of the scene around him. It could all be gone after tomorrow and he wanted to remember everything. Most especially, he wanted to remember the feeling of being important. The feeling of being needed and helpful. He brought his hand up to his cheek. He recalled the memory of when Valerie kissed his cheek and told him he did great work.

In some ways, he was at the top of his game. He was a Solar Knight in training. He had piloted a starfighter—a red-winged beauty no less. He was just starting to get the hang of flinging force fields around. He had been in his first combat and had rescued the man who saw greatness in him. And then there was Valerie...

Hans was right about the Gun Stars. He couldn't find a more fiercely loyal friend than Valerie. He hadn't been paying attention to the scenery for the last few minutes. He found himself beside a wide-open door to a clothing shop. He glanced up to see the sign. The sign read, Wardrobe of the Order. It hung alongside a heraldic arms shield with a blue and white pattern and a hollow eight-point star.

He stepped inside and saw several people perusing the clothes and small trinkets. An older woman in a blue and white dress approached him.

She noticed his squire pin. "Good evening, Squire. Looking for anything in particular?"

"I, uh... I've come to admire the Gun Stars lately. S'pose I'm lookin' for a little somethin' I can carry with me to remind me of the Gun Stars."

She smiled. "You must be Squire Brewer."

"Wha—Serious? You heard about me too?"

"I don't know who hasn't," she admitted. "Right this way."

Vance walked behind her as she showed him to a counter with a great many pins, buttons, and broaches. He scanned the colorful landscape. His eyes settled on a silver pin of two pistols with their barrels crossed. "That's the one! Right there."

She retrieved it and handed it over to Vance. He traced its edges with his finger. He gazed at it a few more long moments. "It's perfect. How much?"

"Consider it my gift to you."

Vance shook his head. "Nah nah nah, I couldn't do that, what do I owe ya?"

"I wish to express my appreciation for what you have done for Sage Vlavskisk's daughter. Please allow me to give this to you in token of such."

Vance smiled. "Thank you, ma'am." He cupped the pin in his hand, hoping that doing so would somehow keep him connected with these experiences. He left the shop and wandered down toward the main hall. Hans stood in the middle of the hallway looking right at him. Hans's eyes lit up and he motioned for Vance to join him.

Vance quickly hustled up to him. "Hans the Bronze, hope I haven't kept you waitin' too long?"

"Not to worry, Vance the Lance, I made sure our reservation was fifteen minutes later than I told you—just to make sure you'd make it."

Vance smiled. "I been meaning to ask ya, everybody on New Carillon seems to know me, have you been tellin' everybody you meet about me?"

"Yes. And it's been quite a bit more effective than I thought it would be, I might add."

"Why you doin' that? I feel like I'm a celebrity or somethin'. Look, I was given this today out of appreciation."

"Vance the Lance, people are just as simple as they are complicated. We all love to root for an underdog, we all love to support an up-and-coming folk hero, and we all love to hear exciting news."

"So this was a big P.R. campaign to promote me?"

Hans smiled. "I told you it was a wild and crazy idea. Can you deny that it has opened doors for your training?"

"Negative, sir. I do appreciate all you've done for me. Especially for the use of your force field generator."

"I know you, Vance, and I know your heart. You will always have a friend in me."

"Thank you, sir."

"So let me see what you were given in appreciation?"

Vance showed him the twin pistol pin. Hans's smile ran off his face. "You're collecting souvenirs in case you have to leave, aren't you?"

Vance nodded. "Hans, what's the worst-case scenario? I get dishonorably discharged from the Navy. How would that affect my ability to train as a Solar Knight?"

"Well, it would exclude you from joining Fire Lance and Virtus Occulatum—they work very closely with the military. Blue Planet and Lily of the Valley would have no problem taking you. Wind Dancers, Rising Sun, and Orbiting Star would require a waiting period. Gun Stars are the odd one out. They judge solely on their interview of the candidate's mettle—nothing else is considered, not even a dishonorable discharge."

"Would I be able to stay on New Carillon?"

"...probably not."

Vance sighed. "It's at least comforting to know I can still become a Solar Knight."

"Well, on the bright side, it *would* narrow down your choices."

Vance smiled. "Yeah, that it would." His smile faded and a somber expression took its place. "Though, I sure would hate to have to leave New Carillon; I'd miss her a lot."

"Miss Vlavskisk?"

"Yeah... that would be a real canner to have to say goodbye."

"Well, shall we go inside for your Last Supper?"

Vance smiled. "'Last Supper'... Well, I *am* hungry, and I sure hope they serve crabs."

Hans smiled. "Vance the Lance, I'm sure they serve all sorts of people."

Chapter 26
THE DEBRIEFING

The Wind Dancers have the most simplistic of designs—and certainly the shortest blazon. The black field is decorated by four white piles, representing the four core principles upon which their order is founded. The resulting effect upon the imagination is either animal claws or teeth against the black background. This perhaps is the only arms of the eight orders capable of evoking the emotion of foreboding in so simple a design.

—FROM "GALACTIC HERALDRY" BY JEAN-CLAUDE ARMAND DUBOIS

Vance stepped into a large open room with a tall and long desk at one end with nine seats. Vance tugged at his green formal vest where it itched. The people sitting in each of the nine seats dressed differently.

He instantly recognized the dress clothes of several of the people present. The red formal uniform of the Fire Lance. The ornate black robes of the Wind Dancers and the purple suit of the Lily of the Valley. Beside them, the green vest and black pants of the Orbiting Star as well as the blue coveralls of Blue Planet. The blue and white silk of the Gun

Stars and the all-black ensemble of the Virtus Occulatum. Lastly, a long brown overcoat that presumably belonged to the Rising Sun.

The ninth and last seat was taken by a man in a military uniform—upper brass, probably a general. But he was not close enough to get a good look at his rank insignia. Hans stood at Vance's side. "Just remember to speak in your best High Novan—whatever that happens to be."

Vance nodded and followed Hans down the short aisle. They took their seats at one of the tables below the seated panel of people. Hans set down a thin folder on the table. He opened it and pulled out a small bundle of papers. "One moment while I give this to the debrief panel." He walked up to the tall desk and handed up the small bundle of papers. He exchanged a few words with the man dressed in purple. Hans then returned to his seat.

Vance squirmed a little in his seat. "Why do I get the feelin' everybody has it out for me?"

Hans shrugged. "Paranoia from touring with Virtus Occulatum?"

"Yeah... maybe. So, do you know those people sitting up there?"

Hans nodded. "From left to right: Star Commander Myles of the Fire Lance, Lord Cantrell of the Wind Dancers, Professor Sansbury of Lily of the Valley, Jonny Valdear of Orbiting Star, Chief Watts of Blue Planet, Sage Jor'del Smith of the Gun Stars, Agent Null of Virtus Occulatum, Mrs. Haufmann of the Rising Sun, and General Eggerton of the United Earth Navy."

Several more people walked in and took a seat at the second table next to where Vance was seated. Vance elbowed Hans. "Hey, isn't that what's-his-name? The Wind Captain from the Banquet Table that goosed me over?"

"Wind Captain Marlon Dawes. It would appear he will be speaking to the debriefing panel too, along with Number 1."

Vance looked for Number 1, but instead, someone else came in through the door at the rear of the room. Dorothy walked in beside Valerie who was walking with the assistance of a crutch. Vance grinned and his heart began to beat more triumphantly.

Hans nudged Vance with his elbow. "They are starting."

Sansbury, the man dressed in purple, pressed a switch on the desk in front of his microphone. "Reverence on the premises, please. This formal debrief is now in session. May I take this opportunity to advise all present that, although decisions on how to proceed henceforth are in the powers of this body, these proceedings are to be of an inquisitive nature and not of a punitive one."

Watts, the man dressed in blue, opened a file folder. "This body is hereby assembled to further understand and disseminate understanding of the incident in question. On the evening of the first day of the month of Tetrad, in the first year Post Exterminium, the advanced aerospace scouts of New Carillon sighted and identified Mori starfighters along with two starlancers. The starlancers were later reported issued to Sky Captain Royce Williams and Sage Dorothy Vlavskisk. The threat of the former was nullified by the actions of the latter." He set down his papers.

"Wind Captain Dawes," Sansbury addressed. "It is the understanding of this panel that you are in possession of certain information that may yet shed some light on these events."

Dawes stood up. "Professor Sansbury, I do have somewhat to disseminate on the recent events which may enlighten further upon what the panel currently understands."

Sansbury pushed his glasses further up his nose. "Please proceed, and spare nothing in light of consequence."

"The Mori starfighters were part of a forward staging post previously unbeknownst to common knowledge. The Virtus Occulatum operative code-named Number 22 uncovered and relayed this intel to Number 1. The alarming information obtained by the said operative revealed an untested tactic newly employed by the Mori to uncover the location of the exodus fleet via stratagem. This involved the abduction of a Fire Lance pilot, Sky Captain Royce Williams."

Dawes took a breath before proceeding. "Sadly, however, a Fire Lance initiate, Squire Vance Brewer, who was touring with Number 1— and I will let Number 1 speak to that end—stole a starlancer and recklessly endangered the life of Sky Captain Williams in an ill-conceived, yet successful, rescue attempt." Dawes sat down.

Vance whispered to Hans, "That isn't what happened! I didn't steal no starlancer! That frazzin canner—"

"Shhhh," Hans placed a finger to his lips.

"Noted," Sansbury stated. "Number 1, will you speak to the nature of the said squire in regards to your care and trust while on tour, and in regards to the statement just made by Wind Captain Dawes?"

Number 1 stood up. "As to what is de-classified, I shall endeavor to make a full account, and touching most delicately nearer any classified matters on an ad hoc basis."

Sansbury nodded. "Proceed."

"On the morning of the first of Tetrad, Squire Vance Brewer was entrusted to my care as Tour Advisor to the Virtus Occulatum. During an educational expedition to the Clarissa Pulsar, the squire's health was called into question and an emergency disembarkation—which later proved providential—was entertained. Thereupon we encountered Number 22 who had intel that Wind Captain Dawes has already apprised. The squire presented an original opinion and prematurely requested assignment. Due to his health concerns, I ordered him to remain on New Carillon and remitted him to the care of his chaperone until the following morning." Number 1 sat back down.

Vance leaned over to Hans. "That canner is tellin' the truth alright, but he's tellin' it in a way that makes me look like a total goose!"

"Patience Vance," Hans advised, "you don't win a war of words with outbursts."

"Noted." Sansbury looked at Hans. "Hans Christian, is this panel correct in the understanding that you are Chaperone Solemn to Squire Vance Brewer?"

Hans stayed seated. "Professor Sansbury, the panel is unquestionably and unreservedly accurate in that understanding."

"Have you anything to contribute to the panel's understanding of the squire's actions post remittance?"

Hans looked up and to the side a moment as if in thought. "Hmm... nope."

Myles, the man in red, straightened up in his seat. "Is the panel to understand that you are in *refusal* to cooperate with this debriefing?"

"Hmm... nope."

"Blast you! This debrief is *not* to be treated like the *joke* your order is!"

"You are out of order, Star Commander Myles!" Sansbury declared.

Myles sat back and clenched his fists.

Sansbury turned back to Hans. "Out of the spirit of cooperation with this panel, we respectfully request that you expound on your previous statement."

"Thank you ever so kindly for taking the time to explain my obligation, Professor Sansbury. I would be overjoyed to be of some relevance to this panel's discovery. On the evening of the first of Tetrad, I was expecting Squire Brewer to be remitted to my care at seventeen-hundred hours. I received word at about thirteen-hundred forty hours that the squire was prematurely released back to me. With the sudden change in schedule, I was understandably employed in procuring the evening's meal in haste. However, the squire was absent upon my return with the food."

"Noted," Sansbury declared. "Is the squire both able and willing to recount his actions to this panel?"

Vance looked to Hans. Hans whispered, "Just remember to tell the truth as respectfully as you can."

"I can't incriminate Valerie."

"Trust me, Vance the Lance, tell what you know—in the most respectful manner.

"I hope you're right about this..."

Vance stood up and cleared his throat. "Sir, members of the panel, when I was in space with Number 1 around the pulsar, I had a weird dream that I think was me accidentally lookin' into the future—"

"Pure fiction," Agent Null, the woman in black, asserted. "Precognition is not something that accidentally happens; it requires concerted effort."

"Beggin' your pardon, ma'am. Then it must'a been a coincidence that Sky Captain Williams was captured by the Mori. Because in that dream I saw Sky Captain Williams say goodbye to me and then fade away. I tried to tell Number 1 that Sky Captain Williams was in trouble. He told me I had no right to think I was somethin' special and ta go home."

"If the squire would please refrain from pontification and restrict his depiction to specific dialogue, it would aid these proceedings greatly," Agent Null again objected.

Vance stood there a moment, "Uh, not sure what you askin' ma'am."

Sansbury answered instead. "What Agent Null means, is that it would be more helpful if you told us the words that were exchanged."

"As best I can recall, sir, Number 1 told me I was inexperienced and had no right to expect him to believe me, sayin' that noble intentions and pulsaric ideals was no match for experience. He then ordered me to go home and rest."

General Eggerton, the general seated on the end, leaned into his microphone. "And did you stay there as ordered?"

"Negative, sir—though, I was ordered to *go* home, not *stay* home, if'n that makes a difference. I left the apartment with the intention that if nobody was gonna help Sky Captain Williams, then *I* had ta try."

"Such a bold undertaking for one so inexperienced," the man in the black robe observed.

"This is a debrief, Lord Cantrell, not an evaluation of the boy's mettle," General Eggerton insisted.

"General Eggerton," Cantrell addressed, "if 'noble intentions and pulsaric ideals' are what the aforementioned was sternly dressed down for, I would assume you, of all members of this panel, would consider it a slight on your very culture. Does not respect, duty, loyalty, selfless service, integrity, and personal courage embody military honor?"

"They surely do, Lord Cantrell, but insubordination violates nearly *all* of those values," General Eggerton replied.

Mrs. Haufmann, the lady in the brown overcoat, raised one hand. "If we may please continue with the squire's statement, it would be most agreeable. We may, of assurity, be at better capacity to discuss the facts once their entirety has been presented."

"Please proceed, Squire Brewer," Sansbury directed.

"I made my way down to the Hangar deck—but I didn't steal no starcraft. I bumped into a friend who helped me with transportation."

"Please enlighten this panel on from whom you received this 'assistance'?" Myles demanded.

Vance glanced down. "I'd rather not get her in trouble, sir. I take full responsibility—"

"It was me!" a voice shouted from the back of the room.

Vance turned around. Valerie had her hand raised in the air.

"Noted, Miss Valerie Vlavskisk answered to the aforementioned description," Sansbury stated. He then looked back at Vance, "Proceed, Squire Brewer."

"With a little work, we found where the Mori were holding Sky Captain Williams and rescued him. Sky Captain Williams set fire to much of the Mori's outpost in our escape. Durin' the fight, however, Miss Vlavskisk was injured. I did my best to fly her starlancer—her mother's starlancer—back to New Carillon. The starlancer took a hit to the afterburner though."

"How much schooling have you accrued in piloting starfighters, Squire Brewer?" Myles inquired.

"None sir, just what instruction Miss Vlavskisk was able to provide in her condition."

"No formal instruction, and yet you fancied yourself capable enough to entrust your life and that of Miss Vlavskisk behind the stick?"

"What was I s'posed ta do? She needed medical attention. Was I s'posed to say 'Sorry miss, the regs are more important than your life'?"

Jonny Valdear, the man in the green vest, quietly smiled. Sansbury held up one finger. "Squire Brewer, this panel expects better respect than what has just been displayed."

"Sorry sir. It won't happen again."

Sansbury looked over to Myles. "That standard, of course, will be followed by everyone present." He looked back to Vance, "You may be seated, Squire Brewer."

Vance sat down and exhaled nervously.

Sansbury turned to the man in blue. "Chief Watts, where does this panel stand on understanding how the events unfolded?"

Watts set down his pen and picked up the packet of papers. "A few discrepancies to mitigate. It appears Squire Vance Brewer is not guilty of theft of a starcraft, only disobedience. So—"

"Upon technicality," the Mrs. Haufmann interjected. "If the members of this panel will entertain me, the order given to the squire was to *return* home, not to *remain* home. I would ask if we are to judge the correctness of his action based upon what the order *implied* or what it *stated?*"

Jor'del Smith, the man in the blue and white silk shirt, raised a few fingers in the air. "I would, of principle, need to concur."

General Eggerton shook his head, "I'm confident he knew what the order meant. You don't expect every commanding officer to have to specify, 'go home, *and* stay here, *and* follow all the other regulations while you're at it'?"

Agent Null nodded her head. "I concur with the general."

Myles leaned back. "Upon conflict, I find this extraneous prattle of the utmost importance to the squire's condition. Whilst I disapprove of the squire's actions, I must concede that it would appear the aforementioned did in fact comply with the precise declaration of his order. I must, upon principle, side with Mrs. Haufmann's assessment."

"I believe you'll find an official review board would conclude to the contrary!" General Eggerton snapped.

"May I remind the members of this panel," Sansbury addressed, "that this is an official debrief and not a punitive court."

"Very well," Watts concluded. "The squire is not found to have committed theft, nor disobeyed a direct order, per se." He scribbled a note on the packet of papers. "The full implications of these events can now be discussed."

"Are we to understand," Agent Null sneered, "that the squire is to have no repercussions for being the cause of what could have been a disaster? We could be now preparing three funerals due to the actions of the aforementioned!"

Sansbury took off his glasses and set them on the desk. "At the risk of my words sounding as would a broken record, this debrief is not—"

"Not a punitive court," Agent Null interrupted. "Then let this debrief at least uphold the regulations of a knight's training. We've seen where a disruption in the proper order of training can lead! I demand the squire be remitted to flight school before he embarks on any further tour of the orders; what was seen as a necessary deviation has proven detrimental."

"Just a moment, Agent Null," Watts said, "the flight school was reduced to cinders and magma by the Mori; it would be impractical to commit any squire to an indefinite wait."

"It will not be indefinite," Myles interjected. "The new flight school is currently under design, and within a few short years will be assembled and ready to take on new students."

Vance whispered to Hans, "They want me to stop training for several years?"

Hans closed his eyes and sighed.

Vance heard a voice in his head. *Number 13, it doesn't have to be this way.*

Vance turned and looked at the adjacent table. Number 1 looked right at him. *You know what I hate,* Vance thought, *I hate playing cards; 'cus I'm always being dealt clubs, clubs, clubs.*

Number 1 smirked. *But the jack is wild. You still remember the basics I have taught you.*

Vance nodded as he thought, *I rescued Sky Captain Williams; why you tryin' ta give me the can?*

Rescued? Number 13, what you did was botch an undercover mission. Do you know just what it would mean to the remnant of humankind if we knew where the Mori were stationed? Or if we could know where they would send their ships? Do you have any idea what it would mean if we could learn to read the Mori language and peer into their databases and glean their secrets?

Negative, Vance thought, *but I'm bettin' you're gonna tell me.*

Number 1 nodded. *Survival, Number 13. As the intelligence arm of the Solar Knights, it is our burden to carry the backup plan if we cannot breach the Great Frontier of the Ancients.*

How come Sky Captain Williams didn't tell me he was on a secret mission? Vance thought.

That's because he was never told. To fool the Mori, it needed to look realistic. Therefore, the kidnapping needed to be real.

That's just plain wrong, Vance thought.

This isn't about right and wrong, Number 13, this is about the human species being dangerously close to extinction. If I have to sell my soul to save humankind, I would do it a thousand times over.

Vance shook his head. *Usin' someone as bait just doesn't seem honorable, Number 1.*

I don't believe you are qualified to judge me. Besides, it isn't smart to bite the hand that feeds you. You see, I am offering you an olive branch; a way to continue your training instead of waiting around several years for a new flight school to be constructed.

Vance looked down and thought, *what would I have to do?*

Just continue touring with me. That's all.

Vance looked back up at Number 1. *Nah, I don't buy it,* he thought. *There has ta be more to it than that; you wouldn't be doin' this outta the kindness of your heart.*

Number 1 sat and thought a moment before taking a deep breath. *Agent Null is correct, people don't just 'accidentally' peer into the possible future—that is, all except for you. And I want to know why.*

So that's it, Vance thought in conclusion, *you wanna study my head, and in return, I get ta keep trainin' to be a Solar Knight.*

To be precise, you would continue training as a Virtus Occulatum knight. You would have the chance to learn all the techniques of telepathy, precognition, and more. Number 1's mouth pulled into a smirk. *Ask yourself, just how different would your first combat have been if you had had the power to make yourself invisible? Or if you could have snatched from a Mori's very thoughts the location of Royce Williams?*

Vance closed his eyes and breathed deeply for a few moments. *Your offer is more tempting than anythin' I've ever been offered,* he thought, opening his eyes and looking at Number 1. *An' I'd be lyin' if'n I said this was an easy decision.* Vance's eyes began to water. *But at the end of the day, I gotta be able to sleep. And I think bein' in your shoes would keep me up at night. With respect, sir—I mean Number 1, I have to decline.*

Number 1's eyes narrowed. *You're condemning yourself to—*

"I will train him!" a voice called out from the back of the room.

Vance and Number 1 turned around. The entire room stared at Royce, who stood from his chair in the back row.

Sansbury put his glasses back on. "Sky Captain Royce Williams, it's quite unusual to interrupt the proceedings of a formal debrief."

"Forgive the impropriety of my actions, Professor Sansbury, but I offer a solution to the deliberations of this panel in regards to Squire Brewer. His training has been declared on hold until such a time as he can attend flight training, and with the absence of a proper school, the squire is left without redress for several years to come. I offer to personally train the squire to fly. I am the most experienced pilot in Fire Lance and graduated at the top of my class."

"This is highly irregular!" Myles complained.

"As Star Commander Myles can attest, I am the most qualified to instruct."

Sansbury sat back in his chair and stared at Royce for a few moments. "Your logic is undeniable. Are you then willing and able to answer for the squire's actions while under your direction?"

"I am."

"There must be some degree of oversight," Myles objected, "to ensure adequate training."

"Noted," Sansbury declared. "The squire is to be remitted to Sky Captain Royce Williams for flight training. The order of Fire Lance will ensure the squire's training meets minimum guidelines and thereafter, issue a certificate of completion." Sansbury turned to Myles. "Is it agreeable?"

Myles slowly nodded. "Quite..."

Chapter 27
FLIGHT TRAINING

The duties of a flight wingman are to maintain situational awareness of the battlespace, perform defensive maneuvers to protect the flight lead when engaging an enemy fighter, and coordinate offensive maneuvers against a more maneuverable target or targets (i.e. Grinder, Cat & Mouse, Thatch Weave). A wingman may also be given the tactical lead (TAC Lead) in an engagement depending on the specifics of the engagement.

—FROM "STARCRAFT CARRIER OPERATIONS MANUAL" BY THOMAS J. SUTTON, UNITED EARTH NAVAL COMMAND

Vance sat in the cockpit of a red-winged beauty; a starlancer. He was grateful all the pre-flight checks had already been done for him by the plane captain. He gave a thumbs-up to a plane director standing on the flight deck. She gave him a hand signal with both arms to taxi forward. He'd experienced the launch sequence many times in the last five months of his flight training. Most were in the simulator but his count of actual flights was quickly catching up.

Vance pushed the throttle forward ever so slightly, and the engines roared to life. The starlancer rolled forward. He taxied down a long lane until he saw another plane director motioning for him to turn onto the runway. He steered the starlancer onto the end of the runway and made a few final corrections to his forward angle.

Vance heard the radio chatter in his ear from his helmet. "AberrantStar, you are Training-one-three to Mother."

"Roger Carillon," he replied.

"Training thirteen, cleared for launch. Clear stars today, sir."

"Training, roger and thank you."

A catapult crewman in a green jacket ran up to the nose gear of the starlancer. The twin gigantic electromagnets on crane arms swiveled around behind the starlancer. The catapult crewman then hustled out from under the nose of the craft. He signaled to the flight controller that the nose gear was connected to the launch track.

Vance saluted The Shooter. The Shooter crouched down and signaled with one arm extended forward. A few seconds later, Vance was thrown into the back of his seat. The starlancer was propelled to launch speed in two seconds. He barely saw the space doors fly past before being bathed in starlight.

This is like a dream come true, he thought.

"AberrantStar, this is Firefly. About time you got off the runway."

"Sorry for the delay, sir. I didn't want another repeat of what happened in the simulator last week."

"It could have happened to anybody."

"Oh come on, sir, who else busts their nose gear while taxiing onto the runway?"

"...point taken."

"Oh, and it bugs me how Mother keeps callin' me Training Thirteen? I thought only Virtus Occulatum called me thirteen. Havin' the tower also call me thirteen is kinda creepy, like Number 1 himself was spyin' on me or somethin'. Where did the tower get thirteen anyway?"

"AberrantStar, it's your starlancer's tail number."

"...ah, right."

Vance looked out the right side of his canopy. Royce's starlancer pulled up alongside. "Sir," Vance said. "Thank you for taking me out into the stars today. I was goin' nuts sittin' in that make-shift classroom day after day."

"I figured you had earned it. Besides, it's been a few weeks since your last round of dogfighting maneuvers."

"You gonna go easy on me this time?"

"Never."

Vance sighed. "That's what I figured."

"I did, however, arrange for you to have a wingman for this exercise."

"What do I need a wingman for?"

"To practice your teamwork skills, of course."

"Right. Right. The one thing I haven't been able to do much of bein' your sole student."

"My my," a third voice chimed in, "fancy seeing my admirer up here in the stars."

"Valerie! Are *you* my wingman?"

"True-blue, sticking with you," her voice replied. "But you'll have to call me by my callsign."

"You got yer callsign? That's so gabb! What is it? I hope it isn't HotHead."

"No," she replied. "It's not HotHead. But I'm pretty sure *you* had something to do with my callsign."

"Me?" Vance asked. "Alls I did was tell the story of how you sacrificed yourself to save Sky Captain Williams to every pilot and flight deck operator I bumped into."

"That means a lot to me." Her starlancer formed up on his left side.

"So you gonna tell me your callsign, or what?"

"Starburst."

"Seriously!"

"If the two of you are finished reacquainting, we can get this exercise underway," Royce directed.

"Sorry sir."

Royce rolled his starlancer and broke off. "We'll start with a low 3 o'clock encounter. Remember, stay with your wingman and work together; the ego of a fighter pilot will make you each easy prey."

"Roger, Firefly."

"Roger, Firefly," she also said. "AbberantStar, I'll watch SEDAR until we engage."

"Roger, Starburst. If it's anything like last time, you won't have ta wait long."

"Speaking of which, Bandit on your 3 o'clock, coming in low."

Vance turned into Royce's path. "Tally on Bandit."

"AberrantStar, watch your turning arc or you'll overshoot at the merge."

Vance watched Royce fly past him. Vance rolled into a tight turn. "Ah kreket; he reversed."

"Don't worry, I'm closing into range."

Vance rolled the starlancer into a wide turn and looked around through the canopy. He caught a short glimpse of Royce's starlancer whiz past, toward his rear. "He's gaining the advantage."

"Keep scissoring, I've almost got him."

Vance pulled around for another pass and kept looking for Royce. "I've lost tally!"

"Tally Bandit. He's forming up on your six."

Vance looked back as far as he could see out the canopy. "Don't you have a lock yet?"

"I tried; he jammed the target lock."

Vance's heart rate accelerated. "I gotta bug out!"

"No! I just need a little more time to close the distance for guns."

Vance pulled into a turn and then quickly reversed, pulling back out and settling into a dive.

"Vance! I almost had him!"

"Yeah, well he almost had *me*!"

Vance leveled off and then quickly checked his SEDAR scope. He gained distance from the other two yellow dots. "Okay, now I'm re-engaging."

Vance rolled and pulled into a tight turn and hit his afterburner. Within moments he saw the two small starcraft in the distance. He flipped the switch on his stick for missile targeting. Royce was right behind Valerie. "Starburst, Bandit on your six!"

He heard a series of beeps in his ear. He looked quickly down to his SEDAR. One of the yellow dots turned gray.

"No AberrantStar, he *was* on my six. Now he splashed me."

"Kreket!"

"You know, it is about time we work on your language!"

"Hardly the time!" Vance sighed and turned his starlancer into the arc Royce was turning. Royce reversed his turn and Vance tried to follow.

"Too soon, AberrantStar! You're putting yourself right into his line of fire!"

Vance quickly rolled and hit his afterburner. He saw the stars zip across the canopy. He looked to his left and spotted Royce, still turning to get behind him. Vance kept tightening up his turn. "I'm starting to get him into the line of fire."

"Yes, but you're sacrificing speed to do so! Reverse and get him into a scissor."

Vance kept pulling the starlancer into an ever-tighter turn. Royce's starlancer came into his 12 o'clock. Vance smiled a moment, and then his smile fell. "He's put too much distance between us."

Royce rolled and circled around. Vance turned to intercept. As Royce came near, he suddenly turned away. Vance turned to follow. Royce quickly reversed the turn and both starlancers crossed paths right past each other.

"AberrantStar, he's got you into a two circle fight; if you can't angle your nose before he does, you'll have to bug out."

"I think I can get him before the next merge." Vance briefly hit his braking thruster and turned hard. Royce flew right across his nose and Vance pulled his trigger. He heard one beep in his ear. He checked his SEDAR. Still a yellow dot. "Blast! I missed."

"AberrantStar, you better pick up some speed, he's circling around to your six."

Vance hit his afterburner and rolled to one side. He looked around but couldn't see Royce. He glanced down at his SEDAR. He heard a series of beeps in his ear. And his entire SEDAR screen greyed out. "Oh not again!"

"AberrantStar, this is Firefly. Take a moment to break out your kneeboard and write down your maneuvers for this engagement. We'll be going over your spaghetti notation during our debrief. Starburst, if you would do the same, it would help."

"Tell it to me plain, sir; where did I goose up?"

"I think you already know."

Vance sighed. "It was when I disengaged and left Starburst by herself."

There was a short pause before Royce's solemn voice responded, "Never leave your wingman."

Chapter 28
THE CARTRIDGE

The Solar Winds Nautical Calendar was first instituted by the Federation of Tradesmen following Sir Edwin Norfolk's discovery of The Solar Winds. The calendar was designed on mathematical principles with thirteen months (months Null through Prinnary) of twenty-eight days each, with the day of Null preceding the Month of Null.

—FROM "GALACTIC HISTORY VOL. IV" BY PROF. EZRA DOUGHERTY

Vance held a pistol at arm's length and fired three times before lowering his hands. He looked at the hanging poster of a man's silhouette. Three holes barely touched the edges of the silhouette. He raised the pistol again and aimed a few seconds before firing another round.

"Nice shot," Valerie critiqued. "Aiming works wonders; you got it inside the black this time."

Vance adjusted the hard plastic ear-muff headset with one hand. "Hard to believe my shootin' has gone downhill since basic training."

Valerie pushed the clear plastic visor further up the bridge of her nose. "That's why we practice." She pointed down range with her finger. "Now let's see if you can get a tight grouping *inside* the black."

"Aye aye miss." Vance held the pistol in both hands, bent his knees, and fired off three more rounds. He sighed and fired off five more shots. "Well, at least they're gettin' inside the black now."

"*Two* of them are in the black."

"Ah, yeah but those two are close together, right?"

Valerie rolled her eyes. "Okay, technically, that could be considered a tight grouping inside the black." Valerie pressed a button on the side of the stall. The small crane arm quickly brought the target poster up close.

"Wait, we leavin' already?"

Valerie nodded. "I want some lunch."

"Well before we go, can I see how well you shoot?"

Valerie looked into his eyes a moment and then added a sinister grin. She pressed the other button and the target poster zoomed back to the far end of the range. "Okay, admirer, you get to count."

"What do you mean count?"

She drew both her pistols and pulled the magazines. She quickly eyeballed the number of bullets in each, then slapped them both back into place. She re-holstered both pistols. "Give me a count down."

"Okay. Three, two, one, mark."

Her hands reached for her pistols. Before Vance could see her draw them, she fired off multiple shots from each pistol. Then she spun each pistol around her trigger fingers and holstered them both.

"Whoa, it didn't look like you even drew your sidearms!"

She gave him half a smile as she retracted the target poster. She detached it and handed it over to Vance.

Vance snickered. "You made him look like a cyclops."

She laughed and gathered up a few things from the firing bench. Vance followed her out the door. Once outside the shooting range, Vance took off the protective visor and ear-muffs and hung them up.

Valerie folded hers up and put them into a small blue and white carrying case.

"Valerie, maybe next time you can show me how ta do some trick shots?"

"You'll first need to learn to hit what you're aiming at."

Vance smiled. "Yeah, that."

They both exited into the long hallway and walked together. Vance looked down as they walked. "About earlier today, I'm sorry I abandoned you during the dogfight training."

"It must have been a little scary up there."

"Yeah, I... sorta panicked." He slowly exhaled. "It's been a little stressful, tryin' ta do good around so many Solar Knights doing such amazing things."

"Vance, you can't compare yourself to seasoned knights. They have had the benefit of years and years of honing their craft. You're just barely scratching the surface."

"I know, I know, I just... I just feel like I'm runnin' outta time."

"How so?"

"Well, I hear Sky Captain Williams talkin' about the Great Frontier of the Ancients, and how the fleets are assembling to try to breach it. My mind sorta wonders if I'll be ready when that happens. I still have two weeks left in my flight training."

"Vance, if you can't learn to trust me, you'll never feel ready."

"What does this have ta do with trust?"

"Vance, no one is a hundred percent. No one can do everything by themselves. Even Royce, as skilled as he is, could not escape from the Mori by himself." She drew one of her pistols and removed the magazine. She popped one bullet out of the magazine before returning it to her pistol. She handed the pullet to Vance. "Look at that."

"A bullet?"

"It's a Thompson-Remmington HyperMag centerfire cartridge. The bullet is only the tip. And as impressive as that bullet is, it can't do anything on its own. It needs a cartridge case with 240 grains and a primer just to be capable of doing anything impressive. But that's still not enough; it cannot unleash all that stored energy without a firing pin from the pistol."

"An' so I need ta trust that all these things work together to make the bullet fly?"

"No, neutron-head, *you* are the bullet. Royce, Hans, and all your friends and mentors are the grains of powder, the primer, and the casing. And destiny—your destiny—is the firing pin."

"I hadn't thought about it that way."

She halted walking and Vance stopped too. Her mahogany eyes penetrated his. "I don't know what you've been through, or who you have lost, but I will not leave you. I want you to know you can trust me."

Vance quickly looked away and sniffled as he took in a deep breath. Once the threat of an embarrassing tear had passed, he re-engaged her eyes. "This war just keeps takin' all my friends away. Back when I was a mechanic, I was really close to a pilot. He was even proud of me when I made Petty Officer 3rd Class. When I became a squire, he turned against me. I guess I'm still scared I'm gonna end up alone."

That means a lot ta me, miss."

Her captivating gaze softened and she smiled. "Okay, now I'm *really* hungry, where should we go?"

Chapter 29

GRAVITY

During the Third Great Horror, the Great Races (the Ancients, Ezsh'der the Doryu, and the Fourth Race) destroyed the Amber Crystal which held open the dimensional tear that allowed The Darkness to intrude upon our galaxy. Following its destruction, the Fourth Race left the galaxy in pursuit of "other matters" now that the Darkness was completely dispelled. The prophet Nomad warned the Fourth Race, to no avail, that The Darkness would again return after a long season. The Ancients then commenced an 832-year-long project, later known as The Great Frontier of the Ancients, to encircle the star systems under their control and to forever shut out The Darkness as well as their one-time allies: Ezsh'der the Doryu.

—FROM "GALACTIC HISTORY VOL. II" BY PROF. EZRA DOUGHERTY

Vance pressed a few buttons on his console display in the back seat of a starlancer. "Firefly, sir, how come you got me flying Rio back here? Shouldn't I be at the stick?"

"You've been through nearly twenty weeks of training. Now I'm introducing you to the last phase of flight training."

"With all due respect, sir, I kinda seen the back seat plenty."

"Look out the canopy."

Vance looked up and saw a brown planet in the distance. "We gonna practice planet landing?"

"Negative. I'm introducing you to gravity."

"Ah geez, gravity and I have a horrible relationship; it's always tryin' ta keep me down." Vance leaned forward. "Was that a laugh?"

Royce shook his head. "No."

"That was a laugh, wasn't it?"

"Negative Squire, I was... clearing my throat."

"If you say so, sir."

Royce pulled the starlancer into a gentle turn and skimmed into a low orbit above the planet. "Up until now, you've been flying in flat space. Now we're going to add some curves into the mix. Gravity changes all the rules."

"Sir, does it change combat tactics too?"

"Affirmative. You have to be aware of the gravitational body and its position. You must back off your turning thrusters when pulling a lead turn or you risk overshooting. Gravity changes everything, and the experienced pilot will use it to their advantage."

He drifted the starlancer closer toward the planet. "AberrantStar, I want you to close your eyes and just feel the pull."

Vance obeyed. "Sir, do the Mori practice much with gravity?"

"The Mori are the most technologically advanced species we've ever encountered. They're also the most complacent and under-practiced species we've ever met."

Vance felt a slight heaviness to his left which gradually became stronger. "We must be getting closer to the planet; it feels like the pull is more pronounced."

"Very good. Keep your eyes closed. Feel where I'm going, and call out my maneuvers."

"Aye sir. An' if I may ask, what is it you think that got them so complacent?"

Royce sighed. "That dates back to ancient galactic history. How much do you know about the age before the Mori?"

"Alls I know, sir, is that before the Mori, the Ancients built the Great Frontier." Vance suddenly felt lighter. "Whoa, you've turned the nose down into a dive."

"The earliest records we have are from a roaming prophet of sorts, known as Nomad. He wrote extensively about ancient galactic history. His record begins with four major powers that spanned the galaxy. Four races which we know as The Ancients, Ezsh'der the Doryu, The Darkness, and The Fourth Race."

Vance then felt heavy. "Okay, now you're in a climb."

"The Ancients built the Great Frontier because of The Darkness. And since the time they built the Great Frontier, they had no external conflict. They had nothing to fear and nothing to fight. They fell into complacency and their great machines kept running all by themselves. Generations later, they digressed into the race we now know as the Mori."

"What? The Ancients are the Mori?"

"Negative. The Mori are all that is left of the Ancients. They have been on top for so long, that they have forgotten how their great machines work. They have not been opposed for so long, they nearly have forgotten how to wage war."

Vance felt his weight shift to the side of the cockpit. "Ah, you're rollin' out to starboard. Sir, can I ask you another question?"

"Fire away."

"You mentioned the Great Frontier of the Ancients was built because of The Darkness. What exactly did The Darkness do?"

"The Darkness, also known as The Intruders or The Madness, was not native to our galaxy. They gained a foothold into our galaxy and waged war on anyone who would not join them. The Ancients, along with Ezsh'der the Doryu, and the Fourth Race, defeated The Darkness and pushed them out. But that war was only the first of four Great

Horrors. After the fourth Great Horror, The Fourth Race left our galaxy."

Vance suddenly felt thrown to the side of the cockpit. "And that's a left break. So why'd they leave?"

"Professor Dougherty has a few theories, but for whatever reason, they left. Then Ezsh'der the Doryu and The Ancients sort of had a falling out, you might say."

"A falling out?"

"That's a whole other topic. But needless to say, they went their separate ways, and yet both were fearful that The Darkness might return yet again. The Ancients built the Great Frontier to forever shield themselves."

The starlancer started rattling and shaking. "What's that sir!"

"Keep your eyes closed, AberrantStar. This is the buffet."

"What's a buff-it?"

"The buffet is the tension line between the pull of gravity and atmospheric lift. It comes on right before the craft stalls. Remember this feeling, AberrantStar. This shaking means you're near the edge; the point of no return."

"It this 'cause we're too close to the planet?" Vance asked.

"It's because we've reached the craft's critical angle of attack. If you try too hard to fight gravity, you wind up losing the lift of the air currents."

Royce loosened up his turn and the shaking subsided. "Flying in the buffet is a majestic dance between the captive pull of gravity and freedom of soaring across the stars. When you find yourself in the buffet, remember to ease up."

Royce pulled the starlancer out of the planet's orbit and rolled into a smooth turn. "You can open your eyes now."

Vance blinked a few times. "Well, I'm not gonna lie, that tale makes me wonder if breaching the Great Frontier is such a good idea."

Royce chuckled. "At least on the other side, we're not being hunted and eliminated." Royce leveled out the starlancer.

Vance looked out the canopy for a few minutes, soaking in everything he had just heard. "Firefly, sir, do you use much gravity when fightin' the Mori?"

"All the time. If you find yourself up against a skilled Mori pilot, throw some gravity into the mix. It'll turn the tables faster than a nosedive. The Mori's impressive technology means we cannot outlast them. But by Nova, we sure can out-think them and out-fly them."

Vance heard a voice in his helmet. "Golden two, Carillon marshal."

Royce switched on the transmission. "Golden two, go."

"Golden two, you are cleared to land. Call the ball."

Royce pressed a few buttons on his console. "Paddles, Golden two, starlancer, 'Firefly', ball, fuel state 9.5, manual."

The voice in his helmet replied, "Roger, ball. You're fast."

Royce eased up on the throttle while keeping his eyes on the indicator lights. Vance watched the space door fly by. The sudden pull of the safety straps dug into his shoulders as the starlancer came to an arrested stop.

Vance then leaned back and rested his head. "Ah, there's nothin' quite like that feelin'.

"You know, I dare say you're becoming a pilot in more ways than one."

Vance grinned. "Why thank you, sir."

Royce taxied the starlancer toward the recovery lane, following the plane director's hand signals. "Vance, remember to practice your maneuvers, your final exam is coming up."

"You don't have ta tell me twice. Wind Captain Dawes is gonna be gradin' me, and I don't think he likes me much."

"I'm sure you'll be just fine."

The canopy slid open. Royce stepped out and descended the stairs. Vance climbed down after him. Valerie stood at the bottom, waiting for him.

"Vance, you're late!"

"Sorry, miss. Sky Captain Williams was introducin' me to gravity."

She smirked. "You didn't crack a gravity joke, did you?"

"I was seriously thinkin' about a gravity joke, but then I decided to drop it."

She swatted him on the arm. "Very funny. Now let's get going. We're already going to be late."

"Where we goin'?"

"Lord Baltris had invited us to attend the Ascensio tonight."

Vance lowered his brow and widened his eyes. "The what?"

"It's where an apprentice graduates to become a master. It's loads of fun. The apprentice performs a display of the different things they can do with The Winds."

"Ah, that sounds gabb!"

Chapter 30

ASCENSIO

Date: 27 Oct
Subject: Continued observation
*Notes: The subject's loyalties have polarized since
the last attempt to acquire him. This is
unsurprising considering his limited experience.
My only concern is his association with that young
Gun Star. It is tainting my results.*

—FROM "DOSSIER #13" CLASSIFIED

Vance stepped into a crowded room with dim yellow lights. All sorts of people cluttered the area, chatting with one another. Some were seated at tables, sipping drinks. Others were standing about exchanging long-winded discussions. Some people were Solar Knights dressed in formal wear, others were military or civilian.

Vance flexed his fingers a few times, readjusting to the formal green gloves. He glanced down to make sure his long sleeveless green jacket hung properly. Valerie adjusted the string-tie on the front of his gold silk shirt. "You look great."

Vance grinned. "So do you, miss. That blue and white dress is what caught my eye in the first place."

Valerie slid her arm around Vance's. "Okay, admirer, let's find a seat."

Vance led them through the sea of people and commotion until a man in an ornate black robe raised his hand. "Miss Vlavskisk, over here."

Vance led Valerie up to the table. "Lord Baltris, sir, you mind if we join ya?"

"Not at all, Squire. And how is Miss Vlavskisk?"

"Thrilled, Lord Baltris. I still remember your last apprentice. His Ascensio was spectacular!"

Baltris nodded. "Master Yoshimo was quite the showman—still is, I hear." He motioned toward adjacent chairs. "Have a seat."

Vance and Valerie sat down. Vance had to resituate his long coat tail. "So Lord Baltris, I haven't yet toured with the Wind Dancers. What do you guys specialize in?"

"How do you mean?"

"Well, sir," Vance motioned toward Valerie. "Gun Stars are shootin' experts. Fire Lance are starfighter aces. Orbiting Star does their force field tricks. And Virtus Occulatum does a lot with the mind. What do Wind Dancers do?"

"That's a fair question. How much do you know already?"

"Well, sir, I seen a Wind Dancer lighting candles with his finger."

Baltris chuckled. "Yes, fire is one of the first things an apprentice learns. Fire is not much more than molecules in motion. A Wind Dancer's studies will focus inward. We learn to quiet the mind and discipline thoughts and behaviors. And as we turn inward, we find we can focus on the minute energy fields within the human body."

"Well, what does that do?"

Valerie snickered. "It lets them light candles with their finger."

Vance turned to her. "When you toured with them, did you ever learn the candle lighting trick?"

She shook her head. "No, a tour is not nearly long enough to learn the hocus-pocus of the Wind Dancers. I spent the entire tour learning to meditate and memorizing rituals."

"That doesn't sound very gabb at all."

"Perhaps not, Squire Brewer. You see, the ability to harness the electrical fields in your own body—to accelerate or rearrange molecules—takes a lot of self-mastery. For this reason, we have rituals to help keep our mind in balance."

Valerie rolled her eyes. "There's a ritual to calm down, a ritual to refocus your thoughts, a ritual to clear the mind. There's a ritual for when you're sad—there's even a ritual for memorizing rituals!"

Baltris laughed. "Well the way you word it, even I would think it excessive. But as you'll see here in a minute, the results are worth the years of training."

"Quiet down everyone!" A woman hollered over the cacophony.

All the people standing quickly moved to their seats. The lights dimmed even more. The woman walked on a low stage with two spotlights on her. "Thank you all for coming, I am Rosa Lorca De Leon, apprentice first-class to Lord Baltris. And while I am most appreciative of his tutelage, I just can't wait to graduate."

The room erupted in small laughter and applause. She nodded a few times before continuing. "Traditionally we light the candles on the tables before we begin. But I am going to break with that tradition tonight. I have incorporated the lighting of the candles into my routine."

She waited for the applause to subside, then she turned to a man at the far end of the stage who held a drum between his legs. She nodded to him and he started beating a fast-paced rhythm. Rosa put a tablet in her mouth and took a drink from a cup on a small table. She then put the hood of her robe over her head, partially concealing her face.

She brought one hand to her face and stared with intensity at her fingers. She slowly brought her hand closer and closer to her face. Suddenly, the air above her fingers burst into a small match-sized flame.

She started moving to the rhythm of the drum, rolling the tiny ball of flame around her fingers and across her hand. The audience clapped as she continued to play with the little flame. She brought it close to her face and then she blew as if she were blowing a kiss. The little flame flew across the room and struck the candle on the center table.

The audience gasped in delight. Rosa threw her hands up high into the air and the candle flame flared into a torch-sized roar. The people seated at that table recoiled in fright while the other tables cheered. Rosa lowered her hands and the flame relaxed back down to a flicker. Then on one drum beat, she waved her hand to the left, and the flame spread to the adjacent candle. On the next drum beat, she waved her other hand to the right, and the flame spread to the candle on the other side.

She continued alternating her hand movements on each drum beat until every table had each candle lit. Then she took a bow as the drum stopped. Vance whistled while following the rest of the room in clapping.

Before the applause completely subsided, the drum started up again. This time it was in a slow archaic rhythm. Rosa slothfully swayed to the drum beats. She reached over to a small table at the back of the stage and picked up a small cup of water. Keeping in time to the beat, she poured it into her mouth and then blasted a spray of water up into the air. The water droplets came raining down as little ice pellets.

Rose threw her hands up. The air above her head shimmered like water as the ice pellets bounced and broke upon the force field. The room broke out into applause.

Vance shot a glance over to Baltris. He whispered, "Wind Dancers can manipulate force fields too?"

He shook his head. "Nothing compared to Orbiting Star. But we do have the ability to create force fields without a generator."

"You *create* them?" Vance said, nearly dropping his jaw.

Baltris shrugged. "It's simple molecular manipulation along with an electromagnetic field."

The drumming stopped and the room cheered. Vance looked back to the stage. Rosa pushed her hood off her head. Another woman in a black robe stood at the other end of the stage, holding a handful of metal knives. Rosa put another tablet in her mouth and quickly took another drink. The drum started up again with a fast four-beat melody.

Vance folded his arms, "That sure could have come in handy when my portable force field generator was hit."

Baltris nodded. "You can, with a few years of dedicated practice and emotional discipline."

"Emotional discipline?" he asked.

Baltris nodded again. "Emotion is far too often spontaneous and unreliable. Every idle thought and dark desire affect our emotions in one way or another." Baltris pointed to Rosa on stage. "The only sure way to manipulate The Winds on that level is with extreme control. The slightest loss of control can be disastrous to a Wind Dancer."

Vance looked at Rosa and watched her dancing to the drum and spinning objects in the air.

Vance's eyes dropped to the table. His heart rate slowed. He felt his heart sink as memories of his battle with Valerie kept resurfacing. All the times she had pulled or pushed him out of the path of incoming fire. He remembered her bandaging up his shoulder. He had looked into her mahogany eyes and admitted he didn't know how he would have managed without her.

Vance looked back up to the stage. Rosa stepped forward in time to the drumbeats. With each step forward the lady on the end of the stage threw a large knife at her. Rosa batted away each knife with the palms of her hands, breaking the knives into several pieces. When Rosa took her last step toward the other lady, she threw her fist upward. The other lady rose into the air as if an invisible hand had grabbed her and lifted her off the ground.

The drum stopped and Rosa relaxed her arm. The other lady dropped back down to her feet. Both women took a bow as the audience cheered and applauded. Vance jumped out of his seat and marched out the door.

He didn't wander far. He leaned his back up against the hallway wall. He stood there, leaning for a few minutes, then he slid down the wall until he was sitting. A few moments later, a hand touched his shoulder. It was Valerie. She knelt beside him.

"Hey, are you okay?"

"Yeah, I just. I guess I just needed some air or somethin'"

"What's going on?" she prodded.

"Well…" He hesitated.

"Vance. Look at me, please."

He looked over at her curly black locks and her glossy lips. He didn't want to look up into her eyes; he felt vulnerable. Her gloved hand on his shoulder strengthened his resolve.

Her mahogany eyes stared into his. "Vance, after everything we've been through together, why can't you trust me?"

"'Course I trust you miss."

"Then why don't you let me in?"

He looked away, breathing heavily. "I keep thinkin' what a goose I was on our first mission together. Everyone keeps thankin' me for saving *your* life when in reality you prob'ly saved *mine* a dozen times over that night."

She gazed at him.

"An' I know I'm not supposed to compare myself ta other knights, but I can't help it! I'm just a grease monkey with delusions of grandeur—well, 'visions' of grandeur is prob'ly more accurate…"

"Vance—"

"An' I keep askin' myself why I'm even here! There are big things ahead. The fleet will be movin' out to the Great Frontier of the Ancients. We have Mori fleets huntin' us down. An' here I am, thinkin' I can be one of you. Thinkin' I can be a Solar Knight." He hung his head. "The funny thing is, I was offered a deal with the devil. Only now, I'm startin' to regret turnin' him down."

"Vance, what are you talking about?"

Vance turned to her. "Back at the debrief, Number 1 offered to train me as a Virt-O. He asked me questions like, how different things could have been rescuin' Sky Captain Williams if'n I had learned their tricks. And I keep wonderin' if I could have been a help instead of dead weight back there if I was a Virt-O."

"Vance, first of all, I wouldn't trust Number 1 if he was the last knight on New Carillon, he gives me the creeps. And second, you have a real identity issue. How can you say you're just a grease monkey? You looked into the future! You found Royce by touching the walls! You stopped a space door! You even beat a Mori in hand to hand!"

Vance shook his head. "Valerie—"

"The man my heart orbits, is a loyal and pulsaric knight that bleeds blue and white." She stood and walked a few steps away.

"Valerie, wait." Vance got to his feet and hurried after her.

She turned and tossed something to him. He caught it in both hands and looked at it. His eyes widened. He glanced back into her eyes. A tear streamed down her cheek.

"I don't know what gravity Number 1 has pulling on you. But I'd say you're in the buffet. So when you figure out which way you're going, you know where to find me." She turned and left.

Vance watched a few speechless moments before returning his eyes to his hands. It was the second bullet she had given him. He fondly caressed the edges of the bullet cartridge with his finger.

Chapter 31
IN THE BUFFET

*Sky Captain Royce Williams always seemed
more than just a pilot to me. He had the heart of a
mentor and enough skill and experience to back it
up. It seemed to me that all the soldiers I'd known
fit into one of two categories: men and toddlers.
The men were people like Royce, and the
toddlers, well... I guess that's why they called it the
infantry.*

—FROM "MEMOIRS OF THE EXODUS" BY HANS THE BRONZE

"Sky Captain Williams, sir. Thank you for seeing me at such a late hour."

"Can I get you something to drink?" Royce offered.

"Mineral water."

"Mineral water?"

"Aye sir. And just in case I'm low on potassium..."

Royce walked back from the small cooler. Vance sat on the couch in the small apartment. Royce handed an opened bottle to him along with an electrolyte tablet. He swallowed the tablet with a few gulps of water. "Thank you, sir."

Royce sat down in a chair off to the side of the couch. "What's on your mind, Brewer."

"It's, it's kinda hard ta explain sir. I know why I'm here, but... I don't know why I'm here."

Royce pulled out a pocket knife from the breast pocket of his red duty uniform and began cutting the peel off an apple. "You mean here in my apartment, or here in the program?

Vance looked down and fidgeted with his bottle. "In the program, sir."

Royce continued peeling the apple.

"It's..." he hesitated.

Royce cut a slice off the apple and put it in his mouth.

"Sir, I don't know how ta say this. I really appreciate what you've done for me. But when I see a Virt-O using mind games, a Wind Dancer alakazaming the unthinkable, and a Gun Star turnin' my target into a cyclops, I can't help but wonder if I'm any good."

"Good at what?" Royce asked, slicing off another piece of apple and eating it.

"...good at bein' a Solar Knight, sir."

Royce sliced off another piece of apple, turned it around in his hand a few times, and then put it in his mouth. After a few silent moments, he swallowed. "Brewer, what's got you in a nosedive?"

Vance took another gulp of his water. "I wish I knew, sir."

"What advice have you received so far?"

"Well, Miss Vlavskisk says I'm like a bullet, and I can't expect to do much on my own. I need my friends and mentors to be somethin'."

Royce cut another slice of apple. "Is that what you believe?"

"I hadn't thought about it in that way before she said it. An' it makes sense, sort of. I see people doin' amazin' stuff and I have to wonder if I will be any good at amazin' stuff. 'Cuz so far, I'm not. Miss Vlavskisk prob'ly saved my life half a dozen times when we rescued you. An' I get hero status for savin' her *once*."

"So, what do you want to get out of this conversation tonight?"

Vance huffed an exasperated chuckle. "Sir, I was hopin' for some guidance."

"Let me put it to you a different way. Brewer, what is it you want?"

He shrugged. "To be important, I guess."

"Tell me about the last time you felt important. What were you doing?"

Vance took another drink of water and stared at the table. "When I saw the dream of you vanishin'. I knew you was in trouble. An' even though Number 1 dressed me down for suggesting I could contribute anythin' of value, I wanted so much ta help. When Miss Vlavskisk took me serious and offered ta help me, I felt important. I didn't realize just how important that made me feel until just now."

"You weren't a Virtus Occulatum, or a Wind Dancer, or a Gun Star. What cause did you have to feel important?" Royce put the last piece of apple in his mouth.

Vance looked into Royce's eyes. "...I'm not sure sir. It was different somehow."

"What made it different?"

He shrugged. "I don't know, sir."

"Guess."

He huffed. "Okay... I suppose I knew what I could do, and I wasn't scared ta do it. No one was expectin' me ta be anything great. I was just me. Doin' what I knew how ta do."

"Thank you for being honest about yourself."

Vance looked down. "You're welcome, sir."

"Brewer, tell me why there are two seats in the starlancer."

A confused expression plastered Vance's face. "Well, one ta fly an' one ta operate SEDAR intercept."

Royce nodded. "And why don't they each have a stick?"

"Wha—That'd be a little redundant. You only need one pilot. And the RIO has his hands full runnin' Intercept and watchin' their six."

"So, what I hear you saying is: if both of them were pilots, half of them would be unnecessary?"

Vance nodded. "Yeah, 'cus—" He blinked and set down his bottle. He looked around, lost in thought. Then he picked up his bottle to take a drink, but instead hesitated and set it back down. "If'n I am the same as somebody else, I'm not necessary?"

Royce set down his pocket knife. "We don't need another Royce Williams. We've already got one. Why did Nova send us Vance Brewer? What is it that he has, that nobody else does?"

Vance took another drink.

"My advice is this: Don't chase down what everybody else is. Find out what you're really good at, grab a hold of the stick, and hit your afterburner. When you become the Ace of what you do best, you will become indispensable."

Vance set down his bottle and stared at it. "Miss Vlavskisk was right. S'pose I *am* in the buffet."

"The buffet is brought on when you are trying too hard. If you fight too hard, you'll stall. But if you power down a little, you can leave the buffet and still change course."

Vance smiled at Royce. "Thank you, sir."

Chapter 32
FINAL EXAM

It is still a matter of debate exactly when the decline of the Ancients resulted in the Mori. With incomplete records and limited accounts to glean, the best date we can estimate is in the one-hundred eleventh year of the Mori (about four-thousand six-hundred and fifty-nine years before the Year of Infamy). The Great Frontier provided complete safety from external threats, which turned their culture into one of idleness and perpetual contentment. That is the generally accepted year that marks the delineation of the Ancients and the Mori.

—FROM "GALACTIC HISTORY VOL. III" BY PROF. EZRA DOUGHERTY

Vance strolled across the flight deck toward his starlancer. He kept his helmet under his arm and walked up to his plane captain, a 32-year-old flight deck crewman in a brown jacket. "Adamson, how is she?"

"Pre-flight is good, sir."

Vance bumped fists with him. "I love that you take such good care of her."

He smiled. "Thank you, sir."

Vance stepped onto the rolling staircase.

"Vance!" Valerie called, running across the flight deck.

He stepped off the staircase. "Valerie, I'm so glad ta see you."

She shook her head. "Royce has been looking for you. Dawes moved up your final exam date to today."

"What? I still have a week!"

"Royce is trying to fight it. But it looks like you're scheduled to take your final exam this afternoon at fourteen hundred hours."

"Kreket!"

She pointed a finger at him. "Vance, don't say kreket anymore. Instead, say Blast it; it's less crude."

Vance ran his hand across his face. "Blast it! I have ta learn ta talk and fly at the same time."

She scowled.

"Sorry, Valerie. It's just turned into one of those days." Something behind Valerie caught his attention. He looked past her and saw Dawes walking across the flight deck. "Hey, miss, that's him. That's Dawes. I'm gonna talk with him."

"What are you going to do? Ask him nicely to postpone?"

Vance smiled. "I got about as much confidence in that as I do sproutin' feathers. But if there's one thing I learned from Hans, you can learn a lot from someone's reactions."

Valerie followed Vance as he hurried over to the starlancer Dawes was approaching. Dawes turned and looked at Vance. Vance stopped and stood at attention. "Wind Captain Dawes, sir, Squire Brewer reporting to ask a question."

Dawes looked at him blankly. "At ease, squire."

Vance widened his stance and put his hands behind his back. "Sir, I have just been informed that my final exam for flight training has been misscheduled. My last day of training is next week, sir."

"There's been no mistake, squire. Your exam date was moved to today due to flight scheduling." Dawes turned to climb the rolling staircase.

"Beggin' your pardon, sir. Wouldn't it have been less taxing on a trainee to move the date *later*, instead of sooner?"

Dawes spun around. "We tolerate only the very best, Squire Brewer. Now if a grease monkey can't muster the skills by the date allotted, then you're wasting everybody's time. Dismissed."

Vance stood back at attention. "Good day, sir."

Dawes ascended the stairs and got into his starlancer. Vance walked with Valerie back to his. She looked at him. "What did you learn from his reaction?"

"It sounds like he still sees me as a junior enlisted, not worthy to join the ranks, so to speak. I think I got some back-to-back training I need ta do. Might I be able ta count on your help, miss?"

"Always," she replied.

They reached his starlancer. "Will you fly in the aggressor role for me? I need ta practice my dogfighting."

She smiled. "I'll change into my flight suit and meet you out there."

Vance smiled back. "Thank you, miss." He turned around and climbed up into his starlancer and strapped in. Adamson gave him a hand signal and he started the engines. The turbines groaned to life. Adamson signaled to a plane director who took over guiding the starcraft. He signaled for Vance to taxi forward. Vance inched the throttle up and the engines roared. His starlancer rolled forward and down the lane. The next plane director guided him over to the runway.

He laid his head back against the headrest. "I am *so* in the buffet." His white knuckles clutched the stick. He took a few deep breaths. "Power back, power back." He eased up his grip. "Power back..." He relaxed his hand and flexed his fingers a few times.

Vance heard the radio chatter from his helmet. "AberrantStar, you are Training-one-three to Mother."

"Roger Carillon."

"Training thirteen, cleared for launch. Be advised there is an ion storm warning in effect."

"Training, roger and thank you." He gave a salute to The Shooter on deck. The Shooter pointed to each of the flight deck operators before dropping to one knee with his arm pointed forward. Vance was thrown back into his seat as the space door flew by. He grabbed the stick and promptly rolled the starlancer upside down and back around.

Freedom, he thought. *If only I could soar through the stars forever.*

Vance settled into a gentle turn and went through each of the basic maneuvers. Then he went through all of the advanced maneuvers. The amount of grace that he performed in each one convinced him his challenge would be in dogfighting.

Vance glanced at his small SEDAR scope and saw an incoming yellow dot. Vance switched on the transmission. "Starburst, this is AberrantStar. Glad you could join the party."

Vance heard a rapid beeping in his ear. He glanced down to his SEDAR and saw the flashing red word, LOCK. "Kreket!" He broke hard right and steered into the path of the incoming starcraft. Both starlancers merged and passed each other. Vance rolled left and circled around. The other starlancer reversed and began circling in the other direction. Vance lightly tapped his braking thruster and managed to get his nose angled toward the other starlancer. He gave his afterburner a short burst and leveled out.

The other starlancer pulled up into a vertical turn. Vance followed. When they reached the top of the loop the starlancer rolled right and dove. Vance struggled to keep up with the turns. Vance flipped a switch on his stick and the missile targeting computer activated. The starlancer broke left and Vance rolled into a tight turn to keep his nose on target.

The targeting computer beeped a few times and then hummed a low pitch. Vance huffed in frustration and flipped the switch over to guns. He gave his afterburner a short burst and followed the starlancer into another fierce set of tight turns. After each turn, he noticed his nose was getting farther and farther out of the attack angle. He tapped his braking thruster once more. His nose lined back up but the other starlancer pulled farther away.

He needed to keep his speed up, but using too much afterburner could cause him to overshoot. It was time for a gamble. Vance hit his afterburner and bolted forward. The starlancer broke left and Vance whizzed straight past. "Krek—Blast!"

He broke right and circled around. The starlancer circled around to his six o'clock. Vance reversed and rolled left while pressing into a dive. He glanced at his SEDAR scope and the yellow dot was at his 4 o'clock. Vance pulled his turn even tighter. The starlancer merged and crossed right past him.

Vance straightened out slightly to gain some more speed. Then he pulled around into another circle. He saw the starlancer coming around right at him. Vance rolled right into the path of the oncoming starlancer. Then quickly reversed and rolled out, pulling the trigger as he did so. He heard a series of beeps in his ear. He merged and passed the starlancer. He looked down at the SEDAR screen and the yellow dot turned gray.

"AberrantStar, this is Starburst. Looks like you got me."

Vance let out a loud exhale. "You really know how ta get a guy's blood pumpin'."

"Well, Dawes did say I could have been one of the best Fire Lance pilots. By the way, that was a very bold shot."

"That was a desperate shot."

"It was effective," she admitted. "And I'm glad you remembered to conserve your speed. You never would have pulled back into a scissor if you hadn't."

Vance pulled out his kneeboard and started writing down the maneuvers of the fight. "I was expectin' a little 'hello, how are ya' before we started."

Valerie pulled her starlancer alongside Vance. "Come on AberrantStar, you know in a real engagement the Mori won't announce they're about to attack you."

"Yeah they will, it's called the moment they show up on SEDAR." They both laughed.

"Would you like to go again?"

Vance finished scribbling in his kneeboard and closed it up. "Yes. Only let's do it near the Crosis planet. I wanna toss some gravity in."

"You won't be graded on a gravity engagement."

"If you didn't much like a student, and you wanted ta make sure they failed, what would you do?"

"You've got a good point," she admitted. "I'll give you a 3-minute head start."

Vance hit his afterburner and rocketed forward.

After a few minutes, Vance saw the speck in the distance. He glanced down to his SEDAR to verify it was the correct planet. He pushed the throttle up to maximum and watched the planet slowly get bigger. "Hello, Crosis. You ready to help me dance?"

A few moments later, Vance felt the pull of the upper orbit. Vance looked down at his SEDAR. A yellow dot approached. "Hello, Miss Vlavskisk," he said to himself. "Would ya care to dance?" He backed off on the throttle and waited for the yellow dot to get closer. Then he hit his afterburner and rolled toward the planet. Valerie swung into his 5 o'clock. He sharpened his turn into the planet's gravity.

The yellow dot on his SEDAR slowly got farther away. Vance suddenly heard a rapid beeping in his ear. He pulled up and sank into his seat as he fought against gravity. The rapid beeping stopped. He rolled left and hit his afterburner. Valerie headed straight for his 3 o'clock. He tapped his braking thruster and angled his nose right at her. They merged, passing each other. Vance reversed his roll and circled around.

Valerie pulled around in a similar circle. Vance quickly glanced back at the planet and took note of its position. Then looked back at Valerie's starlancer. She pulled around and they passed each other again. Vance pulled up into a climb, his starlancer slowed by the pull of gravity. He kept his eyes on Valerie and then rolled into a descent. His starlancer quickly picked up speed. Vance tapped the braking thruster. Valerie pulled up into a climb. Vance rolled and also pulled hard into a climb.

He panted. His vision narrowed.

"AberrantStar, you're pulling too many G's. Level off or you'll blackout!"

Vance obeyed. His vision returned and he started breathing normally again. "Roger Starburst. What just happened there?"

"When you pull away from gravity that hard, you're experiencing gravity many times greater than you're used to. It was pulling blood away from your brain. You don't want to go unconscious in a dogfight."

"I guess I have a little more ta learn about gravity."

"Oh, by the way," she said.

Vance heard multiple beeps in his ear and his SEDAR screen grayed out. "Alright, alright. We're one for one." He pulled into a gentle turn.

Valerie pulled up alongside him. "We'll need to refuel before our next engagement."

"One sec," he replied. "I need to write down my maneuvers from the engagement." He quickly pulled out his kneeboard and quickly scribbled down his arrows and lines.

"And you'll want to get a good lunch before—" Valerie's starlancer lurched forward with full afterburner and started spiraling.

"Starburst?" Vance hit his afterburner and rolled into a short turn and chased after her. "I thought you wanted to refuel before engaging again."

"Vance, I've lost control!"

"Power back your thrust!"

"It's not responding!"

"Can you level out?"

"Turning thrusters are not responding either!"

Vance gripped his stick tighter. "I'll keep you on SEDAR but I have power back. Your afterburner will run through the rest of your fuel in no time. I'll reserve mine so I can tow you back."

"None of the controls are responding!"

"Cut electrical power and restart!"

Her starlancer spun farther and farther away from him. Then her afterburner shut off along with all lights on the starlancer. It continued to roll through space. Then the lights turned on and she ignited her engines. The starlancer leveled out and stopped the spin.

"Good thinking AberrantStar. The restart seems to have corrected the malfunction."

"Just thinkin' like a grease monkey, miss." Vance pressed a few buttons and flipped a switch. He heard a motor moaning as the tow cable hatch opened. "I'm gonna give you a tow. I don't know how much fuel you have left but you should save it for landing."

"Roger AberrantStar."

Vance pulled his starlancer in front of hers and extended the cable. Once he heard it latch, he gently rolled and circled around. "We'll have you back to New Carillon shortly."

"What happened?"

"I don't know, but I intend ta find out." A few minutes later, the specks of the fleet appeared in the distance. "Home sweet home."

"Did you ever see Earth?" she asked.

"Once. When I was small. My mother took me on a vacation trip. It was like a little miracle. Blue water all over the place, green trees. Oh, and the smell was amazing. It was like breathing fresh linen and holly blossoms."

"I never got to see it," she said. "I grew up on Phi Coronae 1. Trips to Earth were too expensive."

"I wish I could rewind time and take you there."

He heard a voice in his ear. "Training thirteen, Carillon marshal."

"Training thirteen, go."

"Training thirteen, you are cleared to land. Call the ball."

"Negative Carillon. Caliber twelve fuel state is critical. Releasing tow."

"Roger Training thirteen. Your signal Charlie."

"Starburst, I'll meet you on the flight deck."

"Roger AberrantStar."

Vance detached the tow cable and pulled into a wide turn, circling New Carillon for another pass. When he finally came back around, he leveled off his trajectory toward the open space door.

He heard a voice in his helmet. "In the groove, call the ball."

"Paddles, Training thirteen, starlancer, 'AberrantStar', ball, fuel state 1.3, manual."

"Roger, ball. Left to line up."

Vance slightly adjusted his heading, keeping his eye on the indicator lights. He flew through the space door and was promptly thrown forward into his safety straps. Once inertia caught up with him, he sat back and looked out the canopy to locate the closest plane director on the flight deck.

He taxied off the runway and down the recovery lane until he was instructed where to stop and cut his engines. Vance opened the canopy and climbed down the rolling staircase. He took off his helmet and looked around for Valerie. She stood next to the adjacent starlancer.

He rushed to her side. "Doin' alright?"

She nodded. "Yeah, I asked for the Aerospace Machinists to give it a rundown."

Vance smiled. "I might know a thing or two about a starfighter's inner workin's."

She leaned her head back. "Oh, that's right. All the grease monkey references."

He handed his helmet to Valerie and climbed up the rolling staircase. He reached into the cockpit and flipped on the rudimentary power switch. Descending the staircase, he put his hand on the starlancer's fuselage. He closed his eyes and moved his hand down the spaceframe and under the wing. He stopped and waved his hand over a sensor panel and a hatch popped open. He lifted the lid and ran his fingers across the circuit boards.

In the distance, the *beep, beep, beep* of the starcraft tractor echoed down the flight deck. It pulled up to the starlancer and a man in a blue jacket hopped out and attached the starlancer to the tractor. Vance closed the hatch and backed off. The tractor driver hopped back into the tractor and started hauling the starlancer over to the machinist bays.

Valerie walked up to Vance. "Did you figure out what was wrong?"

He nodded. "When they run the diag we'll know for sure. But I'll bet you anything it was a massive bit-flip."

"A what?"

"Long story short: your craft was hit with a large dose of ionized particles. It confused your main controller circuit. Looks like that ion storm is rollin' in."

Valerie handed Vance back his helmet. "I guess I kinda ruined last-minute dogfighting practice."

"Negative miss, it was the storm. Could've happened to anybody—well, anybody in that exact spot at that exact time."

She grimaced. "Well, are you hungry for some lunch?"

"Yeah, but I'd better stay and give my starlancer a once-over. I wanna make sure she doesn't give me any troubles during my final exam."

"Doesn't your plane captain take care of that?" she asked.

"Yeah, but I'd feel better knowin' for sure."

"I'll bring you some lunch then."

Vance smiled. "Thank you, miss. I appreciate that."

She smiled back as she left.

Vance spent the next hour inspecting his starlancer. He combed every inch of the spaceframe and circuit boards. Then he pulled out his kneeboard and went over all his notes on the last several engagements.

Valerie walked up with a bundle in her arm. Vance looked up, inhaled, and closed his eyes. "Ah, you brought Randolpho's!"

She smirked. "Oh, don't let me interrupt."

He laughed. "I'm hopelessly distracted now." He put away his kneeboard. "Allow me ta help with that."

Valerie handed him the bundle and she climbed up the rolling staircase. She stepped onto the top of the starlancer. Vance followed and handed off the bundle before joining her. Valerie handed Vance a napkin and spread one for herself. Vance gazed out across the long flight deck. His eyes surveyed the long rows of landed starfighters and shuttles. "You know, Valerie, I don't think I can go back."

She handed him a gyro wrapped in foil. "Back to what?"

He took a big whiff of his gyro and savored the smell with his eyes closed. "Nothin' beats that smell." He took a bite.

"Back to what?" she repeated.

"Back to bein' a machinist. After everything that I've seen and learned. After everything I've done." He shook his head. "By Nova, I've been dancing with starlancers among the heavens! I've been in the jet stream of a pulsar. I've fought by your side against the Mori. I—"

"Saved my life." She said, unwrapping her gyro and taking a bite.

Vance smiled. "Saved *each other's* lives. I just... I don't think I can go back to the way it was before." He took another bite.

"Just promise me one thing, Vance."

"Sure, anything."

"Forget about failure."

He nearly took another bite but hesitated. "It's a pass-or-fail grade. How can I *not* think about failure?"

"Look, I'm not trying to sound half-cocked. But I'm going to shoot it to you straight. When you're up there, not worrying about failure, you're good. But when you doubt yourself, you crumble."

"What do ya mean? I'm always doubtin' myself?"

"No, you're not. When you threw your last force field, you didn't wonder if you'd fail."

He thought a moment. "Yeah, but that was an extreme circumstance."

"Listen to me, when you're shooting from the hip, you accomplish amazing things. I saw you disable a space door!"

He shook his head. "This is not the same thing. This is flyin'. I'm not using The Winds for flyin'."

"Vance, why aren't you? Do you think the Fire Lance fly without using The Winds?"

Vance blinked and stared into space. For some reason, that thought hadn't occurred to him. If all Solar Knights specialized in using The Winds one way or another, it would stand to reason the Fire Lance would use it to aid them in flying. The memory of his first flight with Royce flooded into his mind. "Now that you mention it, I remember Sky Captain Williams rammed a Mori carrier. He put his hands on the side rails and the whole starlancer had a red glow to it. We passed through the enemy carrier like a bullet through canvas..."

"To the Fire Lance, their starlancer is a part of them, a symbiosis. They have an almost spiritual connection to it. They can listen to it, learn its name—"

"Lleona," Vance blurted out. "Sky Captain Williams's starlancer has a name, and I heard it once. And at the Banquet Table, when you heard that, you left. What was that about?"

She looked down.

"...or is that a touchy subject?" he asked.

"I'm not ready to talk about it."

"I understand." He took another bite.

"Vance, what I've been trying to tell you is that even if you think you're shooting blanks, just keep firing. Don't stop to doubt yourself. Don't stop to ask yourself if you're going to make it. Never take your eye off the target and keep shooting until the exam is over."

Vance glanced down. "Kinda like the whole 'do your best, leave to Nova the rest' thing?"

She took another bite of her gyro.

"What if my best isn't good enough?" he asked.

"Squire Brewer." A voice called from below.

Vance looked over the side of the starlancer. "Sky Captain Williams, sir." Vance saw Royce dressed in his red duty uniform with navy blue trim.

"You ready for your final?"

Vance shrugged. "S'pose I'm as ready as I'll ever be." Valerie started gathering up the remains of lunch. Vance climbed off the starlancer and down the staircase.

He heard a voice several paces away. "Hey hey, Vance the Lance!"

He turned around and saw Hans walking over to him. Vance smiled. "Hans the Bronze! You come to watch my final exam?"

"Racing comets couldn't keep me away," he replied, with a wide grin. Hans walked up to Vance and Royce.

"And Royce the Voice! An excellent squire you have here. It's been a privilege getting to know him."

Royce smiled. "Thank you for taking such great care of him."

"My pleasure, Royce the Voice, my pleasure." Hans turned to Vance. "So, you nervous?"

"Yeah, I feel like my nerves are all armed and locked on target."

Hans chuckled. "Nervousness is simply the language of performance. It's your body's way of saying: it's showtime!"

Vance sighed. "Yeah, Miss Vlavskisk has been tellin' me ta do my best and not worry about failin'."

"It's not enough to do your best," Royce said. "You must also *believe* you are the best."

Vance narrowed his eyes, puzzled. "But I'm not the best."

"Says who?"

Vance huffed a slight chuckle. "Says our dogfighting practices."

"Brewer, you'll never be the best until you decide you already are. Your mind is the pilot of your performance. And a craft is only as good as its pilot."

"He's right," Hans said. "Excellence is not something you discover, it's something you choose."

Royce turned to his left and stood at attention. "Wind Captain Dawes."

Vance also turned and stood at attention. Dawes walked up to them. "As you were." He looked at Vance. "There's an ion storm warning, so we'll be starting a few minutes early. You will be tested on handling, reaction time, and precision. Do you have any questions?"

"Negative, sir."

Dawes nodded and looked over to Valerie who was descending the staircase. "Miss Vlavskisk, I have you listed as RIO for Squire Brewer's exam. Is that correct?"

"That is correct."

He turned back to Vance. "See you in the stars, Squire Brewer. Dismissed." Dawes walked on past. Adamson walked around the starlancer and began the pre-flight inspection.

Vance took a deep breath and turned to Hans. "History made me last time. I'm makin' history this time."

"That's the spirit, Vance the Lance."

Vance turned to Valerie. "All right, Starburst, you ready to dance?"

She smiled. "True-blue, sticking with you."

She climbed up the staircase and Vance followed. They sat down in the starlancer and put their helmets on. Vance switched on initial power and assisted Adamson in the pre-flight checks. Then, on his signal, Vance ignited the engines. They roared to life. He flipped a switch and the canopy closed. He taxied the starlancer down the lane, following the signals of the plane directors until he was positioned on the runway.

Vance heard the radio chatter in his ear through his helmet. "AberrantStar, you are Training One-Three to Mother."

"Roger Carillon." Vance switched off the transmission. "Starburst, I want ta thank you for talkin' with me."

"Anytime, AberrantStar."

"Training thirteen, cleared for launch. Be advised there is an ion storm warning in effect."

Vance switched the transmission back on. "Training, roger and thank you." He turned and saluted The Shooter. A moment later, they were thrown back into their seats as the space door flew by.

Vance pulled into a gentle turn and leveled out. A voice spoke through his helmet. "Training thirteen, this is Firefly. I will be monitoring and recording your progress. Good luck."

"Roger Firefly, see you at my winging ceremony."

A third voice entered the conversation. "You'll first have to pass your final exam, AberrantStar."

"Roger, Wind Captain Dawes. Requesting your callsign, sir."

"EarlyDawn."

"Roger EarlyDawn."

"AberrantStar, there will be a series of three engagements; offensive, defensive, and neutral. You are not required to get the kill, although it will earn you more points. You will also follow any directions Firefly gives you during the engagements."

"Roger EarlyDawn."

Dawes pulled in front of Vance a little way ahead. Vance heard Royce's voice in his ear. "On my mark. Three, two, one, fight's on."

Dawes hit his afterburner and rocketed forward. Vance hit his afterburner and followed. Dawes rolled into a turn and Vance pulled in behind. Dawes tightened his turn and Vance struggled to keep his nose angled. Dawes reversed the roll and pulled out the other direction. Vance followed behind and tapped his braking thruster. His nose lined up. He flicked the switch on his stick to arm missiles. He heard the growl of the targeting computer in his ear and Dawes broke right into a tight turn. Vance rolled into the turn but couldn't keep his nose lined up. Dawes slipped out of Vance's 12 o'clock and began a tight circle.

"Kreket!—sorry Valerie."

"Forget your language right now, AberrantStar! Just focus on getting back into the saddle!"

"Ma'am, yes ma'am."

"AberrantStar, he's pulling out of defensive and into a neutral position. We've lost the advantage."

"Not the best way to begin my exam..."

Dawes circled back around as Vance completed his loop. They merged, passing each other. Vance rolled to the right and Dawes rolled left. They looped around toward each other in one large circle.

"Starburst, he accepted the one circle fight. See if you can jam his missile lock, just in case."

"Roger."

"I'm bettin' he's gonna do the same before the merge." Vance flicked the switch on his stick and armed his guns.

Dawes and Vance merged again, passing each other. Vance rolled left and Dawes again rolled right. They looped around in another large circle. Vance pulled hard into his turn and lined up his nose. He realized he was just a little too far away. He gave his afterburner a short burst.

"What are you doing AberrantStar!"

"I need ta close the distance."

"You're going to overshoot!"

Dawes pulled his turn tighter and Vance flew straight past. "Blast it!"

"You're too impatient, AberrantStar. Dogfighting is a dance. Be patient and let each of the loops bring you closer to your target."

"Space it all! What am I thinkin'?" he said. "Even Firefly told me that."

"Bandit is forming up on our six."

Vance hit his braking thruster hard and broke left. The starlancer shuddered a moment. Dawes pulled head-on into the turn. Vance heard a series of beeps in his ear.

"Blast it!"

"AberrantStar, this is Firefly. Level out and bring your throttle back to military. Prepare for the next engagement."

Vance slammed his head back against the headrest. "I just blew the easiest engagement."

"You can throw yourself a pity party later," Valerie said with a slight hint of annoyance. "We're on defensive this time. Bandit is starting at 7 o'clock high."

"On my mark," Royce said. "Three, two, one, fight's on."

Vance hit his afterburner and rolled into a dive. Dawes quickly rolled into pursuit. Vance pulled into a tight turn and then quickly reversed. He hit his afterburner and rocketed away.

"Nice one, AberrantStar. You faked him out but he's coming around."

Vance hit his braking thruster and pulled hard around. "At least now we're in a neutral position." He switched back to missiles and lined up on Dawes. His targeting computer beeped a few times and then hummed a low pitch. "Aw, he jammed me already."

"He's not forgetting you got an early lock on him last time."

Vance switched to guns. "I'll take that as braggin' rights."

Vance and Dawes merged and passed each other. Vance pulled tight into a turn with some elevation. Dawes pulled into a short turn toward Vance. They merged again and passed.

"You've got him into a nice scissor, AberrantStar. Remember, it's a dance."

"Vance the Lance is in a dance..." he said to himself.

Turn after turn, merge after merge, Vance kept pressing but he couldn't seem to get any advantage on Dawes.

"I can't seem ta get my nose on him."

"Don't do it," Valerie said.

"Don't do what?"

"Don't even think about your braking thruster."

"AberrantStar, this is Firefly. Brake off and level out for your next engagement."

"Firefly, sir, the engagement isn't over yet."

"Negative squire. You're essentially in the scissor's version of a Lufbery. You've stalemated. Setup for your final engagement."

"Aye sir," Vance said with his heart sinking.

"It's alright AberrantStar," Valerie said, in a soft voice. "You don't have to get the kill."

"Yeah, but I sure could use some extra points right about now."

Vance broke off and leveled out. "Starburst?"

"What is it?"

"...if'n I don't end up earnin' my wings, could you and I still be close?"

She huffed. "Don't be a neutron-head; my heart orbits *you*, not your wings."

Vance smiled. "I think that could be enough for me."

"On my mark," Royce announced. "Three, two, one, fight's on."

"Okay, talk ta me, Starburst. Where is he?"

"He's on your one o'clock approaching the merge. Do you see him?"

"Negative," he admitted.

"Turn in left a bit and you should be coming in right at him."

Vance gently adjusted his angle. Vance spotted Dawes's starlancer flying low. "Tally on bandit."

Vance pulled up into a climb and rolled around. He leveled off behind Dawes. Warning lights blinked all across Vance's instrumentation panel. A loud screeching alarm blared in the cockpit. "That the—"

"AberrantStar, every alarm on my panel is lit up!"

"Yeah, mine too. Either we're stalling *and* spinning out *and* bingo fuel *and* have a missile locked on us *and* all these others, or it's a major instrumentation failure."

Valerie screamed.

"What? Valerie!"

She groaned in pain. "I got a shock from my instrument panel."

Vance's eyes lit up. "Hold on, miss." Vance killed his engines and cut power to the cockpit. Seconds later, Vance was thrown to the side of the starlancer. The starlancer started rolling, drifting off course.

Valerie clutched her aching hand. "What's going on?"

"The ion storm has arrived."

Chapter 33
ION STORM

Date: 10 Novenary
Subject: Operational concern
*Notes: The asset has proven more resourceful
than previously anticipated. These interruptions
have proved detrimental to the operation. The
decision has been made that the usefulness of this
asset has expired.*

—FROM "DOSSIER #13" CLASSIFIED

The lights in the cockpit lit up. The instrumentation panel turned on. Vance saw the SEDAR screen light up and start tracking. "Okay, this is a bit freaky. I turned the systems off, and yet they're bein' powered."

"You probably just bumped the switch," Valerie said, still in pain.

"Negative, miss. It's still switched off. We're gettin' power from somewhere but not from me."

"From the storm?" she asked.

Vance shrugged. "I guess."

Valerie groaned again.

"Ya know, miss, this is giving me some serious déjà vu."

"Well next time it'll be your turn to be sitting back here in pain."

Vance looked out the canopy. The stars swirled around the starlancer. "Let's see if I can reignite the engines an' stop our spin."

Vance pressed the ignition button and felt all the muscles in his arm instantly tense up. A sharp pain surged through his hand and up his arm. "Ahhh! Kreket! Holy frazzin—" He held his breath a moment, clutching his hand. "...I meant, blast it."

Valerie laughed. "Thanks for remembering."

Vance massaged his hand and wrist.

"AberrantStar, are we spinning faster?"

Vance looked out the canopy and took note of the stars whizzing around. "I want ta say yes, but we can't be. 'Cus the thrusters are offline."

"No, we are definitely spinning faster."

"How? The thrusters didn't fire!"

"Vance! Why are you yelling?"

Vance pursed his lips and closed his eyes. "Sorry miss. I guess today has been less than ideal. What else could cause us to spin faster?"

"Well, gravity," she said. "But I don't see a planet."

"I wonder how far off course we are..."

Valerie pushed buttons and then flipped a switch. The transparent surface of the canopy faded into a red hue followed by a blue hue. A light among the stars flashed as it flew past the canopy.

"Oh, blast! There's our answer," Valerie said.

"But we're nowhere near Clarissa."

"AberrantStar, either that is Clarissa or we've just discovered a new pulsar—either way, we have to get the engines back online."

Vance huffed a sigh of exasperation. "I'd love to, miss, but I've had my fair share of *shocking* revelations for one day."

"Well, we had better do something!"

"I know, I know." Vance leaned his head back and mumbled to himself. "I'm in the buffet, power down. I just need ta power down." Vance turned toward Valerie as best he could. "Okay Starburst, please help me find what I'm missin'. I gotta understand how this storm is affecting us."

"You know more about the storm than I do."

"I need a pair of fresh eyes. For instance, how do we have electricity when I shut down the electric?"

She sighed, annoyed at the task. "I don't know. What makes an ion storm?"

"Please be patient with me, miss. An ion storm is a huge cloud of ionized particles with a magnetic field. It gets ejected from a star. An' I'm prob'ly oversimplifyin' it—"

"Wait a minute, magnetic?"

"Yeah, why? That mean somethin'?"

"AberrantStar, an electric current creates a magnetic field. It also works in reverse. A magnetic field in motion will generate an electrical current."

Vance wrinkled his brow. "Not sure I'm followin' you, miss."

"The moving magnetic field of the storm is generating electricity in the starlancer's wiring."

"Okay, okay. So maybe we can create a magnetic field of our own to deflect some of the storm's field. An' maybe I can ignite the engines without electrocutin' myself."

"The starlancer has electromagnets in the spaceframe for the catapult and the arresting magnets."

Vance shook his head. "We're gonna need somethin' more powerful than that to counteract a solar storm, right?"

"You're the grease monkey, remember? Can't you rewire it or something to enhance it?"

Vance huffed in frustration. "There's not a whole lot I can do from the cockpit!"

"Well, then I hope you brought a jacket because it's a little chilly outside!"

Vance laid his head back and snickered. "I'm sorry, miss, but that was funny."

Valerie crossed her arms. "Well, I'm glad you think I'm funny!"

"Here we are, tumbling into a pulsar's gravity and we're bickerin' like an old married couple."

Valerie failed to suppress a laugh. "Okay, admirer, I see your point. So what do we do?"

"Well, I like your electromagnet idea. Let me see if I can access the wiring from my instrumentation panel." Vance pulled out a small pocket knife from his flight suit pocket. He used the blade in place of a screwdriver. He twisted but the screw stubbornly stayed in place. He twisted harder. *Snap.* "Aw, blast."

"What's wrong?"

"Let's just say these screws aren't exactly hand tightened. I don't suppose you have a pocket knife or somethin' we can use for a screwdriver?"

"I'm afraid not."

Vance rested his head back and mumbled to himself. "Think, think, think..."

"Maybe we can try to use the thrust from one of the missiles—"

Vance shot his eyes open. "I'm overthinking this! Oh, by Nova, I am *so* overthinking this!"

"Are you going to let me in on your little revelation?" she asked.

"Alls we're tryin' ta do is disrupt the electricity bein' generated by the storm long enough to reignite the engines, right?"

"You're going to sabotage the starlancer's electric systems, aren't you?"

Vance smiled. "It's so simple." He felt himself get heavier in his seat. The spinning began pulling on his equilibrium.

"AberrantStar, we're running out of time! We're definitely in the gravity pull now!"

"Wait. I can sabotage the power, but I can't be doin' that *and* ignite the engines! I don't suppose there's an engine ignition back by you is there?"

"No. I'll have to use yours."

She pulled out one of her pistols and eject the magazine.

"Please don't tell me you're gonna shoot it!"

"I'm not going to shoot it." She popped out a couple of rounds from the magazine. "Trust me. Do what you do best, and I'll do what I do best."

"Aye miss." Vance flipped the power switch on, then placed both hands on the canopy side rails. "Oh, wait a moment, wait a moment!"

"What?"

Vance pulled out a gel capsule from a zipper pocket and retrieved a small plastic pouch of water from under his seat. "Pulsars and me aren't on the best of terms."

"What do you mean?"

Vance put the gel capsule in his mouth. Then he tore off the top of the water pouch and drank. "I guess you could say it's a rather revealing relationship." He placed both hands on the side rails. "Okay, now I'm ready." He closed his eyes. He envisioned purple wavy lines passing through the starlancer. He pictured those lines creating yellow dotted lines circling inside the starlancer. He focused his attention on the circling dotted lines. He imagined placing his hands between the purple wavy lines and the circling yellow dotted lines. Then, he imagined the purple lines bouncing off his hands.

Vance heard a bullet thrown at the canopy, bounce, and hit his console. Then he felt the bullet hit his helmet visor. He flinched. *Concentrate Vance,* he thought. *Keep holding it.* Vance heard another bullet thrown against the canopy, bounce, and hit his console. The engine turbines whined and revved up, roaring to life.

Vance opened his eyes and grabbed the stick and throttle. "Great shot, miss!" He rolled the starlancer to correct for the spin and leveled out. He felt the mighty pull of the pulsar fighting against him. "Starburst, I need ta see the pulsar again. Can you do that thing with the canopy so I can see it?"

Valerie pressed a few buttons and flipped a switch. The transparent surface of the canopy glowed red and then blue. Vance saw the flashing light in the distance. He rolled and pushed his throttle to full. The starlancer tugged against the pulsar's grasp. He looked down and pressed another couple of buttons and looked up.

He no longer saw the cockpit. He no longer heard the sounds from the cockpit. It seemed as if he were in a dream. A burning heat flared behind him. He turned around to see high roaring flames in the lading bay of a starcraft carrier. Across the bay, a short dart-shaped Mori starcraft plowed through the open space door and into the flight deck. Explosions sent debris and men flying across the bay.

A voice yelled in the distance, "Foul deck, foul deck!"

"AD3 Brewer," another voice called.

Vance turned around. His old pilot friend from his home carrier stood a few feet away. "Sedston?"

"This is all your fault," he said with an echo. Then the image of Sedston faded away.

"There, you see," a voice said on his left. "The carrier will take damage."

Number 1 stood beside Number 22, watching as they conversed. Something was different about them compared to the other people Vance saw. They didn't seem to fit the lighting, like a poor photo editing job. He didn't see the glow of the fire on them nor did he see any shadows about them. "But there's no guarantee the carrier will be destroyed," Number 1 said.

"No," Number 22 said. "To increase our odds, we would—"

"What is he doing here?" Number 1 demanded, pointing to Vance.

Number 22 shook his head. "It's highly unlikely it's actually him. It's probably just an echo."

"I'd like to be sure," Number 1 replied, taking off his glasses. *Number 13, who were the last three people you met in nightclubs?*

Vance stared at Number 1. "I'm willin' ta bet the jack isn't nearly as wild as what's goin' on right now."

Number 1's eyes widened.

"Vance!" Valerie's voice sounded distant but urgent. "Vance!"

Vance blinked and the vision was gone. "I'm here!" He looked out the canopy and saw the large flashes of the pulsar. They were too close. Vance tightened his grip on the stick. He pulled hard and hit his afterburner. The starlancer pulled against the gravity field but gained no distance. "Ah, blast it! We need more power."

"Vance, are you able to sabotage the missile clamps while flying?"

Vance removed his throttle hand and slapped it up against the side rail. He closed his eyes while keeping the stick pulled hard away from the pulsar's pull. He opened his eyes. "Best I can do!"

Valerie pressed a few buttons and launched the missiles. The missile clamps held on tightly to the missiles. The added thrust inched them farther and farther away from the grip of the pulsar. After a moment, the thrust from the missiles expired and the starlancer suddenly lurched forward as they escaped the pull of gravity.

Vance pulled back on the throttle. Laying his head back, he sighed. "Great thinking, miss."

"What happened to you back there? I kept shouting your name."

Vance blinked a few times. "The funny thing with me and pulsars is they are rather talkative." He looked at his hand and saw it shaking. "And they burn through a lot of electrolytes."

"What did you see?" she asked.

"I think I saw the Mori attackin' the Saratoga, in Alpha Fleet."

"AberrantStar, you have to tell Royce."

"There's more; I saw Number 1 and Number 22. They were talkin' like they were planning on it happening."

An uncomfortable silence hung in the air. "That doesn't make any sense. They are Solar Knights. They're sworn to protect the fleets."

"I know, I know," Vance admitted. "There's a lot that doesn't make any sense right now. I need to talk to someone who is good at solving puzzles."

"Puzzles?" she asked.

Vance thought a moment. "I gotta talk ta Hans."

Chapter 34
THE JACK IS WILD

The Gun Stars have the most practical example of simple elegance in their arms. The alternating blue and white Vair pattern sets the perfect backdrop for their philosophy of destiny. Their hollow golden star (an eight-point mullet) blends the colors into a cohesive work of art.

—FROM "GALACTIC HERALDRY" BY JEAN-CLAUDE ARMAND DUBOIS

Hans walked beside Vance down the hallway. "It does have an unsavory implication."

"But we're all human, Hans. There's no reason anybody should want ta help the Mori. They're tryin' ta kill us—all of us."

"Well, strictly speaking, there's no evidence anybody does."

Vance huffed. His blood pressure started to rise. Stating the obvious wasn't what he wanted Hans for. He needed answers, no reiterations of the problem. "That isn't—" he looked around to be sure his voice wasn't carrying. "That isn't helpful. I need to know what possible reason someone could have."

Hans stared into the distance, thinking. "If I had to guess, I'd assume our whole way of life is going to change once we cross the Great Frontier of the Ancients. And those who have invested their entire purpose into outwitting the Mori might see themselves becoming obsolete."

Vance's stride slowed to a halt. Hans was right. Vance knew from personal experience what it felt like to be needed. He didn't want to stop feeling that way. It was easy, then, to imagine the fear of becoming obsolete. "But that's so backward."

Hans turned around and smirked. "Vance, people do not operate on logic. We operate on emotion. Stop asking why anyone would logically do a thing and start asking why they would emotionally do a thing. That is where your answer lies."

"What should I do? I can't go over his head without any evidence."

"You'll need to talk to her."

"That's easier said than done; I don't even know how to contact her."

Hans smiled. "Do what an Orbiting Star would do."

Vance smiled in return. "I think I will."

After parting ways, Vance made his way over to the main hallway, outside a clothing shop with a sign that read, Wardrobe of the Order. A large black heraldic arms shield, with a gold line in a broken V-shape, hung beside the sign. Vance looked down both ends of the hallway and began pacing. He wasn't sure his idea would work, but if the direct approach didn't work last time, the indirect approach was worth a shot.

Something hit Vance's foot. It was a blue and white checkered ball. He picked it up and looked around for its owner. Three young boys jogged over to Vance. "Hey mister, that's our ball."

Vance crouched. "You got a really gabb ball here, kid. I like the colors too; it reminds me of the Gun Stars."

"That's 'cause it's a Gun Star ball," the second boy said.

"Yeah," said the third boy. "'Cause, it's a Gun Star ball. Do you know why it's a Gun Star ball?"

"I'm guessin' it's because it has this blue and white pattern on it?"

The first boy nodded. "Yeah, 'cause it has the vair on it."

Vance raised his eyebrows. "What's a vair?"

"It's the pattern in the blazon," the second boy answered. "Guess what? I know the blazon for the Gun Stars."

Vance faintly chuckled. "Okay, now what's a blazon?"

The third boy chimed in. "Blazon is—blazon is, like, how you spell what you see on the arms."

"The arms of the Gun Stars, is that the blue and white shield with the gold star on it?" Vance asked.

"Yeah," the second boy said. "And I know the blazon for the Gun Stars."

Vance smiled. "Okay, kid, can you tell me the blazon for the Gun Stars?"

He nodded. "Vair, a mullet of eight points voided interlaced, or."

Vance looked confused. "Or what?"

The boys laughed. "No silly," the first boy said. "Or means the color gold."

Vance handed the ball back. "Okay, alright. Do you boys know any other blazons?"

The second boy turned to the others. "We know all the blazons, huh?" The other boys agreed.

"Okay, squirt, do ya know the blazon for the Orbiting Star?"

"That's a long one," the third boy announced.

"Oh, but I thought you boys knew all the blazons?" Vance said.

The second boy put the ball on the ground and stepped one foot on top. "Um, that one is, per pale nebuly or and vert, an annulet counterchanged, a star or in sinister chief."

"My goodness, you weren't kidding, that was a long one." Vance held up his hand. "Alright, give me a high-five."

The boys stared at him. Vance glanced at his hand. "What? You boys don't do high-fives?"

They shook their heads and one answered, "No."

"Aw, c'mon, my kid brother and I used to always do high-fives."

"Nah, we just do knuckles," the first boy replied.

Vance smiled wide. "Okay, then gimme some knuckles." He bumped fists with each of the boys. "Okay, now what's another blazon you boys know?"

The second boy tried to balance standing on the ball a few times. "Um, Virtus Oco—ocolu—that one," the boy said, pointing to the shield beside the shop sign.

"Ah, the Virtus Occulatum?"

"Yeah, it's easy. It's sable, a chevron inverted removed or."

Vance snickered. "Or what?"

The boys laughed together. "Nah, nah, nah, or just means gold, silly."

The second boy picked up the ball and walked up to Vance. "Are you the squire from those stories?"

"Well, you're pretty smart, kid, what do you think?"

"I think you are, 'cause you're funny," the boy said.

Vance laughed. "Oh, is that why? I guess I need to hear those stories again."

The first boy walked up closer. "Is it okay with your mom if you play with us?"

Black boots step up beside Vance. They belonged to Number 1. The smile ran off Vance's face. He turned to the boys. "It looks like I gotta do my chores first."

The boys nodded with a little disappointment and walked away. As they went off to play their game, Vance's game was about to begin. and Vance needed as many answers as he could get. Number 1 would undoubtedly seek some answers of his own. How much did Number 1 know about the impending attack on Alpha fleet? Was he allowing it to happen? Or, worse yet, was he facilitating it? And could Vance do anything about it? An inexperienced squire with no evidence didn't have much of a fighting chance to incriminate anyone.

Vance stood, motioning toward the boys. "Aw, there ya go, ruinin' my chances ta play with those three boys with their ball and clubs."

But the jack is wild.

"You're sure not very talkative Number 1."

"Well, we haven't seen each other for quite some time, Number 13, not since your formal debrief," Number 1 said as if discussing the weather. "How many weeks has it been? Twenty?"

"Twenty-one," Vance replied. "Oh, hey, speaking of formalities, I just learned your order's blazon. It's somethin' like a stable with a reverted chevron ore."

Number 1's cheek twitched. "The color is pronounced sable. It's black, like the natural color of a pulsar."

"I guess the Virtus Occulatum must have ta visit pulsars often to see their natural color."

"Oh, of course, it's no secret that we use the pulsars to peer into the future. I even took you to a pulsar once. Have you been back to see it since?"

"Well, I kinda been busy with flight training and all. That's why I'm always hopin' you guys are watchin' out for the fleets. Nova knows we don't want to lose any more ships to the Mori before we get the exodus underway."

Number 1 adjusted his dark sunglasses. "Our very mission is to protect humanity. The very soul of patriotism is acting in the best interest of humanity."

"I'm very glad you hear that, Number 1. It makes me feel safe knowin' that if the Mori were ever to attack, we would get advanced warning."

Number 1 folded his arms. "Don't create unrealistic expectations. We don't always get much warning ahead of time."

"Yeah, but sometimes you guys get a lot of warning."

Number 1 scowled. "And what makes you an expert on the Virtus Occulatum? You think a fluke episode with a pulsar makes you an expert on precognition? Let me offer you some advice, young squire, don't let delusions of grandeur cloud your judgment."

Vance wanted to smile but he resisted. It looked like he had pushed the right button with Number 1; he was talking. It now made more sense why Hans taunted Star Commander Myles during the debriefing; knowing which buttons to push revealed a lot of good information. But Vance was still so new at this.

Perhaps there was a quicker way. Perhaps he didn't need to know what Number 1 knew. Maybe just letting Number 1 know that he was not the only one to see the vision would be incentive enough to ensure Number 1 did the right thing.

Vance smirked. "Well, I s'pose I could be havin' some of them delusions, but I'm willin' ta bet the jack isn't nearly as wild as what's goin' on right now."

Number 1 stared.

"Good day, Number 1. I feel safer already." Vance walked back down the hallway.

He fought against his desire to turn around and look. He wasn't sure if Number 1 was still there. It also wasn't clear if his message had been received, but somehow, it felt right to leave. So, Vance wandered back to his apartment.

Hans hovered over the coffee table setting out food from a cardboard container. He looked up. "Vance the Lance, how are you feeling?"

"A lot better after our talk." Vance walked up to the coffee table and smelled the food. The pleasing aroma of shrimp and pasta permeated his nostrils. "Aw, now that's a smell ta come home to."

"It's your victory dinner," Hans said with a smile.

"Well, it might be premature for that."

"I assume you spoke with Royce about the exam?"

Vance slumped onto the couch. "Yeah, Dawes says there won't be a retest. Some lousy rule in the regs. So they're discussin' how ta score the exam. You know, considerin' the storm an' all."

"Good," Hans announced, lifting a plastic cup. "A toast to earning your wings."

"What? C'mon, Hans. I still don't know if I've earned enough to get my wings."

Hans set down the cup and sat beside Vance. "Vance the Lance, when are you going to get it through that neutronium skull of yours. Victory doesn't start out there." He pointed to Vance's head. "It starts in here."

"Right, right," Vance said. "'I think I can, I think I can'."

Hans stared at him.

"What? Look, I know what ta do. I just can't see myself goin' around bein' all stuck up on myself."

Hans crossed his arms. "So that's what this is about."

Vance displayed a confused look on his face. "What what's about?"

"Vance, do you believe that to be confident, you have to be boastful?"

"Well... how can I go around sayin' I'm the best when I know it isn't true? That's what stuck-up people do. They say they're great and that I'm not."

Hans leaned back on the couch and looked away. "You must have had a pretty hard life."

Vance looked down. "I'd rather not talk about it."

"With people always ready and willing to tear you down."

"Hans, please. That's a dark place for me."

Hans took a piece of food with his fingers. "How do you combat the darkness?" He popped the food into his mouth.

Vance indifferently waved his head around and shrugged. "I just leave it be and try not ta wake the bear."

"You like force fields?"

Vance nodded. "Yeah, they're totally gabb."

"Well then here's a pop quiz: how do you invert the field?"

"Simple. Swap the positive and negative."

Hans smiled. "Exactly. To neutralize the negative, you pour on the positive."

Vance sat up straight. "Wait. You kiddin' me? It can't be that simple."

"Why don't you test it and find out for yourself?"

Vance smiled. "Okay, ya sold me. What do I do?"

"We're going to play a little game. It's called 'see how outrageous you can be'."

Vance chuckled. "Sounds like fun."

Hans pushed a plate over to Vance and handed him a fork. "When somebody asks you how you're doing, you say: I'm on top of my game! When somebody says you did nice work, you say: that was left-handed!"

Vance snickered.

"And when something is inconvenient, you say: keep it coming!—and you pretend it's just the way you prefer it. And when somebody asks you to do something hard, you say: give me more, drill sergeant!"

Vance chuckled and nearly dropped his fork. "That might've been useful back in basic; I don't have a drill sergeant anymore."

"Vance the Lance, that only makes it more *outrageous.*"

He laughed and pointed at Hans. "Okay, you're on. I'm game."

Vance swirled up some noodles on his fork. The humor faded and he sat in contemplation. "Hans?"

Hans looked up from his plate.

"This gonna work?" he asked.

Hans picked up a forkful of pasta. "When you get others to believe you, it's deception. When you get yourself to believe it, it's transformation. In a phrase: fake it 'til you make it."

Vance smiled. "Give me more, drill sergeant."

Hans chuckled and handed Vance a cup. "A toast, to your outrageous success!"

They tapped their plastic cups together and each took a drink.

Chapter 35
RETURN TO ALPHA FLEET

*In a carrier task force, the primary purpose of
cruisers and destroyers shall be to defend the
starcraft carrier. Enemy bombers and torpedo-craft
shall be the primary targets for anti-starcraft fire.
The carrier is the heart of the task force and the
most valuable naval asset.*

—FROM "CARRIER FLEET OPERATIONS MANUAL" BY THOMAS J.
SUTTON, UNITED EARTH NAVAL COMMAND

Vance strolled into the ready room along with Royce. Hans also sat at the table. Vance smiled. "Hans the Bronze! What are you doin' here?"

"I've been instructed to attend the briefing," he said with a shrug.

Vance took a seat near Royce. Many various Solar Knights filed into the room and took a seat. He leaned over to Royce. "Sir, this can't be about my grades, there's too many people here."

Royce nodded. "Agreed. I wonder what is going on."

A man in a black robe walked behind Vance and patted him on the shoulder as he passed by. Vance looked up. It was Lord Baltris. Vance smiled and waved. When he turned his attention forward again, Dorothy Vlavskisk entered along with Valerie. He waved but she didn't notice. Once the chairs were all taken, people filled in the standing space. Number 1 entered the room and walk to the front.

He set down a small leather-bound folder on the table. "Knights, we have seen in a vision an impending attack by the Mori."

The room erupted in gasps and mumbled conversation. Dawes pounded the table several times. "Quiet down! Let us hear the rest of the briefing."

Number 1 spotted Vance but quickly diverted his eyes. "Alpha fleet, which has only recently joined with Delta fleet, will be attacked by a Mori patrol. We estimate this will take place somewhere between 3 to 12 hours."

The room again burst out in muffled conversation and elevated tones. Dawes again pounded the table in demand for quiet. Number 1 opened the folder and passed around papers with tactical details. "As you will see from these papers, we plan to shuttle a group of Blue Planet engineers on board the starcraft carriers Saratoga, Ticonderoga, and Hornet. This is to counteract the damage we saw in vision. We'll also be ferrying over a group of Lily of the Valley to assist the wounded. Fire Lance and Wind Dancers will focus on attacking the Mori cruisers and other capital ships. Rising Sun will piggyback with Virtus Occulatum to disrupt the enemy communications and sabotage their defensive systems." Number 1 pulled out a few more papers. "Orbiting Star and Gun Stars will ferry the engineer and medical teams to the starcraft carriers. They will then assist the military in taking out the Mori starfighters."

Number 1 glanced back at Vance, then over to Dawes. "We need all available pilots to participate, including your trainee."

Dawes shook his head. "Negative. Squire Brewer doesn't have his wings. He's not a pilot."

Number 1 pulled up one corner of his mouth. "I'm sorry Wind Captain, but this is not a request."

Dawes jumped to his feet. "This is out of the question!"

Number 1 shrugged and pointed to a stamp on the first page of the packet of papers. "As you can see, this plan has been approved by The Council."

Dawes glared at Number 1 as if his eyes were daggers. Then he slowly sat. Vance whispered to Royce. "Sir, there's no way Number 1 is doin' me any favors. Why is he pullin' to let me fight?"

Royce leaned toward Vance. "Not everyone comes home from a battle."

Vance's eyes drifted to the table. He wondered if there was a plan in place to get rid of him permanently. *Could Number 1 do such a thing?* He thought. *Solar Knights are supposed to be the best of the best.* Whenever he heard Valerie talk about pulsaric virtue and honor, he envisioned any knight would fit that description. He wondered if he was wrong.

Out of the corner of his eye, Hans leaned back in his chair. If Hans was a template of Orbiting Star knights, he could comfortably see all the Orbiting Star knights being friendly and supportive. Beside Hans, a man in a blue and white silk shirt twirled a bullet cartridge around his fingers on one hand. The fluid motion looked like it had been practiced into a nervous habit. Vance knew two Gun Stars, both were loyal and encouraging. These too, he knew fit into his stereotype of Solar Knights.

"Our count is about 87% accurate," Number 1 said, distributing another bundle of papers. "So plan on three enemy carriers with starfighters, and about 57 supporting ships."

A man in a brown overcoat raised his hand. Number 1 looked at him a few moments as if debating. "Question?"

"The Mori are getting smarter about their tactics. Last time they wouldn't let us get close enough to cut their power."

"If that happens again, focus on their fighters."

A grumble came from Vance's left. A woman dressed in a black robe with white trims sat with steam rising from her clenched fists. Admittedly, he didn't know much about the Wind Dancers. All the ones he had met so far were wondrous people.

A man in blue coveralls stood behind Hans. The man reached over to the table and picked up one of the papers. Vance had only met one Blue Planet: Eddison Frank. Although he hadn't realized he'd been talking to the author of the four laws of The Winds, Eddison had seemed very down to earth. As if his purpose was to enlighten and instruct. It would be tough to imagine Blue Planet knights breaking the mold he envisioned of Solar Knights.

"Question?" Number 1 asked.

A man in purple scrubs had his hand up. Vance had only known one Lily of the Valley knight, Dr. Rychen. He was also friendly and seemed interested in helping. If any knight was going to break his mental picture of what a knight was, Virtus Occulatum was the most likely candidate. *The problem with stereotypes*, Vance thought, *is that they're all assumptions*. What if the knights he had met were the exceptions to their orders? He shook his head. He was overthinking it. It was probably better just to go along with Valerie's instinct. She didn't trust Number 1, and when it came down to it, neither did he.

"If there are no more questions," Number 1 said in conclusion, scanning the room. "Then let's prep and be starborne in 2 hours. We are adjourned."

As people filed out of the ready room, Royce turned to Vance. "Squire Brewer, whatever happens, follow your orders."

Vance smiled. "Aye sir."

Royce stood and walked out the door. Vance tried to stand but figured it might be more practical to wait until the room emptied a bit.

"Vance the Lance," Hans said as he followed the flow of human traffic out the door. "Just remember to follow your gut, it won't lead you astray."

Vance's smile dropped. "Yeah...I'll keep that in mind too."

Valerie walked out the door. She turned and looked at him. He smiled and waved. She simply looked the other way and exited. Vance rushed into the crowd of people and got out of the room as best he could. He scanned the corridor and found her walking a short distance away.

"Valerie!" He dashed over to her.

She glanced heavenward and sighed.

"Valerie, didn't you see me wavin'?"

She rolled her eyes. "Yes, Vance. Hi."

"Hey, what's goin' on?" Vance asked. "Your shoulder come outta the freezer or somethin'?"

"Going into battle soon, what's there to be going on?"

"Have I said somethin' wrong? Are we no longer friends?"

She stopped. "This has nothing to do with us being friends."

"Then, miss, what is it about? 'Cause I'm feelin' like you're either mad at me or tryin' ta avoid me."

She bit her lip and glanced down. "Sometimes it's not wise to get close before a battle."

Vance rolled his eyes in exasperation. "What do I gotta do ta prove myself?"

"Vance, you do not have to prove anything."

He crossed his arms. "Oh don't I? Apparently I'm not competent enough ta come back from a battle."

"Vance..." She turned away.

"Okay, I don't have my wings. What else? What else is wrong with me?"

She shook her head. "Vance—"

"Tell me!"

She glared at him. "Fine. You're a terrible shot."

"Keep it comin'!"

"Your force field needs more practice."

"Keep it comin'!"

"You can't control your precognition."

"Keep it comin'!"

"...and you have trust issues."

"Give me more, drill sergeant!"

She shook her head and mumbled under her breath. "Blazing clown thinks this is a joke." She stormed off.

Vance stood, watching until she was out of sight. His jaw quivered and he sniffled. "Give me more, drill sergeant," he whispered sullenly.

Vance turned around as Dawes walked up to him. "Wind Captain Dawes, sir."

Dawes handed Vance a folded paper.

Vance opened it up and glanced at the contents. "Wait..." Vance's breathing grew heavy. "I uh, don't suppose there's anything..."

"I'm sorry, but numbers are numbers," Dawes declared. "Better get suited up for your final flight. Dismissed." Dawes walked on past.

Vance crumpled up the paper and angrily tossed it across the hall. A tear rolled down his cheek. He leaned against the wall and slid down to the ground. He stared at the floor a few moments before looking at his squire pin. He reverently took it off and lovingly caressed its edges with his finger. He took a large breath and put the pin in his pocket.

Vance returned to his apartment and changed into his flight suit and picked up his helmet. Underneath, he saw the dead force field generator Hans had given him as a souvenir. Vance ran his fingers across the charred blue half-moon logo. Memories of his escapade with Valerie flooded into his mind. Vance took a deep breath and forced those memories down. *Now's not the time,* he thought. He exited the apartment and found his way down to the hangar.

He walked onto the flight deck and saw Adamson descending the rolling staircase. "Adamson, how's my starlancer?"

"Nonsense, sir. It's my starlancer; you simply borrow it for a few hours."

Vance laughed and bumped fists with him. A small open vehicle with seven people in the back seats drove up to the starlancer. A heavy-set dark man in blue overalls and a toolbelt hopped out. He walked up to Vance with a wide smile. "Hahaha! As I measure and cut, I get to fly with the famous squire."

Vance snickered. "I'm not sure what stories you've heard, but I promise they're all true."

The man's deep laugh echoed in the bay. "The name is Paulsky; Ronland Paulsky. Science Guild, Electromagnetic Chapter."

He shook hands with Ronland. "Good ta meet ya, Ronland. Squire Vance Brewer, grease monkey chapter."

Ronland laughed and pulled Vance into a brief bear hug. "C'mere you. I get the feeling we're gonna get along swimmingly, Vance. Though I should warn you, it's been years since I flew RIO."

"I'm sure you'll do fine, Ronland. Why don't ya go ahead and climb in." Vance motioned to the rolling staircase.

Ronland nodded. "A pleasure." He fastened on a helmet and climbed the stairs.

Vance turned back to Adamson. "Pre-flight good?"

"Fueled up and performing like a champ."

Vance put on his helmet. "You're the man."

"Oh no, sir. You're the man," Adamson said, grinning.

Vance climbed up the stairs. "Oh no, no. You're the man." He sat down in the cockpit and closed the canopy. Adamson signaled him to start the engines. Vance hit the ignition and the turbines roared to life. As Vance taxied into place, a large refueling starcraft took off down the runway. *I'm glad they think of these things. I've been bingo fuel one time too many,* he thought.

A plane director on the flight deck guided Vance over to the second catapult. The radio chatter sounded in his ear. "AberrantStar, you are Royal one-three to Mother."

"Roger Carillon."

"Royal thirteen, cleared to launch. Clear stars today, sir."

"Royal, roger. And thank you guys for all you do." Vance saluted The Shooter and looked forward. He was thrown back into his seat, watching the space door zoom past in two seconds. Swarms of starfighters formed into squadrons. Never before had he seen so many starfighters in the sky.

"Hey Vance," Ronland said. "You mind if I ask you a question?"

"Sure thing," Vance replied.

"Is it true you learned how to sabotage on your second day of introduction?"

"Oh, you talkin' about the flashlight?"

Ronland smiled. "Yeah, that's the story alright."

A voice spoke in his ear. "Royal thirteen, form up with Royal double nuts, eleven o'clock high."

Vance switched on the transmission. "Roger Carillon." He switched off the transmission and pulled the starlancer into a gentle climb. "Well, Ronland, I figured if I could use The Winds ta complete the circuit, why not use it ta prevent the circuit?"

Ronland chuckled. "That's the kind of out-of-the-box thinking we love in Blue Planet. Have you started your tour of the orders yet?"

"I haven't toured Blue Planet yet. But I'm thinkin' it'll be totally gabb. I hear you guys designed the starlancer."

"Yeah baby, that was us. You should come by some time and see what we have in store for the second-generation starlancer."

Vance's eyes lit up. "Get spaced! Boy, would I ever love that!"

"AberrantStar, this is EarlyDawn. You've been paired up with a Blue Planet. Your mission is to deliver your RIO to the starcraft carrier Saratoga and then eliminate any targets of opportunity."

Vance switched the transmission back on. "Roger EarlyDawn." Vance looked out the canopy and took note of his position relative to Dawes.

"How 'bout you come to the aerospace lab tomorrow. I'll show you the prototype," Ronland said, smiling.

Vance switched off the transmission. "Ronland, you got yourself a deal! I am totally there!"

Ronland chuckled. "Then I'll see you at 0900 hours."

"Royal squadron, this is EarlyDawn. Power back to sixty percent military thrust and follow me to the rendezvous point."

Vance pulled the throttle back and checked his alignment. It would be a while until they rendezvoused with Alpha fleet. He still remembered the long trip he had with Hans. It was smart to pull back the power to conserve fuel. He didn't have to worry about boredom, though. Ronland kept him company with lots of technical details about the next-generation starlancer. The time seemed to speed by like a passing comet.

"Okay, but I'm dyin' ta know if you guys fixed the aeon overflow valve issue?" Vance asked.

Ronland narrowed his brow. "What aeon overflow valve issue?"

"You know, where the flow regulator occasionally sticks from the buildup."

"We haven't had any reports of regulator issues related to the overflow valve."

"Ah c'mon, I been fixin' those valves on a regular basis back on the Saratoga. It's so common that the number one thing we check is that overflow valve. Nine times out of ten, we replace the valve and she's starborne again."

He chuckled. "Vance, I'm gonna put in a special request to have you tour along with me. My team could really use your input." He chuckled again. "I suppose we didn't think to talk to the mechanics in the field."

Vance smiled. "Yeah, well—"

Ronland's console beeped. "Hello there. Vance, we have SEDAR contacts bearing zero-four-seven. I'm not sure if they've seen us yet."

"Royal squadron, this is EarlyDawn. Multiple bandits bearing zero-four-seven. Break and engage. Again, break and engage."

Vance pulled into a gentle turn and throttled up to full. "Okay, Ronland. See if you can get a ranged missile lock."

"Already ahead of you."

Vance heard the targeting computer growl in his ear. "That's it. You got it."

Ronland pressed a red button. "Royal thirteen, fox-2."

The missile clanked as it dropped from under his wing. It rocketed ahead and sped off into the distance. Several other wingmen called out missile launches. Vance peeked at his SEDAR scope but then decided to keep his eyes forward waiting for a visual to engage with.

"Missile is on course," Ronland said. "Bandit is taking evasive...splash one bandit!"

"Woohoo!" Vance cried. "That was left-handed!"

"Getting a lock on the next one..."

Vance saw little dots in the distance. "Tally on bandits. They're jinking." The targeting computer growled in his ear.

"Got 'em locked!" Ronland said, brimming with excitement. "Royal thirteen, fox-2." The missile detached and sprang forward off into the distance. The distant starfighters grew larger as they closed in.

"Missile on course. Bandit taking evasive—Vance, you have incoming bandits, do you see them?"

Vance saw two starfighters heading straight for him. He rolled and pulled out of their direct line. Red bolts of light flashed past him. A voice hollered in his helmet. "Guns, guns, guns, fight's on."

"Royal thirteen, roger," Vance said. He reversed the roll as he merged and passed the two fighters. He pulled around in a large circle. "Ronland, keep tabs on that other bandit, he's gonna try ta get on my six."

"Roger, Vance—by the way, we splashed that other bandit."

Vance smiled. "That was left-handed!"

Ronland smiled wide. "Hooyah!" The SEDAR beeped. "I got tally on bandit two, he does not have an angle. Keep pressing bandit one."

Vance pulled harder into the turn. The Mori starfighter cut straight past him as they merged again. Red bolts of light flew past the canopy. "Frazza-blasta...whatever!"

Ronland chuckled. "Cool your jets, Vance, let him come to you."

"Roger," Vance replied. He rolled into the next turn and circled into a vertical loop.

"Bandit two still doesn't have an angle. Keep pressing."

Vance gave a short burst from his afterburner and widened the loop. They circled around and merged again, passing each other with a wider margin. He reached over to the braking thruster control but stopped himself. *Patience, Vance,* he thought to himself. *Patience.*

He followed the loop around and the starfighter moved into his line of fire. He pulled the trigger and a missile released from the rail and rocketed forward. "Royal thirteen, fox-3."

"Vance, break left!" Ronland said in a panic. "Bandit two now has an angle on us!"

Vance rolled hard left and hit his afterburner, narrowly evading red bolts of light. "Keep it comin'!"

"Vance he's hanging behind us. This guy is good."

Vance pulled into a tighter turn. "Looks like I'm gonna have ta work ta get us into a neutral position."

"The Mori are faster, but they can't hold an extremely tight turn like the starlancer can."

Vance nodded. "Time to get fancy." He tapped his braking thruster, sharpening his turn, and then hit his afterburner.

"Hooyah! Bandit two overshot!"

Vance leveled out and then rolled in the other direction. "I've lost tally."

"I got 'em," Ronland said, watching out the canopy. "He's circling around to our left."

Vance broke hard left and swung the nose of the starlancer around. "Okay, I got a tally now." He hit his afterburner and felt the jolt of acceleration.

"As you come to the merge, Vance, don't let this guy put you into a one-circle fight. This one is skilled with the turns."

"Roger." Vance rolled left as they merged and flew past the Mori starfighter. Vance immediately reversed his roll and circled the other direction. He flicked the switch on his stick to arm the guns.

"What the?"

"Ronland, talk ta me!" Vance said in a panic.

"The bandit just did this crazy slip! He's sliding into our 4 o'clock, we're back on the defensive!"

Vance leveled out and hit his afterburner. "Give me more, drill sergeant!"

"This blazar is good."

"Well nobody ever said I had ta be better," Vance said as he switched on the transmission. "Royal thirteen, got an ace on my six."

"Roger thirteen, royal seven, tally on bandit."

Vance pulled around and looked out the canopy. The Mori starfighter circled around to his rear.

"Royal seven, fox-2."

"Bandit is taking evasive," Ronland said.

"Keep it comin'!" Vance broke hard to the right and tapped his braking thruster. His nose swung around and then he hit his afterburner. "Tally bandit." The Mori starfighter turned into the path of the missile and flew past it. "Bandit evaded."

"I'll see if I can get a lock on him while he's focused on Royal seven," Ronland offered.

"Negative, Ronland. This guy is really good. And while he's focused on Royal seven, I don't want to alert him that I'm forming on his six." Vance resisted the urge to give a little afterburner. Instead, he patiently pulled into each turn the Mori starfighter made.

"It's workin' Vance, you're closing the distance," Ronland said.

The Mori starfighter drifted into Vance's line of fire. He pulled the trigger. "Royal thirteen, guns, guns, guns." The cannon rounds tore into the Mori starfighter. Green gas billowed in a stream from the engine as it veered off course and exploded. "Royal thirteen, splash bandit. Thanks for the assist, Royal seven."

"Roger thirteen."

"Royal squadron, this is EarlyDawn. Bandits eliminated. Form back up and proceed to rendezvous."

Vance settled into a gentle climb and pulled up beside Dawes. He pulled the throttle back to match. A few moments later, he saw the small dots of the fleet in the distance. Something looked wrong. Little flashes of yellow and red light dotted the scene.

"Uh-oh," Ronland said. "Looks like the party has already started."

"Royal squadron, this is EarlyDawn. Get your RIOs to the rendezvous."

Vance accelerated to full throttle. As the dots in the distance grew larger, Vance could more easily see the swarms of starfighters dancing across the whole area. Large turret cannons flashed as they fired from the destroyers. Long plumes of gas streaked across the starry sky from the AEGIS defense system. Instantly, Vance's muscles tightened. This was not an isolated one-on-one skirmish, this was a treacherous minefield of commotion he had to navigate.

"Ronland, I'm gonna need you ta guide me in. This is chaos."

"You got it, Vance." He pushed a few buttons. "Vance, remind me again how to isolate the IFF?"

"Uh...left-hand, third row, second switch."

Ronland flipped the switch. "Okay, come left to zero-eight-nine, and climb a little higher."

Vane obeyed. An alarm screeched while a light on his panel flashed the word LOCK.

"Fox-2, fight's on!" Ronland said.

"A missile!" Vance pulled hard left and nosed down into a dive. "The Mori don't use missiles!"

"Most likely we picked up one of our own that missed its target and was trying to re-engage. On our one o'clock low! Do you see it?"

"Tally, what do I do against a missile?"

"Treat it like a starcraft. Pull into a merge and pass. Missiles cannot maneuver the way starcraft can."

Vance rolled and hit his afterburner. He saw the small dot of the missile out the canopy. It closed the distance very fast. Vance quickly reversed the roll and merged, passing by the missile.

"Very good!"

"That was left-handed!" Vance shouted with glee. In front of him, he saw a Mori starfighter swing into the rear of a wildcat starfighter and shower it with red bolts of light. Venting gas streamed from the wildcat as it spiraled out of control and crashed into the nearby destroyer. Vance's nostrils flared as he rolled and pulled in behind the Mori starfighter. The enemy pilot must have seen him; it started moving erratically.

"Bandit knows you're on to him, Vance."

"Keep 'em comin'!" Vance said. He pulled in tight behind the Mori and flicked the switch on his stick to missile targeting.

Vance heard Dawe's voice through his helmet. "Royal thirteen, break off and deliver your RIO."

"EarlyDawn, sir, I'm almost in the saddle on this Mori."

"Negative AberrantStar. Break off and deliver your RIO."

Vance gripped his stick tight and clenched his jaw. He stared at the Mori starfighter with daggers in his eyes. "Give me more, drill sergeant!" He reversed his roll and leveled out toward the carrier and hit his afterburner.

"Royal thirteen, Allstar marshal."

"Royal thirteen, go."

"Royal thirteen, you are cleared to land. Your signal Charlie."

Vance pulled around in a wide arc, circling around to the back of the carrier.

"Vance, we have a bandit forming up on our six!" Ronland shouted in alarm.

Vance straightened out and hit his afterburner, overshooting the carrier. Then he climbed into a vertical loop. The Mori followed him.

"Vance, we're gonna need more room to maneuver; we're too close to the carrier," Ronland said.

Vance shook his head. "We're not goin' after him. My orders are ta get you on board the Saratoga."

"But we have a bandit on our six!"

"Give me more, drill sergeant, give me more!" Vance tapped his breaking thruster, spinning the nose down, and started into a dive toward the carrier. Vance rolled as red bolts of light streaked past him. "Paddles, Royal thirteen, starlancer, 'AberrantStar', ball, fuel state 2.2, jibber!"

"Roger, ball, jibber. Right to lineup."

Vance adjusted his angle.

"Vance, the bandit is on our six!

"Keep 'em comin'!" Without taking his eyes off the lineup lights, Vance pressed a button. Anti-missile flares popped out the back of the starlancer. He heard the loud *pop pop pop* from the anti-starcraft turrets on the carrier. Still, he kept his eyes on the lights. He flew through the space door at an alarming speed. The starlancer hit the runway with a loud *bang* and slid into a barricade net. His insides wanted to keep going while his safety straps held him back. After a moment of disorientation, Vance looked up. Several firefighters in red jackets ran up to his starlancer with fire suppression tanks. When they got close, they sprayed down the starlancer. Vance opened the canopy and stood. He turned around and gave a hand to Ronland.

"You alright, sir?"

"Yeah, thanks, buddy. Thanks for getting here in one piece," Ronland replied.

As the rolling staircase wheeled over, Vance shut down the engines. Vance and Ronland quickly descended the stairs as a tractor sped up to the starlancer. Vance took off his helmet. A man in the distance yelled, "Foul deck! Foul deck!"

A woman in a white jacket with a red cross rushed over to Vance and Ronland. She ushered them off the flight deck while the tractor pulled the starlancer off the runway. As they hustled off the flight deck, Vance looked back. He saw his starlancer with a broken nose gear being towed away. "Ah, krek—blast it!"

When they stepped into a little room off the flight deck, the corpsman shined a flashlight in Vance's eyes. She asked him a few questions while writing the answers down on a clipboard. Ronland turned to Vance. "You know, I have never met anyone who enjoys their work as much as you seem to. Keep it up; it'll take you far."

Vance smiled. "That was left-handed."

Chapter 36
INVASION

One of the finest examples of graceful design can be found in the arms of the Lily of the Valley. Their simple purple field sets the stage, so to speak, for a white lily. This single charge serves to identify the name of the order (as a canting charge) as well as adorn the field with a beautiful reminder of our one-time home planet of Earth.

—FROM "GALACTIC HERALDRY" BY JEAN-CLAUDE ARMAND DUBOIS

Vance and Ronland hustled across the flight deck and over to the stairwell. When they reached the top, Vance held out his hand. "I gotta go debrief the flight. And I'm prob'ly gonna need to explain to the skipper why I pulled a jibber and goosed up his runway."

Ronland shook his hand. "When you get done, if you're not busy, swing on by the engine room and I'll show you what Blue Planets can do."

"You're on!" Vance said as they parted. Ronland headed through the doorway. As he disappeared up the stairs, Vance remembered the times he had gone through that doorway and climbed those very stairs.

Vance stiffened when Sedston descended the stairs and entered the bay. Sedston wore his flight suit and carried his helmet. When he saw Vance, he stopped and glared at him. "This is all your fault."

Vance pointed to the open space door, toward the raging combat outside. "That? You're blamin' me for that? How in Nova's name is that my fault?"

Sedston's eyes intensified. "It's because of you Solwins that the Mori destroyed Earth, to begin with. And you joined them! You're the reason we're all on the run. Everybody we've lost in this war is because of *you.*"

Vance felt his heart weighing him down. It was like his first flight all over again. But something felt different this time. Anger swelled within. *I will not let Sedston do this to me again,* he thought. He also couldn't show anger, that would be letting Sedston control his emotions. *What would Hans do?* He wondered. He took a deep breath and smiled wide. "Well, you know me, Starwrecker, always gots ta be the center of attention."

Sedston shook his head in disgust and stormed past.

Vance took another deep breath, exhaling with a feeling of light shoulders. *You know what,* he thought. *I really think I could make a great Orbiting Star.* Then a loud *BOOM* echoed in the bay, sending a vibration through the floor. He spun around to see flames roaring in the machinist bays. He dashed across the bay and skidded to a stop. In front of him, his starlancer lay torn apart and burning.

A bell rang and the overhead speakers blared. "Fire, fire, fire! Class bravo fire in compartment 1-75-0-Q. Away the Flying Squad, provide from Repair 3!"

Vance dashed over to the sidewall and opened the fire panel. He took out a fire suppression tank and ran back to his starlancer. He sprayed down the tall flames as the fire suppression team arrived to combat the fire. The flames roared and smoked. Vance coughed and turned away from the heavy smoke in his eyes. He walked out of the heat and looked ahead, across the landing bay to the runway. Another starlancer taxied away from the runway after landing.

Then in a flash of steel, a foreign-shaped starcraft plowed through the open space door and crashed into the runway. The overhead klaxon blared its alert. Vance squinted at the burning starcraft on the runway. The long dart-shaped starcraft with four short wings was undoubtedly a Mori starcraft. Firefighters in red jackets ran up to the starfighter and sprayed it down with fire suppressant. The canopy opened and red bolts of light shot out from the canopy, tearing into the flight crew.

Vance dashed across to the nearby wall and smashed the alarm box emergency glass with his elbow. He opened the panel and pulled the lever. Another alarm rang out. "Security Alert! Security Alert! Security Alert! Away the security team! Away the Back-up Alert force! All hands not involved in Security Alert, stand fast. Intruders in the landing bay!"

Mori soldiers hopped out of the starcraft, gunning down everyone that they saw on the flight deck.

"What I wouldn't give for a force field generator right about now," Vance mumbled.

He hunched down and hustled along the wall to the stairwell, and descended. He peeked around the corner and made his way toward the Mori soldiers. He swiftly walked behind the landed wildcat starfighters, keeping his eye out for the enemy. He saw red bolts of light flashing in the near distance. He ducked under and around the crafts and crept closer. He peered over the top of a metal dividing wall. The Mori soldiers briskly walked in his direction.

Vance closed his eyes and pictured the advancing soldiers. He focused on their rifles. He imagined what the inside of them looked like. He imagined a power cell pulsing with energy. And then he pictured his own hands grabbing the power cell and yanking it out.

Vance heard bullet fire behind. He ducked and looked back. The security team had arrived and were exchanging fire with the Mori. Angry red bolts of light flew through the air at the security team. Vance peeked over the metal wall once more. One Mori soldier inspected his rifle while the other two shot back. *Gotcha!* Vance thought.

He focused on the other two Mori and closed his eyes. He envisioned himself ripping out the power cells of their rifles. He opened his eyes but the two soldiers still shot at the security team. Vance huffed. "Why can't I make it work all the time? I've gotta talk to some of them Rising Suns."

The Mori soldier with the broken rifle tapped his arm a few times and then he faded from view. Vance's jaw dropped. He blinked a few times to be certain his eyes weren't tricking him. Only two Mori soldiers now. "Blast!" he mumbled under his breath. "It's like déjà vu's evil twin."

Vance dashed back the way he had come, ducking under the folded wings of parked wildcats. He climbed the stairwell and bolted for the door. Once in the hallway, he sprinted to the other end of the deck, passing fire suppression teams and security troops. He rounded a corner and plowed into three men, toppling them to the ground.

Vance got to his feet. "So sorry!"

One of the men stood. "What's the frazzin idea, canner!"

Vance looked back and saw the brass metal badge on the man's uniform. He had just bulldozed three Masters-at-Arms. "So sorry, Chief. I gotta get ta the engine room."

One Master-at-Arms drew his Beretta pistol. "Hold it! What you doin' in the engine room in such a hurry?"

"I gotta tell Ronland, there's a zandor'an."

The two other men looked at each other and laughed. "Chief Jenkins, I think we found our intruder."

Vance rolled his eyes. "The Mori are the intruders. They're in the landing bay. Now I really gotta get goin'."

He shook his head. "You're not goin' anywhere, canner."

Vance huffed. "They *gotta* raise the ASVAB score needed ta be an MA."

"Can it! And move."

Vance very quickly found himself behind a solid metal door with a tiny glass window. Vance looked out the little door window from his brig cell. How would he ever get out to warn Ronland about the zandor'an?

He turned around and leaned against the door, sliding down into a seated position. He leaned his head back and rested it against the door.

The white ceiling had only a single light bolted to it. *I don't suppose sabotaging a light would help any,* Vance thought. *What I need is a key to the lock.*

He felt the door with his hand. *Just as I figured,* he thought. *No vibration of electronics.* He surveyed his white-washed cell. It had a cot and a toilet with a petty excuse for a sink. Nothing useful to escape with. *I wish I had some Virt-o skills,* he thought. *Bein' invisible could have come in handy a while back.* He stood and faced the door again.

He sighed and rested his forehead against the little window. He was powerless. He didn't have any way to create a force field, and he couldn't sabotage a physical lock. His heart sank. What would happen to Ronland? What would happen to the ship? The main power reactor was in the engine room. If the zandor'an could overload the reactor, he could destroy the entire starcraft carrier. Five thousand sailors and pilots would die in a matter of moments. But the loss of the starcraft carrier would not be limited to the lives of the crew. The fastest way to cripple a fleet was to destroy the carrier. That one zandor'an could spell the defeat of Alpha fleet.

But what could he do? Even if he could get out of his cell, he would still need to get past the Masters-at-Arms. The proper procedure to clear himself to be released would take too long. He probably couldn't outrun them, not while they were armed with Berettas. Vance came to the unsettling realization that he would have to assault them in order to get away. Could he do that? Then his thoughts returned to the five thousand sailors and pilots on board. He would have to. But what was the point in worrying about them now? He didn't even have a way to get out of his cell. He took in a long breath and sighed. He gazed out the tiny window.

He saw a little red light on the ceiling outside his cell. He moved his head around until he could see its source. The red light was on a smoke detector. He lifted his head and a smile crossed his lips. He put his hand on the window and closed his eyes. A few moments later, an alarm blared. Muffled curses came from voices down the hall. The Masters-at-Arms came running and unlocked the doors, ushering out any occupants. He backed away from the door and a Master-at-Arms unlocked it and pulled him out. He shoved Vance toward a couple of other others who directed him to the exit.

It was time to make his escape. Hopefully, he could pull it off. He clutched his chest and tumbled to the ground. One of the Master-at-Arms picked up Vance and put his arm around their neck and pulled him out of the room. Once in the corridor, Vance closed his eyes and grabbed the man's head. He gave Vance a sharp jab to the ribs. Vance groaned but held on. Then they both collapsed to the floor. Vance coughed and staggered to his feet. "Sorry about that, Chief. Sweet dreams." He hobbled as fast as he could down the corridor, clutching his side.

After stumbling down several passageways, his discomfort eased up, allowing him to walk normally. The bruise in his ribs, however, was still painful. He descended a staircase and halted at the bottom, resting against the railing. He panted and breathed heavily, fighting against the throbs in his side. After a moment's rest, he continued down the passageway and into a large room with big machines and pipes. Several people lay on the floor, motionless. His heart rate accelerated and his breathing shortened. Vance leaned over to one of the bodies on the floor and felt their neck. The skin was warm but he couldn't feel a pulse. With a shaking hand, he picked up a large wrench beside them. It didn't look like much but at least it was heavy and blunt.

Vance cautiously stepped one foot over the next, second-guessing every little sound he heard. He peeked around the next corner. No movement. But then again, would he see anything? His last encounter with a zandor'an flooded into his mind. He pictured the scene in his mind as if it were yesterday. Hans had tumbled off the large machine and onto the gantry and he had scrambled down to the floor to check on him. He remembered the terrible sounds of the invisible killer. A shiver went down his back as he thought of the horrible growls.

Vance walked as softly as he could, straining his ear for any sound that could give him some advanced warning. Then he heard a *clang*. The sound came from down the next corridor. His feet felt glued in place. *What am I doin' tryin' ta square off with a blazin' zandor'an?* He thought. *I can barely shoot, let alone go hand ta hand.*

The thought of going back had a comforting appeal to Vance. Then the image of Ronland shaking his hand flooded into his mind. Ronland had thanked him for getting him to the carrier in one piece. *What do I do for Ronland?* He wondered. *Somebody's gotta warn him.* Vance heard another *clang* and he froze, his heart rate accelerated. *Ronland is a Solar Knight.* He thought. *Surely he has ta be able to take care of himself?* Once again, the thought of turning back felt so alluring.

He took one step backward and his mind flashed back to the stairwell where Valerie bumped into him. He heard her voice once more in his mind: ...your heart only masquerades as a squire, when in reality it bleeds blue and white. What would Valerie think of him if she knew he left a friend to fend for himself? His heart grew heavy. His mind returned again to the thousands of sailors and pilots on board. *But I'm not a knight,* he thought. *I'm just a squire.* He looked back the way he came. The thought to flee gripped him. The memory of sitting in the infirmary in front of Royce cascaded in front of his eyes. He heard Royce's words echoing deep within: Be not afraid of greatness, Brewer, just be believing.

His breathing accelerated into panting. He tightened his grip on the large wrench. He yelled at the top of his lungs. "Give me more, drill sergeant!" He heard his voice echo down the corridor. A sudden realization flashed across his mind. Announcing to the whole ship where he was probably wasn't the smartest move. Fear crept up his legs. He knew if he stayed standing, he would never move from that spot. He took off running toward the strange sounds with the wrench poised to strike.

He charged into the large open engine room. The familiar hum of machinery filled the air. The smell of grease and perspiration assaulted his nose. He heard a thump to his left. Adrenaline shot through his veins and he sprinted away from the sound. He approached a ladder straight ahead; higher ground felt safer. He jumped onto the fourth rung from the bottom and began climbing. The wrench banged against the rungs as he climbed—if only it didn't make so much noise. Fear, however, drove that concern further down the priority list.

His leg muscles tired before he reached the top of the ladder. A feeling of safety came with the extreme height, that is, until he looked down. He clutched the railing. He had climbed to the top of a massive white cylinder in the center of the room. A fall from this height would be fatal. The circular gantry formed a walkway around the giant machine. There was still part of the cylinder that protruded higher than the gantry, obscuring the view of what was on the other side. At least it had a railing, but with it, a very good view of the long drop to the bottom.

He surveyed the landscape of machines below him, hoping to spot Ronland. He squinted his eyes but could not see him. In fact, he couldn't see *anyone* around. *Somethin' is way wrong with this scene,* he thought. *In the middle of a battle outside, this place should be crawlin' with sailors.* He walked quietly around the circular gantry, unsure what he would find around the bend. He heard a *clang* nearby and froze. He lifted the wrench like a club and inched forward around the bend.

As he inched around, a faint shadow moved on the metal grate floor of the gantry. Vance stopped a moment and took a deep breath. Then he inched farther around.

"Brewer!"

Vance jumped. His throat locked up and his heart skipped a beat. He clutched his chest and breathed deep.

"Hey hey, Squire Brewer, glad you came to visit," Ronland said in his deep cheery voice. "What's with the wrench?"

"Ronland, you scared the bejeebies out of me."

"Sorry Vance, I'm just happy I'm not alone up here. I can't seem to get anybody on the radio. And I don't dare leave, because the reactor coolant system keeps going offline for some reason."

"Ronland, there's a zandor'an on board."

"A what?"

Vance rolled his eyes. "Oh c'mon, I can't be the only one who knows about this." He took a step closer.

"Careful," Ronland warned, pointing to a yellow sticker on the cylinder wall. "This is a containment field area."

Vance lowered the wench he was carrying. "A zandor'an is an invisible Mori saboteur."

"Invisible huh?"

Vance nodded.

"Well, if he's invisible, how do you know he's on board?"

"'Cause I saw him pull a frazzin David Copperfield in the landing bay! One minute I saw him, the next I didn't."

Ronland held up his hands. "Okay, okay, Vance. I trust you if you say there's an invisible Mori soldier on board."

"Mori *saboteur*," Vance corrected. "How long have you been fighting that coolant thingy?"

He looked back at the computer terminal mounted to the wall. "The better part of an hour." He smiled. "Hey hey, looks like whatever was causing the coolant system to go offline has cleared up. The coolant system appears stable."

"Unless," Vance said. "Unless you've been fightin' with the zandor'an for an hour. And s'posin' he got fed up and went lookin'." Vance looked over the gantry railing down to the distant ground below. "And me makin' all that racket leadin' way up here..."

"Do you smell starcraft fuel?" Ronland asked.

Vance sniffed the air. It held an unmistakable odor of burnt starcraft fuel. Vance turned back to Ronland. "Now that you mention—" Vance saw the air behind Ronland shimmer and move. "Behind you!"

Ronland turned around in time to hear the wild roar of the zandor'an and get backhanded. Ronland tumbled and fell on his back. Vance yelled and charged at the zandor'an. He swung the wrench and struck the enemy's arm. He swung again and again. Each time the zandor'an blocked the strike and backed up. On the fourth strike, a few sparks flew from the zandor'an's arm. His large head with off-set eyes and jagged teeth faded into view. "I guess that's another way ta sabotage," Vance said, proud of his work. "Now you're just an ordinary Mori."

Vance swung again. The Mori growled and batted the wrench away. It slipped from Vance's hands and tumbled through the air. It landed with a distant clatter against the ground below. The Mori punched Vance square in the chest. He toppled backward and tripped over Ronland's unconscious body. Vance hit the gantry floor as the Mori casually walked toward him with clenched fists.

Vance hastily staggered to his feet as the Mori backhanded him over the railing. Vance felt the solid metal of the railing at his back as he tumbled over the edge. Vance desperately grasped at anything in reach. The fingers of his right hand caught hold of the ledge. His feet swayed in the open air, high above the ground. His sore rib muscles complained with a sharp sting. He looked up at the Mori taking the last few steps up to the railing.

This wasn't how he pictured leaving this world. He had always hoped he would have had a chance to get closer to Valerie. He hadn't even had a chance to tell her how he felt about her. So many unfinished things he always thought he would have time to get around to. If only he had taken the opportunity when he had it. His breathing shallowed as he braced for the end. Another step and the Mori would make sure he tumbled through the air and smashed against the floor below.

Then Vance saw it; the yellow sticker on the wall behind the Mori's head. The inscription read, Caution, containment field area. It had a blue half-moon logo next to it. His heart rate climbed as a sense of hope suddenly surged through his body.

He smiled at the Mori. "Hey blazar, say hello to gravity for me; it's a real canner sometimes." Vance threw his free hand toward the Mori. The air behind the Mori shimmered like water and slammed into his back, pushing him into the railing. The impact of the force field broke the railing and the Mori fell forward over the edge of the gantry. He roared an awful sound as he plummeted to the distant floor and landed with a loud *thump.*

Vance reached up with his free hand and grabbed the ledge just as his other hand slipped off. "Ronland! Ronland! I need you!" His fingers ached and his other hand started to shake. He reached up and grabbed the ledge with his other hand too. The strength in his fingers continued to diminish. His hands trembled under the strain. "Give me more, drill sergeant," he muttered under his breath as his fingers slipped off.

For a moment, he felt weightless as he fell from the gantry. Time seemed to move in slow motion. Then he felt a firm grip on his wrist and a strong tug on his arm. "I got ya, Vance," Ronland said in a strained voice. Vance looked up into Ronland's face, blood running from his nose. Ronland hoisted Vance back onto the gantry, overlooking the ground far beneath.

Vance sat with his back against the cylinder wall. "Thanks, buddy, I owe ya one."

Ronland nodded. "Anytime Vance, except I should be thanking you."

Vance smiled. "Feel free to mention it anytime."

Ronland laughed with Vance. "Let me guess, that was left-handed?"

Vance laughed again until his ribs reminded him that wasn't such a good idea. He rolled to his side and stood up, steadying himself with the bent railing.

Ronland stood and peered over the ledge at the body of the Mori on the ground far below. "I guess I'm real lucky you had one of those portable force field generators on you."

Vance shook his head. "I don't," he pointed to the blue half-moon logo near the yellow sticker on the wall. "Which is why I'm so glad the reactor comes with one."

Ronland glanced at the sticker. "As I measure and cut..."

"You gonna be okay up here if I head back to the landing bay?" Vance asked.

"Vance, you should take a rest. You've taken a beating," he replied.

Vance took a few breaths. "Give me more, drill sergeant."

Ronland stared into his eyes. "You're one dedicated knight, Vance, I'll give you that."

Vance smiled. "Don't forget, after this is all over, I'm comin' ta see you and the new prototype."

Ronland laughed. "You're on."

Vance made his way back to the landing bay. Swarms of damage control personnel were busy patching up the runway to get it functional again. The muffled *pop pop pop* sounds of the anti-starcraft turrets firing away still permeated the air. Across the flight deck, sparks flew as metal plates were welded to the runway. A wildcat taxied down the lane. His eyebrows rose. *They got the runway patched up already?* He wondered.

A muffled rattling of metal pieces sounded behind him; the remains of his starlancer being cleared out of the machinist bay. *Oh blast,* he thought. *That's right, I can't do what it is I do best right now. My starlancer is toast.*

Vance walked over and picked up a few charred pieces. He flipped one over and saw a partial inscription. The words didn't mean anything to him, but the feel of the metal was wrong. He handled the metal of starcraft spaceframes all the time, and they were a particular metal alloy. This felt different. It was rough and clunky. Nothing like the sleek lightweight alloy of starcraft metal. The whine of a starcraft engine roared to life across the bay. The wildcat catapulted to take-off speed and raced out the space door.

Vance pocketed the metal fragment and walked over to the edge of the balcony overlooking the flight deck. A starlancer was parked below him. Vance jogged over to the stairwell and descended. He rounded the corner and found the starlancer. Walking up to the red-winged beauty brought back memories of his first flirtation with destiny. He ran his hand all along the folded wing until he saw the inscribed pilot name on the side rail. He blinked to be sure he read it correctly. Then he quickly turned to leave but instead stared into those mahogany eyes he wasn't sure he was ready to see.

Vance's muscles stiffened.

She stared back. "Squire Brewer."

"Miss Vlavskisk."

"What were you doing with my craft?" she asked.

Vance took a breath. "This is where it all began for me. It just seemed fittin' that it's where it all should end."

She returned a confused look. "What do you mean?"

Vance looked away a moment. "Wind Captain Dawes gave me my final exam score."

"And?"

He shook his head.

Valerie placed a consoling hand on his shoulder.

He looked down and took another deep breath. "This is my final flight." He returned to her eyes and smiled weakly. "Give me more, drill sergeant..." He wiped away a tear and sniffled. "And my starlancer is toast, so I figured maybe I could fly RIO with you?"

"I'm sorry Vance."

He shrugged. "It's not all bad. I mean, I won't get ta stay on New Carillon, and I can't be a Fire Lance. But at least I'll still be a Solar Knight."

Valerie waited for a wildcat to taxi past. "Where will you go?"

Vance tilted his head back and breathed deep. "It's all-new territory ta me. I'll come up with somethin'."

"Well if this is your final flight, let's get into the stars and make a mess of the Mori."

Vance sniffled and smiled. "Thank you, miss."

"Go ahead and take the stick." She nodded toward the cockpit.

He shook his head. "I appreciate the offer, miss, but this time I'm here ta support you. This time I'm not the bullet. This time I'm the powder."

"You'd seriously take RIO over the stick?" she asked.

He smiled. "True blue, stickin' with you."

Valerie failed to suppress her smile. "Alright, admirer, there should be a spare helmet in the back.

They climbed into the cockpit and she started the pre-flight checks. Vance switched on the transmission. "Allstar tower, AberrantStar."

"Allstar tower, go."

"Starburst, starlancer, tail number one-two. Request permission to launch and re-engage the enemy."

"Roger AberrantStar. Standby for flight direction."

When the pre-flight was complete, Valerie followed the directions of the plane directors, taxiing over to the repaired runway. The radio chattered in Vance's helmet. "Starburst, you are Caliber one-two to Mother."

"Roger Allstar," she replied.

"Caliber twelve, cleared to launch. Go get 'em."

"Caliber, roger and thank you." She looked out the canopy and saluted The Shooter. Vance grabbed onto the side rails and leaned his head back. A moment later he was thrust into his seat as the starlancer soared through the space door and into the debris-ridden starry landscape.

The anti-starcraft turrets belted out their volleys into space. Starfighters zoomed all around. Valerie pulled into a climb. Vance looked down at his SEDAR. "Two bandits bearing three-one-five."

Valerie rolled to the right and hit her afterburner. Vance watched out the canopy and saw both Mori starfighters chasing a pair of wildcats. "Starburst, they're tailin' some friendlies."

"Tally on bandits," she said.

"Lemme see if I can patch in ta their frequency." Vance punched a few keys on his console. The transmission erupted with chatter. It was permeated with pilots talking and command staff directing attacks. Staff personnel were even heard in the background.

The missile targeting computer growled in their ears. Valerie pulled the trigger and a missile detached and rocketed forward. "Caliber twelve, fox-2."

The Mori starfighter broke left and veered into the missile's path and fired red hot bolts of light. The missile exploded prematurely and the starfighter passed by Valerie's starlancer. Valerie pulled hard right and followed.

Vance watched the Mori out the canopy. "If you tighten up a little more, you'll gain the advantage."

Valerie pulled harder into the turn. "Tally on bandit."

The starfighter pulled into a vertical loop and Valerie followed. The second Mori starfighter pulled around behind. "Bandit two is on our 5 o'clock, he doesn't have angle. Keep pressing bandit one," Vance said.

Vance glanced down to his SEDAR. Two more red dots closed in on them. "Keep it comin'," he mumbled. He looked back at the tailing Mori. "Bandit two still does not have angle. Keep pressing."

He looked out the other side of the canopy and saw the other two starfighters coming in. "Starburst, Break left! Two more bandits on our nine o'clock!" Valerie rolled hard to the left. The two starfighters pass by the canopy. Valerie pulled her turn into a wide circle. Vance followed the starcraft with his eyes. "Bandit two overshot. Bandits three and four are looping into a one-circle fight."

Valerie reversed her roll and tightened up her turn. They merged again and passed, pulling into another large circle. Vance glanced back to his SEDAR. "Hey Starburst, I can get a lock on bandit two."

"Take him out!"

Vance tapped a few buttons and flipped a switch. Vance heard the growling in his ear and pressed the red button. "Caliber twelve, fox-2". A missile dropped and rocketed away as Valerie pulled into another tight turn. Vance looked back at the first starfighter pulling around behind them. "Bandit one is forming on our six. He doesn't have angle yet. Keep pressing."

Valerie reversed her roll and pulled hard to the left and lined up on the starfighter she was chasing. "Caliber twelve, guns, guns, guns." The starlancer's cannon pelted the starfighter and it veered off, trailing green gas. "Splash bandit three," she announced.

"Splash bandit two as well," Vance said, watching the SEDAR. He glanced back out the rear of the canopy. "Break right! Break right! Bandit one has angle!"

Valerie broke into a hard turn and pushed into a dive. Vance looked out the other side of the canopy. The fourth starfighter circled around behind. "Starburst, bandit four is back on our 5 o'clock. No angle. Keep pressing bandit one."

Valerie pulled into a climb and hit her afterburner. Vance glanced at his SEDAR again. "Miss, we got another bandit takin' interest in us. No angle yet, keep pressin'."

"What else is new!"

Vance smiled and whispered to himself. "Keep 'em comin'."

Vance looked out the rear of the canopy at all three starfighters closing in on their tail. He laughed.

"What's so funny?" she demanded, with a hint of annoyance.

"We got three bandits all competin' with each other tryin' ta take us out. Who'd a thought we'd be so popular?"

"Gruesome five, I have an ace on my six," a voice called out over the transmission.

"Where is he?" she asked.

Vance looked at his SEDAR screen. "Bearing zero-eight-nine, low."

Valerie switched on the transmission. "Roger Gruesome five, Caliber twelve. Tally on bandit." She hit her afterburner.

"We got three bandits on our six, miss."

"If I can't shoot the ones behind me, I'll shoot the ones in front of me."

Vance shrugged. "Sounds good ta me. Just remember ta jink, bandit one is good."

Vance glanced back to his SEDAR. "Gruesome's bandit is in long-range for missile lock."

"Take him out."

Vance flipped a switch, waited for the screen to confirm the lock, then hit the red button. A missile dropped off the rack and rocketed away. "Caliber twelve, fox-3." Vance looked back through the canopy. "Miss, bandits one, four, and five are getting an angle on us."

Valerie pulled into a climb and then quickly rolled into a dive.

"Great maneuver, miss, bandits four and five overshot."

"Bandit one still pressing us?" she asked, with noticeable stress in her voice.

"Affirmative, miss."

"Blast, this blazar is good!"

Vance widened his eyes and smiled. "Starburst, take us in closer to that destroyer."

"Not enough room to maneuver," she replied.

"We're not gonna need ta maneuver. Take us along the port side."

Valerie reversed her turn and rolled into a climb. Vance looked out the back of the canopy. The other two starfighters pull back in behind them. "Okay miss, now it's time for you ta do what you do best."

"I've never done it in a starfighter before."

"You got this, Starburst," he said. "You're the best shot I've seen. I know you can do this. Just be believing."

She pulled the starlancer into a circle, looping toward the side of the large destroyer. "Call out their angles!"

Vance glanced back to the SEDAR and flipped a switch. "Compared ta us or compared ta the ship?"

"To us *and* the hull of the destroyer!" Valerie rolled as red bolts few past the canopy from behind.

"One is 43, four is 92, five is 118!"

Valerie tightened her turn toward the destroyer. "Caliber twelve, guns, guns, guns!" She held the trigger down and the starlancer's cannon roared, spraying the side of the destroyer. The cannon rounds ricocheted off the hull of the destroyer, showering the oncoming path of the trailing Mori starfighters. Green gas billowed in long trails from the enemy starfighters. Large pieces fell away and tumbled through space.

"Great shot, Starburst! You nailed bandits four and five!"

"What about bandit one?"

Vance looked back. "He's still behind us. He's almost got an angle. He's loose on his left turn."

Valerie broke left and hit her afterburner. "I can't keep running from this blazar!"

"Yes we can, miss. We came out all fueled up. The Mori had to spend a bit of fuel getting over to the fleet. Their starcraft are also smaller. Guaranteed, he will run out of fuel before we do."

Valerie rolled into a dive as red hot bolts of light streaked past the canopy. Vance watched out the back. "That's good miss, make him pay for every inch he gains."

She broke right and hit her breaking thruster. Vance's helmet hit the side of the canopy. Red bolts streaked past as the starfighter flew by. "You did it, miss, bandit one overshot."

"Blast it!"

A light flashed on his instrumentation panel. "Blast it is right, looks like we took a hit to the right aileron thruster. We can't roll, so we're gonna have ta stick close to the capital ships. We can use them to break line of sight."

Valerie started her long circle around toward the destroyer. Vance looked out the canopy behind them. "Bandit one is comin' around."

"We're not going to make it, are we?"

"Don't talk like that, miss, of course we're goin' ta make it. We still have one missile left. We can use that idea of yours, usin' its thrust to turn us quicker."

She shook her head. "It's on the wrong side."

Vance opened his mouth to offer another suggestion, but nothing came to mind. He looked back at the trailing starfighter and then looked forward at their angle. "There's gotta be somethin' we can do..."

"Vance, if we don't make it—"

"We're goin' ta make it," he said, grumbling.

"—I want you to know I am very sorry for walking out on you."

"Don't worry about it, miss, I prob'ly had it comin'."

She shook her head. "No, Vance. Loyalty is a very big deal for a Gun Star."

Vance swallowed. "I don't think it's necessary, but if you need ta hear it, all is forgiven. I got no hard feelin's." He reached down and pulled a large red lever. "Sequence active. You ready to eject?"

She placed both hands on her seat handles. "What are the chances the Mori won't see us?"

"I like ta think there's always a chance," Vance said in a weak tone.

Vance looked through the back of the canopy and saw the starfighter closing in on their six o'clock. "Valerie?"

"Yes?"

"If'n I don't get ta tell you later, back durin' our first mission together…"

"Yes?"

"What I wanted ta say ta you—"

"…yes?"

"…bandit one is bugging out! Woohoo! He's prob'ly bingo fuel!"

Valerie huffed and hit her afterburner. She pulled into a wide arc toward the carrier.

Chapter 37

ACE

*Ah, yes, a pilot's final fight. Although it's always a sad day to watch a pilot walk out onto the flight deck knowing it's their last flight, at least it's better than the pilot walking out onto the flight deck **not** knowing it's their last flight.*

—FROM "MEMOIRS OF THE EXODUS" BY HANS THE BRONZE

Valerie flew through the space door of the Saratoga and touched down. The safety straps dug into Vance's shoulders as they came to a complete stop. An awkward silence hung in the air as Valerie taxied the starlancer along the recovery lane. It felt like being in grade school, waiting outside the principal's office.

At a hand signal from a plane director, Valerie shut down the engines. The staircase rolled up to the cockpit and Vance put his hands on the side rails, preparing to stand up. He waited for Valerie to open the canopy. Then, he waited some more.

"Vance," she began.

He slumped back into his seat. It was apparent, that he wasn't going anywhere.

"I promised you I would not leave you," she said. "Are you really going to leave me?"

She wasn't talking about the starlancer. She was talking about the unfinished conversation. And as awkward and nervous as it was, she deserved the rest of the conversation. "Valerie, I—"

A man knocked on the canopy. It was a Master-at-Arms. Vance glanced past him at the flight deck. Four more MA's waited, one of them talking with Dawes. "Yeah...I've got quite a bit of explainin' ta do."

Valerie huffed in exasperation and swatted the canopy control. The canopy slid open, and Vance descended the stairs behind the Master-at-Arms. They stopped in front of Dawes. Dawes sternly look at Vance. "These are some pretty serious accusations."

Vance swallowed. "I couldn't let the zandor'an get to the main reactor, sir."

"Go with the MA's and give them a hundred and ten percent cooperation while I sort this out."

"Aye sir." Vance walked with the Masters-at-Arms back to the brig. The biggest irony was that he wound up in the very same cell. He walked up to the bunk that was bolted to the wall and sat. Strangely, he didn't feel the same sense of helplessness he had earlier. The ship was safe, and that gave him some degree of comfort. He laid back and let his muscles relax. His fingertips still tingled from clinging onto the gantry ledge, and his ribs still complained. The air smelled fresh at least.

For the next several hours, he lay there, replaying the events of the day in his mind. Someone knocked on his cell door. "Squire Brewer, you have a visitor."

Vance lifted his head. He had finally got comfortable. "Aye, Chief." He sat up. The door lock clanked. A Master-at-Arms escorted Valerie into the cell. "Ten minutes," he said, closing the door behind her. She took a few steps forward. Her pistol holsters were empty, but she still carried herself as if she were armed.

"I guess you really want to finish talkin'," he said.

"Unless you want to tell me you have anything better to do."

Vance smiled. "Nah, I don't have anythin' better ta do." He got up and motioned to the bunk. Here, you can have a seat."

She sauntered over and sat.

Vance took a breath. "You told me once, miss, that I do real good when I shoot from the hip. So, I'm just gonna say it straight—and I apologize in advance if I say somethin' wrong."

Valerie nodded.

Vance cleared his throat. "Valerie, I can't stop thinkin' about you. I've never before had a friend like you. You stick with me so stubbornly I'd swear you were welded on."

Valerie blushed.

Vance took her gloved hand. "I think I can say with confidence, miss, that I am hopelessly caught in your gravity. And that kinda scares me."

She frowned. "Scares you?"

He gave her hand a little squeeze before letting go. He paced in a circle. "Up until now, I've had a lot on my plate. I was worried about flight training, qualifying for Fire Lance, makin' sense of these visions, coming ta terms with my confidence issues, yadda yadda yadda—oh yeah, and saving the fleet was thrown in there for good measure I s'pose."

She muffled her giggle.

He continued pacing. "Then I meet you—and I really like you. And if you really like me too, then... then... then I gots a whole other set of things ta prepare for. I'm just startin' to get used to thinkin' of myself as a Solar Knight. I don't know if I'm ready to add on some real adult responsibilities."

She walked over to him and touched his arm. He turned to her and stammered for something more to say. "And since I can't stay on New Carillon, I gotta find some way to be with you."

She put her gloved finger to his lips. "Shhhh. I think you're overthinking this. First off, you're not alone; you have me. And second, we don't have to figure everything out all at once. It's okay to just take it one day at a time."

His gaze sank deeper into her mahogany eyes. She took a step closer. The air seemed to thicken and his heart beat faster. He took a shallow breath and reached a hand toward her cheek.

The cell door clanked open and a Master-at-Arms stepped in. "Time," he announced.

Vance glanced heavenward in annoyance. "Shootin' from the hip," he muttered. He turned to the Master-at-Arms. "Aye, Chief. One sec." He returned to Valerie, placed his hand on her cheek, and kissed her.

"Squire Brewer," a familiar voice called from the door.

Startled, Vance spun around and stood at attention. "Wind Captain Dawes, sir."

Dawes stepped inside and took a few steps closer to Vance. "I don't recall lipstick being a part of the uniform regulations."

Now that Dawes mentioned it, his lips did feel a bit glossy after kissing Valerie. He quickly wiped his mouth.

"That's better," Dawes said. "The preliminary investigation has concluded. The charges are being dropped."

Vance blinked. "Wait, but I assaulted a fellow officer."

"The official reason is that the MA's didn't follow proper procedure."

"And the unofficial reason?" Vance asked.

"The unofficial reason may have something to do with preventing the destruction of the Saratoga." Dawes glanced over to Valerie and then back to Vance. "So, if you're finished here, you are ordered back to New Carillon. And I want you in my office at o-eight-hundred hours tomorrow morning."

"Aye sir."

Vance was disappointed to learn that Dawes had prearranged transportation back to New Carillon. He would rather have flown home with Valerie. When he got to bed that night, he didn't sleep very well. His brain was stubbornly active, wondering what his life was going to look like after New Carillon. The next morning, Vance made his way to Dawes's office.

Vance knocked on the metal door with two thumps of his knuckles. It still felt surreal that it had only been nine hours since he was flying his last mission. He had soared through the stars in pursuit of the enemy and even engaged in hand-to-hand combat in the engine room. It had been a terrifying experience, yet somehow, he longed to be back there. When he was there, he felt useful. He felt needed. It was like he belonged. Now that his flying days were over and his time on New Carillon was coming to a close, he felt old somehow. *I wonder if this is what retirement feels like?* He thought.

He heard a voice call from behind the door. "Come in."

Vance opened the door and stepped inside. He walked up to Dawes's desk with small deliberate steps. He stood at attention. "Sir, Squire Brewer reporting as ordered."

"Sit down, son." Dawes gestured to a chair on the other side of his desk. Vance sat down. Dawes set aside a manila folder and picked up another one that looked thicker. He opened the folder and then leaned back in his chair. "Well, son, it seems you had one gabb fine flight."

"Thank you, sir," Vance replied.

"You foxed three bandits and gunned a fourth. That's four confirmed kills. And you were climbing into the saddle of a fifth when I instructed you to deliver your RIO. That fifth kill would have made you an Ace."

"Believe me, sir, that fact was not lost on me."

"Instead, you broke off and delivered your RIO as ordered." He leaned forward in his chair. "Now I want you to know, that those four kills do not impress me."

Vance's eyebrows raised. "They don't?"

"Son, I've been doin' this frazz for more years than you've been alive. Hotshot pilots racking up a quick kill score do not impress me. What *does* impress me is, that despite losing your opportunity to get your fifth kill, you followed your orders. You were willing to sacrifice becoming an ace to do what you were told. *That's* a pilot I can trust. *That's* an asset I can use."

Vance wrinkled his brow in confusion. "What does this mean for me, sir?"

Dawes riffled through the pages in the folder and removed one. It was his flight instruction final exam score. Dawes reached over and picked up a small wooden handle with a rubber stamp on the bottom.

He thumped the stamp on the paper before returning it. Vance tilted his head to see what was stamped on the paper. It was a single word in red ink: Rejected.

Vance's heart rate started to climb. Dawes scribbled a note across the bottom of the page and signed his name. "I am officially overriding your exam score in favor of your performance during the battle."

A deep breath forced its way into Vance's lungs and his hands trembled. Dawes continued. "I'll admit, my first impression of you was a junior enlisted masquerading as an officer. But you've proven to me that I was wrong. You're courageous, resourceful, and you don't give up." Dawes returned the paper to Vance's file. "Besides," he said, closing the file folder. "Far be it for me to deny an ace his wings."

Vance swallowed. "Ace?"

Dawes picked up the previous folder and opened it. "I finally got around to reading Sky Captain Royce Williams's report on your first engagement. You destroyed a Mori starfighter with the Clarissa pulsar. That makes a total of five confirmed kills."

Vance's eyes darted around, searching for something to say. He blinked a few times. Was this for real? Was he going to suddenly wake up from a dream? "An ace..." He looked back at Dawes, blinking to keep his eyes clear of the impending moisture. "I get my wings?"

Dawes's face softened. "That's affirmative, son. You earned your wings." Dawes pulled out a leather patch from a drawer and set it on the desk in front of Vance.

Vance picked it up and fingered the gold-leaf impressions. He recognized the design though he had never been close enough to touch one. It was the 'soft patch' wings that Velcro to the pilot's flight suit. Vance lifted a trembling hand and wiped away a loose tear. "Thank... thank you, sir."

"You'll get your official gold insignia at your winging ceremony, which will be held on the third Tuesday of Novenary. Then you will report to Eddison Frank on the following Monday, to begin your tour with Blue Planet."

Vance held a shaky smile and nodded. "Aye, aye sir."

"And last but not least, that was some pretty impressive flying you did with Miss Vlavskisk. The two of you took a lot of pressure off those wildcat pilots."

Vance smiled. "She is an excellent pilot, sir."

"She could have been one of the best Fire Lance pilots."

Vance looked at the desk. "Did she ever say why? You know, not becoming the best Fire Lance."

"We each have our demons to face. That will be all."

Vance nodded before getting out of his chair. He stood at attention. "Good day, sir."

Dawes nodded and Vance about-faced and exited.

Once in the hallway, he pulled out his squire pin from his breast pocket and pinned it back on. A broad smile crossed his lips and he took in a large breath. His shoulders felt light as if they would carry him up into the stars.

Vance walked down the hallways with a renewed bounce in his step. As he came to an elevator, his arm brushed up against an odd shape in his pocket. He unzipped the pocket and pulled out the strange metal fragment from his starlancer's wreckage. He turned it over in his hands a few times. Something was definitely off about that metal fragment. He entered the elevator and pressed a button. As the elevator descended, he again inspected the inscription. It looked like nothing more than a partial serial number and perhaps the last part of a manufacturer's name. Or maybe it was a partial part number and the last half of a model name. Either way, it meant nothing to him yet.

The elevator concluded its trip and Vance exited. He briskly walked down the hallway and rounded the second corner. He walked into a tall room with workbenches and scaffolding. People in white lab coats and safety goggles worked all around the room.

"Hey Vance!" a voice called from the other end of the room.

Ronland jogged up to Vance and wrapped one large arm around him. "As I measure and cut! Long time, no see, buddy!"

"It's good ta see you too, Ronland."

Ronland released Vance. "I'm afraid the prototype is not available right now. It's getting the new guidance system installed."

Vance grinned. "That's okay, Ronland. I actually have somethin' else I wanted ta run by you." He held up the metal fragment.

Ronland took it. "Dense metal, by the heft of it. This discoloration here looks like it's been under some intense heat."

"Found it in the wreckage of a starlancer."

"Okay, an explosion would explain the discoloration. But if I'm not mistaken, starcraft spaceframes are built out of lighter metal."

"A lot lighter. And a sleeker feel. So that begs the question of what this would be doin' on a starlancer."

"Doesn't sound like I'm telling you anything you don't already know," Ronland said, half surprised.

"Yeah, well that's all I know about it."

Ronland flipped it over and looked at the inscription. He called out to a coworker at another workbench. "Hey, Phill! Come here, take a look at this for me, will ya?"

A skinny pale man walked over. He took the metal fragment with his long bony fingers and held it up to the light. "ANFO bomb casing." He pointed to the inscription. "You can even make out the explosive rating."

Ronland turned to Vance. "Makes sense. Probably a fragment of a missile still attached to the starlancer."

Phill shook his head. "No, ANFO is a commercial explosive. If you want military-grade, you'd go with RDX or something with a lot more kick. Missile warheads are in a whole separate ballpark in comparison." He handed the fragment back to Ronland and returned to his work.

Ronland shrugged and handed the fragment back to Vance. "Okay, you got me. Beats me why you'd get that in a starfighter's wreckage. It doesn't seem to belong."

Vance turned it over and over in his hands while staring past Ronland. "I'm startin' ta wonder if I've known all along..." He cupped it into his hand and turned back to Ronland. "So, how'd ya like ta come to my winging ceremony next Tuesday?"

Ronland smiled. "Ha ha ha, wouldn't miss it for anything! Congratulations, Squire!"

Vance smiled. "Thanks. I'll see ya there."

"Hey, you take care, man."

Vance exited the room and pocketed the metal fragment. He made his way back to his apartment and sat down on the couch. He stared at the ceiling, dozens of new questions swarming around inside. He reached over the arm of the couch and picked up a ball of yarn and a small metal rod.

Hans walked in and set down a steaming box on the coffee table. "What's that?" he asked, pointing to the yarn.

"What? You said I should take up a craft that would work on my dexterity skills."

Hans blinked. "You chose knitting?"

Vance shook his head. "Nah, it's called crachit."

Hans stared a moment. "Do you mean crochet?"

Vance stared blankly for a few seconds. "Oh, that's how you say it? No wonder the lady was lookin' at me all weird."

"I thought you'd pick pottery or origami," Hans said.

"Hey, with this I get ta make somethin' useful."

"Really?" Hans asked.

"Yeah," Vance said holding up his work. "I made a square."

Hans chuckled. "And here I stand without a square joke. Vance the Lance, I'd say you really are loose as a goose." He sat down beside Vance and began opening up the box of food. "So, what did Marlon Dawes want with you?"

"Not much," he said as if discussing the weather. "Rundown on my flight performance, said my kills didn't impress him, and my winging ceremony is next Tuesday."

"That's typical. Those overly uptight Lancers wouldn't know—" Hans blinked a moment. "Wait, what?"

Vance smiled and held up his soft patch wings.

Hans threw his arm around Vance and jerked him into a sideways hug. "I knew you'd do it!"

"Careful of the ribs," Vance protested.

"I knew you would pass the exam."

Vance shook his head. "Actually, I failed the exam."

"What?" Hans asked, letting him go. "Well then, how did you..."

Vance smiled. "Wind Captain Dawes overrode my exam score in favor of my battle performance."

"Get spaced! Are you serious?"

Vance nodded. "I can hardly believe it myself. I thought I was done for."

"What made the difference?" Hans asked.

"I'm not sure," he admitted. "But bein' outrageous sure made acceptin' life a whole lotta fun."

Hans smiled. "That, Vance the Lance, is my personal recipe for confidence."

Chapter 38

WINGS

Qualification for the Naval aerospace aviation insignia shall be dependent upon completion of flight training and being designated as qualified to pilot military starcraft. The student shall be presented with their "soft patch" wings (gold-leaf impressions on a leather patch that will Velcro to the flight suit) immediately after completion of their flight training. The official Naval aerospace aviation insignia (gold metal pin to be worn on the dress and duty uniforms) shall be presented later at the Winging Ceremony.

—FROM "STARCRAFT CARRIER OPERATIONS MANUAL" BY THOMAS J. SUTTON, UNITED EARTH NAVAL COMMAND

Vance stood in a shallow maintenance closet with a single light overhead. He ran his finger across the electrical panel until he found the cable marked, Block C Sections 12-14. He wasn't sure exactly which was the right room, so he chose a couple of adjoining rooms. He tapped his wristband and the time lit up. Once he set the timer, he placed his hand on the power cable and closed his eyes. Several minutes later his timer sounded and he removed his hand.

That would send the message all right, but he could not guarantee who would reply. All he could do was hope the correct person responded. *All right, Hans,* he thought. *I sure hope she gets the message.* He closed up the maintenance closet and snuck back out to the hallway. He casually leaned against a wall and tapped his wristband once more to watch the time. He didn't have to wait long.

Vance heard a voice in his head. *Number 13, small-scale power failures are rarely limited to one specific set of living quarters. Let alone lasting for precisely thirteen minutes.*

Vance smiled. He had enjoyed that little prank more than he ought to. It was a rather bold move, but he needed to get answers. And in order to get answers, he first had to get someone's attention. The voice in his head didn't sound quite like Number 1—which was a good thing since that was not whose attention he was trying to get. But to be on the safe side, he figured he should issue the challenge anyway.

Well, you know me, he thought. *It's like golfin' with my three favorite clubs.*

I assume you had a purpose in doing it?

Vance noticed his challenge wasn't answered and concluded that it wasn't Number 1.

Yeah... an overly dramatic calling card prob'ly wasn't the best way of introducin' myself. But I wasn't sure how else ta meet with you.

Wardrobe of the Order, in fifteen minutes.

Is anyone else able ta hear our conversation? Vance thought.

Not while I control it.

Then the 'challenge', Vance thought, *is the 'message is sent'.*

Your 'answer', then, is 'it took thirteen minutes'.

Until then, he thought.

Vance smiled as he made his way down the long hallway toward the shops. He entered an elevator and heard a familiar voice in his head. *A rather audacious way to get my attention, Number 13.*

Well, you know me, Vance thought. *It's like golfin' with my favorite three clubs.*

But the Jack is Wild.

I'm flattered you noticed, Number 1, He thought. *I was rather fond of my starlancer.*

I heard you had a mishap.

Vance pulled the metal fragment out of his pocket and turned it around in his hand. *About that mishap, what I can't figure out is, what's so troublesome about this delusional squire?*

What you insinuate, if it can be proven, would be treason.

Or patriotism; actin' in the best interest of the people. How convenient a definition, Vance thought.

If only you knew something about the best interests of the people.

The elevator stopped and more people stepped inside. *Speaking of best interests, there shouldn't be any more mishaps, should there?* He thought. *We wouldn't want the insinuation proven, now would we?*

If you intend to draw battle lines, you had best be sure you're on the winning side.

Winning side be canned! He thought. *If it ain't right, it's wrong.*

Oh, don't pretend to preach morals to me! If life is so precious to you, then every Mori you kill is another nail in the coffin of your conscience.

That's different. That's combat, Vance thought.

What a convenient definition.

The elevator stopped again and Vance stepped out.

Your bravado won't get you very far with me, little squire. This is a dangerous game you're choosing to play. Just keep in mind you're playing for two now.

Vance smirked. *Weak threat, Number 1. You and me both know she can take care of herself.*

Time will tell...

Vance made his way down to the main plaza and stood in front of the Wardrobe of the Order shop for Virtus Occulatum. He tapped his wristband to make sure he was still on time.

He looked at the metal fragment in his hand once more. Then the little hairs on the back of his neck stood up. Vance looked around. He saw no one. "It's hard ta tell if the message is sent."

A voice immediately to his left responded, "It took thirteen minutes."

Vance was startled when he saw a woman beside him dressed in black leather and sunglasses. "Agent Null. Either you're very quiet or I'm pretty noisy."

"You have some nerve contacting me directly," she said.

"I know. And I do apologize for the impropriety, but you guys don't exactly have a directory and you're the only other Virto-O I know."

"Your Tour Advisor is Number 1. Why didn't you go to him?"

"I didn't think he would help."

She eyed him up and down. "You're a bad liar. You think he's trying to eliminate you."

Vance huffed. "Yep."

"And you think you can trust me? I spoke out against you during the formal debrief."

"Believe me, Agent Null, if I thought I could get a clear answer any other way, I would have. At least I know you don't have a vested interest in manipulating me."

She eyed him curiously. "What is it you want?"

Vance held out his hand and Agent Null took the metal fragment. She looked it over for a few moments. "You found this in the wreckage of your starlancer, didn't you?"

Vance nodded.

"But you didn't turn it over to the authorities. And what I don't understand is, why. Why must you be personally involved?" she asked. "Despite the opposition, you rescued Sky Captain Williams from the Mori, earned your wings, and saved an entire starcraft carrier. As I see it, you have accomplished everything you set out for. Is this vanity then? Another notch to add to your belt?"

"I'm in over my head in this area. And somethin' tells me that isn't enough to prove anything." Vance said.

"You're right. If you're going to get evidence that will hold up in court, you're going to need something a lot stronger than this." She tossed the metal fragment to Vance.

"That's where I was hopin' you would come in."

Agent Null eyed him up and down. "It's a dangerous game."

"So I've been told," Vance said. "Why am I in the crosshairs?"

"You're not, as far as I am aware," she declared. "Then again, Number 1 operates a tight cell, and my control over the various operative cells is not what it used to be."

"How am I a threat to anybody?"

Agent Null lifted an eyebrow. "An ignorant peasant who can earn the respect of the Fire Lance. A savant that stumbles upon the powers of the Rising Sun. An unpracticed student that can effortlessly peer into the possible futures. My dear Number 13, just who couldn't you threaten?"

"I can tell jokes, too," Vance added with a smile.

She smirked. "And you can tame the heart of the young Vlavskisk."

Vance flushed. "Jeez, does everybody know about that?"

"My dear Number 13, it doesn't take a Virtus Occulatum to figure that one out."

Vance took an exasperated breath. "So you gonna help me or what?"

Agent Null pondered aloud as she walked a slow circle around Vance. "This squire is outside the organization—off the SEDAR so to speak. And his natural talent with The Winds can make him a very useful asset—I might even regain control of the cells. Yes, a quid pro quo would be acceptable."

She stopped and looked him directly in the eyes. "For the time being, revel in your victory, Number 13—Nova knows you've earned it. In return for information on Number 1, you will perform certain favors for me."

Vance nodded. "What do I do?"

"When the time is right, I'll be contacting you, *Agent* 13." She turned and left.

Vance took a deep breath. His nerves were a little shakey but he was glad the encounter ended up the way he wanted. He now had an ally inside Virtus Occulatum.

A sudden sense of panic surged through him. He tapped his wristband. He still had time before the ceremony. He hustled back to his apartment to change into his formal clothes. Then he made his way toward Valerie's apartment. He knocked and Dorothy opened the door. Her face lit up. "Vance Brewer, come in."

Vance entered. "Thank you, ma'am." He cleared his throat. "I uh, offered ta walk Miss Vlavskisk to the ceremony."

"I'll let her know you're here. Make yourself at home," she said.

Vance nodded and walked into the center of the living room. Ornate lamps and picture frames decorated the table and nearby shelf. A few knick-knacks adorned the coffee table and the top of the bookcase. Vance walked up to the shelf and looked at the many picture frames lined up. They seemed to be of various family members. One picture, in particular, caught his eye.

He looked closer at the picture; it was of a little girl. His mind flashed the memory of his second vision before his eyes. He remembered seeing that girl clinging to him for comfort while at the other end of his pistol, he saw Number 1 fall to the ground.

Dorothy walked back into the living room. "She'll be out in a moment."

He pointed to the picture. "You know, I might be crazy, but I think I've seen this girl."

She smirked. "Yes, you've been seeing quite a lot of her."

"Oh, you mean that's..." Vance felt the blood rush to his cheeks. "Of course." He smiled sheepishly.

"Well, Admirer, are you ready to go?" Valerie asked.

Vance turned to her. She wore the same blue and white dress that he had first seen her in. Her curly hair was pulled up into a bun with glittering barrettes. Her earrings dangled and teased his attention.

"Wow. Now there's gravity," Vance said.

She blushed.

"I think you two should start walking," Dorothy said.

Valerie put her arm in his and they exited, walking down the hall toward the banquet hall.

Vance cleared his throat. "Miss, would you mind now tellin' me about Lleona?"

She sighed. "Lleona was my first starlancer."

Vance returned a confused look. "That's funny, that's also the name of Sky Captain Williams's starlancer."

"It's the same starlancer," she explained. "It was reassigned to Royce when I transferred out of Fire Lance."

"You mean when you finished your *tour* with Fire Lance?" he asked.

She shook her head. "No, that was after my tour."

"Wait... you mean you were an actual Fire Lance knight?" he asked in amazement.

She lowered her gaze. "It's rare for any Solar Knight to request re-assignment to another order. It's not the kind of thing that people like to talk about. Some knights see it as a black mark on their record as if they failed as an instructor."

"You must have toured with Wind Captain Dawes," Vance said.

She nodded.

"That must've been hard on you too."

She stopped and glanced into his eyes. "I'm sorry I didn't tell you sooner. I hope you don't think less of me."

Vance smirked. "Now you go throw that neutron-brained idea out of your head. My heart orbits you, not your past."

She beamed.

Vance and Valerie filed into the banquet hall. It was the same large room where Vance had had his first Banquet Table and met Valerie for the first time. The room was absent of tables this time; instead, it was filled with chairs. Vance took a seat in the front row with Valerie by his side. He had to re-situate himself to not sit on the long coattails of his formal green sleeveless jacket. He wasn't sure he'd ever get used to formal wear but he did look good in it, and it doubled as his uniform.

Royce sat down on the other side of him and put a hand on his shoulder. "This time, Squire Brewer, you have not had greatness thrust upon you. This time, you have become great. Congratulations."

Vance smiled. "Thank you, sir. Thank you for believin' in me."

"Thank you, for believing in yourself."

Royce nodded to Valerie. "Miss Vlavskisk."

She smiled in return.

Royce wore his formal red uniform with white trims. The formal white hat with red trims that he wore had a golden emblem of his rank on the front. Vance felt a sense of panic; he didn't have a hat.

"Sir, my Orbiting Star uniform doesn't come with a cover. How am I gonna salute?"

Royce smiled. "Not to worry. It's going to feel a little strange, but you are allowed to salute uncovered if you're still in the military and your Solar Knight uniform doesn't come with a cover."

A voice called his name called from the back of the room. "Vance the Lance, and Royce the Voice!"

Royce motioned for Hans to join them. Hans strolled up to the front row wearing the same formal clothes as Vance and took a seat. Vance glanced back at the large number of people filing into the room. "Hans, who are all these people?"

He shrugged. "Probably everyone who's heard of your stories." He pointed to a man on the sixth row. "There's the tailor who fitted you for your formal suit."

Vance looked farther back and saw two of the little boys who had invited him to play ball. He also saw Dr. Rychen, Lord Baltris, and Ronland. Dorothy took a seat a few rows back. Vance waved and she waved back.

When all the seats were filled, a few people stood in the back. Dawes stood at a podium and set down two little boxes. As with Royce, he wore his dress red uniform with a hat. He turned to a woman dressed in a neatly ironed pencil skirt and matching jacket. She walked over to Dawes with perfect posture. Dawes stood at attention until she shook his hand and exchanged a few words. Dawes nodded and pointed to Vance. She took note of him and continued talking to Dawes.

Vance squirmed in his seat. Then whispered to Royce. "Who's Wind Captain Dawes talkin' to?"

Royce leaned over. "That's NAVSEC Barbara Thorman."

"The Secretary of the whole Navy! What's she here for? I know winging is a big deal, but I didn't think it was *that* big."

Royce shook his head. "It's usually not, but this is *you* we're talking about. Your training has been about as abnormal as can be."

Vance looked down at his formal Orbiting Star uniform. "Somehow, it seems now that I should be in dress whites."

Valerie muffled her giggle.

Royce quietly chuckled and shook his head. "You are appropriately dressed for a Solar Knight."

"Do I salute her?"

Royce shook his head. "But be sure to shake her hand."

Vance nodded.

Dawes cleared his throat. "Soldiers, sailors, knights, and guests. On behalf of the Knights of the Solar Winds and the Earth Navy, I would like to thank you all for attending this Winging Ceremony. Now, since this is not strictly a Solar Knight ceremony, we'll spare you the High Novan and talk normally." A slight chuckle circulated through the audience.

"Normally, this ceremony is held at graduation from the flight school. Unfortunately, the flight school was destroyed by the Mori." He motioned toward Royce. "So Sky Captain Royce Williams has instructed Squire Brewer in flight training. And if that doesn't sound odd enough, Squire Brewer has already started touring with the orders of the Solar Knights. He has also been involved in two major aerospace skirmishes, earning him the status of Starfighter Ace."

Dawes paused. "So I'm sure we can all agree, it's about time he got his wings." The audience chuckled. "Secretary of the Navy, Barbara Thorman has a few remarks." He turned and motioned for Barbara to take his place at the podium.

Barbara walked up and looked around at the audience. "Now, here comes the part where I give a long-winded speech about dedication, hard work, and courage. And while I can certainly deliver a great speech to that effect, I felt this time, it would be more inspiring to tell a story." She looked at Vance. "Squire Vance Brewer, it's time to stand up here."

Vance walked over to her side and stood at attention. She looked back at the audience. "I want to tell you a story about a young aerospace aviator trainee, who as fate would have it, wound up in a combat situation. This trainee pursued a Mori saboteur aboard the starcraft carrier Saratoga. This trainee followed a specialized enemy soldier while unprepared and unarmed. And according to reports, had this trainee not acted, the enemy would have sabotaged the main power reactor. His actions saved the entire carrier and the estimated five thousand crew on board. And to top it all off, this trainee immediately hopped back into a starfighter to continue engaging enemy starcraft."

Vance felt the blood rushing to his cheeks. He stood more rigid.

"What does this story have to do with Squire Brewer receiving his wings, you might ask? Well, let's just say I've heard enough stories about Squire Brewer that I'm thrilled I finally got to tell one." She turned to Vance. "Next time, Squire, take either a Beretta or a Sig Sauer pistol with you." The crowd erupted with laughter and applauded.

Barbara waited for the applause to die down. "Now, my first instinct was to give this pulsaric trainee a field promotion. But seeing as he is already a commissioned officer and hasn't met time in rank yet, that wasn't really an option." She picked up a small felt-covered case from the podium. She opened it and showed it to the audience. "Squire Vance Brewer, for gallantry in action against an opposing armed force, you are awarded the Silver Star." She handed it to Vance. He took it and then shook her hand.

She grinned. "Normally, we'd have a proper award ceremony but since we're in a time crunch for the Exodus, I hope you don't mind I just slipped it in here."

Vance smiled. "Don't mind a bit, ma'am."

Barbara looked at Dawes. "The floor is all yours."

Dawes stepped up to the podium and picked up the second, and smaller, velveted case. He opened it up and looked at Royce. "Sky Captain Williams." He held out the case to him.

Royce walked over and took the case, then stood beside Vance. Dawes looked over at Vance. "Congratulations, Squire Brewer, you are an aerospace aviator. Always fly above the best."

Royce removed the gold-colored pin. It looked like an anchor behind a shield on top of a pair of wings. Royce pinned it on Vance's formal jacket. The audience applauded. Vance sniffled and shook Royce's hand. Then he saluted Royce, who returned the salute.

Dawes picked up an ornate red saber scabbard from behind the podium. He pointed the saber handle toward Royce. Royce drew the gold-handled saber, the red and gold tassels dangling from the handle. Vance dropped to one knee.

"Squire Vance Brewer, do you vow to uphold the statutes of Earth government and of the Knights of the Solar Winds?"

Vance sniffled again. "This I pledge with my life, my fortune, and my sacred honor."

Royce touched the flat of the blade to Vance's right shoulder. "I hereby dub thee a Knight of the Solar Winds." He touched the blade to Vance's left shoulder. "And I charge thee to uphold the conduct of the Knights of the Solar Winds."

Vance stood as Royce returned the saber to its case. The audience stood and applauded.

The ceremony concluded with countless people walking up to Vance. Some congratulated him while others asked if he would be telling that story at the next Banquet Table. Valerie gave him a warm hug. At that moment, he felt like he was flying across the stars. He was where he belonged.

Dawes waded through the crowd of people and leaned over to Vance. "Squire Brewer."

Vance stood at attention and saluted. "Wind Captain Dawes, sir."

Dawes returned the salute. "Squire Brewer, Alpha and Delta fleets have arrived. As of 0600 hours tomorrow morning, we will officially be a single fleet under the direction of President Lanquist. Then at precisely 1130 hours, the Exodus will officially begin. I know I had assigned you to fly patrol, but you seem to have made a name for yourself and the President wants you as an honored guest when we set out."

Vance smiled. "Aye sir."

"You'll need to be on the command deck of New Carillon by 1030 hours. And dress formally. Any questions?"

"Sir, do I gotta say anything?"

Dawes shook his head. "No, but you'll probably be mentioned in his speech and the press will most likely want to show your face on camera."

"Understood sir."

"That will be all."

Vance turned to Valerie. "I wonder what I got myself into now?"

She simply smiled.

Chapter 39
UNDER WAY

On the eighteenth day of Novenary in the four-thousand seven-hundred and seventy-first year of the Mori, known to us as the first year (or year one), the last of the human ships had gathered, and the long exodus to the Great Frontier of the Ancients officially began.

—FROM "GALACTIC HISTORY VOL. IV" BY PROF. EZRA DOUGHERTY

Vance kicked a blue and white soccer-sized ball. It tumbled a short distance to a small boy who kicked it back. The ball rolled past Vance. "Ah nah, that's another one for you."

A second boy nodded. "Yep. We gots four and you guys gots two."

Vance turned to the third boy standing beside him. "Don't worry, we'll get 'em this next time."

"You're not very good when you wear those funny clothes," he replied.

Vance smiled. "It's my dress uniform, sorta. I gotta keep it clean. I'm visitin' with some important people in a little bit." He tapped his wristband and looked at the time. "Okay, we got time for one more."

The second boy kicked the ball toward Vance. His teammate intercepted the ball and kicked it high. The first boy swatted the ball down and then kicked it back.

"Hands!" Vance called out. "I saw it. That's another point for us."

"We still win," the boy called back. "We still gots one more point than you guys gots."

Valerie walked up. "When you said you needed to go play, I thought you were kidding."

Vance smiled then turned back to the boys. "Okay, I gotta haul jets. I'll see you boys tomorrow." He bumped fists with each one before turning to Valerie. "Oh," he said pulling a cloth out of his pocket. "This is for you."

She unfolded a crocheted square cloth.

"I figured maybe you could clean your pistols with it or somethin'," he said.

She smiled. "It's lovely."

They strolled down the hallway, which dead-ended with a reinforced security door. Vance patted down his pockets. "...where did I put..." He pulled out a small metal card and inserted it into a narrow slot beside the door. The door opened. Vance walked inside, past two marines posted at the door. A young lady held her hand out. "Credentials?"

He handed her his metal card. She waved it over a small device in her hand. She glanced up. "Welcome on deck, Squire Vance Brewer. And is this your guest?" she asked, motioning to Valerie.

"She sure is."

She nodded. "Mike will show you to your designated seats." They stepped over to the next person in the line.

"Arms out to your side please," Mike said, holding a long electronic rod.

Vance held his arms out and Mike waved the rod all around Vance. It beeped once.

"Is that good or bad?" Vance asked.

"It's just picking up your rank pins." He waved the wand over Valerie before motioning for them to follow him. He led them over to the front row and pointed to the center two chairs. Valerie took her seat and Vance took his. Vance glanced at the lady on the other side of him and stared.

The lady looked at him and he quickly looked away. "You find something to be the matter?" she asked.

Vance sat still. "Many apologies your ladyship. I wasn't expectin' ta be sittin' next ta the Supreme Grandmaster of the Orders."

Anna-Lexa smiled. "I inspire your nervousness then?"

Vance felt his cheeks getting hot. "If'n I could compare my feelin' ta joining a party, I'd be the one who arrived under-dressed."

"Well, be not afraid of greatness Mr. Brewer, you don't seem to be that same young squire I saw in the Great Council. On the contrary, you've made quite the public impression."

"I appreciate that, your ladyship."

A tall thin man entered from the door across the room. He wore flawless hair and a practiced smile. He strolled up to Anna-Lexa and shook her hand. "Lady Novinensky, I'm glad you were able to make it. Your presence here is a powerful reminder of the faith and commitment of the Solar Knights to the human people."

"A pleasure, Mr. President."

President Lanquist turned to Vance and shook his hand. "And you must be the famous squire I've heard so much about."

"Whatever you've heard, I promise it's all true," he replied.

President Lanquist chuckled. "Good to have you aboard, son." He turned to Valerie. "And you must be the young Miss Vlavskisk?" She smiled as he shook her hand. He then moved on to the man sitting beside Valerie.

"Mr. President," a man said, wearing headphones and a name tag. "You're on in 5."

President Lanquist finished his short conversation and then approached the podium. An older woman walked up and handed him a packet of papers. "I numbered the pages, so you can skip around if necessary."

"Thank you, Denise."

"10 seconds," a voice called out.

A man operating a large mounted camera counted down on his fingers. When the last finger dropped, President Lanquist smiled big. "Centuries ago, our forefathers wrestled with the decision to dissolve the political bands which tied them with other nations. Today we stand on a precipice overlooking another great political band that must be dissolved. Not of men or of nations, but of location. Our home space, as we have come to call it, is no longer where the future of mankind lies. Our beloved star system and the constellations that have embedded themselves in our very culture embody the great sacrifice we must now make. We indeed..."

Vance turned to Valerie and whispered. "You know, all that time I spend worryin' about not bein' ready when the Exodus starts? Now that I'm here, that all seems so silly."

"Thank you for trusting me," she said.

"...that we should be so blessed to have such a dedicated Solar Knight along with us for the next leg of our journey." President Lanquist turned around and walked over to Vance. Vance stood and shook his hand for the camera before sitting down.

He whispered to Valerie. "It does make me wonder, though, what we're gonna find on the other side of the Great Frontier of the Ancients. After all, it was built to keep somethin' out. Maybe I should see about talkin' with that Professor Dougherty that Sky Captain Williams mentioned..."

"You're missing the speech," she said.

Vance joined the audience in applauding the President's most recent remarks. The camera panned to show members of the audience. Vance reached his arm around Valerie. "Pose for the camera," he whispered.

She smiled warmly.

After the camera had passed, she leaned over. "Don't worry about the Great Frontier or what lies beyond. You and I make a great team. Whatever is out there, we'll face it together."

Vance smiled.

They joined in a standing ovation after the President's address. A wall-mounted screen showed a camera view of the many ships in the combined fleet. They all started rocketing forward, attempting to stay in formation.

"After seven months of planning, the Exodus of Mankind has begun!" President Lanquist declared. Music played from the overhead speaker and balloons fell from a ceiling net.

Vance looked into those enchanting mahogany eyes and time seemed to slow down. He didn't hear the music anymore, nor did he notice anything but floating balloons from his surroundings. At that moment, all that existed was Valerie. The light glinted off her dangling earrings. He leaned toward her, and she closed her eyes. Her hair smelled of honey blossoms. He kissed her softly as a balloon gracefully rested on their heads.

They looked up and smiled as the balloon continued its journey to the ground. He pulled her into an embrace, and she rested her head on his shoulder. Standing there with her, he felt whole and complete. And in many ways, the luckiest man alive; he had the perfect wingman.

He turned the metal fragment around in his right hand, remembering his conversation with Number 1. He grinned and whispered to himself, "Bring it on."

Appendix

HERALDIC ARMS

Argent (silver)	Or (gold)	Gules (red)	Sable (black)	Azure (blue)	Vert (green)	Purpure (purple)	Murrey (mulberry)	Sanguine (blood-red)	Tenné (tawny)

Fire Lance

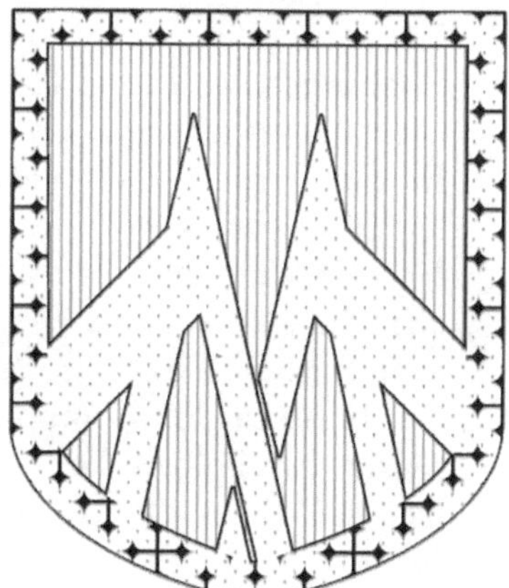

Established: 18 Ternary 0 PE (Year Zero, the Year of Infamy, Post Exterminium)

Blazon: gules, two chevronels interlaced or, a chevron disjointed or, a bordure crusilly or and sable.

Notable Mentions: Sky Captain Royce Williams, Squire Valerie Vlavskisk, Wind Captain Marlon Dawes, Twin-Star Commander Alan DeCampbell, Star Commander Uulan Myles, Lieutenant Esther Black.

Wind Dancers

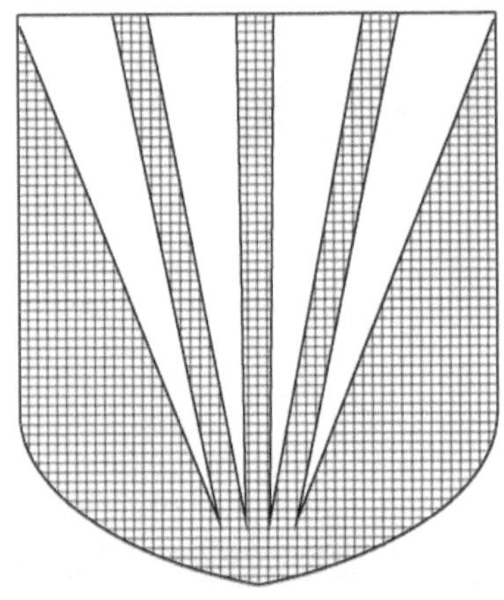

Established: 28 Null 172 AE
(Ante Exterminium)
Blazon: sable, 4 piles argent.
Notable Mentions:
Lord Baltris, Lord Cantrell,
Master Yoshimo Haruto, Rosa
Lorca De Leon, Li Feng,
Huang Shu, Alice Ursomb.

Lily of the Valley

Established: 22 Tetrad 169 AE
(Ante Exterminium)
Blazon: purpure, a lily argent
leaved vert seeded or.
Notable Mentions:
Grandmaster Surgeon Dr.
John Rychen, Professor Carl
Sansbury, Dr. Phi Combes,
Master Psychologist Dr.
Jacques Monet, Dr. Quinn
Mallory.

Orbiting Star

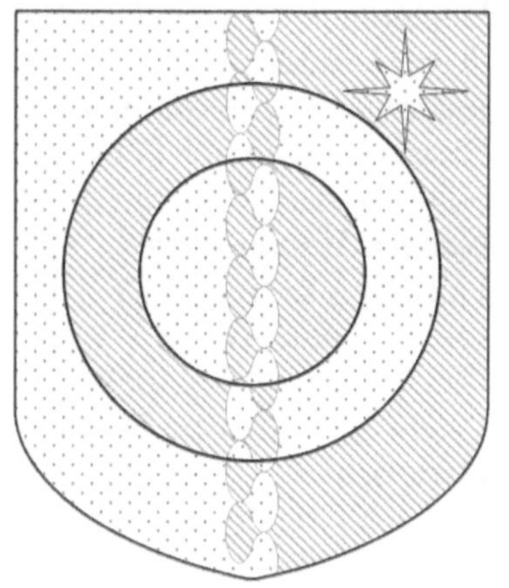

Established: 13 Monoprim 112 AE (Ante Exterminium)
Blazon: per pale nebuly or and vert, an annulet counterchanged, a star or in sinister chief.
Notable Mentions: Hans Christian, Johnny Valdear, Reginald Owens, Jimmy Hoin, Chuck Walters, Sue McArther.

Blue Planet

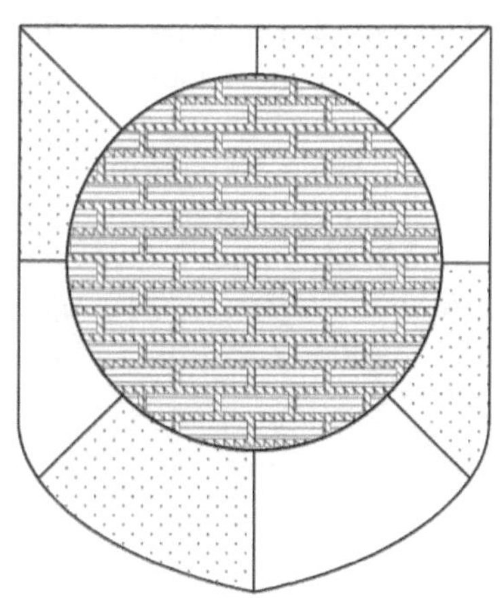

Established: 28 Null 172 AE (Ante Exterminium)
Blazon: gyronny argent and or, a roundel azure masoned tenne.
Notable Mentions: Chief Engineer Eddison Frank, Chief Engineer Byron Watts, Senior Scientist Ronland Paulsky, Senior Scientist Elain Greys, Senior Scientist Sarah McGlothlin.

Gun Stars

Established: 20 Tetrad 0 PE (Year Zero, the Year of Infamy, Post Exterminium)
Blazon: vair, a mullet of 8 points voided interlaced or.
Notable Mentions: Sage Dorothy Vlavskisk, Sage Jor'del Smith, Valerie Vlavskisk, Scott Fredrick Crandall III, Umathi Kines, Erica Bauler.

Virtus Occulatum

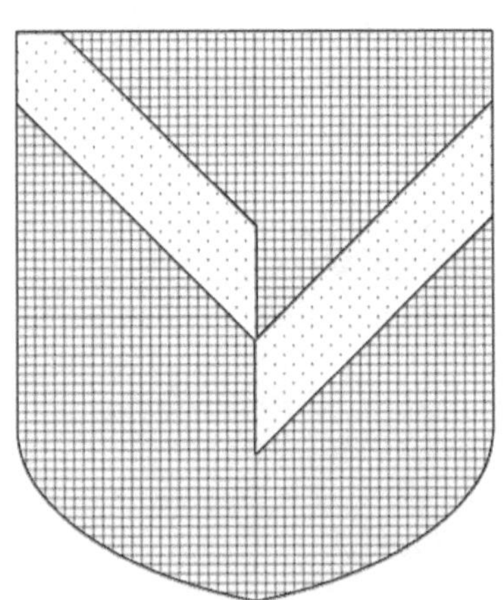

Established: 18 Ternary 0 PE (Year Zero, the Year of Infamy, Post Exterminium)
Blazon: sable, a chevron inverted removed or.
Notable Mentions: Number 1, Number 22, Agent Null, Agent 13, Number 2, Number 25, Agent 9.

Rising Sun

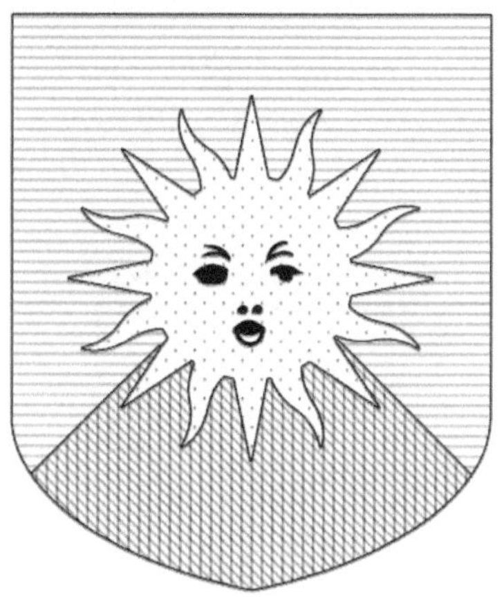

Established: 3 Pentad 0 PE (Year Zero, the Year of Infamy, Post Exterminium)
Blazon: per chevron azure and tenne, a sun or.
Notable Mentions: Mrs. Anna-Lexa Novinensky, Mrs. Natalia Anuje, Mrs. Sarah Haufmann, Mr. Karl Yaeger, Miss Francis Livres, Mr. Pierce Hammonds

SOLAR WINDS NAUTICAL CALENDAR

0

0 Null

1	2	3	4	5	6	7
8	9	10	11	12	13	14
15	16	17	18	19	20	21
22	23	24	25	26	27	28

1 Prime

1	2	3	4	5	6	7
8	9	10	11	12	13	14
15	16	17	18	19	20	21
22	23	24	25	26	27	28

2 Binar

1	2	3	4	5	6	7
8	9	10	11	12	13	14
15	16	17	18	19	20	21
22	23	24	25	26	27	28

3 Ternary

1	2	3	4	5	6	7
8	9	10	11	12	13	14
15	16	17	18	19	20	21
22	23	24	25	26	27	28

4 Tetrad

1	2	3	4	5	6	7
8	9	10	11	12	13	14
15	16	17	18	19	20	21
22	23	24	25	26	27	28

▢ Events of the book

Did you know?

- It is considered good luck to be born on Null day.
- When the new calendar was being planned, the day Sir Edwin Norfolk discovered The Solar Winds was chosen as "Day Zero", or Null day.
- Vance Brewer became Squire to The Solar Knights on 21 Ternary.
- Vance first fought a Zandor'an on 23 Ternary.
- Vance first met Valerie at The Banquet Table on 28 Ternary.
- Vance and Valerie rescued Royce Williams on 1 Tetrad.

5 Pentad

1	2	3	4	5	6	7
8	9	10	11	12	13	14
15	16	17	18	19	20	21
22	23	24	25	26	27	28

6 Senary

1	2	3	4	5	6	7
8	9	10	11	12	13	14
15	16	17	18	19	20	21
22	23	24	25	26	27	28

7 Hebdoman

1	2	3	4	5	6	7
8	9	10	11	12	13	14
15	16	17	18	19	20	21
22	23	24	25	26	27	28

8 Oct

1	2	3	4	5	6	7
8	9	10	11	12	13	14
15	16	17	18	19	20	21
22	23	24	25	26	27	28

9 Novenary

1	2	3	4	5	6	7
8	9	10	11	12	13	14
15	16	17	18	19	20	21
22	23	24	25	26	27	28

10 Primilul

1	2	3	4	5	6	7
8	9	10	11	12	13	14
15	16	17	18	19	20	21
22	23	24	25	26	27	28

Did you know?

- Valerie first kissed Vance on 1 Tetrad.
- Valerie's birthday is on 26 Senary.
- Valerie flies as Vance's wingman for the first time on 27 Oct.
- The battle of Norfolk's Nebula took place on 10 Novenary.
- Hans's birthday is on 12 Novenary.
- Vance's winging ceremony was held on 17 Novenary.
- Vance's and Valerie's first mutual kiss was on 18 Novenary during the celebration that marked the beginning of the Exodus of Mankind.
- Vance's birthday is on 28 Novenary.

11 Moniprim

1	2	3	4	5	6	7
8	9	10	11	12	13	14
15	16	17	18	19	20	21
22	23	24	25	26	27	28

12 Prinnary

1	2	3	4	5	6	7
8	9	10	11	12	13	14
15	16	17	18	19	20	21
22	23	24	25	26	27	28

Did you know?

- Royce's birthday is on 24 Moniprim.
- The new mobile flight training school finishes construction on 4 Prinnary.

Timeline of Galactic History

There is no known recorded history prior to AE 8687 (Ante Exterminium)

The Age of the Ancients (ANC) lasted from AE 8687 to AE 4771

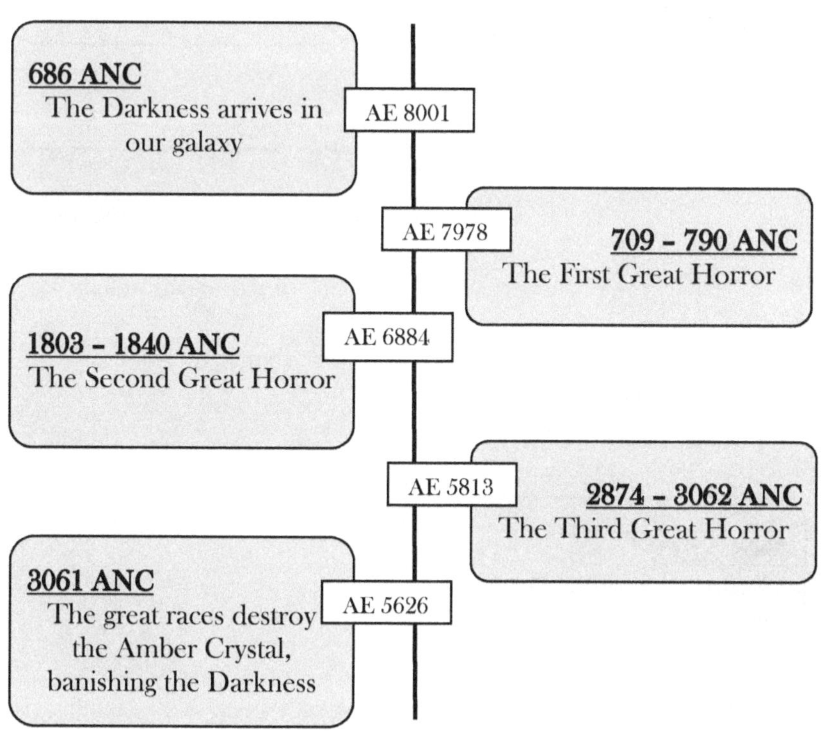

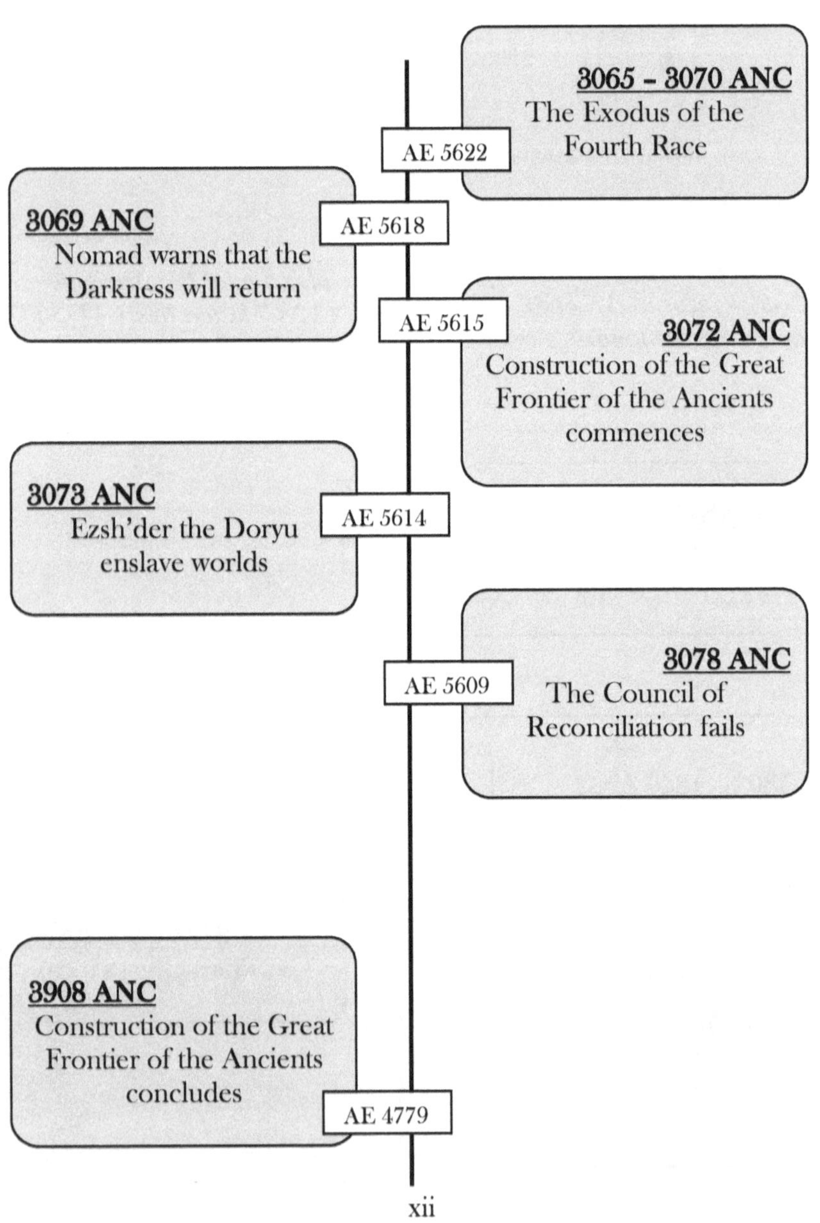
AE 5622
3065 – 3070 ANC
The Exodus of the
Fourth Race
AE 5618
3069 ANC
Nomad warns that the
Darkness will return
AE 5615
3072 ANC
Construction of the Great
Frontier of the Ancients
commences
3073 ANC
Ezsh'der the Doryu
enslave worlds
AE 5614
AE 5609
3078 ANC
The Council of
Reconciliation fails
3908 ANC
Construction of the Great
Frontier of the Ancients
concludes
AE 4779

*The Age of the Mori (MOR)
lasted from AE 4770 to 319 PE
(Post Exterminium)*

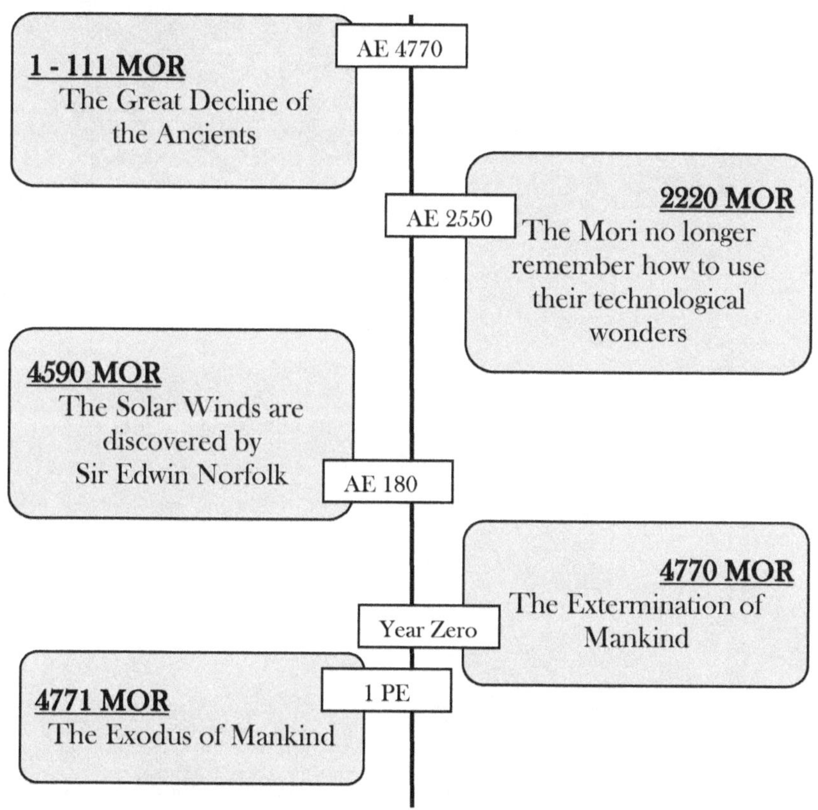

About the Author

BENJAMIN BOEKWEG

Some men see things as they are, and say why. I dream of things that never were, and say why not. — Robert Kennedy

I was born a long time ago, in a galaxy far, far away...okay maybe not—but you've got to admit it would be pretty sweet to claim that! It would certainly make for a more interesting introduction. My name is Benjamin, and I love to tell stories of far away and the impossible. I enjoy a good sci-fi space opera or time travel story. My first introduction to fantasy was Brandon Sanderson, and I fell in love with his books. I simply love Sanderson's Rules of Magic.

Clean language? Why not? This is science fiction and fantasy; I can make up whatever words the characters use for "harsh language" and it doesn't have to offend me or my readers.

Buckle up; there's no Walmart where we're headed... My stories reside far outside the realm of normal modern life. They don't explore what we know, but what could be out there.

I believe the best stories are the ones that can send your emotions on a roller coaster and provide some humor as well.

Website: https://benjaminboekweg.com